Praise for Jillian Hunter

and

Fairy Tale

Books by Jillian Hunter

Fairy Tale
Daring

Published by POCKET BOOKS

JILLIAN HUNTER

DARING

POCKET STAR BOOKS
New York London Toronto Sydney Tokyo Singapore

An *Original* Publication of POCKET BOOKS

A Pocket Star Book published by
POCKET BOOKS, a division of Simon & Schuster Inc.
1230 Avenue of the Americas, New York, NY 10020

ISBN: 0-671-00158-2

First Pocket Books printing March 1998

10 9 8 7 6 5 4 3 2 1

POCKET STAR BOOKS and colophon are registered
trademarks of Simon & Schuster Inc.

Cover art by Robert Hunt

Printed in the U.S.A.

Chapter

1

Edinburgh, Scotland

It wasn't the best night to be breaking into a house, especially when that house belonged to the most powerful man in Scotland. Everything had conspired against her from the start. A thunderstorm, an inexperienced partner, a series of mishaps which could only be interpreted as an evil omen. Maggie kept reminding herself that an innocent life was at stake. The thought failed to counteract the stark terror that had settled in her spine.

"I can't believe that I let them talk me into doing this," she whispered to the gangly young man poised like a gargoyle on the ledge of the three-story town house beside her. "I've never done anything this daring or stupid in my entire life."

"I dinna see why you're so nervous," he whispered back. "I told you I know what I'm doing."

"We barely made it up onto the balcony without breaking our necks, Hugh." A crackle of thunder drowned out her quavering voice. "What if he should catch us?"

"What if he does? He's only a man."

"Yes, and just this morning the newspaper named him the most powerful man in Scotland. That makes him different than the rest of us. It makes him more . . . more—"

"Powerful?"

"Exactly."

"Well, powerful or not, Maggie, it isn't as if he's going to do us bodily injury."

"He could if he decided to make an example of us," she said miserably. "He's influential enough to do it in public and not suffer the consequences. People would probably claim he acted in self-defense. He'd probably persuade them he feared for his own life."

Maggie was utterly convinced of this. The ruthless Highlander she intended to rob would show her no mercy. He might be a nobleman on the outside, but it was a well-known fact that he had the heart of a barbarian, a beast. He enjoyed punishing people. He'd established his reputation on it.

In fact, his professional rivals were complaining amongst themselves that his power had exceeded acceptable boundaries. In private, however, those same men conceded that he was the most brilliant criminal lawyer in Europe.

They said that once he decided in his black heart a man was guilty of a crime, no defense on earth could save that man from conviction.

They said he had made a pact with the devil, exchanging his soul for his unparalleled success. Several witnesses, who begged to remain anonymous, swore they had seen him transacting the deal. It had happened on a foggy All Hallows' midnight seven years ago, in the graveyard near Princes Street.

To this day a group of then-recently graduated medical students, strolling back to their lodgings on the ill-fated evening, insisted that their watches had stopped on the stroke of twelve as the bargain was sealed.

They said that for good luck he seduced a virgin on the eve of opening every trial. That was the part that Maggie found the most unsettling.

Despite these aspersions on his character, slews of admirers thronged the courtroom to watch the master in action and to applaud his recent appointment as Lord Advocate of Scotland. Crime had increased in the country. People needed a champion, and Connor Buchanan had all the makings of a latter-day warlord.

Arrogant and irresistible, he played to his audience with

unabashed charm. He was a gifted performer, with the power of the populace on his side. His voice could carry through the gallery like thunder, or move a jury to tears with its subtle persuasion.

That same deep-timbred voice now drifted out onto the balcony ledge through the half-open door to the two young housebreakers flattened like fledgling bats against the town house wall. The topic of conversation was another ancient art at which, as rumor went, he also excelled.

"No one is going to believe you were helping me choose a cravat all this time, Ardath. By the way, you have your drawers on backwards."

Yes, indeed, the man had more supporters than critics. There were even some people who thought he was a hero, who called him the Last Lion. There were some people, mostly women, grandmothers, maidens, and housewives, who claimed they slept better at night for his existence. Apparently, he did have a few redeeming qualities. But unlike the rest of Edinburgh's female population, Maggie Saunders had managed to remain blissfully unaware of his lordship's infamous existence until yesterday.

Guardian and protector of the innocent, or heartless scoundrel? Rogue or knight in shining armor?

Actually, no matter what you chose to believe about Connor Buchanan, and Maggie had reason to believe the worst, she wished to heaven she hadn't volunteered to break into his house.

She took a breath and edged another inch along the ledge. She tried not to dwell on the three-story drop to the street. On how much it would hurt to break every bone in her previously law-abiding body. On whether she would remain conscious long enough to feel any pain after she hit that stone wall, bounced off the row of parked carriages, and rolled down the embankment.

She couldn't bear to think what would happen once she reached the cesspools.

A chilly raindrop trickled down her forehead and hung suspended on the tip of her nose. She gave her head a desperate little shake to dislodge it. "This damned thunderstorm isn't exactly helping the situation," she whispered resentfully through chattering teeth.

Neither was the woman teasing Lord Buchanan in the darkened bed chamber Maggie and Hugh had been hoping to enter. She could hear Buchanan's muted laughter, his unsuccessful efforts to restrain his exuberant partner. Then there were those disturbing stretches of silence that piqued the imagination. God only knew what immoral acts were going on behind those cream brocade curtains.

At least she could attempt to protect her young accomplice's virtue. "You mustn't listen, Hugh," she said from the side of her mouth.

"I'm not," he lied.

A blast of wind brushed the wall. Maggie reached protectively for the boy's hand. She studied the hay cart they had dragged under the window as an emergency precaution. "We'll have to jump," she said in resignation. "They sound like they're settled in for the night."

"They might be taking a nap."

"A nap!" Maggie's voice rose in indignation. "You'd think they'd have a little more consideration, behaving in such an unseemly manner in his lordship's very own bedroom with a party going on."

"Except that it's probably his lordship in there," Hugh pointed out. "A man does have certain rights in his own house."

"Not when that house is full of people. It's indecent."

A grin crept across Hugh's narrow face. "Sinful is what it is. Still, perhaps it isn't what it seems. They might just be playing charades."

"Charades? Are you daft?"

"All right then. Blindman's buff."

Maggie bit her lower lip. "The press reporters were still waiting for him outside the courtyard when we walked past. The man obviously has only one thing on his mind, and it isn't his job." She refrained from mentioning that if Hugh's mind had been on *his* job, they wouldn't be in this pickle.

Hugh rubbed his ear on his shoulder to disperse a spray of raindrops. "I'm sorry I dropped that rope."

"I suppose it couldn't be helped," she said in an irritated

4

whisper. "At least you have the crowbar to jemmy open the door on the other balcony."

Hugh was silent.

Maggie craned her neck to stare at him. "You do have the crowbar, don't you?"

"Well, I did have it, Maggie, but I forgot about the hole in my pocket. I reckon it fell out when that dog chased us across the links."

"Then all I can say is that it's a damn good thing you brought that skeleton key."

He gave her a sheepish smile. Maggie closed her eyes and prayed for forbearance. "You lost the skeleton key too?"

"Of course not." He looked down between his feet to the street. "I left it right there in the hay cart so it would be safe."

"You *what?* Oh, damnation, Hugh. Now we *will* have to jump and sneak in through the servants' quarters, assuming we're capable of walking without assistance afterward. I'll stand guard downstairs and meet you—"

Hugh lifted his head from the wall. "What was that noise?" he whispered.

Maggie dug her bare toes into the ledge and peered down into the street. She had been wearing white satin pumps until several minutes ago when the man in the bedroom had cracked open the balcony doors, presumably to cool down the passionate atmosphere inside. Fearing discovery, Maggie and Hugh had scrambled like squirrels to take cover on the ledge behind the branches of a tree.

One of her white shoes sat right in the middle of the balcony. The other had fallen into the street along with the rope. She'd been forced to take off her stockings so she wouldn't slip. They were dangling on the lower limb of the horse chestnut tree that grew against the ledge.

She stared down in apprehension as a heavyset servant in black and gold livery emerged from the house. To judge by his stomping footsteps and muttered curses, he was not a happy man.

He picked up Maggie's shoe and hurled it over the gate like a javelin. "Shoes in the street. Do they care that poor sods like me have to pick up their belongings where they drop them? Do they care that I canna draw a breath for bein' trussed up like a Hogmanay turkey?" He came to a halt, shouting to himself: "And who's the big imbecile who left this hay cart in front of the house?"

The thunderstorm threatened to erupt into a full-blown storm. Wind lashed the gray stone walls of the elegant town house. It teased Maggie's curly black hair loose from her chignon to blow in a blinding tangle around her face. It rivaled the chaotic emotions that clamored inside her, the anxiety she was struggling to suppress.

"I'm frightened, Hugh," she said aloud. "Something bad is going to happen. This storm is a sign from God."

"All in the name of justice, Maggie."

"Justice." Her voice caught. "I'm a criminal now. Me, the daughter of a duke, who's never stolen so much as a scone before."

Except for once. She paused, shivering, as the bittersweet memory of that embarrassing experience years ago flickered through her mind. Tonight undoubtedly marked another low point in a life that had not been easy for a long time now. She only hoped that her parents, those bastions of noble breeding, would look down at her from heaven with understanding and not horror. She hoped they would forgive her for helping a homeless old man who would be condemned to death if she did not make an effort to prove his innocence.

They had forgiven her, eleven years ago, for stealing her older sister Jeanette's earrings.

Her family had been visiting Maggie's elderly aunt and uncle in Scotland for Christmas at the time. The following year the small but tightly knit clan, Scots and French, Saunders and de Saint-Evremonds, planned to celebrate the holiday together in the river château in France where Maggie lived with her immediate family.

Less than an hour after stealing the earrings, Maggie was apprehended with the pilfered pearls and banished, in shame, to the drafty attic while everyone else feasted below on Christmas dinner.

She accepted her sentence with the calm stoicism one expected of an ancient family. It wasn't the first time a de Saint-Evremond had been led astray by a pretty bauble. More than a few courtesans and king's mistresses figured in Maggie's lineage.

Her banishment to the attic would have been an effective punishment, too, except that Maggie's older brother, Robert, took pity on her and sneaked her up a heaping bowl of Christmas trifle. Then Jeanette began to feel guilty, remembering how she'd taunted her little sister with the earrings. She brought up a plate of roasted lamb and tender potatoes as a peace offering.

Before Maggie knew it, the entire family was celebrating Christmas in the cold musty attic, and it was the best Christmas they had ever enjoyed together.

It was also the last.

Yes, it was wrong to steal. She'd realized that even then. She had been disciplined for her misdeed. It was fair.

But she never understood, years later, why everything and everyone she loved and needed had been stolen from her. Why she, alone, of that close warmhearted family, had been allowed to survive and make sense of the loss.

Evils she'd never known existed had crushed her world in a cruel fist during the course of a single evening.

It hadn't been fair at all.

Her parents had taught her right from wrong. They had instilled their noble ideals and compassion in her heart. She wished they had also warned her that justice did not always come when it was merited.

Sometimes it, too, had to be stolen.

The sound of the majordomo shouting in the street startled her back to the present. "Move this damned hay cart out of the driveway!" he was ordering the two footmen who'd been roused from their station on the entrance steps.

The footmen pushed. The hay cart rolled like a prehistoric beast down the street; it took Maggie's only hope for escape with it on its bumpy, undignified descent into darkness. There was no choice now but to forge ahead with the robbery.

"Hell," she said in frustration. "What else can go wrong?"

Hugh leaned forward. "I'll jump anyway and get the rope."

"You will not. We'll wait until they're done in that room. They can't take—"

Before she could finish the thought, there was another

trill of laughter from inside the bedroom, the balcony doors flew open, and a woman with red flowing hair burst outside with her arms outflung as if to embrace the rain.

"Oh, look," she cried over her shoulder to the man in the room. "How wonderful. How perfect. We're having a storm to celebrate your success!"

She raised her arms to the inky sky like a pagan goddess and twirled, reveling in the rock-hard pellets of rain that pelted her voluptuous figure. Maggie couldn't believe her eyes; she'd just realized that the demented creature was dancing around in her underwear. And the man was right—she did have her drawers on backward.

"For the love of God, Ardath, get inside before someone sees you."

The man's voice, gruff with amusement and annoyance, did little to deter his uninhibited partner. The woman was now performing a very strange ritual around the perimeters of the balcony. Clapping her hand over her mouth, prancing around in circles. Making loud ululations to the sky.

"What the blazes are you doing, Ardath?"

A large shadow moved into Maggie's peripheral vision. She huddled into her cloak, too terrified to breathe. Was this the infamous Connor Buchanan, literally in the flesh?

The shadow strode forward, straight into Maggie's range of vision. He was powerfully built and he moved with riveting self-assurance, his long dark blond hair stirring in the wind. Thankfully, he was fully dressed, in black broadcloth evening breeches and long-tailed white linen shirt with a cambric cravat, which he was casually trying to arrange. Maggie couldn't see his face, and it was probably a good thing. Even from this distance he emanated a dangerous energy that she'd rather not encounter.

"Have you lost your mind, Ardath?" he said calmly.

He leaned his hip against the railing, his elbow protruding onto the ledge. If he happened to turn his head, if he looked up closely enough through the tree, he would see the two figures on the ledge.

As it was now, the wind was blowing the ends of his hair into Maggie's cloak. A leafy branch provided the only unreliable barrier between them. She stole an anxious look at his profile; its rugged contours carved a silhouette against the night sky that was anything but reassuring.

So *this* was Connor Buchanan, the man who had sold his soul to the devil for success. He was more formidable in person than even his reputation claimed.

"I am doing the pagan Gubong rain dance that Professor Macbean showed us during this month's lecture," Ardath told him. "He lived with a family of natives on a little volcanic island for almost a year."

"Your professor lectured on lions and unicorns last summer," he said wryly. "I suppose he lived with them too?"

"You're too cynical. You don't believe in anything. Stop trying to spoil my fun."

"Come inside now, Ardath," he ordered her. "You'll have the Reverend Abernathy waking me up at dawn to complain about the strange goings-on in my house. As usual, I'll be the one blamed."

Maggie squeezed her shoulders to the wall, every muscle in her body tightening in response to his deep authoritative voice. She had gotten her first glimpse of the notorious Connor Buchanan only yesterday afternoon. A tall, dominant figure in long black robes and a wig, he had strode right past her to the courthouse, larger than life, commanding attention.

Maggie had been too short to see above the eager crowd. She'd gone unnoticed in the crush of smitten young women, press reporters, and legal clerks who rode the wake of his charismatic personage. She could still remember the strange current of excitement his presence stirred. She'd been so impressed she had forgotten she was supposed to hate him.

There was a murderer running loose in the city, and newly appointed public prosecutor Lord Buchanan had charmed a confession out of the suspect.

Unfortunately, the suspect was one of Maggie's dearest friends, an elderly vagrant with diminished mental capacities. Maggie, in a moment of compassionate indignation, had been talked into helping Hugh steal the old man's confession from Buchanan's house. A disgruntled maid who was a friend of Hugh's had provided the tip that the confession could be found in his lordship's private study.

"A rain dance is supposed to make it rain," Connor pointed out to his partner, drawing back under the eaves. "It's already raining, you're not a Gubong, and we're both getting soaked. Not to mention the guests arriving."

"But it's not raining very hard," Ardath protested, waving her arms in weird patterns above her head.

He raised his voice. "It's bloody pouring. What do you want, a flood?"

As if he had commanded it, thunder rumbled in the distance over the dark bulk of Edinburgh Castle on its rise of basalt rock. Lightning flickered above the castle. A bright flash illuminated the ledge in pitiless detail. Maggie swallowed a gasp and willed herself invisible inside her black waterlogged cloak, every moment of waiting straining her composure.

Her white shoe shone like a beacon on the balcony floor, proclaiming an intruder's presence to the world. It was only a matter of time before Connor or his partner discovered it. A knot of fear lodged in her throat. Why had she ever thought she had the nerve for this sort of thing?

Ardath shrieked in delight. "Look at the lightning! Isn't it exciting?"

Connor grunted, distracted by the carriage rolling up the drive directly below them. Guests alighted with groans of dismay as rain splattered their fine silks and tweeds.

"For God's sake," he muttered. "This is all I need. I don't have privacy anymore. My enemies are dying for the chance to destroy me." Exasperated at her antics, he stalked onto the balcony to pull Ardath out of public view.

It wasn't exactly an easy task.

Ardath attached herself to him like an octopus, her white arms flailing everywhere—over his chest, his face, his shoulders, disarranging the cravat he had finally folded to his satisfaction. Chuckling helplessly, he finally caught her wrists in one hand and held them immobile above her head.

She closed her eyes, shivering in anticipation. "I used to love it when you dominated me this way."

"I'm never letting you drink whisky on an empty stomach again."

"Ooooh. Women adore it when you use that masterful voice to put them in their place."

"You're going to have one hell of a headache in the morning."

"Put us in our place, you big muscular beast, you Viking warlord, you Dutch pirate. Why do you have four eyes all of a sudden? You look like a spider."

He tightened his grip on her hands. "Has it occurred to you that someone might be watching us?"

"Someone—" She went very still. "You mean someone dangerous? . . . Someone like the murderer you're trying to trap?"

"No. I meant someone even more frightening, like your mother, or one of my sisters."

Ardath gave him a wicked smile, walking him backward into the opposite railing. "It was a night like this the first time you conquered me."

"Well, it wasn't on a balcony."

"You ravished me in the rain."

"I don't think so, Ardath. There wasn't a cloud in the sky that night, as I recall."

"You seduced me by starlight?"

He raised his brow. "I sincerely hope the guests can't hear any of this conversation."

"Loved me like lightning?"

He laughed reluctantly, a deep warm vibration that contrasted with the austere masculinity of his face. "Get inside, you lunatic."

"The newspapers don't know the half of it." She lowered her voice to a teasing whisper. "If they think you're a lion in the courtroom, they should have seen you—"

His head lifted abruptly, all traces of humor vanishing from his face. "Did you hear that?" he said.

"Did I hear what?"

"It sounded like someone choking—I'd swear it was a woman."

He dropped Ardath's hands to push around her and stare down into the street. In the process he stepped right over Maggie's white dancing pump. She cringed, waiting for the inevitable moment when he paused to wonder how a strange woman's shoe had gotten onto his balcony.

Ardath, apparently, was not a threat. She was too busy catching raindrops on the tip of her tongue to notice anything. Then, as Maggie had feared, Connor turned slowly from the railing and walked right over to where the shoe sat, practically screaming for attention. Good Lord, if it had been a snake it would have bitten him, but he still didn't seem to see it.

Then Connor looked down suddenly at the shoe. He frowned for the longest time. Maggie tensed and mentally prepared herself for a disastrous outcome. She was too afraid to jump.

"Ardath." He picked up the shoe and casually tossed it back into the bedroom. "I wish you'd stop leaving your clothes around the house when my sisters are visiting. Norah is still complaining about finding your corset in the coal scuttle. She doesn't understand our friendship."

"Norah is a narrow-minded nitwit. She was delighted when I told her I hadn't been your mistress for almost a—"

"Be quiet." His voice cut like a whip through the gusting wind. "I *swear* someone is watching us." He strode to the opposite railing where he paused, still and forbidding. Then, as if obeying the devil's own intuition, he lifted his head to the large tree whose wind-lashed branches fluttered wetly against the ledge.

A shiver of foreboding jolted through Maggie as she felt the full impact of gazing straight down into his face. It was a face imprinted with the invisible scars of a hundred hard-fought battles and all but few won. Harsh angles. Strong bones. The arrogance of a Celtic warlord.

It was a face you would never forget.

She studied him in quiet horror for a fraction of a second before he turned away. In bone-melting relief she realized he hadn't seen her. But the aftermath of the impression he had made left her feeling as weak as if she'd just been washed ashore by a tidal wave.

Just as riveting and magnetic as her first glimpse of him. Probably as ruthless, too, if given the opportunity.

The newspapers had just named him the most powerful man in Scotland. His influence was unlimited: military, political, civil. His brilliant successes had already been recorded in history books. But in the disreputable streets where Maggie had found an unlikely home, they called him the Devil's Advocate.

And she had a horrible feeling she was going to find out why.

Chapter

2

Connor caught Ardath by the waistband of her drawers and dragged her back into the privacy of his bedroom. "I've got an idea," she said, stumbling up against his chest. "Let's play charades again, but this time we can only do Shakespearean characters. I promise not to cheat."

He sighed and closed the door behind them with a decisive click, Ardath's laughter echoing in the room. "You are one insane woman, Ardath Macmillan. I'm convinced someone was watching us out there."

"Would you prefer to play blindman's buff?"

She gave him a naughty grin and reached for the tumbler of whisky on the nightstand. Before she could raise it, Connor trapped her in his arms and gently forced her back against the closed door.

"Thank you for being here tonight," he said quietly. "I know you and your professor had plans to go off hunting Pictish artifacts."

She swallowed to cover her emotion and tangled her fingers in his unfashionably long hair. "What kind of friend would I be to miss your victory celebration? Anyway, Matthew understands the situation. Just because you and I are no longer lovers doesn't mean we have to become enemies."

Connor lifted his brow. "Is he coming tonight?"

"I invited him, but you know how he confuses dates. Besides, he's busy planning our haunted castles of the Highlands expedition."

"Poor old bastard," he said with a rueful grin. "No—lucky bastard, to have earned your loyalty."

"He does need me," Ardath admitted with a sigh. "The darling man is so disoriented, I'm afraid one of these days he might set off on an excursion and never return. You should come with us this next time, Connor. You have a good month before you take office."

"No, I don't," he said in a heavy voice. "I haven't heard a word from Rebecca since last summer, and the last time she did bother to write, she sounded rather lonesome. I thought I'd leave for Kilcurrie as soon as the verdict comes in on the Campbell rape case. I'm hoping I can persuade her to move back here where she can at least meet people her own age."

"I'd forgotten about Rebecca." Ardath's tone was subdued. Rebecca was the second eldest of his sisters, lame since childhood from a riding accident and living alone with a menagerie of hurt animals she'd nursed back to health in her lonely cottage on the edge of Connor's isolated Highland estate. "I think she's safe enough with her little creatures. Your neighbors watch over her, don't they?"

Connor frowned. "Yes, but I worry about her all the same, and it isn't natural for a young woman to live alone in the woods. Now get dressed, and don't you dare do that rain dance around the table."

"Honestly, Connor, have I ever embarrassed you in public before?"

"Not if I don't count the time you pinched that footman on the behind at the Lord Justice-Clerk's funeral."

She sniffed. "It's Sheena you need to worry about."

The reminder of the differences between him and his errant youngest sister broke the playful mood. His face troubled, Connor picked up his black satin waistcoat and tailored jacket from the bed. "She seemed happy enough this morning," he said after a thoughtful silence.

"She was miserable last week. She really loved that man."

Connor shrugged his massive shoulders, an impressive figure in the evening clothes that emphasized his masculine elegance. "I refuse to believe it. How in God's name could a sister of mine fall in love with a convict? He swindled old women out of their life savings."

"He only did it twice, Connor. He served his time and he's trying to repay his victims. You've done a few things in your life that you're ashamed of, haven't you?"

His face darkened in warning, but Ardath pretended not to notice. Connor had forbidden her to discuss his past. "I know you had your reasons," she said soothingly. "I know it wasn't the same thing, but she *loves* him. She's convinced he's reformed."

"She'll *love* the young viscount I've invited tonight to meet her. Sheena doesn't know what's good for her."

Ardath held her breath as his strong fingers began to hook the back of her gown. "Few of us do."

"I curbed my self-destructive tendencies a long time ago," he said in an even tone. "I know I've been hard on my sisters, but it was for their own good."

"I promised myself I wouldn't argue with you tonight." She suppressed a sigh as he brushed a stray curl from her neck. "Don't let's talk about this anymore, or we'll really miss the party."

"And I'll really miss the fun we've had together. You're the most honest woman I know, Ardath."

She compressed her lips. "You're going to make me cry," she whispered. "It's not as if we'll never see each other again, but it is time you found someone nice and stable to settle down with. We have agreed on that, haven't we?"

"Yes, we agreed."

He could hear the regret in his voice. Ardath had lent him money when he was broke. She had introduced him to influential people when he was struggling to make his mark. She'd stood by him when he had suffered his first professional failure.

In return he had protected her, by his presence, from men

who would take advantage of her generosity, and in an age when a woman enjoyed little freedom, he had encouraged her eccentricities and intelligence with indulgent humor. He had also comforted her when her only son committed suicide five years ago.

Trust, sexual compatibility, mutual respect. They hadn't fallen in love, they hadn't even made love with each other in a month, but their friendship would endure forever.

Besides, Ardath had her professor and charity functions to fill her life, and no desire to remarry after twenty years in a loveless marriage.

She insisted Connor needed a wife and family. Recently he'd begun to wonder if she was right. Success. Power. Fighting the good fight. Something essential was missing from his life. No one saw him as he truly was.

Aye, he'd heard the rumors about his reputation. He tended to either fascinate or frighten women, and quite frankly his notoriety embarrassed him. He was a Highlander at heart, a man of simple needs and strong emotions which life had taught him to restrain.

He waited, his face impassive, as Ardath deftly twisted her hair into a figure eight at her nape, and covered her tempting cleavage with a lace fichu. Then, to make the transformation complete, she put on a pair of unflattering iron-rimmed spectacles and nodded to herself in the mirror.

Connor was always astonished by the contrast between the spontaneous woman she was in private and the facade she presented to the public.

"Behold, Mrs. Ardath Macmillan," she said lightly, "wealthy widow, benefactress of the Orphans' Aid Society and—"

"Pagan Gubong rain dancer," Connor said, shaking his head in amusement. "My God. Talk about not trusting appearances. I'm tempted to believe there are two of you."

She pinched him on the buttocks as she moved past him to the door. "It wasn't the footman, by the way. It was the pallbearer."

He stopped, on impulse, to kiss her on the cheek in the doorway. Ardath primly resisted, conscious of the guests gathering below. Despite her earlier antics, she did care about Connor's professional image. "Enjoy tonight," she said softly, disentangling herself from his arms. "You deserve it."

"Do I?" He gave her a boyish grin, but his eyes were cynical in the half-light of the hallway. "Are you sure you don't want to marry me?"

"And spoil your reputation as a rogue? I wouldn't dream of it."

She edged around him. Connor drew back inside the room to give her time to make her escape. Then he glanced around, distracted by a sudden gust of wind rattling the balcony doors. He'd managed to shake off the unpleasant feeling that had crept over him outside. He was prepared to sacrifice parts of his personal life for public office but not to that extent. He resented being spied on.

Yes, Ardath's mother might have been watching them. The woman probably didn't have anything better to do. More likely, though, it was one of his six troublesome sisters looking for mischief. The young demons had delighted in making his life misery for years. Tormenting him had become a habit with them by now.

Yet, for all their differences, they were a close family. Their parents had been proud Highland people, loving and kind. Connor's father, a Sheriff's Advocate, had dedicated his life to keeping peace, and he'd enjoyed his work, instilling a strong sense of responsibility in his only son. His untimely death at the hands of a hunted felon had proved too much for Connor's mother to accept.

She had died heartbroken seven months after losing her husband.

Those first years raising the girls alone had been sheer hell for a bewildered young boy on the verge of manhood. Connor hadn't had a clue how to handle them; he couldn't handle his own unpredictable urges. His first priority, of course, was keeping the family safe.

He rubbed the muscles tightening at the nape of his neck. God, he couldn't believe the terror and trauma the girls had put him through. Running around with reckless young men. Defying him. Squandering the little cash he'd saved on perfumes and silk hankies. Rebecca riding an unbroken horse and fracturing her hip when she was twelve.

They were a spirited lot, those Buchanans, and Connor had sewn a few wild oats himself on the side.

Well, with any luck, he was getting rid of the last sister tonight. Sheena was the youngest, the most rebellious, and his biggest problem. Still, Connor hadn't come this far in life without mastering the art of persuasion. He wasn't above a white lie or two. He had painted such an appealing picture of Sheena's virtues that Viscount Lamond already imagined himself half in love with her.

Connor hoped to hell he could marry Sheena off before the end of the year. He had his hands full trying to find the murderer who'd thrown the city into a panic; his friends on both sides of the law had been working around the clock to prove who had stabbed an elderly banker and his assistant to death in an alleyway last month.

His colleagues were already congratulating him on wangling a confession out of the befuddled old peddler he'd visited in jail only yesterday. The confession was sitting on the desk of his private study, which adjoined the bedroom.

Confession or not, the poor wretch hadn't brutally robbed and murdered those two people.

Connor was as convinced of that as he was that someone had been watching him and Ardath on the balcony.

But he didn't want to ruin the evening's celebration by contemplating murder and prosecuting criminals tonight. He'd be living and breathing courtroom drama soon enough. For this evening, for the next month, in fact, he was going to relax and enjoy his success. He was planning a hunting holiday in the Highlands after he visited with Rebecca. He was going to enjoy his party.

Trouble would have to wait.

In the street below the Lord Advocate's balcony a lone figure lowered his walking stick to the wet cobbles and skewered the pale object glistening in the gutter. He lifted the stick into the hazy aura of the lamplight for closer inspection.

A woman's white satin slipper dangled by its badly scuffed heel.

He studied the slipper for several moments, then looked up thoughtfully at the balcony.

"Well?" a cultured voice demanded from the depths of the carriage parked across the street. "Did you find something?"

"A woman's slipper." He gestured upward with his stick. "If I am not mistaken that is also a pair of stockings hanging from the tree. I think it's safe to assume that the woman herself is in the house."

Chapter

3

～

Sheena was missing. Connor should have guessed that she would cause trouble tonight. The storm clouds of rebellion had been gathering for weeks, ripening for an outburst. She hadn't forgiven him for forbidding her to see her convict, and social embarrassment was to be the rain of her revenge.

He strode down the gaslit hallways of his home. His face was dark, resolute, silencing the few servants who had sought to speak with him on some trivial matter. Ardath would cover his absence at the party; he'd left her coaxing a donation from the Solicitor-General for the Infant Pauper Asylum. Ardath's mother, Bella, was flirting shamelessly with the viscount Connor had been hoping would take Sheena off his hands.

Presumably Sheena was hiding in a pout to punish him. He wondered irately how she could expect to be treated like a woman when she acted like such an infant. Yes, he knew he'd dealt sternly with her in the past, but it was for her own protection, because she'd never shown an ounce of common sense.

He came to a dead stop outside the door to the small withdrawing room. A candlelit shadow at the sideboard

21

drew his attention. On closer inspection he realized it was a woman's silhouette. A woman he had never met, he was certain. All his hot-blooded male instincts went on the alert. Something in her manner caught his interest.

Graceful and delicate. An air of intrigue. Who was she?

"Sheena?" he said into the silence, even though he knew damned well that the slight figure who turned in surprise at his voice couldn't possibly be his statuesque blond sister. "Sheena," he repeated, entering the room, "is that you?"

She stood frozen at the sideboard like a deer trapped in the flare of a hunter's torch. He suppressed a grin as he studied her face in the candlelight; she looked as guilty as sin of something. Perhaps she had just been scolded by her papa for some social blunder. Her vulnerability only added to her allure.

His gaze went from the hand she'd hidden behind her back to the platter of chocolate éclairs and bottles of iced champagne in the silver bucket on the sideboard. He chuckled to himself, welcoming a reprieve from another confrontation with his wayward sister. Meeting this girl held infinitely more appeal.

His first thought was that she looked like a medieval princess in a French tapestry, with her classic features and that tumble of curly midnight hair down her back. There was something pure about her. Something unique and enchanting. He couldn't resist.

A mystery. A conquest. A beautiful young woman caught in the act of demolishing the dessert course. He was fascinated by her aura of secrecy. Was she waiting for one of his friends? Or hiding from them? He could just imagine the young lawyers he worked with circling around her like a pack of wolves.

A droll smile twisted his mouth. "Excuse me. Obviously you aren't Sheena."

She didn't answer. Her eyes were wide with mistrust. He closed the door behind them, aware of a strange tension crackling in the air. In spite of convention, he wanted to enjoy this introduction all alone. He wondered where she had she come from, if she could be Aaron Elliot's daughter, fresh from boarding school in Marseilles. Aaron had said he was going to bring the girl. He'd neglected to mention she was an exquisite beauty.

He regarded her finely shaped features in curiosity. "You don't have Elliot's nose."

She crept back another inch, a cautious little thing. "Don't I?"

He glanced past her to the sideboard. Amazed, he realized that she must have packed at least a dozen pastries into her petite frame. There was a tiny smudge of chocolate on her chin; he pulled out his handkerchief to gently rub it away.

She caught her breath as he brought his hand to her face.

"The evidence," he said, his voice low and teasing, Sheena and the party suddenly forgotten in the pleasant anticipation of the moment. Then, reaching casually for her arm, he said, "Have you tried the champagne?"

"Of course not." Which wasn't a lie, exactly.

Maggie hadn't actually sampled the expensive champagne. But she did have two bottles of it tucked under each arm beneath her specially designed cloak, which was lined with numerous oilskin pockets.

Stealing the champagne was her only concession to turning felon, and a present for the Chief back in Heaven's Court, although there wasn't anything remotely divine about the family of assorted criminals who called the shabby sanctuary home under the leadership of a crusty old Highlander named Arthur Ogilvie. In fact, Maggie wished Arthur were here right now to handle this mess. He was as accomplished in his chosen career of vice as Connor Buchanan was in upholding justice.

Actually, Maggie was one of only a few people aware that Arthur was secretly a gentle giant who befriended the downtrodden. Her first month in the city after her aunt's death, Maggie had come to his aid when he'd been hit by an omnibus while supervising a swarm of amateur pickpockets. Arthur had broken his ankle and gold watch. To hear him swearing in the street you'd have thought he was mortally wounded.

She'd spent the last of her money on cab fare to see him to his house, and Arthur had been her unofficial guardian ever since. The Chief always repaid both insults and favors.

He had offered the frightened young exile a home, protection, security, and the strangest family she had ever seen.

Connor's voice broke the silence that had fallen, sending a little chill down her back. "Are you sure you won't try the champagne?"

"I don't drink anything stronger than tea," she said, wondering frantically what was taking Hugh such a long time, and how to get herself out of this situation. She couldn't think of anything more disastrous than facing the devil alone. How had he found her?

His gaze drifted over her, warm and personal, confident of a conquest. "Really?"

She gave him an admonishing look. Good heavens, he wasn't flirting with her, was he? What a dreadful complication. "Yes, really," she said, her lips tightening.

He chuckled. Before she knew it, the handsome beast was sliding his arm around her shoulders. "Let me take your cloak. I'm Connor Buchanan, by the way, and you must be—no, don't tell me. I'm good at remembering names. You are—"

"Freezing to death. Leave my cloak alone. Brrr." She blew out her cheeks and stamped her feet, thinking of the trouble she'd have explaining not only the champagne, but also the dozen chocolate éclairs she had wrapped up in his nice monogrammed napkins and hidden inside her bulky cloak. The children of Heaven's Court rarely tasted such treats. She couldn't believe anyone in his house would miss them.

He cast a puzzled glance at the blazing fireplace. "Freezing?"

"Cold as an icebox in January tonight, isn't it? It must be the rain."

Connor stared at her, charmed and confused. She was like a shadow that would elude him if he tried to catch her, a reflection in a moonlight pond that might vanish forever if he came too close. "Why haven't we ever met before?" he asked in amusement.

Maggie glanced at the door, avoiding his eyes. What on earth was taking Hugh so long? Had something gone wrong? She was supposed to create a diversion among the guests in the event he ran into any trouble, which would be damn near impossible with his lordship hovering over her like a dark angel. It had been difficult enough sneaking down the stairs unnoticed.

"I don't get out much," she said distractedly, realizing he expected some kind of reply. "I'm a . . . a recluse."

"Tell me that it isn't so."

She frowned, slowly looking away from the door. "I don't like people."

"But you like chocolate éclairs."

Maggie lifted her gaze to his face in reluctance, steeling herself for the power of her reaction. Hazel eyes. Heavy eyebrows, chin with a deep cleft. Experience had honed any hint of softness from his features, leaving only strong angles and a sense of ruthless elegance. Everyone said he was a hard man. But no one had mentioned the good-natured warmth that lurked beneath his dark intensity. She'd seen it herself in the way he indulged that woman on the balcony. He was human after all, but no less dangerous than she'd been warned.

"You look like you could use a glass of champagne," he said lightly. "It's the best, yellow label."

"Clicquot-Ponsardin," she said with a sigh. "Papa's favorite."

Connor was surprised by her remark. He'd always assumed Aaron Elliot to be a bit of a social oaf, the type to quaff beer from a bottle and belch at the table. But certainly Aaron's daughter looked expensive, with her fragile bone structure and intriguing shyness.

He made a mental note to contact his florist in the morning. Something unusual, a bouquet of hothouse freesias, lilies, and Queen Anne's lace, a tribute to her appealing delicacy.

"Drink to my success," he urged her.

Maggie groaned inwardly; apparently he wasn't a man who took no for an answer. "Perhaps after supper."

"The champagne won't last that long. Everyone is looking forward to it."

Anxiety, the fire's warmth, and his dominant presence were making her feel light-headed. Of course, she couldn't take off her cloak, not without explaining the stolen champagne and éclairs underneath. Anyway, she didn't want to encourage a sense of intimacy between them.

"Half of the bottles exploded on the way from France," Connor explained. He didn't give a damn what they talked about as long as he could keep her in the room. "It's the secret sedimentation process—it's what keeps the fizz. Apparently, the corks can burst with such force that the vintners have to wear masks when they walk through the vaults. It's an unpredictable phenomenon."

Blood was beginning to rush to Maggie's head. The pleasant scent of bay rum soap and rain on his skin briefly distracted her. "I really shouldn't . . ." He'd have her transported to Tasmania if he found out she was a thief. The Chief had said they had vampire bats there that sucked the blood from your toes while you slept.

Her toes. Good Lord, what if he noticed she was barefooted?

"Yes, you should. We'll have a private toast." He reached around her for a bottle and expertly cut the string that secured the cork. The depth of his interest in her bothered him a little. It was a new experience, a woman unsettling him. For a moment he couldn't decide what to do next. Experience took over where his emotions failed.

There was a loud pop. Maggie jumped reflexively, then suppressed a shiver as he handed her a flute and filled it. A toast tonight, Tasmania tomorrow. She took a hesitant sip, then gasped as he unexpectedly set down his glass and snagged her arm.

"You said you were cold. Let me get you settled in front of the fire. I want to show you something."

Nervous tension churned in her stomach as his shoulder brushed her cheek. "I'm not cold anymore—did I say I was cold? I'm warm as toast, overwarm, to tell the truth." She fanned her face with her free hand. "Whew. It's like an oven in here. How can you stand it? I think I'll just slip outside for a breath of air—"

He laughed, refusing to let her go. "Why don't you take off that wet cloak instead and finish your champagne? That way you won't risk running into any people on your way out."

She looked away, taking another deep gulp of champagne.

He was a charming devil, she'd give him that. There was going to be hell to pay when he discovered the missing confession, and Maggie for one didn't want to be in the vicinity when it happened.

"Your guests must be missing you, my lord," she said pointedly.

Connor refused to be discouraged. She had an elusive quality about her that was driving him mad. Besides, he was dying to know what she looked like under that cloak. She had small bones, he could tell that much from her hands. The mystery of her tantalized him. "You're one of my guests, aren't you?"

She swallowed, trying not to choke. The uninhibited warmth in his eyes made her feel breathless. And aware. Suddenly she was suffused by her awareness of him, his size, his power and reputation.

"It's my place to see that all of my guests are happy," he said smoothly.

She could have hit him. "I'll be happy walking outside, my lord."

"In the thunderstorm?"

Damn, she thought. The thunderstorm. He was a lawyer to the last detail. "I love the rain," she said. "I love walking in a thunderstorm more than anything in the world."

He gave her a strange look, and no wonder. Lord above, she sounded just like Ardath with that remark. She hoped that Jamie appreciated what she was doing on his behalf, which of course he wouldn't. Jamie was such a helpless old soul that he'd have confessed to murdering Julius Caesar if you'd dressed him in a toga.

"I'll walk with you," Connor said, surprising even himself at the offer.

"But you can't leave your own party," she said in alarm.

"Why not?" He put his hand on the small of her back, guiding her closer to the fireplace. "Look at that wall hanging first."

Maggie obeyed, staring up at the old tapestry above the mantel, but she didn't really see it. She couldn't concentrate on anything but the pressure of his hand on her back. Strange things were happening to her body. The sheer maleness of him overwhelmed her senses.

"It's a tapestry," she said at last. A millefleurs tapestry of a young noblewoman with a lion resting its head on her lap. A unicorn hid behind a tree, watching the woman and the beast. Behind the unicorn stood a huntsman with his bow and arrow aimed to shoot.

"A friend of mine bought it for me when I won the appointment," he said in a quiet voice. "It's called *The Princess and the Lion.* In the next tapestry of the series, the beast is supposed to spring up and protect her from the huntsman. I believe the final tapestry is missing so I don't know how it all ends."

Maggie was impressed against her will by the erotic intimacy between the woman and the beast. "I'd have thought the princess would protect the lion," she said after a moment. "She looks enamored of him."

"But he would give his life for her." He turned without warning, lifting the glass from her hand and placing it on the mantel. His smile was captivating, a tiny bit self-conscious, as if he were embarrassed to be talking about something as ridiculous as an imaginary romance. It was hard to believe the power and cold ambition that his charm concealed. "Legend says that the lion was attracted to her virginal purity. She looks a little like you, don't you think?"

She blinked. "Attracted to her *what?*"

"The untamed is drawn to the ethereal." He grinned boyishly at her shocked expression. "Only a virgin could capture him."

"A virgin. Fancy that."

"Sexual attraction is what got him killed."

Maggie quickly stepped behind a footstool. All this talk of virgins and killing while she was in the act of committing her first crime was making her a nervous wreck. Aside from swearing a lot, which was the worst habit she'd picked up in Heaven's Court, she considered herself a model of decorum. "This is all very fascinating, my lord, but—"

He nudged aside the footstool with the tip of his shoe. "Sexual attraction is a very powerful force."

"I'm sure it is."

"Powerful enough to destroy kingdoms and topple empires," he continued conversationally.

It had also done in a few of Maggie's ancestresses, those

wicked women who'd bucked tradition to follow their hearts. "Well, it's been lovely meeting you, but I have to—"

A door slammed somewhere upstairs, followed by a few angry shouts and the sounds of a scuffle. Maggie glanced across the room, holding her breath in apprehension.

"It's nothing." Connor brushed his knuckle against her pale cheek. Amusement glinted in the depths of his hazel eyes, amusement and unapologetic male aggression. He wanted this woman. "My sisters have never met a door they didn't slam. Do you still want to go for a walk?"

She suppressed a shudder. It wasn't his sisters making that commotion upstairs. She could have told him that if she'd been capable of thinking clearly. But he was seducing her with his smile, with the touch of his strong fingers on her cheek, her chin, her throat. She felt the power of that touch all the way down to her toes. The bare toes that would be the death of her when he transported her to Tasmania for housebreaking.

"Walk with me in the rain," he said quietly. "We'll sneak—"

"Connor! *Connor!*"

The deafening bellow from the hallway interrupted them. He drew his hand away from Maggie in annoyance a split second before his sister Norah threw open the door. She was tall, attractive, fair-haired, and extremely upset.

"Connor, dallying in the dark with a woman, for God's sake. Well, am I surprised? Come, quickly. There's a criminal in the house. Ardath and the chambermaid have got him trapped in your study."

Maggie turned a ghastly shade of gray. Connor, misinterpreting her reaction as fear, squared his shoulders, the public prosecutor about to spring into unofficial action, the lion ready to protect.

"Don't go away," he said in an undertone. "It's probably just a drunken guest who wandered into the wrong room. But wait here anyway. I wouldn't want anything to happen to you."

Maggie could only nod in agreement. She was practically shaking with relief. In fact, she had to restrain herself from pushing him out into the hall. She couldn't very well create a diversion for Hugh hiding inside this room.

Then suddenly Connor stopped at the door and pivoted to stare at her. Norah was shouting out orders behind him. "I know who you are," he said with a grin of satisfaction. "I know your name."

Maggie closed her eyes. It was all over now. "Please, God," she whispered, "don't let him send me to Tasmania."

"It's Philomena."

She opened her eyes in bewilderment. "What?"

"Philomena Elliot. Your father is always talking about you." His grin faded, replaced by a look of regret as Norah dragged him out into the hall. "I knew I'd remember—don't go away."

Chapter

4

⌒

"You ought to be ashamed of yourself." Norah forged ahead of him like a drill sergeant, arms swinging, voice strident. "We've been looking for you for ages. Everyone was asking where you were."

Connor scowled and slowed his stride to straighten his white cambric cravat. "I'm sorry you found me. You have the worst sense of timing in the world."

"That young woman's parents wouldn't have thought so," she said dryly.

Her parents. Connor's eyes narrowed as he spotted Aaron Elliot in the crowd of guests milling around the bottom of the stairs. Aaron was a mediocre civil lawyer at best. Connor had always secretly thought he was a silly clod, but he was damn well going to pay more attention to him in future.

"I wanted to call the police right away," Norah said in a miffed voice. "But Ardath, your former *mistress*, insisted I be discreet and find you first."

"Bellowing like a buffalo is hardly discreet. Anyway, Ardath was right. We don't want to embarrass an inebriated guest. She could well be holding the Lord President pris-

31

oner. The old coot is as blind as a bat. He was probably looking for the privy."

He strode to the foot of the stairs, pretending to acknowledge the concerned remarks that followed him.

"Be careful going up there, your honor."

"Best to let the police handle these things."

"Can you believe the arrogance—breaking into the Lord Advocate's house?"

"It'll be Tasmania for the dirty devil! Shouldn't you take a gun with you, sir?"

No one would dare break into his house during a party. Connor was sure of it. The whole thing would turn out to be an embarrassing mistake. He put his arm around Elliot's shoulders, drawing the shorter man up the stairs with him. "Good to see you, Aaron. I'm so glad you could come."

"You are, my lord?" Elliot said, clearly surprised to have been singled out by his eminent host.

"Yes, and I've just met Philomena. What a lovely young woman. I don't blame you for hiding her away in France all these years."

"Philomena?" Elliot struggled to keep pace with Connor on the winding stone staircase. "A lovely young woman?"

"A shy little violet, isn't she? I suppose she learned the art of deportment in school."

"Shy?" Elliot echoed, his footsteps slowing. "Deportment—*my* Philomena?"

"Yes, she's intelligent and amusing too. Has she always been a recluse, or is this a recent affliction?"

At that Elliot came to a dead halt on the stairs and stared at Connor with blank confusion on his round, perspiring face. "Philomena, a recluse, my lord?"

Connor frowned at him over his shoulder. "What is the matter with you, Elliot? You sound like a blasted parrot."

Before Elliot could frame a reply, Ardath began shouting from his study. "Are you coming to help us or not, Connor?"

"Yes, yes. I'm coming."

With a last look at Elliot—Good God, it strained the imagination to think such a dull nondescript man had sired that beautiful child—Connor continued up the stairs. He resented this intruder, whoever he was. He resented his own party because it took him away from *her*.

He paused outside his bedroom door. He could hear Ardath and the chambermaid shouting for him, but they seemed to have the situation under control.

Hell, what if he'd frightened the girl off? Had he overwhelmed her with his obvious interest? He couldn't remember acting like that with a woman he'd just met. As a matter of fact, he usually didn't give seducing a woman that much thought. He followed his instincts, or could it be that he had never cared about making a good impression before?

At any rate, something about her had thrown him off balance. Fortunately, even if he had frightened her away, he knew where to find her. Philomena Elliot. Lord, what a name. She'd probably been warned about his reputation. Sheltered in a private school, she had no experience to use as a defense. He'd have to temper his aggressive tendencies the next time he saw her.

He stared at the bedroom door.

Was he losing his mind? He didn't want to go to his own party. He wanted to walk in the rain with a woman who made him smile. He wanted to talk about French tapestries and drink champagne in front of a fire. What good was his success if he had no one of his own to share it with? When she learned to trust him a little, he would put her at ease, loosen her inhibitions, then kiss her soft rosebud mouth, the white arch of her neck, those graceful shoulders. He would discover exactly what she looked like under that awful cloak.

And then—

Ardath flung the door open in his face. Her red hair was disheveled; her glasses dangled from the tip of her nose.

"What on earth are you doing, Connor?" she demanded.

I'm fantasizing about a woman who looks like the princess in the tapestry you gave me for my birthday. I think you'd approve of her, Ardath.

He frowned, rubbing his bruised cheekbone. "I was coming to help you. Is all this drama necessary? I hope to God you don't have Hubert locked in my closet."

"It's a boy," she said in a strained voice, drawing him inside the room; she and the chambermaid had barricaded his study door with every available piece of furniture, the dressing table, a desk, the wing chairs—

"The bed," he said in astonishment. "You moved the bed."

"He looked like a very rough sort, Connor," she said, straightening her spectacles. "I'd come upstairs to fetch the necklace I'd forgotten when I surprised him."

Connor glanced at the half open balcony doors, wind blowing the brocade curtains inward. The chambermaid was sitting in the middle of the floor, looking terrified and exhausted.

"He was looking for jewelry?"

"No," Ardath said. "That's the most disturbing part. I caught him rifling through your papers."

"My papers?" Connor's face hardened. "Then he was probably looking for cash."

She lowered her voice. "He'd gotten hold of your portfolio—the one on the Balfour murder case. There were so many papers stuffed up his shirtsleeves and trousers that he looks like a scarecrow. He knew what he was looking for, Connor. And it wasn't money."

Chapter

5

Maggie didn't waste any time making her own exit after Connor rushed off to investigate the commotion. As she ran through the house, she felt as though she were a princess in a story awakening from a dark spell, escaping an even darker prince.

Connor Buchanan was not only a lovely-looking lion of a man, he was also perceptive and possessed of a personal magnetism that even she had found difficult to resist. Not that she had much experience in such matters. Most men were too afraid to flirt with her. The Chief intimidated the few suitors brave enough to show any serious interest in courtship. Overprotective, suspicious by nature, he behaved the same way with his young daughter, Janet. Maggie never ceased to marvel that a man who made his living in vice could be so morally minded.

An unconscious sigh of pleasure escaped her as she remembered the unique sensation of Connor's fingers stroking her throat. Of course, if she ever saw Lord Buchanan again, he'd be putting those strong hands around her neck to strangle her. He wasn't likely to forgive her for making a fool of him. A shiver of terror jolted through her at the thought of their meeting again, as prisoner and prosecutor, in a court of law.

Suddenly she stopped, realizing she had no idea where she was. She'd always had a hopeless sense of direction; the Chief tucked a compass in her basket every time she went to market. Somehow, avoiding the party guests, she seemed to have ended up in a private courtyard off the main withdrawing room.

The outer doors had been left open to the terrace, but the room appeared oddly deserted. Perhaps everyone had gone off to search the premises for more dangerous intruders, such as the one his lordship had trapped upstairs.

The rain had stopped, and Maggie wondered wryly whether this would be a great disappointment to Ardath. And what exactly was the woman's relationship to Lord Buchanan?

She knew she needed to create a disturbance so that Hugh could escape, but short of setting a fire in the basement, she couldn't imagine what to do. There wasn't time to run back to Heaven's Court to ask the Chief for advice. If she hadn't encountered Lord Buchanan, she would have had a chance to think.

She whirled, startled out of her thoughts, as a wand-slim woman appeared on the terrace steps beside her.

The woman gave Maggie a long assessing look. Maggie looked right back at her, summoning the de Saint-Evremond hauteur to conceal the humiliating fact that she was a housebreaker with twelve pilfered chocolate éclairs and two bottles of champagne under her cloak. Her heart pounded against her breastbone.

There was something a little familiar, a little unsettling about the woman—oh, blast, she looked like a paler version of Connor Buchanan. She must be another one of his sisters, judging by that tall thin frame and Nordic elegance.

The woman didn't seem to have Connor's self-confidence, though. In fact, she struck Maggie as rather sad and anxious, a woman with worries enough of her own. The impression deepened as she asked, "Who are you?" in a high-pitched voice that sounded as if she were on the verge of tears.

Damn. "I'm—I'm Elliot's daughter."

"Philomena?"

"Yes. Philomena."

A puzzled frown furrowed the woman's brow, but then it was gone, her own troubled thoughts clearly taking precedence.

A maid came out of the house to bring the woman a shawl. Maggie stared up thoughtfully at the house. She could throw a stone at his lordship's window and break it, but that wouldn't be enough of a distraction for Hugh to make it downstairs. She could—

She pivoted in alarm. A large black carriage careened around the corner and barreled into the courtyard. The driver narrowly missed colliding with the gate. Panic gripped her, paralyzing her reflexes. What if Lord Buchanan had already sent for the police to take Hugh away?

The woman glanced at Maggie, her voice shrill and unnatural above the clatter of wheels. "Look at the way that coachman is driving. Doesn't he realize he could hurt someone?"

A chill of apprehension darted down Maggie's spine. There had been a large black carriage in her own past. A carriage commissioned by Napoleon's police, who had arrived in the middle of the night to arrest her aristocratic parents for treason.

Papa had died of a heart attack on the front lawn of the château, struggling to stop the police from dragging Maman away in her nightclothes. But they had taken her anyway, and they had taken Papa's body with her in that carriage. Maggie had been left on the steps, in shock, with her older brother, Robert. Her sister, Jeanette, had remained in the house with Papa's secretary; Maggie had run inside to warn them.

The rest of that night remained a mysterious blank in her memory, a void of darkness with shadowed figures and voices too distant to make out.

The de Saint-Evremond butler, Claude Villiers, had whisked Maggie off before morning to his brother's cottage in LeHavre. She never found out what had happened to her brother and sister. They had completely vanished from her life. From France, Claude and Maggie had escaped across the Channel, smuggled between brandy barrels, to Scotland. Maggie's elderly Aunt Flora had given them a home until her death five years ago. She had changed Maggie's name and kept their whereabouts a secret for fear their political enemies would find her. To this day Maggie had never discovered why anyone would bother to hunt her down. She knew nothing of spying. In fact, this past year she had decided she would no longer try to hide her identity.

She forced herself to take a breath. From habit she suppressed the sorrow and rage that welled up—a black wave of overwhelming emotion. For the most part she refused to let resentment over life's injustices ruin the present. She was alive. She had her friends, and faithful Claude, who was getting on in years. She had found love and loyalty in unlikely places.

But then at the most unexpected moments the smallest thing would trigger a memory. A woman walking down the street wearing a bonnet like Maman's. A young boy who looked like Robert hurrying off to school. A girl with Jeanette's beguiling grin.

Where were her brother and sister now? she wondered. The pain of not knowing their fate had grown unbearable over the years. Did they think of her, remember her? Were they even alive? Not an evening passed that she didn't remember them in her prayers. Several times she had tried, unsuccessfully, to trace them, but it was as if they had ceased to exist after that night. Had they tried to find her?

The family estates had been confiscated. The château was apparently unoccupied and had fallen into disrepair.

And now she was a thief who lived with thieves and gave deportment lessons for a living.

The carriage horses came to a heaving stop in the courtyard. The clamor broke her trance. The carriage door clattered open, and a man in a black velvet domino jumped out. The maid standing behind Connor's sister gave a fearful shriek, pulling at her mistress's arm. Maggie's heart began to race; an eerie sense of déjà vu immobilized her. This wasn't a costume party.

Something was horribly wrong.

The coachman wore a mask too.

For a moment the other man stared in silent assessment at the three women standing as still as statues on the terrace steps. The next thing Maggie knew he had lunged forward to grab Connor's sister and drag her across the courtyard.

Their movements looked staged and jerky, like a marionette show, the timing off.

Then the woman started to scream, and so did the maid, their voices echoing in the still aftermath of the storm.

Maggie's own breath felt trapped in her throat against a cry for help. The woman's shawl had fallen in a puddle of rainwater. The man in the domino seemed to be having trouble hoisting her into the carriage. Apparently, she was heavier than she looked.

Maggie thought of Maman, crying in fear and shame as they carried her off, shivering in her thin nightclothes. She thought of Papa staggering between the policemen, his hand pressed to his heart. No one helped him. No one lifted a blessed finger to save his life.

The maid had uttered one final, useless shriek before fainting behind the fish pond. The carriage door closed. The curtains were swiftly drawn to obscure the interior. The driver snapped his whip to circle the four horses back toward the street.

Kidnap.

Abduction.

There was a murderer running loose in the city.

My enemies are dying for the chance to destroy me.

But Connor Buchanan was *her* enemy.

If she got involved in his sister's kidnapping, she'd have to explain her presence at his party. He would probably work twice as hard to get a death sentence for Jamie, and then he would turn his considerable talents on prosecuting her and Hugh. Her life would be over.

I have to help. This time I won't let them hurt her.

She didn't know where the strange thought had sprung from, or even what it meant. She only knew she couldn't let this happen.

She started to run after the carriage without any idea what she could do to stop it. But she had to try, even if she ended up in prison. God help her, even if she got transported to Tasmania and did penal servitude with hardened convicts for the rest of her life. She was so afraid for that woman.

She was so angry at what had happened to her own family that an almost supernatural strength flowed through her.

The coachman had slowed to pass back through the porte cochere. He was startled out of his wits when he glanced down and saw a wee curly-haired woman climbing up into the box beside him, her face bright with angelic wrath.

"Here," he said in alarm. "What do ye think ye're doing?"

"Stop this carriage." She reached into her cloak. Then she raised a bottle of champagne, of all things, over his head. "Stop this carriage, and let that woman out, or I'll bash you from here to Friday."

"What's going on?" the other man inside the carriage called out in a muffled voice. "Get us the bloody hell out of here before that devil Buchanan comes."

"There's a girl up on the box with a champagne bottle," the driver shouted. "What do ye want me to do with her?"

The bottle came crashing down on his head, but the damned thing didn't break, even though the woman had thrown her entire weight into it. He swore, and when she came at him again, he put up his hands to protect himself, jerking back on the reins in the process. The horses obediently took off at a sharp trot. The bottle slid down between his feet.

He winced as the woman went flying backward off the box. He didn't wait to watch her hit the ground. This was a bad business, this abduction. He'd said it from the start. He hadn't wanted any part of it, and now he had a bruised skull into the bargain. There was a woman lying on the ground like a fallen angel, and it was his fault. The maid who'd fainted by the fish pond had started screaming bloody murder again, and people were pouring out of the house to investigate with that cruel bastard Connor Buchanan shouldering to the front of the crowd.

Maggie stared at the receding carriage in shock. She felt bruised and disoriented from the fall. Her left shoulder ached too much to even lift. Dear God. Her chest was burning too. She wondered if she'd been shot, remembering the strange *pop* she'd heard when she landed. The driver could have pulled a pistol and shot her because she'd hit him on the head with the bottle. She felt physically sick at the thought of that girl inside the carriage, alone with her captors. Had they hurt her, too?

She felt the ground vibrating beneath her. From the corner of her eye she saw a large gray stallion thundering across the courtyard into the street. She recognized the rider as Lord Buchanan right away, his broad shoulders rigid, his face a study in ruthless determination. He didn't notice her, and she was relieved. She hoped fiercely that he would hunt down and punish the men who had taken his sister.

Her thoughts drifted into blankness, curiously detached and unafraid. It crossed her mind that she might be dying. Listen to that maid screaming. What an undignified noise to usher you into the afterlife. Shadows were closing in on her. She didn't try to fight the loss of consciousness.

The sounds impinged on the shadows: a muddle of voices, footsteps, the maid babbling between screams that her mistress had been abducted and that the brave woman lying dead by the gate had tried to rescue her. Maggie had no idea how much time had elapsed since she had seen Lord Buchanan cantering past her.

Suddenly there was a crowd of people in evening clothes standing over her, lamenting her demise, Sheena's abduction, the wicked state of the world that two innocent women should come to such an end.

"I'm not dead yet," she said weakly, but the party guests were so engrossed in putting together the pieces of the heinous crime that Maggie's voice went unheeded.

"The murderer has struck again," one man said with a sort of grim satisfaction.

"It might not be the murderer," another retorted. "This could have been one of Connor's rivals taking revenge, or warning him off. He's Lord Advocate now and can expect this sort of thing."

"Is there a ransom note?"

"Let's take this poor lassie's body inside. Look at the wee thing. What a tragedy."

"I'm not dead," Maggie said in a stronger voice, scowling up at the concerned faces.

"Who is she, anyway?"

"Did the maid get a description?"

"Norah said she was Elliot's daughter."

"She's not my daughter," Elliot said from the back of the crowd. "Philomena's still inside trying to get that caviar off her dress."

Maggie sat up, so irritated that she scarcely felt the sharp pain in her shoulder. "I'm not dead, damn it, but I will be soon if somebody doesn't help me."

Lazurus rising four days from the tomb had probably not caused such a commotion. The guests gasped as if they had seen a ghost. They took a collective step back, stumbling against one another.

From the safe distance they stared down at Maggie in dumbstruck silence.

She sank back onto her cloak with a faint groan, aware once again of the deep pain in her shoulder. She had made her point.

"I think I've been shot," she said with a grimace of pain. This wrung another gasp from the guests.

"A man in a black mask took Lord Buchanan's sister," she added.

"Took her where?" someone had the stupidity to ask.

"They didn't say. It—it was an abduction. I was hurt trying to stop them. Lord Buchanan went chasing after them too."

"Oh, my God. Connor!" A large-figured attractive woman in her fifties, with auburn hair, broke from the line of stunned guests to kneel at Maggie's side. "Don't worry, my dear. We'll take care of you. Where were you shot?"

The woman smelled heavily of powder and orange water, and her raspy voice was kind and concerned. The fan dangling on her wrist hit Maggie in the face. Her sable boa floated down to tickle her nose, but the worst part was that she kept leaning all her weight against Maggie's left shoulder, which hurt like blue blazes as it was.

"What is it, Bella?" one of the guests said.

Ardath abandoned Connor at the fountain to investigate. "What happened, Mother?"

"One of Connor's young guests was shot trying to stop

Sheena's kidnappers," the woman named Bella answered in a whisper.

Maggie breathed out a sigh. "I suppose you could say I deserved this, turning felon and breaking into a house, but my motives were pure. I think I was shot in the shoulder. I'm not entirely sure. My head feels awfully queer. I must be hallucinating—I thought I heard an angel singing."

"That's one of the cats that got locked up in the carriage house during the confusion," Bella explained gently.

"Dear heaven," Ardath said. "Somebody fetch the Lord Advocate."

The color drained from the older woman's face as she gently drew open Maggie's cloak. "Lord help us. She's only a wee thing. *Connor.*" Her voice was deep and urgent, attracting the tall figure from the fish pond where he and Norah stood questioning the maid. Evidently his search for his sister had proven unsuccessful, and he had returned alone.

Ardath stared at Maggie with tears welling in her eyes. "How bad is it, Mother?"

"Someone send for the doctor," Bella said gruffly. "Elliot's daughter has been shot. To judge by her color, it doesn't look good."

"I knew it," Maggie whispered, and closed her eyes in resignation as people began running to and fro.

The end must be very near, she thought. The head groom of Lord Buchanan's household brought her a horse blanket and tucked her up in its smelly warmth. Patting her hand, he backed away with a tragic shake of his head.

Then the Lion himself was kneeling over her, an intimidating man even in that humble position. Imprisoned in the perimeters of his shadow, she felt small, protected, and terrified of his latent power all at once. His presence momentarily eclipsed her own fear. A breath shuddered out of her chest.

He was distraught and furious over his sister's abduction—Maggie wasn't quite so far gone that she could remain unaffected by the raw emotions that tightened his riveting features. Shock washed over his face when he recognized her from their recent encounter. His hazel eyes burned with the fires of hell's vengeance as they met hers.

"It's all right," he said quietly, touching his big hand to her forehead. "You're a very brave girl, and I'll take care of you. I'm going to find the men who did this. Try to rest." He dropped his tone to a whisper. "Oh, lass, why didn't you stay where I left you?"

His voice sent shivers down her spine. It was a voice as warm and wonderful as whisky drunk without restraint on a winter night. His hand felt cool in contrast. His fingers were skilled and soothing, stroking her temple, evoking the most delicious sensations in her already overwrought nervous system. His strength comforted her.

"If I'd known earlier this was going to happen," she joked weakly, "I would have drunk another glass of champagne with you."

He swallowed hard. "Hush now. Save your strength, Philomena."

"I hate that name," she whispered with a frown. "It's even worse than Marguerite."

"You shouldn't talk, lass." He looked as if he were waging a fierce war within himself to contain his anger. "Just let me help you."

"I'm not really a recluse either," Maggie confessed.

"It doesn't matter."

"No. I suppose it doesn't, does it?"

"Ask her what the men looked like," Norah prompted over his shoulder.

Connor hesitated, struggling to control his emotions, to recover from the shock of realizing that not only was Sheena missing but that this was the girl who had enchanted him such a short time ago. He couldn't think straight. His mind was reeling. His body still pulsed with outrage and the sick fear of riding across Edinburgh after the mysterious carriage that had disappeared into the night.

He hadn't found his sister. Was she already dead? He wanted to throw back his head and roar like an animal in frustration.

He wanted to take action, to make everything as it was before. Sheena was the baby, the wild child of the family. She wouldn't know how to defend herself. He couldn't bear to think of anyone harming her, or of never seeing her again.

Guilt tore through him as he remembered wishing her out of his life only an hour ago.

What if she were wandering about hurt and frightened, abandoned in a dirty alley? Would someone help her?

Someone had tried.

He stared down in wonder at the girl lying so still before him. Her bones felt fragile beneath his fingers, like finely wrought porcelain. Her skin reminded him of moonlight, fair and translucent, without a trace of warmth. He frowned, pressing his thumb against her lower lip as if to still the sigh that fluttered out. She had been so vibrant earlier.

"Why?" he wondered aloud.

Why had this happened? He could understand someone attacking him, but not Sheena. And this girl who'd made him laugh and feel like a fool—had he finally found someone he could give his heart to only to lose her in a twisted stroke of fortune? For an irrational moment he almost believed the rumors of his reputation. *Had* he sold his soul somewhere along the way? Did tonight, his celebration of triumph, mark the beginning of the price he would have to pay?

He set his jaw, refusing to let the irrational thoughts take root. He concentrated instead on the anger burning in his blood, a potent emotion he would use to punish the men who had done this. It made him want to kill with his bare hands to see her lying here like a broken doll, and to imagine Sheena in even worse circumstances. He could only blame himself. Because he dealt in danger, two innocent women could lose their lives.

"Do you remember, lass?" he asked, not pressuring her, brushing back the black curls that lay against her cool ashen cheek.

She frowned as she fought to bring back the details. "It was a large black carriage," she said slowly. "The driver had gray-brown hair, I think. But I didn't see the man who took your sister. He had on a mask, and—"

She stopped in mid-sentence, biting the inside of her lip. Everything was so confused in her mind, superimposed with the memory of her parents' arrest, the police who had stood like sentinels of death on the château lawn. Then that curious blankness, the gap in recall, images suppressed like tender shoots in black soil, pressing against layers of protective consciousness.

"I can't remember much more than that, but I won't lie to you anymore, my lord," she whispered fiercely. "I'm not really a criminal—we had to get the confession. Jamie Munro is a dimwit but he's no killer, no matter what the papers say. Please don't prosecute him. Whoever murdered those people is still running free."

Connor's hand went deathly still on her cheek.

"The poor lassie is delirious." Jacob, the old groom, shook his grizzled head in sympathy. " 'Tis from the shock and the blow to her head, no doubt. I've seen it happen on the battlefield. They go all dotty in the end. All we can do is make her comfortable."

Maggie shuddered, fearing the prospect of death even less than she did the unnerving chill that had frosted Connor's eyes. Streetwise eyes that offered no redemption, that had seen too much, sharpened over the years into dangerous sophistication. His mind had latched onto every condemning word that had come out of her mouth. Had she really imagined any hint of warmth in their hard hazel depths?

Suddenly she understood his reputation for conquering his opponents in the courtroom. His gaze raked her like a sword that would lay bare her deepest secrets. He studied her with the unholy perception of a predator.

But even worse than the cold glittering anger was the glimpse of disappointment, the death of a dream, that he had briefly allowed to show. The roguish charm, the concern, the vulnerability, all gone and crystallized into cynical suspicion.

When he looked at her now, he didn't see a tapestry princess. He saw a shameless little thief, a woman not worthy of his trust and tenderness.

He still hadn't said a word. He just stared down into her face while everyone else clucked in concern and cursed the slowness of physicians and the heartlessness of this crime.

His silence alarmed her. She searched his face for mercy, for understanding, and found a barren plain. A frisson of foreboding crept down her back, forming sharp icicles of fear in its wake.

She sat up without warning and threw off Connor's hand. Her vision was a little blurry. Her ribs hurt, but the pain in her shoulder had become bearable. Everything paled in comparison to what she imagined her fate would be if this man unleashed his wrath on her.

"I'm going home now," she said, her voice shaking. If Hugh hadn't taken advantage of all the furor to escape, she couldn't do anything to help him. "I want to be by myself."

The old groom glanced at Connor in concern. "Dinna let her move around, my lord."

Connor forced her back down onto the blanket. Even though he did not hurt her, there was an underlying strength of steel in the gesture that warned her she wasn't going anywhere without his permission.

"Lie still, Miss . . ." His deep voice paused on the faintest note of irony. "I don't believe I ever did catch your name."

"I thought you told me she was Elliot's daughter," Norah said, interrupting her distressed pacing by the gate to intervene. "Oh, thank God, here's Ardath with the doctor now."

Maggie closed her eyes. She pretended that she was having a relapse and hadn't caught the menacing undertone in Connor's last remark. The image of his face in all its ruthless beauty blazed in her mind. She almost felt sorry for whoever had abducted his sister. Connor Buchanan looked capable of tearing them apart limb by limb.

"The doctor is here." Ardath glanced at Maggie in distress. "Connor, get out of the way. How can the girl breathe with you hovering over her like that?"

Maggie stole a peep at him through her eyelashes. He stood, reluctantly, watching her in brooding silence as if he expected her to vanish like smoke if he looked away. She lifted her eyes up the seemingly endless length of his legs and torso and gazed into his face. He stared back with all the warm reassurance of a monolith, the accusation in his eyes raising gooseflesh on her arms.

"Well, well, what have we here?"

The cultured gruffness of the doctor's voice struck a familiar chord in Maggie's memory. Curious, she looked to his bearded face as he knelt to make a discreet examination of her shoulder.

"Maggie?" He stopped in astonishment, motioning for his

assistant to bring him his medical bag. "It isn't you, is it, lass? What are you doing lying injured in Connor Buchanan's courtyard?"

She sucked in a ragged breath. The enormity of what had happened deepened her voice. "It's me, Dr. Sinclair. You won't believe what I've done."

"Knowing you, my dear, it can't be any great crime."

"Oh, yes, it can."

"I doubt it," he said, smiling to distract her as he began a gentle probe of her shoulders. "But let's worry about it later, shall we? Your well-being is the thing for now. I can't seem to find where the bullet went in."

Connor frowned, looming over the tender moment like a conqueror in a Celtic legend. "You *know* this woman, Dr. Sinclair?"

"Of course I know her," the doctor snapped; while he might harbor a soft spot in his heart for Maggie, he treated everyone else, patient, prince or pauper, with unfailing rudeness.

Ardath gave Connor a strange look. "Why did you invite her to your party if you don't know her?"

"I didn't." Connor glanced down at Maggie, feeling that same earlier spell of inexplicable attraction, tainted now by his concern for his sister and the dark thread of suspicion running through his mind. "I thought she was Elliot's daughter," he said in a hard voice.

"Not that again." Maggie vented a tired sigh. Then her heart took a frightened plunge as she saw Dr. Sinclair studying her shoulder with a look of utter bewilderment on his face.

"I've never seen anything like this before," he murmured.

She swallowed hard. She couldn't bear the sight of the dark stains on the cotton gauze he gently withdrew from her shoulder. "Is it that bad? Have I lost much blood?" she asked in a whisper.

He lowered his voice so only she could hear him. "Maggie, my darling little dunderhead, you have a nasty cut on your head, but this isn't blood I'm cleaning away. It's chocolate, melted chocolate and something else that looks a bit like vanilla cream."

"Choc—oh, hell, the éclairs," she whispered. "This is the

most embarrassing moment of my life. I was taking them back for the children—they've caught Hugh, you know. We were breaking into his lordship's house to get Jamie's confession. Then his lordship's sister got abducted. I tried to help her, and I'll probably go to prison for my trouble."

Dr. Sinclair glanced up in reluctance at the tall figure hovering over them. "He's a devil of a man to have made your enemy, Maggie," he said quietly.

Connor stared in horror at the dark-stained cloth the doctor quickly stuffed back into his bag. The thought of anyone doing that to this woman, whoever the hell she was, whatever she had done, stirred a wild fury in his soul . . . and terror that Sheena was in deadly danger. "What is all this whispering about?" he demanded. "Is she going to be all right or not?"

Dr. Sinclair straightened his stooped frame, scowling up at Connor with his own brand of professional arrogance. "The woman has a serious head injury, possibly a dislocated shoulder and a bruised rib or two. She'll need to be made comfortable and watched throughout the night. Let's get her inside."

The skin over Connor's cheekbones tightened as he glanced down into the delicate face that less than an hour ago had seemed like the vision from a dream. He couldn't believe that her appealing innocence hid any dark motives. But neither was he naive enough to ignore what he'd heard with his own ears.

Criminal. Confession. She'd mentioned Jamie Munro. Damn it. Damn the newspapers. Half of Scotland had already judged the old fool guilty, which meant that the real murderer might never be apprehended and brought to trial.

He looked up at the doctor. "Wait a minute. Did you just tell me that she *didn't* get shot?"

"No, she didn't," Sinclair said reluctantly, with the thought crossing his mind that it might have been better for her if she had, breaking into *his* house, of all the insane schemes. Connor Buchanan might fight like a lion for justice. He might be a brilliant lawyer, but more than one of his colleagues had privately observed that black demons drove that brilliance. A man like Buchanan would make table scraps out of an inexperienced young girl like Maggie.

He snapped his bag shut. "Why is everyone standing about? Have the servants make a stretcher to carry her inside. I didn't say she wasn't hurt."

"We don't need a stretcher," Connor retorted. Deep beneath his anger and suspicion was a relief so sharp it made him feel weak. He didn't know why, it was irrational, but he clung to the hope that if the kidnappers hadn't tried to hurt this woman, then they wouldn't hurt Sheena either. "If she isn't shot, she isn't dying. I'll carry her inside myself."

Before Maggie or the doctor could object, he knelt and gathered her into his arms. It was a spontaneous act. He wasn't sure why he felt compelled to do it. He'd been attracted to her earlier, and even though he didn't trust her now, he refused to let anyone else be responsible for her. If she knew anything at all about Sheena, he would soon find out.

Nothing like this had ever happened in his life.

"Mind her ribs, Connor," Ardath scolded behind him. "You're going to crush her, holding her like that."

"I am not," he said in annoyance. He glanced down at Maggie. Her eyes were squeezed tightly shut, no doubt to avoid his. He couldn't tell if she was in physical pain or simply terrified. He felt cold with fear himself, shock and anger clashing inside him.

Norah hurried after them. "Why aren't the men back with Sheena? What if they can't find that carriage? Ask her again what the kidnappers looked like, Connor. She's the only one who got a close look at them."

Connor remained silent as he carried Maggie across the courtyard. He was too engrossed in his thoughts to pay any attention to Norah's anxious questioning. God knew he shouldn't have been surprised that something like this would happen. Perhaps he'd grown immune to the occasional threats that usually amounted to nothing, except for the one defendant's wife who'd stabbed him in the wrist with a salad fork at a dinner party after he'd prosecuted her husband for arson.

But the burglary and his sister's abduction in one night? Were they connected? Why would anyone take Sheena except to hurt him? He swallowed over the lump of helplessness in his throat and wondered who hated him so much he would avenge himself on an innocent family.

He hazarded another glance at the woman in his arms. She weighed next to nothing; she looked soft and frightened, hidden in his shoulder, but she had condemned herself with her own words. Disappointment, regret, and wounded pride dug talons into his heart, uprooting the treacherous seeds of tenderness that had begun to sprout.

Who was she? Certainly not Elliot's daughter.

Why had she come here tonight? Not to celebrate his success.

As he moved, his steps mechanical, he could feel her unbound hair brushing his arm, sensual, feminine, teasing. Even bundled up awkwardly against his chest, she possessed a delicate grace and dignity that reminded him of the tapestry princess. The virgin who would lure a beast to its death, who would betray the image of innocence that had attracted him. Dear God, when had he started believing in romance? His own naiveté infuriated him. His vulnerability came as a shock.

He stopped, drawing a deep breath. "Where the hell am I supposed to take her?" he said in such an angry growl that Maggie lifted her head to stare at him.

"Take her upstairs where she'll have quiet and privacy from curious eyes," Ardath said in a cool voice, following behind Norah with Bella and Dr. Sinclair.

"Privacy?" Connor snorted. "Not in my life."

His bachelor uncle came running out of the house as Connor resumed walking past the doors to the drawing room. A tall portly man in his early sixties, the Earl of Glenbrodie had spent all but the last decade of his life traveling around the world as an amateur botanist.

He'd been in the basement brewing an herbal remedy for one of the party guests when the excitement had exploded. Connor had long ago realized that the man lived in another world from everyone else.

"I just heard about Sheena." The earl brushed a sprinkling of loose soil from the gardener's apron he wore over his jacket; his cheeks were ruddy above his trim white beard. Then, noticing the slip of a girl in Connor's arms, he lowered his voice in disapproval. "Well, everyone criticizes my behavior, but I must say, this is a fine time to be carrying a woman around in the courtyard with a housebreaker upstairs and your sister Sheena stolen by a stranger."

Connor scowled. God, he could feel the start of a killer headache throbbing behind his left eye, and now people, important people, were peering at him from behind his own windows. "Apparently the girl was injured trying to rescue Sheena," he said through his teeth. "The doctor wants her made comfortable."

"She tried to rescue Sheena?" The earl's face softened. "For heaven's sake then, don't just stand out here in the damp with her. Do what the doctor told you. Who is she, anyway?"

Connor met Maggie's gaze, hardening his heart against the unexpected power of the innocence in her eyes. "Nobody seems to know," he said. "All I can say for certain is that she isn't Elliot's daughter."

"The poor child could be in shock," the earl said with a reassuring smile for Maggie. "What is your name, my dear?"

Maggie sighed in resignation. There was no point in trying to hide the truth. His lordship hadn't recovered from her earlier deception. It had to be difficult for a man of his stature to admit he could be victimized.

"My name," she began bravely, "is—"

"Maggie!" a familiar young male voice shouted down from the balcony that led into Connor's bedroom. "Judas, don't tell me they've caught you, too? I swear I didna breathe a word. I said I was housebreaking all by myself. I didna let on for a minute that you were the mastermind. I told 'em the slipper on the balcony was mine. I said I'd stolen it."

A dead silence met Hugh's revealing outburst. Everyone seemed afraid to break the devastating tension that held Lord Buchanan spellbound. Maggie cringed as she felt his arms tighten around her like bands of iron, but she couldn't bring herself to look up at his face. The anger that emanated from him like smoke forewarned her of a dangerous fury seething beneath his surface composure.

Two male servants emerged from the bedroom to try to drag Hugh off the balcony.

"Make a run for it, Maggie," the boy shouted, adding fuel

to the fire he'd started. "Remember the rumors about him—you're done for if you dinna get away from the devil."

It sounded like good advice to Maggie. She wouldn't have a lambchop's chance once the lion dragged her into his den. "I think you ought to put me down, my lord," she told Connor, straining against his arms.

There wasn't a flicker of cooperation on his face. "Who the hell are you?" he said in a low, furious voice.

Ardath tugged on the tail of his evening jacket. "Just put her down, Connor. You're probably hurting her. You don't know your own strength. I've told you that before."

"The girl might have sustained internal injuries, Lord Buchanan," Dr. Sinclair said in a stern tone. "I can't allow you to manhandle her like this. She requires careful treatment."

"Put the girl down, I say." The earl had taken Maggie's side along with the others. "As far as I can make out, she's the only one who lifted a damn finger to save Sheena. The family owes her an enormous debt."

Maggie's pulse began to pound in panic. He was backing away from his friends and family like a cornered animal. Clearly he didn't give a damn what anyone said. The cruel gleam in his eyes foreshadowed unimaginable punishments. The most powerful man in Scotland, and she was at his mercy. He wasn't going to listen to reason. He wouldn't care that she'd only wanted to help a friend. All the dreadful things she'd heard about him were true.

The situation called for desperate measures.

She broke out of his arms with such an unexpected burst of energy that Connor, taken off guard, almost lost his hold on her. For a breathless moment she believed she had a chance at freedom. She actually thought she could escape him. Then he snagged a handful of her cloak just in time.

Maggie's toes never even touched the ground. He lifted her in the air with the amount of effort it would have taken him to pluck a daisy from a flowerpot.

She gasped, her feet dangling between his legs, his large hands clamped around her waist. To make matters worse, Dr. Sinclair hadn't stuffed the stolen éclairs back into her pockets and they were sliding free. Fortunately, in all the commotion, an insignificant thing like a few pastries falling to the ground went unnoticed.

Unfortunately, she couldn't say the same for the other bottle of champagne she'd crammed in the pocket of her cloak. It was a wonder it had survived her fall from the carriage.

His mistress was right. The man obviously did not know his own strength.

When he yanked her back toward him, and into the darkness, the bottle finally dislodged and hit the stone walkway with the force of a lead ball hurtling from a cannon. The cork exploded in midair. The silence amplified the deafening pop.

Ardath uttered a startled shriek. "Good Lord, a gunshot! Someone's shooting at us."

"The boy on the balcony," Norah cried. "I thought I saw something in his hand!"

The earl threw his arms around Ardath's mother and began dragging her down the steps. "Everyone on the ground! Connor, protect that girl—we need her help. Guard her with your life."

The old groom came running up from the courtyard, drawn by all the shouting. "What's the matter? Are the kidnappers back?"

"Someone is shooting at Connor," Ardath said breathlessly, picking up her skirts to run. "Take cover, Jacob."

The groom stumbled down the steps, shouting back at the servants who were spilling out of the house. "Someone is trying to assassinate the Lord Advocate! Save yourselves."

Maggie never had a chance to explain. All of a sudden she was flying backward, sailing over the steps, with Connor's big hard body breaking the fall. She credited his reflexes that he reacted so swiftly. She'd been too stunned to do anything but stare.

He rolled her beneath him, cushioning her head with his arm. The impact knocked the breath from her body. A monument of muscle, bone, and sinew smothered her, making it impossible to move. The man might have been sculpted out of stone. His straight blond hair tickled her chin. His massive chest crushed hers, their hearts beating in wild harmony. She groaned to protest her discomfort.

"Lord Buchanan—"

"Don't talk."

"But there isn't—"

"Damn it, be quiet, would you? This is a life or death situation. Someone wants to kill us."

The others had all taken cover under the row of topiary animals that surrounded the darkened terrace. Ardath and her mother were crouched arm-in-arm under a spread-winged evergreen dragon; Norah, the earl, and Dr. Sinclair huddled together in fear of their lives under a bush trimmed to be a pair of Minoan bulls.

Maggie winced inwardly as she heard the champagne bottle roll down the terrace steps toward them, where it began spinning like a Chinese firecracker.

Champagne sprayed through the air in a bubbling mist. Connor raised his head, muttering, "What the hell?" just as a final jet of yellow-label hit him full in the face.

Mortified, Maggie watched his expression of alarm transform into outrage as he realized what had happened. He pushed up on his elbows, allowing her the space to gasp for a breath, but not to escape. A shudder of apprehension seized her as he stared down at her in silence. She almost wished an assassin *would* appear.

Time stopped, ticking by in a slow agony of seconds. Even if he had released her, she couldn't have broken the power of his heartless gaze. She was his prisoner in more ways than one, enwrapped in a web of suspense.

Champagne dripped down his lean cheek to tremble in the cleft of his chin. She could hear the scrape of footsteps behind them—the other guests emerging from their hiding places. She could hear the harsh rhythm of Connor's breathing, as if words failed him, as if the anger that consumed him had pushed him beyond the point of coherent speech.

Brazen it out, bairns, that master criminal, the Chief, would say as he shoved his little band of pickpockets into the streets. *Never admit your guilt to the law even if you're caught red-handed. Maintain your innocence to the end.*

So, with a self-possession that would make her venerable Highland friend proud, she slipped her hand inside Connor's vest pocket to remove his handkerchief and soak up the Clicquot-Ponsardin on his jaw. His body stiffened in reaction. His facial muscles felt like granite under her fingertips.

In fact, if he glared any harder, his face would probably crack.

"Oh, my." Ardath dipped her knuckle in the effervescent puddle on the step and tasted it with a baffled look. "It's champagne. I believe you've just been christened, Connor."

"Help the girl up, Connor," the earl called down the steps. "Neither of you can be comfortable in that position."

"Champagne?" Bella said in a puzzled voice, plucking a leaf from her boa. "You mean that someone was trying to assassinate Connor with a bottle of champagne? What will these criminals think of next?"

Connor didn't answer. He was terrifyingly still.

Maggie drew a breath. Her gaze lifted for an instant to the balcony where Hugh was hanging over the railing laughing his head off at the scene below. The two male servants who'd been ordered to restrain him were having a hard time controlling their own sniggers of amusement.

Connor still hadn't moved. She could feel the imprint of his body through her clothing. Intimate, angry, invasive. She wondered if they were going to stay all night in this humiliating position.

She dabbed at the spot of champagne on his chin that she'd missed. It seemed like the least she could do. "Well, you were right about one thing, my lord," she said in a confidential tone. "It did keep its fizz."

For the first time in a decade Connor's mental faculties failed him. All he knew about this woman was that she had broken into his house, in an incredible act of daring, captivated and deceived him, and apparently played angel of mercy to his sister. Now, to add insult to injury, she was dabbing stolen champagne off his chin and damn if deep down in that irrational male part of his psyche, he didn't find the act mildly arousing.

His face forbidding and cold, he peeled the soggy handkerchief from her fingers and lifted her to her feet, glancing down hard at the pastry that had fallen between them. He bent to pick it up, studying it in disbelief.

"What the—God above, it's one of my own damned éclairs."

The earl stepped a little closer, shaking his head in admonishment. "I can't believe you'd eat dessert at a time like this. Don't you care about anything except your own selfish pleasures?"

Connor vented an uncivilized curse.

Ardath straightened slowly, her voice placating and low. "Connor, it was only champagne."

He ignored them all, rounding on the petite girl who stood in a puddle of moonlight. God help him, she was exquisite, her eyes huge in that fragile face. But he should have known better. Life had taught him that much. A tapestry princess was too good to be true.

"Who are you?" His voice blasted across the terrace like a blizzard as he strode toward her. "Damn it, you will answer me if we have to stand here all evening."

She raised her chin, eyeing him with the aristocratic disdain which reduced him to the social equivalent of a snail, and which, over the past few decades, had gotten most of her ancestors beheaded. "I am Marguerite Marie-Antoinette de Saint-Evremond. In deference to the Scottish side of the family, I go by the name Maggie Saunders. Not," she added as an afterthought, "that it's any of your business."

Chapter

6

Connor squeezed back against the railing to allow the procession of servants to pass him on the stairs. He, the master of the house, had ceased to exist. His staff barely spared him a glance. They were too busy vying for the honor of serving the courageous woman who had single-handedly taken on the kidnappers. It was the talk of the whole street, if not the city. Her brave act had taken on epic proportions.

Towels, heated water, pots of tea, Norah's nightclothes. Not a luxury was denied the dubious heroine who, against Connor's ignored complaints, had been installed in the recently refurbished guest chamber.

"Oh, sir, would you mind carrying these before I ruin 'em?" a chambermaid said over a mound of pillows, struggling to thrust a bouquet of scraggly Michaelmas daisies at him. "It's the best we could do at such short notice to brighten the poor mite's room. You must be so proud of her, sir, trying to save your sister."

Stunned, Connor stuffed the flowers under his arm as the maid barreled around him. "This woman has had a very unsettling effect on my entire household," he explained to the bewildered young Welsh police inspector who tried to follow him up the crowded stairs. "Not that either my family or my staff go out of their way to respect my wishes, but her presence has definitely made things worse."

"I can see that, my lord." The inspector leaned his halberd against the banister. "Were she and your missing sister acquainted by any chance?"

Connor paused. "Not that I know of, but you've brought up a good point. A connection between the housebreaking and Sheena's abduction did cross my mind. You'll have to question the girl in depth. I'm afraid my first reaction was impulsive, and probably not wise. I tried to follow the carriage on horseback, but it had already disappeared. No one I questioned on the way had even seen it. I should have kept my head and summoned help right away."

"Few of us know how we would react in such circumstances, sir."

Connor's expression was grim. "Perhaps, but I should have known better."

He led Inspector Davies to the luxurious suite of interconnecting rooms usually reserved for the families of visiting judges or Members of Parliament. It might have been occupied by a foreign princess for all the excitement buzzing through the house. Connor would have been amused at any other time.

"Take heart, sir," Davies said, reassuring him again. "We're having all the seaports watched and the city gates barricaded. Your colleague Donaldson has already provided us with a list of known criminals and felons with a grudge against you. Your sister will turn up in time."

"I hope to God you're right," Connor said. "She could be anywhere by now."

His face dark with worry, he opened the door. The sight that greeted him briefly wiped every other thought from his mind.

Maggie reclined amidst a sea of lace-embroidered pillows in the middle of a lofty four-poster bed with feathered finials, accepting all the attention as if she were Cleopatra on her royal barge. She looked perfectly natural in her luxurious surroundings. She looked more at home than Connor had ever felt in this fussy room with its gilt-lacquered wardrobe and flocked wallpaper depicting angels and frolicking shepherdesses.

His uncle sat at her bedside, discussing his travels. Ardath was arranging a pink silk ribbon around the bandage on the little usurper's head. Bella and Norah were trying to decide which wrapper Maggie should wear over her nightrail. God forbid she should take a chill and start to sneeze during the night. Dr. Sinclair stood at the dressing table mixing a headache powder for her with the absorption of an alchemist turning base metal into gold.

Maggie herself was gazing blankly at a selection of chocolates in the large box on her lap. Her blue eyes narrowed when Connor entered the room, then widened in astonishment as she noticed the police inspector behind him.

I knew it, Connor thought, refusing to acknowledge a surprising stab of disappointment. This isn't her first run-in with the law. She's probably a professional. Damn her. She was good. He would have sworn she had been gently bred. He could usually read people at a glance.

"I assume you have already met Inspector Davies, Miss Saunders?" he said, not bothering to hide the derision in his voice.

Before she could answer, the young Welshman made a beeline for the bed. "What has this man done to you, Maggie? Why are you wearing a bandage on your head?"

Connor straightened, unable to believe his ears. "Did I miss something?" he said archly, turning to Ardath.

Maggie raised her face to receive the affectionate kiss Inspector Davies planted on her cheek. "I thought you'd gone to Glasgow, Thomas. How are the children?"

"On their way back here with Gladys, and missing you something dreadful. But never mind them." He cast a suspicious glance over his shoulder at Connor. "Housebreaker indeed. What power does to some people. What happened to your head, Maggie love?"

The earl gave her a grateful look. "She banged it up trying to rescue my niece from her abductors. We're lucky we didn't lose her."

Connor came up behind them. "By the way, that's the niece whose abduction you're supposed to be investigating, Inspector."

"You have to find her soon, Thomas," Maggie said, her forehead creased in concern. "It was such a horrible thing to witness—I couldn't stand by without trying to do something, could I? She was so helpless."

"Do you have any other convictions?" Connor demanded.

"Convictions?" Maggie paused to think. "I was raised a devout Roman Catholic. Does that count?"

He gave her a rather nasty smile. "I meant do you have any past criminal convictions."

"How dare you. What an impertinent thing to ask."

Inspector Davies straightened his narrow shoulders. "It's just as I suspected, Lord Buchanan," he said with satisfaction. "Maggie Saunders had nothing to do with any abduction."

Maggie gave him a fleeting smile. Connor watched her in reluctant fascination, trying to see beneath the surface. How did she do it? For a criminal she looked incredibly sweet with her hair streaming in soft waves over her shoulders. No wonder she had fooled him. The girl apparently enchanted everyone she met.

"Are those for me?" she asked him unexpectedly, motioning to the bedraggled flowers stuffed under his arm.

He glanced down at the mangled daisies and vented a deep sigh. In all the furor, he'd forgotten he was even holding them. "Yes. Take the damn things."

He dropped the flowers on the bed. Maggie bit her lip in confusion, wondering why he'd made such a nice gesture as bringing her flowers only to dump them in her lap. "I tried to tell his lordship I was only an innocent bystander," she explained in a small voice to the inspector. She paused to straighten one of the daisies' twisted stems. "He wouldn't listen."

"There's no telling my brother anything once he's made a decision," Norah said. "I've always claimed it's easier to move a mountain than to change Connor's mind. He's been that way ever since I can remember."

Maggie shook her head in sympathy. "It's probably too late to change him now. At his age character is well established."

Connor crossed the room to the window, his shoulders stiff with tension. He'd removed his evening jacket and black velvet waistcoat. The party was obviously over. He frowned in annoyance. What did the girl mean, 'at his age'? And God, where *was* Sheena?

"How many men are out searching for my sister, Inspector Davies?" he asked curtly.

"Every man under my command is looking for her, my lord, including the entire brigade of volunteers."

"I'm going to join them," he muttered.

"You're probably wiser to stay here," Davies said. "Just in case this was an attempt to lure you out into the open where some lunatic might be lying in wait for you. And, I hate to bring it up, sir, but the kidnappers will probably send a ransom note to the house."

Connor turned, his face shadowed with anxiety, and just a touch of irony. "And you are convinced that this woman didn't have anything to do with Sheena's abduction?"

"Did you have anything to do with the abduction, Maggie?" Inspector Davies asked her with an indulgent smile that indicated how ridiculous he found the question.

Maggie drew herself upright in the bed. "I did not."

The inspector turned back to Connor. "She denies any involvement in your sister's abduction, my lord."

"I heard perfectly well what she said," Connor snapped. "But that still doesn't explain why she and her young hoodlum friend broke into my house." He stared down his nose at Maggie. "Does it?"

"Don't be bullied into believing he can keep you here against your will," Ardath advised Maggie under her breath as she pretended to plump up the pillows. "It's called 'wrongful imprisonment.' "

Maggie looked directly at Connor. "I'm not ignorant, my lord. I know what you're trying to do to me. It's called 'wrongly imprison us.' "

Connor made a rude noise in his throat.

"Don't answer any more questions, dear," Ardath said. "Not without a legal agent present. It isn't wise."

"Connor is a legal agent," the earl pointed out. "He's a damn fine one too, even if he does have the devil's own temperament. But don't worry your pretty head about court representation, Miss Saunders. If you have trouble with the law, my nephew is the man you want."

"I am not representing this woman," Connor said quickly. "It's more likely I'll end up prosecuting her than defending her."

"Prosecuting me?" Maggie turned white at the very idea, a daisy drooping in her hand.

The earl's bushy eyebrows gathered into a frown. "How could you even *mention* prosecuting her after all she's done for Sheena? I didn't see *you* attacking that carriage driver in your sister's defense."

"I didn't even see the damned carriage driver," Connor retorted. "Do you think he'd have gotten away with Sheena if I'd been in the courtyard?"

"Be that as it may," the earl continued, "bravery must be rewarded. There's too much apathy in the world. It would be better for everyone if we concentrated our efforts on finding Sheena instead of harassing this young woman. She only meant to help, and we must do the same in return."

Connor rubbed his face, refusing to be drawn into a debate he could never win. No matter how many triumphs he claimed in the courtroom, no matter that the rest of the country regarded him with awe, he had never won an argument with his own bullheaded family. They were his personal cross to bear. And now this girl, this urchin-princess, with the beguiling blue eyes and incredible arrogance—what was he supposed to do with her?

He drew Inspector Davies to the door. "Tell me what I can do to help find Sheena. I can't stay in this house another hour."

"There's nothing much to do at this point but to wait," Davies said somberly. "There's no chance your sister knew the assailant, is there?"

"How would I know?" The ugly blade of reality was cutting through Connor's composure to fray his nerves. "Look, I'm sorry," he said. "Yes. It's a valid question. Sheena didn't have many friends, and I disliked the ones she brought home. Until recently she was engaged to marry a convict, completely against my wishes, of course."

"A convict? Dear me."

"I made certain he left for Italy over a fortnight ago," Connor said, his face darkening at the memory of the ugly scene that had ensued. "Sheena saw his ship off and hasn't spoken a civil word to me since."

Davies pursed his lips. "I see. Well, there are quite a few people who still hold grudges against you, my lord, if you know what I mean."

"Yes, I do know." Connor hated the thought that, just now, in her own way, Sheena was one of them. But she would come around. She would see the wisdom of his decision and forgive him. If—*when* she was found. She had always been a sad child, beyond the scope of Connor's capacity to influence. Sometimes he suspected she deliberately tried to upset him, to make him prove he cared.

He glanced toward the bed at the pale girl who watched him in guarded curiosity. Had one of his enemies sent her? Was her innocence the subtle weapon that would break him down when more brutal tactics had failed? No. No. It didn't make sense. But then nothing about Miss Saunders did, her allegedly noble background and connections to the criminal underworld, her presence in Connor's house. She was a mystery. Unfortunately for her, however, solving mysteries was his strong point.

He returned to Maggie's side after a moment's deliberation. He refused to be moved by the sight of the bandage wrapped around her head. He refused to worship at her tiny feet like everyone else in his blasted household. She had been caught red-handed in a criminal act. He knew how to treat her type. The thought counteracted the sting of guilt he felt as her eyes met his, bright with alarm.

He ignored the faint start she gave as he towered over her, his stance purposefully intimidating. To his frustration he couldn't decide if he was more angry because she had broken into his home, or because he had started to fantasize a romantic future with her on the basis of their one absurd encounter. He must have sounded like an utter moron to Elliot.

"Excuse me, Miss Saunders, if that is indeed your name," he said in a dry voice. "When you're finished holding court to my household, do you think you could try to recall a few more details about my sister's abduction?"

Maggie would have taken offense at his tone if Ardath

hadn't leaped to her defense before she had the chance. Maggie was rapidly amending her earlier impression of the woman. Ardath might enjoy such unconventional pastimes as dancing about half-dressed in the rain, but she did have her good points. She was highly intelligent with strong maternal instincts. She believed in speaking her mind.

"Don't you dare start upsetting her again," Ardath said from the other side of the bed. "Upsetting her won't make her remember. Just look at her, Connor. She has a bandage on her head. One makes exceptions for the injured."

"Not to mention her bruised ribs," the earl added in concern.

Dr. Sinclair turned from the dressing table, shaking a phial of powder. "She's also got—"

"A hell of a lot of nerve," Connor said loudly, finally losing his temper.

The echo of his voice resonated like thunder in the silence that fell over the room. The chambermaid, who had just brought up a warm comforter, thumped a pillow in disapproval. Ardath crossed her arms over her chest and gave Connor a shaming look.

Maggie put down the bouquet of flowers, watching Connor with a curious mixture of sympathy and foreboding. He was rather magnificent, if you could overlook his beastly reputation and penchant for putting people in prison. He certainly knew how to command attention. She admired that in a man. It indicated character, and to be fair she had to concede she probably wasn't seeing him at his best.

"I was about to say that she has a concussion." Dr. Sinclair's voice was curt. "There's a knot on her head the size of an orange. If she does not remember everything that happened tonight, I wouldn't be at all surprised."

Connor gritted his teeth, staring at Maggie in open suspicion. "She broke into my house to steal a legal document—"

"Excuse us, my lord," a polite male voice interrupted from the door. "The trays are here."

"What trays?" Connor looked up with a scowl. "I don't remember ordering any trays."

Ardath motioned pleasantly to the man in the doorway. "Bring it in, Forbes."

The butler opened the door all the way to admit a train of

servants pushing a trolley and carrying several trays. Connor stared in disbelief as Forbes swept past him to display a silver platter on the trolley for Ardath's inspection. You'd have thought a royal banquet was in progress. He'd never dreamed his staff was capable of such service. He practically had to beg for a biscuit, but then Connor had always considered it one of life's little ironies that his own employees and family didn't seem to have a clue of his importance.

"Cook suggested this to revive our little patient, Mrs. Macmillan," the butler said in a conspiratorial whisper.

Ardath nodded in appreciation. "And very nice too. Give Cook my compliments."

The butler whipped off the domed cover with a flourish and sank a carving knife into the crisply browned skin of a roast turkey bulging with dressing. Connor shook himself out of his astonished trance. It was too much.

"That is a roast turkey, Ardath."

She smiled, shaking her head. "Nothing escapes your notice, does it, Connor?" She glanced warmly at Maggie. "Dark or white meat, my dear?"

Maggie sat up, her blue eyes wide with incredulity. Was it possible, she wondered, to sneak an entire turkey back to Heaven's Court? "Oh, I couldn't—is that chestnut dressing?"

Connor raised his voice. "That is the roast turkey we were serving at the party."

"Well, there isn't going to be a party." The earl slid his stool aside to let Forbes position a tray on Maggie's lap. "Not with your sister abducted, and everyone too distraught to enjoy themselves. Everyone except her own brother, who is probably the reason she was abducted to begin with."

Inspector Davies took out his pen and notebook. "A revenge abduction, you think, Lord Glenbrodie? Did anyone hear mention of a ransom note yet?"

A pair of maidservants bustled around the bed, forcing Connor back toward the door. "Mind you dinna burn yerself with this tea, miss."

"Do you take sugar, Miss Saunders, or do you prefer bein' called Lady Marguerite?"

Connor straightened abruptly. "Excuse me—*Lady* Marguerite?"

"Our Miss Saunders is the daughter of a French duke who was working as a secret agent against Napoleon," Ardath explained quietly. "She was living in exile with an elderly Scottish aunt until a few years ago. She isn't just anyone off the street."

"Really, Ardath?" Connor said, pretending to look impressed. "I wonder how many other housebreakers in the city are actually deposed aristocrats and foreign spies in disguise? Could it be—should I check whether our chimney sweep is actually the King of Siam?"

Maggie released a sigh as Dr. Sinclair handed her a small glass of brown medicine. "I don't think his lordship believes me. Not that he doesn't have good cause. By the way, my lord, I don't expect preferential treatment. You may call me Miss Saunders. Oh, this dressing is delicious. I hope everyone will forgive me for eating with such abandon. I haven't had a meal like this in years. It must have cost a fortune."

The earl and Ardath shared sympathetic looks. "You eat to your heart's content, lassie," he told her. "My nephew can certainly afford it."

Connor was jostled back to the bed as the door opened to admit a maid bearing a platter of imported fruits and cheeses. A muscle ticking in his jaw, he watched Maggie make room on her tray for the light dessert course. Bending on the pretense of picking up a napkin, he said in an undertone, "Going into hibernation, are we?"

Maggie didn't answer. How could she? She was stuffing a Spanish orange into her mouth like a greedy little squirrel. Hell, Connor wouldn't be surprised if the bed gave under her weight. He couldn't begin to guess where she would put it all, but she had been served enough food to sustain an army of Highlanders on a winter march.

But then suddenly she expelled a weary sigh and dropped her head back against the pillow. Her appetite apparently had been sated after a few hearty bites of fruit and cheese. Her delicate fingers were wrapped around the turkey drumstick she had yet to taste. Connor straightened slowly, a crosscurrent of emotions catching him unaware. Empathy, attraction, curiosity—all overlaid with a logic that told him she was a very clever, very pretty little fraud whose appearance tonight probably had nothing to do with Sheena's abduction. He'd gone hungry more than once in his own life, and he couldn't help putting himself in her place. Wouldn't he have taken advantage of a similar situation?

"I want everyone else out of the room," he said unexpectedly, cutting off the treacherous tendril of sympathy before it strangled his ability to think. "I want to be alone with Miss Saunders."

Everyone started to protest at once, except for Maggie, who was suddenly too exhausted to worry about the ramifications of surviving a private interrogation with the most powerful man in Scotland. She felt a stab of understanding at the stark emotion in his eyes. He wanted everything to make sense. So did she. Yet some force beyond their control had begun to weave the threads of their lives together whether they wished it or not. The image of the medieval tapestry took shape in her mind. The elements of danger and physical attraction, the lion and his lady in their unguarded intimacy.

Did that tapestry somehow foreshadow the future?

"I don't think this is wise, Connor," Ardath said in a quiet voice. "Not in your current frame of mind."

"We want the lass to regain her memory," the earl said, rising from his stool as if to protect the small figure in the bed. "We don't want you frightening her out of her wits."

Dr. Sinclair opened his mouth to add another objection, but apparently changed his mind at the rigid determination on Connor's face.

"Out," Connor said, pointing to the door. "Everyone—now."

One didn't argue with Connor Buchanan when he used that tone of voice, his Lord Advocate's voice, the voice that condemned murderers and vindicated the innocent. Not even Ardath dared cross him when his voice dropped to that deceptively even baritone, when that hint of a Highlander's deep Scottish burr crept into the cultured inflection. The few who'd been foolish enough to challenge Connor at such a time had learned to regret it.

They scurried from the room, mice escaping as the lion stirred, a victim trapped in his lair.

Slowly he turned to stare at Maggie.

Candlelight caught the deep hollows in his face, emphasized the masculine elegance of his frame. With an impatient gesture he loosened his starched collar and pulled off his cravat. For countless moments he stood at the foot of the bed, his blond hair loose on his wide shoulders as he surveyed the unmoving figure below him. Again he felt that annoying pull of attraction, the spell of sexual and emotional magic that he could not explain. This time he fought it, refusing to acknowledge that she stirred something dangerous inside him.

His face reflected none of his inner conflict; with a practiced detachment that had become second nature, he allowed nothing to soften his expression. In his considerable experience, he could intimidate most of the criminals he handled with a deliberate silence, a look, a few well-chosen words.

It would be child's play to break down this girl.

Maggie wished with all her heart that she were anywhere but in this room. Electricity crackled in the air, a primal force that mirrored the dark energy of the man who confronted her. She had seen the disdain in his eyes when she'd dared to eat his food, but she had lived in deprivation for too long to let pride overcome temptation, and she hadn't wanted to hurt the others' feelings. His family was kind.

He was not.

He loomed at the foot of the bed in condemning silence, as if he were looking through her. A stab of fear pierced her exhaustion, but she willed herself not to show it. Her head ached so badly that she could barely focus on his face. She wanted to close her eyes and pretend—

"You will look at me when I address you, Miss Saunders," he said in a voice that compelled her to obey.

Her heart gave an apprehensive lurch as he moved to the side of the bed. Then he sat down, and all of a sudden she didn't have to struggle to stay awake. Her senses started to clamor like a fire brigade. Alarming thoughts and impressions clanged like bells through her mind. What should she believe about him? Somewhere amidst all the horrifying rumors there must be at least a grain of truth.

"What have you done with Hugh?" she asked suddenly, making a futile effort to balance her tray and scoot to the other side of the bed.

Connor stretched out across the comforter, deliberately holding her captive with the weight of his body. "Your partner in crime is downstairs with my sister's husband and the constable. The last I heard he was trying to convince them that he'd wandered into my house by mistake looking for a lost cat."

"Which is the absolute truth." Maggie pounced on the alibi without blinking an eye. "That stupid tomcat is always running off, and poor granny so attached to the ugly old thing. He must have hidden in your house to escape the storm."

Connor's voice was tart. "I believe your partner claimed it was a pregnant cat that belonged to his crippled sister."

"His sister's cat ran off too?" Maggie said in feigned astonishment. "That old tomcat must have lured her away with him. Male cats are just like that, my lord. Totally amoral and—"

"On furthering questioning, your friend admitted there was no cat, amoral or otherwise. It was Jamie Munro's confession he was after."

Maggie's face crumpled under his unwavering stare. "I knew I should have come alone," she whispered, looking down at her lap in surrender.

Connor's gaze flickered over her downbent head. "You mentioned Munro yourself in the courtyard."

"I wanted to get the confession you forced out of helpless Daft Jamie yesterday morning." Temper darkened her eyes to indigo as she raised her face to his. "It wasn't right, making a helpless old man admit to a murder he didn't have either the wits or wherewithal to commit."

"What," he asked, enunciating each word like the crack of a bullwhip, "were you going to do with that confession once you got hold of it?"

Maggie's fingers tightened around the drumstick. She was taken aback by the absolute lack of understanding in his eyes. "Well, I'm not absolutely sure. I think the plan was to convince an honest criminal lawyer to take on Jamie's case out of the goodness of his heart."

"And why was a girl sent to execute such a brilliant plan?" he asked with mild contempt.

Maggie felt her temper rising again. "Because I was the

only one in Heaven's Court with the aristocratic background to blend into your party, in the event Hugh needed a distraction."

Connor studied her with unnerving intensity. "You were a distraction, all right," he said crisply. "You distracted me into making a damned fool of myself from the moment I met you. Furthermore, that confession was never meant to fall into anyone else's hands."

Maggie sat forward, gesturing with the drumstick to make her point. "Look, I don't care if you *are* the Lord Advocate. Just because Jamie was found at the scene of the crime with the murder weapon in his hand doesn't mean he stabbed two people to death."

"Do you mind not waving that turkey leg in my face while I question you, Miss Saunders? I feel like I'm talking to Henry the Eighth."

"Turkey—" Embarrassed, Maggie carefully placed the drumstick on the tray between them. "I didn't even realize. I'm not at all myself tonight."

He gave her a droll look. "And who precisely are you—when you're being yourself, that is?"

"I told you before."

"You claim to be French, but you do not have any discernible accent. How can this be?"

"My mother was Scottish," Maggie said. "And when I came here, my aunt forbade me to speak any French for fear I'd be recognized." Her voice sounded suddenly thin and unconvincing. The beast was making her doubt her own identity. He intimidated her, sitting there on the bed in all his riveting masculinity and using the courtroom demeanor that had won so many cases before his rivals could strike a blow at his strategy.

"My name is Marguerite Marie-Antoinette de Saint-Evremond, but everyone calls me Maggie Saunders. Saunders was my mother's maiden name. She was from Inverness, actually."

An infuriating smile played across Connor's face. "Let's try again. We're all alone now. I'm not going to eat you. I probably won't even press charges, as long as you cooperate. In fact, to those who trust me I can be a very good friend."

"That isn't what I've heard," she muttered, trying covertly to tug the comforter out from under his massive thigh.

"Did you know my sister?"

"Which one?"

"Sheena, the one you allegedly tried to rescue. Would you please stop putting your hand under my leg, Miss Saunders?"

"I'd never seen her before in my life. I wish I'd never seen you either. This is a nightmare."

"We'll try again," Connor said patiently. "What exactly did the carriage driver say to you during the abduction?"

"I'm not exactly sure." She subsided back against the pillows, surrendering the comforter with a belligerent sniff. "I think he asked the man in the carriage what he was supposed to do with me. It all happened so fast. The man inside the carriage called you a devil—"

"Yes."

"Well, that would indicate to me he knew who you were."

"An act of revenge against me," he said as if reluctant to admit the possibility aloud.

"It's a distinct possibility," she said. "It's a widely known fact that quite a few people dislike you."

"Thank you for the reminder, Miss Saunders." His voice was cynical. "It does go with the profession."

"Some of them really hate you," she added innocently.

"Obviously."

"Quite frankly, my lord, if you treat others in the same fashion you have treated me tonight, I'm not surprised."

"Neither am I."

The grim resignation in his voice aroused her compassion. She realized suddenly how hard it was for him to admit he was helpless.

"Could the abduction—could it have anything to do with the murderer?"

He frowned as if he regretted having revealed even this small facet of his feelings. He narrowed his gaze on her face, reminding himself she couldn't be trusted. "More to the point—did my sister's abduction have anything to do with you and Jamie Munro?"

Maggie's face looked endearingly earnest beneath the top-heavy bandage. "Not as far as I know. How could it? I know Jamie confessed, but he didn't understand what he was saying. He's a bit dicked in the nob, as they say."

The nightrail she'd borrowed from Norah was several sizes too large for her slight frame. Connor stared in unwilling absorption at the curve of her shoulder where the end of the bandage had entangled in her hair. She had such a pale creamy complexion. He resisted the urge to run his hand up her arm, to learn the texture of her skin. He imagined that she would bruise easily. Her delicacy, however, hid an astonishingly forceful personality. Did it also hide a deceitful heart?

He noticed the tiny purple-blue vein that fluttered in the base of her throat. She was agitated, afraid of him. In fascination he traced the path of her pulsebeat with his gaze until it disappeared between the cleft of her breasts. She had generous curves for a slender woman. She was made for seduction, not thievery.

"Dicked in the nob?" he said, forcing his gaze back to her face.

Maggie stared down into her cleavage as if she wondered what he'd found so interesting. "Jamie shouldn't even have been allowed to confess until the court appointed a lawyer to defend him," she said passionately. "At least that's what the Chief said, and Lord knows his lodgers have been in prison for every crime under the sun."

Connor leaned another inch closer only to put his elbow down on the tray between them. The turkey drumstick rolled across the bed. They both pretended not to notice.

"*The* Chief." Connor looked incredulous, suddenly realizing what she had said. "Don't tell me you work for Arthur Ogilvie."

Maggie hesitated, unsure of how to explain her peculiar association with Arthur. "I don't exactly work for him. I live with him. In his house, that is. I'm one of his boarders. Actually, he's been like a godfather to me."

Connor didn't know how to react as he struggled to forge a connection between a tapestry princess and the clanless Highland chief whose old town sanctuary housed the bulk of Edinburgh's criminal underworld. Heaven's Court, as it was known, provided a haven for both retired and working criminals who had pledged their allegiance to Arthur Ogilvie. Connor battled the old rascal in court on a regular basis—he as a prosecutor, Arthur as either a heckler or hostile witness; the Chief was too crafty to get caught himself.

The two men were always trying to outwit each other. They were both the best at what they did, icons of influence and power, on opposite sides of the law. Now they had this unusual girl in common, a guttersnipe who claimed she was the daughter of a duke. His mouth twisted into a faint smile at the irony of it.

"Are you all right, my lord?" Maggie asked, watching him as warily as you would a wild animal that might attack at any moment.

He could only shake his head. Dear God, he'd met the woman less than two hours ago. Yes, he had wanted her on sight—he had wanted her badly, in his bed, to be blunt. But not like this. Not with her lying before him injured, under a cloud of suspicion, and his sister stolen on the night he hoped to celebrate his success with his closest friends.

His friends.

A spark of realization broke his reverie.

His *friends*. His friends, the silly bastards, must have done this to him. They had been threatening to pull a trick on him ever since he'd made the news of his appointment public.

It hit him like a thunderbolt, the absurdity of it, so obvious he was embarrassed not to have caught on earlier. A boyish grin broke across his face. The creases in his cheeks deepened in amusement, easing his expression. A joke. The evening must have been one extended joke. What else could it have been? Relief surged through him as he reviewed the events of the past few hours in a humorous light. He'd been duped.

"God, I should have seen it all along," he said with a low chuckle of appreciation. "I'm always telling them they have no sense of humor at the courthouse. This was their way of proving me wrong."

Maggie smiled uneasily, wondering what on earth had come over him. She was distracted by his change in attitude as much by the seductive warmth of his laughter, and the shock of sensation she felt as he casually began to untangle the bandage from her hair. She looked down suspiciously at the long elegant fingers he laid on her forearm. Then she glanced up again into his face, his chin practically touching her cheek, and a warning tingle shot down her spine.

"I've no idea what you're talking about." She eased out of his grasp and tried to slide to the other side of the bed. "But I do know that you can't keep me here by force. It's against the law."

Connor caught her by the wrist before she could disentangle herself from the comforter. "You did a wonderful job, Miss Marguerite Marie-Antoinette Whatever de Saint-Evremond Saunders." The deep Scots burr had crept back into his voice. "I'm very impressed."

"You're a little unbalanced too, my lord."

She pressed herself back against the headboard, preparing to defend herself as he fell backward across her lap in a paroxysm of deep uncontrollable laughter. His big shoulders shook with a rich rumble of uninhibited sound. In fact, the whole bed shook with it. She stared down at him in alarm.

"Oh, you're . . . very good." He could barely force the words out for laughing to himself. "Chocolate éclairs, confessions, trying to assassinate the Lord Advocate with a champagne cork. You must be a professional."

"I beg your pardon?"

"Don't look so upset—you'll start me laughing all over again." He wiped a tear from his eye, grinning and in good spirits. "This is too clever—I meant professional actress. Ardath and Donaldson put you up to this, didn't they?"

Maggie stared past him, judging the distance to the door. The poor man was delusional, cracking under the strain. She felt sorry for him, but who knew what he might take it into his head to do next? "I think we ought to call Dr. Sinclair in now," she said carefully.

Connor wagged his finger under her nose. "Sinclair, you naughty girl. I can't believe you got that old curmudgeon to play along. I wouldn't have dreamed he had a humorous bone in his body. No wonder he pretended to know you, and that police inspector."

"They do know me," Maggie said curtly.

"I want to know you too."

"No, you don't."

"Yes, I do." His voice had deepened to a rough baritone.

Jillian Hunter

Sensuality smoldered in his eyes like smoke. "In every sense of the word."

Maggie's heart began to pound in panic. "I think you're sitting on the turkey," she whispered.

"I'm going to start by kissing you," he said, touching his thumb to her lower lip.

Maggie shivered. "No, you aren't."

He grinned seductively. "Oh, but I am."

Chapter

7

He slid across the bed, drawing her resistant little body into his arms. "I wanted to kiss you before I found out how talented you are, but now I'm obsessed with the idea. I've been thinking about you all night. You have the most tempting mouth in the world."

Maggie felt heat flooding her face. "Stop it right now," she whispered. "Stop this nonsense before I—"

He brushed his mouth back and forth across hers, his long hair falling across her cheek. He parted her lips before she could order him to stop. A jolt of unadulterated pleasure shot through her as his tongue touched hers, slipping inside her mouth to silence her tiny gasp. This man knew exactly what he was doing. The unexpected power of his kiss stole Maggie's breath from her body.

It stilled the clamor of her thoughts. Sinful. Delicious. She resisted the urge to relax deeply into the pillows and enjoy herself as he eased his arms around her, possessively tilting her to him. Kissing him was more decadent than stolen champagne and chocolate éclairs. She felt her eyes drifting shut. She was a feather floating in a storm of sensations, gliding on an air current above the clouds. For a dangerous moment, she lay unmoving, immobilized by terror and temptation, by the shameless assault of his mouth moving down her jaw.

Decadent, a voice whispered in her brain in belated warning. The Devil's Advocate.

She pushed at his chest, her hands encountering an immovable wall, his hair tangling with hers. But Connor waited until he was good and ready to break the kiss. He waited until desire flashed like wildfire through his veins, until he was satisfied that he had made his mark on her, that she would never forget what it felt like to be kissed by him. The sensation of her soft body in his arms intoxicated him. He had to force himself to stop. He suppressed a shudder of physical reaction as tenderness and black lust mingled inside him, ebbing away to a painful ache.

"There," he said, drawing an uneven breath. "That was the first thing I felt like doing when I found you alone in the drawing room."

Smiling slightly at her dazed expression, he released her to fall back like a windblown petal from a flower against the pillows. He was certain she'd never been kissed like that before, if at all. Unfortunately, the way his belly had twisted into a knot, you'd think he was the one experiencing his first kiss. He hadn't expected her to affect him like that.

He studied her with renewed interest, his mood lifting at the thought of the evening ahead. "I wouldn't put it past Donaldson to come barging in here to cause more mischief," he said in amusement. "God, what a great joke. I can't believe they went to so much trouble. I hope they paid you well for your performance. You certainly deserve it."

She sat up stiffly, burning with humiliation and not certain she would ever recover from the events of the past hour. "They didn't pay me anything, you big overbearing idiot. Get off my bruised rib. I'm not an actress. I'm just a poor working girl with bad judgment and the wrong friends."

"I imagine Ardath picked you because you look like the princess in the tapestry." His dark eyes dancing with appreciation, he curled his forefinger around the ribbon loosely threaded in the collar of her nightrail. "You have very delicate bones," he said quietly. "I'll have to be careful when we make love. I don't want to hurt you."

"You're going to feel very stupid in a few minutes, Lord Buchanan," she whispered, unable to express a shudder when he touched her.

"Take that silly bandage off your head," he commanded gently. "It looks uncomfortable."

"A concussion is uncomfortable, isn't it?"

He nudged her chin upward with his knuckles, forcing her angry face to his. "I just had an idea—would you like to go to the Highlands with me for a month?"

"Would I—"

He was dead serious. "Do you like to go hunting?"

"I detest everything about it," she said through her teeth.

"Good." He gave her a lazy, heart-stopping smile, and dipped his head to nuzzle her soft white neck. "Then we'll spend all our time in bed."

For the first time in her life, Maggie's power of speech failed her.

Her eyes widened as he tugged the nightrail off her shoulder, exposing the swell of her breast. He groaned as he drew his head lower, his lips teasing the nerve endings of her skin. She froze in fascinated apprehension. Lord, the man did sinful things with his mouth. Interesting, inventive, wonderful things that she had never experienced before. She floundered for a moment in a haze of humiliation and unabashed anticipation, afraid to imagine what could happen if she didn't stop him.

She didn't understand this man at all, torn between reluctant sympathy for his situation and the sheer terror of her own. Again she thought of the lion in the tapestry, a big beast who rarely showed the world his vulnerability. She remembered the hunter in the background, the sense of evil that surrounded him. Was it possible that she, like the princess, was playing an unwitting part in luring Lord Buchanan into danger too?

She didn't know at first what made him stop. Only gradually did she become aware of his unnatural silence, then the mechanical stiffness of his movements as he levered up onto his elbow.

A frown furrowed his brow as he stared at the length of blood-flecked gauze in his hand. His gaze flickered to hers, both accusing and brimming with guilt.

"No," he said thickly. Then he threaded his long fingers into her hair, lifting it to stare in dread at the knot on her scalp. "Dear God, you *have* been hurt."

"Of course I've been hurt," she practically shouted. "I fell on my head."

It was a moment before he could speak again. "It wasn't a joke, after all. I'm a fool."

He turned his head to the wall; he looked so bereft of hope that Maggie felt tears of remorse sting her eyes. "I wish it *had* been a joke," she whispered. "I'm sorry, for both of us."

"But it wasn't." His voice fell on a note of finality. He sounded stricken, shaking his head in shocked denial. "Oh, lass, I'm sorry too."

She brushed away a tear. "It's sorry I am for breaking into your house. I knew it was wrong. But I also know Jamie isn't a murderer, and I . . . I believed the things I heard about you."

He ran his hand through his tousled blond hair, the realization of what he had to face slowly sinking into his dazed mind. "In future you might try coming to me personally rather than believing what is said behind my back."

"It's probably a good idea," she agreed meekly.

Not content to accept her contrite attitude at face value, he dug the knife of his disapproval a little deeper. "It would have spared us both a load of embarrassment if you had, for example, simply knocked upon my door last night and requested a private interview."

Maggie nodded miserably. "Isn't that the truth, my lord?"

He glanced back at her, swallowing a groan as she scrubbed another tear from her cheek. He couldn't believe that he had almost seduced a hurt and helpless woman. A few more minutes, and he would have taken her innocence and dear Lord, he shuddered to imagine the scandal that would have ensued. "Don't cry, damn it," he said stiffly.

There was a knock at the door, Dr. Sinclair asking, "Is everything all right in there, Maggie?"

"Everything is fine," Connor said in a toneless voice.

"No, it is not," she whispered, raising her knees to hide her ravaged face.

Connor observed her in bewildered silence, reaching his

hand out to comfort her before he could stop the impulse. "There, there." He patted her awkwardly, amazed that a common little thief could arouse his protective instincts. Innocence, or ingenuity? He grunted, deciding it didn't matter. She looked so upset that he couldn't help himself. "Hell," he thought aloud. "What a mess, and you and I are in it together now."

She nodded again. "I only broke into your house to steal the confession. I suppose you have every right to put me in prison." She hesitated, her voice a thread of sound. "Do you mind not patting me so hard? I know you mean well, but that's the shoulder I hurt when I fell."

Connor released a sigh and pulled his hand back to his side, rising as if in a daze to his feet. "You're not going to prison." God, what was he saying? What kind of example was he setting? He took a step away from the bed, hitting his own shoulder against the bedpost. Was this really happening to him? He caught an unwelcome glimpse of himself in the mirror. Long hair disheveled. Cravat pulled loose. Shirttails hanging around his hips. This—this was the man who bore sole responsibility for the safety of Scotland? He looked like a barbarian. He felt like one. He frightened himself.

Ardath pounded on the door. "It's too quiet in there, Connor. What on earth is going on?"

He forced out a breath and took a moment to tuck in his shirt. He pivoted slowly, stumbling over a pillow on the floor. "I'll still need your cooperation, lass," he said heavily. "And by the way, I am the senior advocate the Crown appointed to advise the young lawyer who is handling Munro's defense. That confession was never intended to be used against him. He's only being held for his own protection. I was working to help him for free."

Chapter

8

≈

Maggie gasped as if he'd dealt her a physical blow, raising her small white face in shock. Good Lord, she had become a felon—she'd committed her first crime—for nothing. He had been helping Jamie all along. She was going to throttle the Chief if she ever got back to Heaven's Court, which seemed highly unlikely to judge by the unforgiving look on the Lion's face. One daring mistake, a misjudgment, and her life was in ruins.

"Where are you going?" she asked him in apprehension as he reached the door.

He lifted his shoulders in a shrug. "To try to find my sister again."

"And what am I supposed to do in the meantime?"

"Eat me out of house and home to judge by the past hour."

She pressed her hand to her heart. "But you can't keep me here. Can you?"

He glanced at her over his shoulder, his face haggard, his smile merciless. "Not unless you want to change your mind about prison. Malicious mischief. Theft aggravated by house-breaking. Drunkenness. Why, it's enough to have you transported to Tasmania. As bad as I am, I think you'll agree you're better off in that bed, lass."

She wondered about that, remembering the violently pleasurable sensations he'd just aroused in her. Yet even though he intimidated her, even though his behavior had proven unpredictable, she was more afraid to be left alone. "But the newspapers said you were going to prosecute Jamie," she said in confusion.

"The newspapers made a mistake," he said coldly, thrusting his arms into his jacket. "I don't broadcast the cases I take for the poor."

"Whyever not?"

His flashed her another pitiless smile as he opened the door. "Because it isn't good for my image."

Her expression of despair gave Connor little satisfaction. He strode from the room, cursing his helplessness and feeling more numb than anything. The anxious faces that awaited him in the hallway destroyed any lingering hopes he'd held that tonight had been a practical joke. If someone wanted to punish him, they'd made a damn good start. For all his complaining, he cared more about his sisters than he'd ever admitted.

It was Connor who, at thirteen, had raised his orphaned family of six little girls. A half dozen fussy, demanding, endearing, emotional females who had driven him to the brink of madness so many times he'd earned a place of honor in Bedlam. He'd gotten four of them settled down; although Rebecca had never married, she claimed to be happy enough in her solitary life. But none of them had ever given him half as much trouble as Sheena: Sheena who had never really known their parents and who had taken their death the hardest, whose grief had left her emotionally scarred and grasping for affection.

Just let her be safe. Even if she never speaks to me again. Even if she bedevils my life until the day I die, just let her come home unharmed.

He rubbed the muscles corded along his neck, frowning to make sense of Ardath and his uncle's voices, talking at once, telling him what to do. Connor had wanted to be a lawyer ever since he could remember. He had raised himself from the ashes of poverty and abandonment to achieve his success after his parents died. But if his early experiences had toughened his character, they'd also destroyed the last of his boyish idealism. He had grown up hard and fast, relying on his fists as much as his wits. Cynicism had begun to corrode his heart even in childhood.

Ardath moved around him, darting him a guarded look. Her face suspicious, she poked her head into the guest suite as if to scrutinize Maggie for battle scars. "She looks horribly upset."

"With good reason," Connor said flatly.

She turned on him, her skirts rustling in the awkward silence. "What did you say to her?" she whispered. "The girl has been crying."

"Leave me alone," he said. "I'm trying to think."

The earl approached him; in the confusion he'd neglected to remove the gardener's apron tied around his waist. "The inspector claims he has something important to show you, Connor," he said quietly.

"Where is he?"

"Downstairs with Norah's husband and the girls."

His face grave, Connor nodded and strode to the top of the stairs. A short woman with bouncy blond ringlets and a large bosom bumped into him on the uppermost step, emitting a tiny shriek of excitement in his ear. He curbed his impatience and moved aside politely to let her pass. He'd completely forgotten he was supposed to be hosting a party.

"Daddy told me everything," she said in a breathy little-girl voice. "I have to admit it came as quite a surprise. I never dreamed you harbored such strong feelings." She batted her lashes at him. "You sly devil."

Connor just nodded absently. He didn't recognize her, she was quite peculiar, and he assumed she was referring to his sister's abduction. "It is a bad situation," he said in a dismissive tone. "Now if you'll excuse me, Miss—"

She clamped her hand down on his arm in a grip of steel as he started around her, refusing to let him go. "Call me Philomena." Her bosom quivered on a deep sigh. It drew Connor's attention to the damp caviar stain on her dress. "I'm not really a recluse, you know," she said with a self-conscious giggle. "I adore parties."

Connor almost lost his footing on the stairs, forcing a smile to hide the unpleasant jolt of realization. "Of course you do. Philomena . . . Excuse me a moment, won't you?"

Hell, what an annoying creature. She reminded him of an empty-headed china doll. To think he'd ever toyed with the idea of stating his interest to Elliot. The woman would drive him mad in a matter of minutes.

He pulled his arm free, spotting Aaron watching them from the bottom of the stairs with an idiotic smile of approval. But even the frightening prospect of a romance with the unappealing Philomena faded from his mind as he noticed his brother-in-law Charles and the inspector pushing through the small throng of guests to greet him. Norah, Caroline, Sarah, Jennie. His four sisters safe, at least for now. He wondered fleetingly about Rebecca. He'd feel better having her here, just knowing she was safe instead of living unprotected in those Highland wilds. A woman needed a man to take care of her.

His chest tightened at the look on Charles's face. He hurried down the remaining stairs. Everything around them dimmed into a distant fog. Something bad had happened, some news about Sheena. He felt it in the terse silence that engulfed him. "What is it?"

Inspector Davies handed him a folded piece of parchment. The tightness in Connor's chest turned into a vise that squeezed his heart as he recognized the broken rose seal. Memories clutched at his mind, dragging him into the past like claws. "This was just found on the front steps," Davies said. "I took the liberty of opening it, sir. I think you'd better read it."

The man removed his mask and rubbed at the thick scar tissue that marred the left side of his face. It was an unconscious gesture, as if he wanted to erase the pain of his original injury. He knew his appearance repulsed certain women and held an inexplicable attraction to others. He wondered if the woman who called herself Maggie Saunders would recognize him beneath the mask.

Maggie Saunders. His scarred lip flattened in disdain. What a common name. A French tutor by day and amateur thief at night who'd gotten involved in an abduction, a thief who was being hailed as a heroine for attacking a man with a champagne bottle.

He stared past the unlit grate to the older man who sat across from him. "Are you sure she's still in his house?"

His companion stroked his thin mustache and nodded slowly. "Of course I'm sure."

"Then why are we waiting? I told you I want to get out of the country."

"It isn't that simple," the other man replied with infinite patience. "Buchanan has reason to be cautious now. As far as I can gather, his family is taking care of her. She'll be frightened, suspicious of strangers. The abduction is fresh in her mind." He spoke with the confidence of a man accustomed to subterfuge. "I thought we'd agreed this must be done carefully."

A sound from the outside of the door of the quiet inn interrupted their conversation. The first man picked up his mask and automatically covered his face. His companion sighed and glanced at his watch. "I'll meet with Buchanan tomorrow. I'll find out exactly what his plans are. He trusts me."

"Well, I don't trust him," the man in the mask said bitterly. "The sooner we get her away from him, the better."

His companion rose and pulled on a pair of gray leather gloves, then reached for his walking stick. "You've waited this long. Another few weeks isn't going to make that much difference."

"You don't know that." The man's blue eyes glittered from the mask with unholy resolve. "He isn't called a devil for nothing, is he?"

Chapter

9

❧

Maggie was drifting in the depths of a laudanum-laced dream when the ungodly shouting in the street awakened her. Her mind in a fog, shivering from the nightmare she'd escaped, she crawled off the bed and staggered across the darkened room to investigate. She guessed she had a good hour left before it was time to get up for work.

This was the first time in years she'd overslept.

As she struggled to open the window, she wondered dimly which moron in the boardinghouse had taken it upon himself to move all her furniture during the night. The portion of her fuzzy brain that appeared to be functioning registered the fact that it was drizzling outside, she'd never had so much trouble with this wretched window, and Lord, had she fallen out of bed last night? She ached all over, starting with a dull throbbing at the back of her head.

In fact, she felt like she'd been run over by a coach and four.

She stared down into the misty street, blinking to clear her blurred vision as she searched for the familiar landmarks of Heaven's Court. Her gaze lit on a man in a dark cloak and cleric's collar standing by the gate.

She frowned, drawing back slightly. Who on earth had cleaned up all the mess, the broken-down carriages, the wheelbarrows, the barricade of whisky kegs while she slept? The Chief would have a conniption. He believed criminals should keep up criminal appearances.

"Be sober!" the man shouted. "Be vigilant, because your adversary the devil, as a roaring lion, walketh about, seeking whom he may devour!"

The man noticed Maggie in the window. He stopped, apparently satisfied he had dragged at least one sinner from her bed. He stomped forward until he stood directly beneath her, banging his Bible with his fist.

"There is no peace for the wicked!"

Maggie glanced down in bewilderment at the unfamiliar nightdress that had twisted around her bare feet. "There's no peace for anyone, you old windbag, spouting Scripture at this hour," she shouted back in annoyance.

"Who is this that gives counsel by words without knowledge?" the man quoted, his voice rising into a bellow. "Gird up now your loins, like a man, for I will demand it of you, and answer thou me!"

A turnip came flying through the air from the side of the house, followed by the irate order to, "Belt up, you silly sod!"

Maggie brought the window down with a satisfying bang, muttering under her breath, "Gird up my—"

"Loins," said a tired and disturbingly familiar voice from the opposite corner of the room. "The Reverend Abernathy has taken a rather perplexing interest lately in more than just the state of my immortal soul."

She pivoted, staring in amazement at the long, shadowed figure unfolding from an armchair to loom over her. A sick feeling washed over her as flashes of memory flooded her mind from the previous evening. It *had* been real.

Connor Buchanan, the legend, larger than life, her captor, her victim. Her unwilling ally against an enemy neither of them could name. She took a step back, frightened by the intensity of emotion in his eyes.

Disoriented, disbelieving, she caught a glimpse of her own reflection in the cheval glass on the other side of the room.

There was a bandage on her head. She looked as grim as death herself. She closed her eyes, then opened them again, hoping the horrifying image would disappear. It didn't.

"Perhaps you ought to lie back down, lass," he said gruffly.

She turned slowly. She felt unsteady and faint, tiny flashes of light dancing before her eyes. "How long have you been here?" she asked in a dry voice.

He stretched his muscular arms over his head before answering, straining as if to ease the tension that gripped him. With athletic grace he advanced across the room until he stood before her in the glow of the dying coals.

She took another instinctive step back toward the window. With his harsh, unshaven face and rumpled evening clothes, he looked as if he'd spent the better part of the night living up to his bad reputation.

"When I wasn't following false leads to my sister's disappearance, I was watching over you." His voice sounded thick with overuse and discouragement. "Ardath and I took turns. The doctor was afraid you might slip into a coma."

She lifted her hand to her head, still stunned that it all was real. "You didn't find your sister?" she said hesitantly.

"No. Apparently a black coach was spotted on the way to the Highlands during the night."

"Was there a ransom note?"

"Yes. Ten of them, actually," he said in a hard voice. "There was also an anonymous letter threatening that my sister Rebecca will be the kidnappers' next victim."

"Could it be a hoax, my lord?"

"I believe it is. But I've been concerned about her anyway and cannot afford to dismiss it. I intend to visit her without delay."

His face like flint, he brushed by her to the window. Maggie caught a whiff of whisky as he passed, whisky and bay rum, a potent but not unpleasant combination. The reverend's rantings grew dimmer in the background. A maidservant in rag curlers had chased him off with a broom.

The sudden quiet made Maggie aware of the blood thrumming in her ears, of the fact that she'd spent an entire night in this man's house. A wave of light-headedness swept over her. She couldn't think of what to do next.

Connor turned; the grainy light played up the shadowed fatigue on his face. "Do you remember anything more?"

She rubbed one foot against her ankle, feeling a shiver ripple through her. "Nothing helpful." She decided it was his penetrating gaze that made her feel so cold. "I swear I'd tell you if I could remember."

"Would you?" he asked wearily.

"Of course," she said, bristling. "What do you think I am?"

"That seems to be quite the mystery. According to everyone else, you've achieved nothing less than angel status during your short but amazingly eventful life. Deposed aristocrat turns street urchin. Isn't that the story?"

"You still don't believe me?"

He gave her a noncommittal shrug. "Don't take it to heart. All I have are your criminal tendencies to go on. As far as I know, you're nothing more than a thief and a housebreaker."

She was also beautiful, he thought irrelevantly, admiring her in the ghostly light. Even Norah's unflattering flannel nightrail couldn't prevent the damage her softly alluring shape did to his male libido. She looked young and vulnerable, her face frightened and appealingly fragile. Connor might have stirred up a measure of sympathy for her if she had broken into anyone else's house. He couldn't remember a time he'd been more attracted to a woman, or a time when attraction had been more inappropriate.

"I don't care if you're the most powerful man in the world," she said suddenly, surprising him with her boldness. "I'm twenty-three years old. You can't keep me locked in this room forever."

"That old? How interesting. I told you I could have you put in Carlton Jail if you'd prefer. Somehow I don't think you'd get much pampering there, though. No roast turkeys, no flowers or champagne."

Expelling her breath in an irate huff, she pushed around him to examine herself in the mirror. "What have you done with my dress?"

He propped his elbow back against the windowsill, his features drawn. "I believe the laundress is trying to remove the chocolate stains—chocolate from the éclairs you were stealing. Anyway, lass, you're in no condition to be leaving this house."

A look of panic crossed her face. "But I can't wait for the laundress. I've just remembered—"

He straightened, his fatigue lifting. "You've remembered—"

"Help me," she cried shakily, pulling at the bandage. "Help me find some other clothes. It's almost dawn. There isn't much time left."

Connor assumed she was talking about Sheena's abduction, that she remembered some crucial detail. Speechless with relief, he started to rush around the room, throwing open the doors to the wardrobe before he realized that they were empty, and besides, he had no intention of allowing her to set foot outside this room. He wheeled, half afraid she would forget what she wanted to tell him.

"I can't find anything here," he said impatiently. "Sit down, for God's sake, and I'll ask Ardath—"

He broke off as he noticed that her eyes had fluttered shut and the blood seemed to be draining from her face, her head lolling forward onto her chest.

"Miss Saunders," he said in alarm, reaching out to catch her a split second before she slumped to the floor in an untidy heap.

Chapter

10

"I swear I never laid a hand on her. We were having a rational conversation. She got upset because she'd remembered something important. I was trying to find her clothes. Then all of a sudden she passed out on the floor."

"You intimidated her, Connor," Ardath said in an admonishing voice. "You always do that to people. Imagine telling a duke's daughter you were going to put her in prison. The shock could have killed her on the spot."

Connor frowned down at the still woman on the bed, more concerned by her pale appearance than he could admit. He'd nearly had a heart attack himself when she had collapsed in his arms. Despite what she'd put him through, he still felt that irrational sense of responsibility toward her. Watching her during the night had been a trial. He'd checked her repeatedly to make sure she hadn't lapsed into a coma. He'd laid his head on her chest to listen to her heartbeat, ignoring the sweet scent of roses on her skin, the soft female curves that aroused him on a fundamental level.

He had studied her classical features, her slender neck and shoulders, wondering about her past, about what part she would play in his future. He'd been tempted more than once to touch her, not only to tread the dangerous waters of attraction between them, but to reassure himself she wasn't slipping away from him. And he'd smiled ruefully as he remembered their absurd conversation in the parlor, that only a few hours ago he'd offered to walk with her in the rain.

"I thought she remembered something about the abduction," he said defensively.

"Anybody would faint, waking up to see you hovering over them. You look like a . . . a scoundrel. You really ought to shave and change those clothes."

Maggie opened her eyes at that moment, her attention drifting from Ardath to Connor. "What happened?" she whispered dryly.

"Go back to sleep, dear," Ardath said.

"I can't sleep," Maggie said in panic, her gaze still transfixed to the forbidding male figure who stood before her. "I have to go to work in a half hour. I'm very dependable."

"Work?" Ardath pronounced the word as if Maggie had just confessed she had a terminal illness. "Did you hear that, Connor? On top of everything else she's endured, the poor girl thinks she has to work."

"It happens to the best of us," he retorted, folding his arms over his broad chest. "Besides, that's why she fainted. On top of the concussion, she worked herself into a state over being late. I told you it wasn't my fault."

Ardath bent to tuck the covers around Maggie, her face a study in concern. "Gracious, she's as cold as ice. Help me get her settled in and stop behaving like such a beast."

He looked anything but pleased as he moved to the other side of the bed. "I don't have time for this," he said in a gravelly voice, dragging the comforter over Maggie with all the enthusiasm of an undertaker arranging a shroud. "I have two more ransom notes to investigate, and briefs to review, not to mention getting ready to leave for the Highlands after court tomorrow."

Maggie pushed the comforter off her nose, piqued by his indifference. "Don't let me stop you."

"Did you hear that?" Connor scowled at Ardath. "Concussion or not, there isn't a damn thing wrong with her mind."

"You've offended her," Ardath said in a stage whisper,

which Maggie was obviously to pretend she didn't hear. "You do it all the time. It's your way of talking down as if the other person is either dense or deceitful."

"Unfortunately in my experience one or the other is usually true."

"Listen to you." Ardath released a rueful sigh. "Perhaps all that power has gone to your head. My mother warned me, but did I believe her?"

"When have I ever talked down to you?" Connor demanded, glancing at Maggie from the corner of his eye. She was watching him with unabashed interest. It unnerved him. He never knew what the girl was thinking, but the glint in her pretty blue eyes assured him she didn't miss a thing.

"When haven't you?" Ardath replied, clearly miffed.

"I suppose your professor treats you like a doctor of philosophy, does he?" Connor dragged his attention away from Maggie, annoyed that she was witnessing yet another private scene from his life. "I suppose you sit around all the time playing chess and translating Greek tragedies into English."

Connor and Ardath started to argue in earnest. Maggie sighed, glancing from one to the other as if she were watching a tennis match. Did he care for Ardath? she wondered. Did he really dislike the professor, or was his male pride only piqued? She couldn't imagine Ardath choosing another man over Lord Buchanan. He was breath-catchingly handsome, and for a few wonderful moments last night, before he'd realized she was a housebreaker, he had stolen a piece of Maggie's heart with his unabashed charm.

He wasn't as mean as everyone said he was, either. More than once during the night she had felt him watching over her. She'd felt his hand brush her face. She'd sensed his worry, the inner struggle of a man who wasn't used to a situation he could not control, who wasn't used to showing his weaknesses to the world. She hadn't been sure at first whether or not she was dreaming.

In the midst of the argument, the Earl of Glenbrodie popped into the room. "And how is our little patient doing today?"

Ardath stopped scolding Connor long enough to answer. "She thinks she's going to work. Of course Connor isn't allowing it."

"Work? The daughter of a duke going to work?" This horrifying prospect brought the earl right into the room. "She must mean charity work. Dr. Sinclair said she's a regular angel of mercy at the Infant Pauper Asylum. I'm surprised you've never met her before, Ardath."

"Actually," Maggie said, struggling to sit up, "I give French and deportment lessons to old women and impolite children. It doesn't pay well, but it's decent employment. You see, I'm saving to have the family name and château restored. You wouldn't believe the cost of legal counsel and court complications back and forth across the Channel."

She paused. The three of them—Maggie, Ardath, and Glenbrodie—stared briefly at Connor as if he, by dint of his elevated position, were somehow personally to blame for the problems of jurisprudence between the two countries.

"The Chief helps whenever he can," she added. "But even a man of his stature can't cut through the bureaucracy. The worst part is that I've been unable to trace my older brother and sister. Everyone has to work in Heaven's Court—it's really only fair."

There was another moment of deep silence as if the others were mourning her loss of dignity and lapse into reduced circumstances. The earl shook his head and sat at her side, taking her hand in a gesture of fond affection.

"Never mind, my dear. Those degrading days are behind you now."

She sneaked a look at the Lion's face to confirm this statement, but his stern expression wasn't exactly encouraging. "They are?"

The earl and Ardath exchanged meaningful looks. "You mean Connor hasn't explained the Arrangement to you yet?" the earl said, his thick white eyebrows raised in disapproval.

"No," Connor said in a testy voice. "Connor hasn't explained the Arrangement to her yet. Connor hasn't had a chance. He's been busy investigating the ransom notes. He hasn't had any sleep, either."

The earl frowned. "Are these outbursts of bad temper quite necessary?"

"You're doing it again, Connor," Ardath said under her breath. "That just goes to prove my point."

Connor didn't bother defending his position; he had to save whatever fight he had left in him to continue looking for Sheena, and to give his final argument in a rape case later this morning. It was a highly publicized trial, the plaintiff a young cleaning woman in a theater.

The defendant, or panel, a popular actor, was as guilty as they came, the evidence presented against him indisputable. But since rape could be a capital crime, it was a battle to win a conviction from an all-male jury.

"You are in danger, my dear," the earl said to Maggie. "Grave danger."

Studying Connor's face, she didn't doubt that for a moment. His black scowl was the most intimidating thing she'd ever seen. "May I borrow something to wear to work please?" she asked quietly. "The Kennedy twins are going to Paris at the end of the week, and I've taught them just enough French to get them into trouble."

"The children can wait," Ardath said somberly. "Your life is at stake, and it would be irresponsible of Connor to let you leave this house without protection."

The Kennedy twins were in their nineties and probably couldn't wait. But Maggie decided not to point this out in light of Ardath's alarming revelation about Maggie's own impending doom. "How could my life be in danger? I admit it was wrong to break into—"

"She isn't talking about the housebreaking." Connor had flung his big frame back into the armchair as if he resented being part of the discussion. "Inspector Davies has convinced everyone that since you were the only one to witness my sister's abduction, there is a chance the kidnappers will return for you. To stop you from identifying them."

Ardath lowered her voice. "To silence you."

"You mean—"

"Permanently," the earl concluded, drawing his hand across his throat in a grim gesture.

Maggie stared in horror across the room at Connor, hoping she had misunderstood. "But I don't remember what they looked like. Why would they want to hurt me? I couldn't possibly identify them."

"Well, they don't know that, do they?" He stretched out his long legs, his voice sharp with frustration. "After all, you got close enough to the driver to bash him over the head with a bottle. Of my best yellow-label."

"And that's why your life is at stake," the earl added darkly. "We don't have any idea what sort of monsters we're dealing with. Connor has helped convict the worst of them in his day. Cutthroats, murderers, arsonists."

Maggie eased up higher against the headboard, her heart thumping against her bruised ribs. Her life wasn't only in danger—it was literally in Connor Buchanan's big hands. Unexpectedly his enemies were her enemies, and she'd become a pawn like his sister in their dangerous game. A tingle of primitive fear shot down her spine as she stared across the room at the man who refused to look at her and who held the power to decide her fate.

Connor gazed into the fireplace, more disturbed by the conversation than he showed. Cutthroats, murderers, arsonists. His uncle was frightening the girl to death. Still, Connor couldn't deny there was a chance, a slim chance, that she might be in danger, depending on who had taken his sister, and why.

His instincts told him that Sheena had not been kidnapped by someone with a past grudge against him. Still, once, a long time ago, only once, his instincts had betrayed him, and the cost had been a helpless old woman's life.

The memory haunted him even now, eight years later. The shock of learning how wrong he could be. That power gave him the ability to not only help people, but to hurt them.

He rarely thought about that time in his life, it was a painful wound, but he'd never forgotten the details of his first and only legal failure.

Early in his career he had defended a brash newspaper editor named William Montrose against a charge of brutally murdering a prostitute. A rose had been found in the abandoned warehouse where Montrose had left the woman's body. Connor fought passionately to prove that the highly educated Montrose was innocent.

He had nearly burst with pride at his first legal victory. He'd paraded his exonerated client around like a trophy. He'd even invited Montrose to his home and granted him an exclusive interview—until the night the police caught the man strangling his landlady, claiming she had tried to cheat him.

The woman, frail and in her seventies, had died with a black silk rose in her hands.

Over the years that black rose had become an emblem of revenge for Connor's rivals, a cruel blow at his recovering confidence. They would never let him forget his one mistake, no matter how high he climbed.

Neither would he. He would never forgive himself for what had happened to that old landlady. A prickle of cold sweat broke out on his back at the thought of his sister meeting a similar fate. Sheena was so blasted impetuous, too much like him for her own good.

He released his breath, refusing to let the dark thoughts dominate. His spirits lifted unexpectedly as he sent an unwilling glance at the girl ensconced in his bed. How ridiculous, how unfair for Miss Saunders that by a quirk of timing and character she alone held the key to identifying the men who'd taken Sheena.

She looked infinitely vulnerable as their eyes met, and he experienced an unwelcome stab of raw longing, remembering how her lithe body had fit so snugly into his last night. She might be an amateur thief, but in sexual matters she was still an innocent. Connor would stake his reputation on that. Her response to him had been artless and infinitely arousing.

But a duke's daughter? He doubted it.

Perhaps she'd grown up as the offspring of a favored servant in a fine household, which would account for the airs she gave herself. A diamond in the gutter made for a nice fairy tale, but he questioned her story. The Chief was known to protect his "clan" of criminals, and she was apparently under Arthur's protection. Connor was surprised the man hadn't already put in an appearance, demanding her release.

Still, he had to admit Miss Saunders was standing up well, all things considered. She had borne the shock of everything better than he had, in fact. His embarrassment over his behavior last night made him cringe. Trying to impress her with the merits of his imported champagne while she was stealing bottles of the stuff under her cloak. Seducing her like a bastard when she lay injured and defenseless under his alleged protection. No wonder she watched him with those wide eyes like a little girl being chased by a wolf in the woods.

All of a sudden it wasn't seduction he had to worry about. It was survival.

"We don't know anything yet," he said, his voice deliberately impersonal as he came to his feet. "The ransom notes have all turned out to be fraudulent."

"There's Rebecca to worry about now," the earl said quietly. "I can't bear to think of her so isolated, physically incapable of running from an attacker who might stalk her."

"Neither can I," Connor said.

The image slashed through his composure like a serrated dagger, reminding him that his influence only reached so far. And even if the note threatening Rebecca's life was a hoax, the kidnappers could easily target her as their next victim. The carriage had been spotted headed for the Highlands. Was it on the way to his home in Kilcurrie even now?

Who was he up against?

Fortunately, after a hellish night of following false leads and interviewing trusted sources from the docks to the upper-class districts, he had reassured himself that it was not a ghost who had returned to wreak revenge.

William Montrose, the murderer who had fooled and betrayed him, *was* dead. Connor had derived vicious satisfaction from watching the man's body being lowered into a grave eight years ago. He had cursed Montrose's soul with every clod of Highland dirt that condemned him to eternal darkness.

He set his jaw. No one had noticed his lapse in attention, no one except the girl who stared at him with shadowed blue eyes that held too much sadness for him to ignore.

All right. He would be fair. What if Miss Saunders *had* embellished the facts of her background? It was still to her credit that she had survived in the underworld among the hardened criminals whom Connor had sworn to sweep from the city like dirt. It was to her credit that she'd managed to retain that aura of absurd innocence like the lopsided halo of an angel who had fallen a little short of heaven.

Despite everything, he was unwillingly touched by her silly

scheme to help a friend in trouble. He valued that sort of stubborn loyalty. And no matter how much chaos she had added to his life, he had no desire to see her hurt.

She was an innocent drawn into a bad situation, or so he hoped. To his astonishment, something inside him wanted to believe the best of her. Just as he wanted to believe that Sheena was still alive.

Ardath's voice pulled him abruptly from his thoughts. "Tell her about the Arrangement, Connor, before you leave for the courthouse. Explain what you and she will have to do to escape the kidnappers."

Chapter

11

⟨⟩

For a moment Maggie couldn't move, mesmerized by the look of raw anguish she had glimpsed in Connor's eyes. It eclipsed her own emotions, the confusion and embarrassment of finding herself in this wretched situation with no one to blame but herself.

He might behave like a heartless scoundrel, but even she could see he was genuinely worried about his sister. He was a hard man, but not inhuman. Even if he deserved his reputation, he didn't deserve to suffer like this.

Suddenly she felt obliged to help him, to atone for her misjudgment. His concern for Sheena was rather endearing. It was an emotion she fully understood. Wouldn't she give anything just to know her own brother and sister were safe?

She frowned, ignoring the bands of tension that tightened around her temples. She had to think, concentrate, *remember*. She tried to picture the courtyard, Sheena standing beside her, to recall any minute detail about the kidnapping.

"What is the matter?" Ardath asked in concern, but her voice was as distant and indistinct as wind blowing across the end of a tunnel. A tunnel of darkness.

Maggie groped through that darkness. The images became

sharper and sharper. But suddenly she was no longer in the room. She wasn't in Connor's courtyard. She was ten years old and running up the vast stone staircase of the old château; she was calling her sister's name in panic as Napoleon's police ransacked the vast rooms below for documents to incriminate her father.

The staircase seemed endless. Her heart threatened to burst as she stumbled up the last step; she realized she'd been followed. She hesitated, staring down the long hallway to Jeanette's room. Candlelight showed through a crack under the door. Maggie felt a man's hand grab her skirts.

A light flared, bright as the sun, engulfed her in heat, then was hastily extinguished. Darkness enveloped her again like a blast of black wind that drove its cold breath into her bones.

"For God's sake," Connor said, leaning over her in alarm, tempted to shake her out of the frightening trance. "What's the matter with her? Why does she look so white?"

The concern in his voice broke through the darkness. It drew her out of the ice-cold shadows and back to the safety of the present. She gazed around the room. Then she raised her eyes to the tall figure at the foot of the bed.

Her heart was beating wildly; she was still transfixed with the distant terror of standing at the top of those stairs. Fire and ice. A fear so profound it left her shaking over a decade later.

"You remembered something?" he asked, straightening as the color began to return to her face. "Something about Sheena?"

She tried to swallow over the constriction in her throat. "No. Nothing beyond what I told you. I'm so sorry. I really tried."

He nodded stiffly. Perhaps he was even a little relieved. He had not wanted that traumatized fear in her eyes to be associated with Sheena's disappearance. He couldn't help wondering what had caused it; for an instant he had wished to step inside her mind to protect her from whatever seemed to threaten her.

He said none of this, of course. It perplexed him that he had even entertained such an outlandish thought. "I have to leave for the courthouse now," he said stiffly. "I have to change my clothes."

Maggie thought he looked just fine the way he was, a little scruffy and disreputable, a distraction from the chilling memory she had just escaped. She wondered if he would take the time to shave before he left the house. His dark shadowed jaw made him look more like a pirate than a public prosecutor. She could just imagine the women in the courthouse gallery sighing in pleasure as they watched him. She of all people understood the importance of keeping up appearances. It was practically a de Saint-Evremond family code.

But last night had thrown both their lives into turmoil. She had awakened this morning from a dream into a nightmare.

In fact, she should be neatly making her own little bed right now, her poodle nibbling at her toes. Claude, her elderly butler, would be laying coals on the fire; as usual the task wouldn't be completed until she was flying out of the house, choking down the cup of hot chocolate he insisted she drink for sustenance.

To save cab fare she would walk all the way to where the Kennedy sisters lived in a house that was a mausoleum from the previous century. No one would dare bother her on the way because she was under the Chief's protection.

The two old women would insist she take tea. Their false teeth would clack like castanets while they conjugated French verbs. Their time-worn clothes would smell of camphor and lavender. They dreamed foolish dreams, but they were kind, unlike Maggie's other younger pupils and their demanding parents, who treated her like a menial. Still, having to work for a living had brought her a sense of humility, which was definitely *not* a family trait.

"I shouldn't stay here," she said awkwardly, the challenges of the real world closing in around her. "I do have obligations to meet."

The earl made a sound of distress. "It's out of the question."

Ardath had found a comb in the dressing table and began to tug out the tangles in Maggie's hair, glancing sharply at Connor as he returned to the chair for his rumpled evening jacket. "Aren't you going to tell her about the plan you and Inspector Davies worked out, Connor?"

Maggie watched him as he turned, the movement wooden

and reluctant. He looked as if the burden of the world had fallen on his powerful shoulders, but if anyone could bear the weight, surely he was the man.

"I was hoping that your memory would have returned this morning, or that my sister would have been found." His unsettling hazel eyes held her spellbound. "Since neither is the case, it seems that you and I might be forced to go into seclusion, Miss Saunders. As the sole witness in a capital crime, you are entitled to protection, and by law your full cooperation is required."

Seclusion. Protection. Cooperation. The solemn words spoken in his deep Scots burr sounded so grave they gave her the shivers. She struggled to make sense of what this would mean in practical terms, the impact on her simple life. Her mind could not grasp the enormity of it.

"Are you saying that I won't be able to give French lessons for a living?" she finally managed to ask, trying not to sound too hopeful.

"I'm afraid not." His voice was very formal, giving Maggie the impression that he had been coerced, perhaps even tortured, into making this decision. "Naturally," he added with the coolest nod, "your needs will be taken care of."

"I see," she murmured, wiggling her toes under the silk-lined comforter. She hadn't slept under silk since she was a child in the château. She doubted that his lordship would consider such a thing a need. How did he intend to protect her, anyway? Would she be carted off to some castle tower and kept under guard? Hidden in a potato cellar?

"We realize this is a tremendous sacrifice," the earl said. "But you do need protection, and we would do anything to have Sheena home safe in the bosom of her family where she belongs."

"And is Lord Buchanan himself going to protect me?" Maggie asked, unwillingly intrigued by the thought.

Connor gave her a look which indicated he would rather eat a breakfast of live worms every day for the rest of his life. "I've been advised that it is necessary."

Maggie stared up at the ceiling, considering her options. She could grow accustomed to this kind of existence. After all, she *had* been born into it. She thought again of her other life, the people who cared for her. The Chief would be dead to the world at this hour, unless Claude panicked at her absence and woke him up, in which case Claude was the one who would end up dead. Hell broke loose in Heaven's Court when the Chief wasn't allowed to sleep off his whisky. Had anyone missed her yet?

"Would I have to stay inside this house with Lord Buchanan all the time?" she asked thoughtfully.

"Of course not," the earl replied. "Connor has a splendid estate in the Highlands where he'll keep you safe and entertained."

A deep scowl darkened Connor's face. "I will keep her safe. I am not a traveling circus."

Maggie slowly lowered her gaze, her heartbeat accelerating. All alone with him. The scene between them last night on this same bed played through her mind. Her pulse began to race as she remembered the rough gentleness of his mouth against hers, the latent power of his body. She had never let a man touch her like that before. Wouldn't she be safer on the streets than in his house?

"His lordship doesn't look very happy about it," she murmured.

"One does what one must," Ardath retorted, giving Maggie's hair a final flick of the comb. "I know this is a lot to ask of you, disrupting your life, but even Connor believes it's for the best, and he was going to the Highlands anyway."

Maggie hesitated, aware of the tension building in the air. Disrupting her life. What life? "I don't know," she said quietly.

"Take your time to consider," the earl urged her.

Connor stirred, his voice sardonic. "Yes, by all means don't rush into making a decision, Miss Saunders."

She frowned at the derision in his voice, his pose as languid and impatient as a Viking conqueror's as he leaned against the door. Heavens, what was there to decide?

Hidden away in the Highlands, guarded by the most powerful (and probably the most handsome) man in Scotland. No more nasty children mangling the French language. No more pinching pennies. Servants at her beck and call instead of petty criminals parading through the lodging house at all hours. Chocolate éclairs instead of stale digestive biscuits, and silk sheets. There were definite advantages, if she chose to look at the bright side of a bad situation.

It wouldn't last long. Only until his poor sister was found, and the men who had abducted her were caught. But, oh, how she needed a rest from the hardships of real life. She vented a deep sigh. She was awfully tempted.

"We've overwhelmed you," the earl said gently. "Is there anything we can do, any questions we can answer to reassure you that this is the wisest decision for everyone involved?"

Maggie ran the tip of her tongue over her teeth, trying her best to look overwhelmed and in need of reassurance. The Lion at the door was watching her, waiting to spring on her answer. But she was less afraid of him now than last night. In fact, she'd grown rather fond of him, bless his beastly heart.

Still, the point was that he needed her, and she certainly did need his protection. She shuddered at the thought of being pursued by the men who had abducted his sister, men who thought nothing of using a girl as a tool for revenge. But for all the danger Maggie had placed herself in, she wasn't sorry she had tried to help. At least she didn't have that burden on her conscience.

"I won't be back until early evening." Connor opened the door as if he couldn't wait to escape. "Miss Saunders can give me her decision then."

"I've decided." She bit her lip; she hadn't meant to sound so eager, but she didn't want to give him time to change his mind.

"What?" He turned in mock astonishment and gave her a look that should have turned her to stone. "You've decided already? My, my, what a surprise."

Maggie swallowed at the unnerving look he gave her, reminding herself they would be dependent on each other's company for an unspecified time under the most strained circumstances. It was highly improper, but then Heaven's Court was hardly a haven of social decorum. "Sometimes one has to make a sacrifice for the greater good," she said somberly. "If everyone else believes it's for the best, I suppose I'll have to go with you to the Highlands."

Connor snorted softly. She made it sound as if he were dragging her to the guillotine. "The lady has spoken," he said, his voice laden with irony. Then he glanced at Ardath and his uncle. "I am leaving now. I'm sure you won't let anyone harm a hair on our precious little houseguest's head."

Connor left the room abruptly, closing the door with enough force to resonate like a thunderclap in the room. As he reached the hall, his temper cooled a few degrees and he told himself he shouldn't take out his frustration on her. He thought again of the gripping terror on her small face, and his gut tightened. Her fear had touched him in a visceral way, triggering impulses he refused to act upon, the urge to comfort, to defend—but against what? She hadn't looked that traumatized last night when he'd found her in the courtyard.

But even if everything else she'd told him had been a lie, something had hurt her in the past, and he struggled to subdue that part of him that wanted to soothe her pain. He wouldn't soften toward her, though. She'd brought this recent grief on herself.

And so, in a strange way, had he. After all, he'd only gotten what he wished for last night. The chance to have her all to himself.

Well, he'd gotten that and more, he thought wryly, hurrying down the stairs. In fact, it was now his official duty to be alone with her. God help him.

Unless he could figure out a way to foist her off on someone else, he had just become her self-appointed bodyguard.

Chapter

12

Maggie had begun to doze off within minutes after Ardath and the earl had tiptoed from the room to let her rest. She awakened with a start as the door opened and a robust young housemaid in a crooked mobcap clumped up to the side of the bed with a tea tray. It was Emily, Hugh's "contact" in the house.

"It's me, Maggie," she whispered, glancing back nervously at the door. "I'm not supposed to be upstairs, but I thought you might need help."

Maggie opened her eyes all the way. "Help to do what?"

"To escape his lordship, of course. The man is so wicked when it comes to women that I fear for the loss of my virtue nearly every night I spend in this house."

Maggie arched her brow, thinking that the girl's virtue had probably been lost, or at least misplaced, quite a few times already. "You shouldn't be here, Emily," she said under her breath. "His lordship will think we're plotting to rob him if he catches us together."

Emily plunked her tray down on the bed, undeterred by the warning. She'd been caught robbing a coach six months ago, and Lord Buchanan, knowing her father was a minister, had offered her the chance at reform by working in his house. Emily hadn't committed any other crimes lately, although she still had close friends in Heaven's Court.

"I haven't stolen a damn thing in ages," she stated.

"You gave Hugh the information about where Lord Buchanan kept the confession," Maggie whispered. "He's going to think you were in on the conspiracy."

"Well, I was," Emily retorted honestly. "But it isn't my welfare I've come to discuss. It's yours."

Maggie laid her head back against the pillow, seized by an involuntary shudder of fear. "You mean the kidnappers?"

"The who? Och, no. I mean a more immediate danger." Emily pushed the tray aside, positioning her plump bottom on the bed. "I'm talking about his lordship. There are things about the man you have to know, seein' that the pair of you have been forced into such an intimate association."

Maggie's sleek black eyebrows drew into a frown. "What are you blethering about?"

"You've heard about his penchant for seducin' virgins on the eve of opening a trial, haven't you?"

"Yes, Emily, I have, and I was quite worried about that trait last night before I met him. But I must say that I've given the matter a little thought, and I doubt there are enough virgins left in the city to meet such a demand. Besides, now that I've met him in person, he's not that big a beast."

"I think I might be too late," Emily said in chagrin. "Listen to you defend him. You know what they say about the pact he made with the devil seven years ago, don't you?"

"I might have heard some nonsense about selling his soul to Satan in a graveyard."

Emily lowered her voice to a tantalizing whisper, leaning over the tea tray. "It isn't nonsense. 'Tis the gospel truth. The deal between them stopped the watches of the passersby. A friend of Hugh's even saw one of the stopped watches himself, when the Chief had a terrible bunion and they had to drag a young doctor into Heaven's Court to operate. The doctor kept it as a souvenir."

Maggie pretended nonchalance as she poured herself a cup of tea. "The bunion?"

"No, the watch." Emily picked up a freshly baked scone

and bit into it with a meaningful shake of her head. "Both hands were stuck dead at midnight, and the crystal face was shattered."

"Stop filling my head with this claptrap. The man makes her nervous enough as it is. Anyway, there aren't really any demons."

"Yes, there are," Emily said with conviction. "And they do say that where there's smoke, there's fire."

"Or where there's sulfur, there's brimstone," Maggie added unthinkingly.

Emily nodded in satisfaction, munching the scone. "My father gave a sermon on demons once. I remember he suggested ringin' a church bell in the possessed person's ear while the person is asleep. It's supposed to drive out evil spirits."

"I might try a less drastic method myself," Maggie murmured.

"Well, I've considered puttin' a nail in his lordship's socks. According to Mrs. Macmillan's professor, demons can't abide iron."

"Not too many people enjoy walking around with a nail sticking in their feet, Emily. Isn't there a better way?"

"The only other thing would be to have him chase you across a burn. The devil can't cross runnin' water, or so I've heard."

"That would only prove he's a devil," Maggie felt obliged to point out. "It wouldn't make him less of one."

"No, it wouldn't." Emily pondered the matter for the moment. "I wonder if I could persuade Papa to perform an exorcism. Of course, if his lordship caught on, he'd probably dismiss me on the spot."

"I should think—"

Maggie broke off in embarrassment to see Connor suddenly standing in the doorway, his frame casting a giant shadow on the floor. His face suspicious, he stared at her for several seconds before entering the room. Maggie tried not to look guilty. Only last evening she herself had been willing to believe the gossip about him, and she had to admit that she still perceived a streak of darkness in him that gave her pause.

But would a man with a black heart stay up all night

watching over someone who had caused him so much trouble?

"I forgot my portfolio," he said curtly. "Emily, I believe Cook is looking for you to slice leeks for some broth."

That message delivered, he strode past the bed to the armchair, glancing at both girls surreptitiously in the mirror. He must have guessed they were talking about him by the utter silence that had fallen, the furtive way Emily edged off the bed to her feet. Maggie marveled at the breadth of his shoulders beneath his black greatcoat. She tried to remember what he'd looked like in his wig and legal robes. A sigh escaped her. A man like that made any costume seem masculine.

"I don't really think he's evil," she whispered to Emily as soon as he left the room.

Emily was backing into the hallway. "Well, don't say I didn't warn you."

"Warn her about what?" Ardath squeezed through the door, glancing curiously from one girl to the other. "You're not gossiping about his lordship again, are you, Emily?"

"Of course not, ma'am," Emily said indignantly. "I never gossip. Excuse me now. Cook needs me to slice her leeks."

The girl fled. Ardath raised her brow in amusement and approached the bed. "I hope she wasn't filling your head with that nonsense in the newspapers. If you want to know any of Connor's dark secrets, you've only to ask me."

"He doesn't really have any dark secrets, does he?" Maggie asked in an undertone.

"I'm afraid anything I tell you about him will sound rather banal in comparison to the kitchen gossip," Ardath began slowly. "But perhaps you do have a right to know."

Maggie's heart skipped a beat. "A right to know what?"

Ardath stared across the room. "Connor is a difficult man to understand. He's struggled almost his entire life just to survive. His father was a Sheriff's Advocate in the Highlands and was beaten to death while hunting down a child murderer. Connor and Norah found their father's body in an abandoned wagon. Connor was only eleven at the time, and she was two years younger."

Maggie put down the cup. It wasn't easy to picture the strong, self-confident man, who could be alternately cruel and charming, as a child faced with such a senseless tragedy. Unfortunately, she knew just how he felt.

"That's horrible," she said.

"You must pretend you don't know. Connor has never told me this himself, understand. Norah did. You see, their mother died shortly after her husband's death. Connor was thirteen and left with the raising of six young girls, if you can imagine such a thing."

"How did he manage?" Maggie asked.

"He lied about his age," Ardath said. "He moved them around from parish to parish before the authorities could catch on."

"So that the family would not be torn apart," Maggie said reflectively.

"Connor knew what could happen to a child on the streets, the workhouses, prostitution, and servitude."

"Why was it allowed?" Maggie asked. "Weren't there any relatives to take them in?"

"Only his uncle, who was off on some tropical island picking flowers. The authorities never caught on because Connor kept moving his little family before anyone could realize there were no parents. He supported them all by whatever means he could."

Ardath paused, sighing deeply. "I never asked the girls what 'whatever means' meant, and I'm sure they'd never tell. Apparently Connor was forced to do a few things that damaged his male pride. No one is allowed to discuss it."

Maggie thought about this. Ardath's revelation put Lord Buchanan in an entirely different light. "So he hasn't always been a ruthless bastard. I suspected as much."

"Apparently not," Ardath said.

"But how did he get to his position of power? It couldn't have been easy."

"His uncle returned from his botany adventures and beat Connor within an inch of his life for the 'whatever means,'" Ardath explained. "Then he sent him away to school. Connor achieved the rest himself on sheer talent and determination."

"At least the story had a happy ending," Maggie said with a sigh.

"That remains to be seen." Ardath's voice was troubled. "I worry about Connor's future."

"Are you and he—"

"No," Ardath said firmly. "Not anymore. In fact, I have been encouraging him to find a nice girl to settle down with. Someone just like—"

A muffled scream from the adjoining chamber where a young Irish maid was dusting interrupted her. Ardath glanced up sharply to listen. Maggie, who had found the conversation strangely reassuring, held her breath.

"Lord help us!" the maid shrieked.

There was a little thud, then silence. Ardath and Maggie glanced at each other in alarm, thoughts of abductors and avenging murderers running through their minds.

"I'll sneak out to fetch help," Ardath whispered, already halfway out of the room. "Maggie, hurry—hide under the bed. The kidnappers must have waited until Connor left the house to come for you."

Chapter

13

⤛⤜

"I appreciate your coming," Connor told the slender middle-aged man who seated himself across the desk in the cramped courtroom antechamber. "I wasn't sure if you were still in the country."

"By the end of the week I might not be." The man laid his silver-knobbed walking stick against his chair. His face devoid of expression, he studied the dozen or so letters Connor slid to him across the desk.

"You look exhausted."

"Last night my sister was—"

"Yes, I heard. What a frightening business."

Connor leaned back, composing his thoughts. He shouldn't be surprised. The retired French spymaster he knew simply as Sebastien had the omniscience of a hawk when it came to keeping an eye on the criminal activities in the city.

"This is the thirteenth ransom note I've received."

Sebastien gave him a wryly sympathetic smile. "The story has already appeared in the newspapers. I'd expect more of the same before the excitement dies down. You're a public figure now, Connor."

Connor shook his head. "They appear to all be fraudulent. This last one is from a goldsmith who still holds a grudge against the government for the fine he had to pay last year. As far as we can tell the others are all pranks. Including the one with the black rose seal." Connor's mouth tightened at the corners. "For a few moments I almost believed in ghosts."

"William Montrose," Sebastien said slowly, studying Connor's face. "The notorious murderer who died years ago?"

"Yes. Incredible, I know. Lord, my brain is so tired. Why would someone take Sheena? To complicate matters I have a houseguest, a woman. The unbelievable creature broke into my home to steal a confession from an old tramp I might have to defend in the Balfour murder."

Sebastien's soft outburst of laughter startled Connor. "Marguerite de Saint-Evremond, isn't that what she calls herself? The little transplanted French daisy struggling to survive among society's thorns."

"You know her too? Good God. Am I the only man in the city who hasn't fallen under her spell?"

"Perhaps you're moving in the wrong circles." Sebastien paused. "Not that I believe it for a minute, but street gossip has it that you're holding her against her will in your bedroom, Connor."

"My prisoner was being served a breakfast of buttered toast, eggs, and sausages in bed when I left the house," Connor retorted dryly. "She's milking her role as witness for all it's worth. Anyone would think she really believed all that nonsense about being a duke's daughter."

Sebastien's amusement faded. "That nonsense just might be true. A tragic story, if you believe it. She claims her father was involved in a British-supported plot to assassinate Napoleon. I have yet to talk to her myself."

Connor was intrigued. "And?"

"And more than that, the young woman would have to tell us in person. Perhaps certain details of her past are better forgotten."

Connor frowned. He never asked how Sebastien garnered his endless treasure trove of information. Popular rumor claimed that he had been a double agent for France and England a decade ago, that he had turned British informant to repay the moral debts he had incurred while dealing in deception. He had appeared in Edinburgh less than a year ago, an enigmatic figure who flitted between polite society and the underworld. Connor would have trusted him even without the personal letters of reference from the Prime Minister and Foreign Office.

But why all this mystery about the audacious Maggie Saunders? How could a girl who consorted with thieves have caught the ear of a man who had made his mark in espionage?

"She's my only link to Sheena's disappearance," he admitted reluctantly. "And all she can remember is that my sister disappeared in a black coach. The driver was an older man who's probably sporting a nasty bruise on his noggin, courtesy of a champagne bottle."

"How—"

"Don't ask. Miss Saunders seems to think he knew me."

Sebastien toyed with the tip of his walking stick. "There's something peculiar about all this, Connor. What happened to the man Sheena wanted to marry?"

"I bribed him to move to Venice. The greedy bastard left without looking back."

They stared at each other in silence, ignoring the conversation of clerks and lawyers in the outer chambers, the muted cries of hot-eel sellers in the street.

"I suppose Sheena's kidnapping could be tied in with the Balfour murders," Sebastien said thoughtfully. "Lord Montgomery might be hoping to deter you from bringing charges."

"All the more reason to pursue the investigation," Connor said quietly.

"I wouldn't want to be in his place." Sebastien rose from his chair, his green eyes glittering. "I'll make all the inquiries I can about your sister. In the meantime, take my advice and treat this Miss Saunders well. You wouldn't want to risk offending her many friends."

"What am I supposed to do with her?" Connor asked darkly.

Sebastien smiled. "They call you a protector of the innocent, don't they?"

"Among other things."

Chapter

14

Given a choice, Maggie would have fled the room with Ardath rather than face the kidnappers alone. Whoever would dare to break into Connor Buchanan's house in broad daylight had to be desperate, dangerous, and determined to find her.

She ignored the pain in her shoulder and wriggled under the bed as the door to the adjoining room slowly opened. A pair of scruffy black boots crept into her line of vision. Was he a killer the kidnappers had hired, a man paid to ensure her silence?

Praying that Ardath would return before he found her, she waited in anxious silence as he walked cautiously around the room. Every so often he would stop and tap the side of his right leg with a heavy wooden cudgel.

Then suddenly, through her haze of fear, she realized that the gesture seemed familiar. When she heard him start muttering to himself, she gave a sigh of relief that shuddered through every constricted muscle in her body.

"Maggie?" The intruder was peering behind the mahogany dressing screen. "Where are ye hiding, lass? What has the bastard done to ye?"

"What are you doing here, Arthur?" she whispered, easing out from under the bed. "Aren't I in enough trouble as it is?"

He scowled at her like an irate father forced to extricate his child from an embarrassing situation. "I should have guessed ye'd make a mess of everything."

"Was it my fault Hugh got himself caught?" She stood, her face defensive. "Was it my fault a woman got herself abducted with me as a witness? And Lord Buchanan is on Jamie's side?"

"Abduction or not, there was no call to be makin' a heroine of yerself. Any more good deeds, and ye'll be ruinin' the Court's bad name."

Arthur was an enormous man, as huge as a hill with a thick muscular body and long apelike arms. He was terribly nearsighted, but he refused to let anyone outside the court see him in spectacles because he said it would weaken the impact of his appearance.

In decades past he had actually been a respected chief in wild Caithness, before a smallpox epidemic had wiped out most of his clan and family, his beloved wife, brother, and sons. With a handful of scraggly followers, he'd moved his young daughter and aging sister to Edinburgh where, unskilled and desperate, he had fallen into a career of crime. Within a few years he had risen through the ranks of the underworld to command a small force of petty criminals, vagrants, and displaced persons.

"Let's go, lass. I came to take ye home."

"It's not that simple," she whispered in frustration. "I can't just leave without permission. I'm a witness now, and you can't stay here, either. They'll have you arrested for housebreaking like they did Hugh."

"Hugh is waiting for us down in the cart, but ye're right. We havena got all day. Here." He took off his heavy black cloak and draped it over her shoulders. "It shocks me senseless to find you half dressed in the devil's own bed, defendin' him, no less."

Maggie pulled away, alarmed by the rumble of activity rising from below. "I don't want you to get hurt, Arthur. Look, it's supposed to be a secret but Lord Buchanan is going to hide me away in his Highland home until the men who kidnapped his sister are found. He thinks they might come after me because I'm the only one who could identify them."

"Balderdash." Arthur gave his cudgel an experimental swing. "I'll protect ye, little one. I always have."

"I have a moral obligation to help Lord Buchanan's family."

"Moral obligation, my arse. Don't let Connor intimidate ye, Maggie."

"I was caught breaking into the man's house," she said quietly. "He has the power to have me put in prison for—"

She and Arthur glanced around simultaneously, their argument forgotten. There were voices filtering from outside the door, footsteps pounding up the stairs.

"You'd better get out of here the same way you came in," Maggie whispered, pulling off his cloak. "They'll never believe you weren't one of the kidnappers last night."

"I'm not leavin' without ye," Arthur said firmly. "For one thing, no one can hold a member of my family hostage. For another, that old butler of yers is fretting his bowels into bowstrings over yer absence. Then there's that silly wee creature that tries to pass itself off as a dog. None of the lads would be caught dead takin' care of a French poodle."

Maggie caught her breath. "What are you saying?"

"I'm sorry, Maggie. But they'll be out on the street tonight if you don't return. I'm not runnin' a charity institution."

Maggie turned away in distress, picturing Claude, frail, loyal, with failing eyesight and the painful rheumatism that plagued him. She could never abandon him. No one would employ a man of his age and infirmity. He would be lost and bewildered if he found himself on the streets. He lived in the past, still clinging to a world of wealth and privilege that had disintegrated over a decade ago. He and her little dog, Daphne, were all Maggie had left of her old life.

"This is blackmail, Arthur," she said angrily.

"Aye. That's my specialty." He flashed her an unapologetic smile, revealing two rows of teeth as irregularly spaced as tombstones. "Will ye be goin' down the rope before or after me?"

Chapter

15

Connor had ventured into the depths of Heaven's Court more than once in the course of his career to seek out informants. He had met with murderers in underground cellars and interviewed witnesses in abandoned warehouses.

But never in his life had he with such single-minded determination gone looking for a girl, a girl he'd offered to protect against his better judgment and who had betrayed him in return.

He'd hurried home from a hectic day in the courtroom to find Ardath, Norah, and his uncle half hysterical, the chambermaid ranting that Miss Saunders had been stolen away in her nightwear by a big monster of a man with a fierce scarred face, a man, the maid babbled, who had a nose like a sausage.

Connor deduced by this absurd description that she could only have been taken by Arthur Ogilvie. While Connor was relieved that the kidnappers hadn't gotten her, he resented the fact that the old rogue had broken into his house. That she was gone.

It had been almost twenty-four hours since Sheena's kidnapping. In court he had functioned like an automaton.

Right up until the very moment he left his chambers in Parliament house, he'd expected one of the clerks to confide in him that Sheena had been found unharmed and brought home.

Not a word.

The fraudulent ransom notes had stopped. He had traced every route out of the city. Late that afternoon a cattle driver had come forward claiming he'd spotted a carriage on the road to the Highlands during the night. He remembered seeing a woman's face in the window.

The information didn't give Connor much to go on, but coupled with gut instinct, it told him that Sheena's kidnappers had fled Edinburgh. How would he find her? She could be hidden in one of a hundred obscure shieling huts on the road to the Highlands. His young protégé, Donaldson, so eager to prove his worth, had already begun to alert every judge, sheriff, and magistrate from Dumfries to Dunnet Head about the kidnapping. But the prospect of tracing her looked dim.

Shadows stirred as he turned into a darkened alleyway. He realized suddenly he was being followed. Windows creaked open above the dark twisting wynds like the slitted eyelids of a slumbering beast resenting the disturbance. He had just crossed the invisible boundary and entered no-man's land. When a pile of bricks came crashing down at his feet from a gabled rooftop, it wasn't a welcome sign.

He quickened his pace.

It was said the Chief's home could only be reached by a secret tunnel that ran beneath a series of interconnecting cellars below the city. Connor hated to think of Maggie Saunders living in some subterranean hovel, to realize that Arthur might turn her appealing vulnerability into a talent for vice. How had she fallen into such an existence?

The footsteps behind him had grown bolder.

He didn't carry a weapon. He half wished that someone would pick a fight so he could vent the frustration he had been forced to suppress all day.

His wish came true a little sooner than he expected.

He'd barely turned the corner when a trio of burly teen-age boys jumped him from behind, two grabbing his arms, the other butting into his back like a goat. A fist came flying at his face. A stiletto flashed in the moonlight.

"Damn it." He grunted, ducking to avoid the punch and the knife. "You'd better not tear my evening coat." Then he slammed all three of them at once against a stone wall, feeling immeasurably better as they stared at him in stunned silence before stumbling over one another to flee.

He backed away from the wall, straightening the cuffs of his ruffled evening shirt. Just ahead he could see the way barred by a mountain of rubbish: wheelbarrows, empty barrels, piles of rotting lumber, the corpse of an old coach.

Then someone whistled. Obscure shapes moved, resolving themselves into human features. A pistol poked Connor in the ribs. He refused to acknowledge it, staring in exasperation at the girl in a man's shirt and trousers who had just popped out of the coach roof like a jack-in-the-box.

She hopped down nimbly onto the rubbish heap, grinning from ear to ear. Two fat chestnut-brown braids framed her long freckled face. "Who dares to enter my father's private sanctuary?" she demanded in a friendly voice. "Speak, stranger, before I blow yer head off."

Connor leaned back against a wheelbarrow. "It's a bit late for you to be out, isn't it, Janet? Children are supposed to be in bed at this hour."

She grinned rudely. "Oh, it's you, Buchanan. I'm not used to seeing ye without yer wig and long black dress. How are things on the good side of the law?"

"You'll be seeing me in that costume in the courthouse soon enough if you don't let me pass."

"Rules are rules, and I'm not lettin' you into Papa's headquarters unless ye know the password."

"This is a legal matter, Janet, and if you don't let me in, I'll return with a search warrant and every policeman in the city."

She gazed at him for a moment, hands on her hips. "I'd like to make an exception in yer case, Connor. But I really can't. What's the password?"

Connor raised his voice to a deafening roar. "How the bloody hell should I know?"

A delighted grin split her impish face. "That's it," she said, sweeping her arm over the rubbish heap as if welcoming a royal prince. "Ye should have told me in the first place. Get the blindfold, lads. The Devil's Advocate is paying us a visit."

Connor stumbled through the darkness, his dignity wounded beyond belief. His trouser cuffs were soaked from splashing across some kind of noxious underground stream. He saw stars from hitting his head on a crossbeam, which no one had thought to warn him about. The lawless girl, Janet, kept prodding him in the rear with a pistol.

But he suffered in silence because he was determined that Miss Saunders would atone for the trouble she caused him and deep beneath his damaged pride, he was curious about the Chief's criminal sanctuary.

None of his legal cronies had ever been allowed into the Chief's secret stronghold. The dubious honor might serve Connor well in the future. He might gain access to untold subterranean connections.

"Here we are, yer lordship."

She gave him an encouraging shove up a series of steps and yanked off his blindfold as he staggered across a threshold. The warmth of a bright coal fire enveloped him. The scent of freshly baked scones teased his nostrils. Blinking, he tripped over a tapestry stool embroidered with the Biblical quotation: GOD BE MERCIFUL TO ME A SINNER.

He found himself standing in the center of a cozy candlelit parlor. The Chief was sitting in a wing chair by the fire, contentedly darning a linen shirt. A well-fed orange cat dozed in the mending basket at his feet. When Arthur recognized Connor, he pulled off his spectacles and cursed ferociously, shattering the domestic scene.

"What the hell is that man doin' here, Janet?" he said in an angry grumble.

"He knew the password, Papa," she answered from the doorway, polishing a crab apple on the seat of her trousers.

Connor strode over to the fire, standing with his back to the flames to stare down at Arthur. "You can't interfere with my witness, Ogilvie."

The Chief scowled at him. "Nobody is supposed to get by my guards. This is an unforgivable breach of criminal ethics."

There were four other people in the parlor, seated at a table sipping tea and playing whist. They regarded Connor in mild astonishment for several moments, then went back to their game. Connor vaguely recognized the three men present—a former embezzler, a pimp, a habitual shoplifter. The only female was a frail-looking woman with fluffy white hair and a woolen shawl secured with a broach around her stooped shoulders. She gave Connor a smile.

He guessed she was the Chief's elderly aunt from Caithness; Connor had heard that the woman had no inkling her nephew was a notorious criminal, and Arthur wanted it kept that way. This secret gave Connor a bit of leverage, which he would use to his advantage if Arthur forced his hand.

He glanced past the table to the curtained alcove that presumably led upstairs to Maggie's room. Was she listening there in those shadows? Would she come down to confront him, or had she already been warned to escape? He'd never live it down if word got out he'd lost his own eyewitness.

The elderly woman laid down her cards to take a closer look at Connor, nodding approvingly. "With that manly physique, he must work with ye down at the dockyard, Arthur."

"The dockyard?" Connor said in puzzlement.

"Where we work, Connor. Don't you remember? Auntie Mabel knows all about us." The Chief stabbed his needle into the shirt. "Janet, get upstairs and into bed. Ye'll need to be up bright and early for your dancing lessons."

"But, Papa," she protested over a mouthful of apple, "I don't take dancing—"

"Upstairs, girl. Honor thy parent, at least in front of company."

Auntie Mabel turned her attention back to Connor as the girl sulkily stomped from the room. "Sit down, young fellow. I'll pour ye a nice cup of tea." She rose to shepherd him into the chair opposite Arthur. "You look a bit out of sorts."

Connor didn't doubt it. In the tussle with the Chief's street thugs, he'd lost a button off his gray woolen coat, and he suspected he had pulled an important muscle in his groin, which would play hell with his golf game, not to mention other more personal activities.

He sat awkwardly, not wanting to hurt the old woman's feelings as she brought him a cup of tea. "Bide here by the fire, laddie," she said. "I'll brew a fresh pot and bring a plate of scones."

"What do you want with us, Buchanan?" the Chief said the instant the woman left the room.

"I want Miss Saunders," he said bluntly.

"Have you pressed charges against her?"

Connor frowned. "No."

"Then ye've no legal right to detain her, and certainly not in yer home."

"She isn't under arrest." Connor stared into the fire. "But there's a damn good chance whoever abducted my sister will try to prevent her from identifying them."

"I can protect her," the Chief said gruffly.

"I don't think you can."

Arthur leaned forward at this open affront. In the firelight shadows, they looked like a pair of warring giants brought together on the grounds of their mutual concern for a girl half their size. Sensing a confrontation, the three men at the table quietly tipped back their chairs and slipped out of the room.

Connor looked up from the fire, scrutinizing the battered features of the man opposite him. "Do you know anything about my sister's abduction?"

"I never prey on women or children, Connor. You ought to know that by now. Whoever took yer sister acted on his own. 'Twas none of my men."

Aunt Mabel returned to the room at that moment, her wrinkled face wreathed in a blithe smile. "Och, it does my old heart good to see ye big blusterin' lads making friends. Or is it wee Janet ye've come to visit, Connor?"

"It's Maggie he wants to see," Arthur said with a sigh.

"Maggie?" The woman poured Connor a cup of tea and slowly carried it over to him. "She's a popular one lately, isn't she?"

Connor balanced the cup on his knee. "Popular?"

"Why, yes." Mabel returned to the table. "Just this morning when I was at the market, another fellow in a big black carriage was asking after her. Persistent, he was."

"What are you saying, Mabel?" The Chief glanced at Connor.

"A man asked after Maggie in the market when I was

shopping for supper. He wanted to know where she lived and what time she would be at home."

Connor released the breath he barely realized he'd drawn. "What did he look like?"

"I don't know," the woman said in confusion. "He spoke to me from the carriage window, and I couldna see inside. Besides, Arthur has warned me not to talk to strangers. He said the city is full of criminals."

Connor put his cup down on the hearth. "Do you know what the carriage looked like?"

"A nice one, I'd say. Black and—" Mabel broke off as if sensing something was wrong. "Goodness, I'm not sure. It was barely light, and I didn't think to pay attention. Was he a bad man, then?"

"Tell Maggie I want to see her now," Connor said, gazing at the alcove.

The Chief rose, his enormous frame eclipsing the fireglow. "Find Claude, Mabel."

Connor's head began to pound. "Who the hell is Claude?" he wondered aloud. "The family executioner?"

"He's Maggie's butler," Arthur said curtly. "Give me yer coat while he fetches her."

Connor didn't respond. A butler? A street thief had a butler? He couldn't imagine it anymore than he could Maggie living in this place, a rare pearl hidden away in a veritable bed of sin.

"Take off yer coat, Connor," Arthur repeated.

Connor shot to his feet. "What the hell for?"

"So I can sew on another button before she sees ye. Maggie notices that sort of thing. And you may as well sit back down. Claude moves as slowly as a snail in a snowstorm."

Ten minutes passed before Connor lost the last of his patience, pacing the confines of the parlor like a mountain cat in a cave. Criminals of every description had paraded in and out of the house to take a peek at him. It wasn't every day that they could watch the Chief sewing on buttons for his nemesis.

Arthur studied the tall figure over the rims of his spectacles. "Fetch her for yerself, lad," he said at last. "Yer prowling is gettin' on my nerves."

Connor didn't need any extra encouragement, reaching the curtained alcove in a giant stride. No one stopped him, and as he suspected, the passageway led directly to a narrow wooden staircase. He'd feel like the biggest fool in the world if he'd been watching Arthur sew on buttons while that girl gave him the slip.

He took the stairs two at a time, slowing only on the landing when he encountered an elderly man who was making a labored effort to continue the climb. With his trim build, pinched face, and silver-gray hair, he exuded a dignity that belied his position—this had to be Maggie's "butler."

"Pardon me," he said. "Are you going up or down?"

The butler gave him a disdainful look. "I am going up, sir," he said in heavily accented French. "There is some man in the parlor, a man from the Scottish wilds, who has come to see my mistress. It is my suspicion he is a policeman in disguise. I am sure he brings trouble."

Connor dropped his voice to a confidential whisper. "Perhaps he wants to help your mistress."

Fear darkened the man's faded blue eyes. "That has not been her experience with such men of his profession in the past."

A ray of understanding broke through the clouds of Connor's irritation. The police—her enemies? Could this man be referring to Napoleon's notorious secret police, who had ruined so many Royalist families years ago? He wondered suddenly whether there was a grain of reality in the fairy tale after all. What could have so terrorized the daughter of a duke that she would seek refuge in a nest of criminals?

Connor patted the man's frail shoulder. "I'm not a policeman. Don't worry, I have no intention of hurting your mistress."

"But, monsieur—"

"She'll call you if she needs you," Connor said reassuringly. Then curiosity got the better of him and he searched the man's shuttered face for the truth that kept eluding him. "What did the police do to make your mistress so afraid?" he asked very softly.

But Claude only shook his head, grim-lipped and not about to reveal any personal secrets to a stranger, if indeed there were secrets to reveal.

"I will wait outside the door," he said as if to warn Connor that Maggie was under his protection. "I will stand guard until you go away."

By the time he reached the top of the stairs, Connor could hear her talking gently as if to a child. He traced the intriguing sound to the tiny room at the end of the hall. He didn't know what he expected to find by barging in on her unannounced, but she was mistaken if she thought she could defy his orders. He was going to show her who was in control.

He pushed the door open to the candlelit room, hesitating as the small figure rifling through the armoire gave a startled gasp. But it was Connor who suffered the greatest shock. The sight of her in a white silk chemise with billowing lace petticoats wreaked more havoc on his composure than all the effort involved in penetrating Heaven's Court. She looked like a beautiful white blossom. Like something fresh and pure, tempting him to touch her, to savor her innocence.

He exhaled slowly. The stress of the previous evening's events conspired with an unwelcome shot of sexual tension to tighten his muscles. He felt like hell and probably looked it too. His head was pounding hard enough to explode. His body ached from riding half the night in a futile search for his sister. He didn't know where he found the energy to be so aroused.

"Miss Saunders." He clenched his jaw unconsciously as he glanced around the room to see who she'd been talking to in that beguilingly tender voice.

Maggie gave him a reproachful look. "In case you hadn't noticed, I am wearing nothing but my undergarments."

He'd noticed, all right. He'd noticed everything from the tiny pink silk rosebuds stitched on the hem of her petticoats to the swell of her full white breasts through her chemise. He turned to the wall, warning himself to behave. Dear Lord, what a preposterous dilemma, and here he was thinking he'd lived through just about everything.

His gaze fell suspiciously on a leather-bound trunk by the door. Feminine garments spilled like seafoam from its bulging edges, evidence of her impending escape. His anger flared, bright and hot. "Caught in the act again," he said furiously. "I see you haven't been wasting any time."

"Of course not," she said in a muffled voice as her head vanished into the gray velvet bodice of the dress she'd tugged from the armoire. "You convinced me this morning how dangerous the situation is—you don't mind carrying that trunk, do you? It would take Claude a fortnight to haul it down the stairs and you, being such a hale and strong Highlander, could do it so much easier."

He wheeled in astonishment. "Are you asking *me* to help you shirk your responsibilities as my witness? Well hell, if that doesn't take—"

She stared at him. "I don't know what you're talking about. I only came back to pack a few necessities, and to get Claude and Daphne, of course. I couldn't just abandon them, could I?"

He took a breath to cool his anger as she darted past him to the dressing table. The scent of roses followed her like a scattering of crushed petals. For a moment he was too distracted by her femininity to continue, by the movement of her hands like a pair of butterflies as she twisted her curly hair into an intricate knot. He noticed how slender her neck was, and wondered if she had recovered from her fall— Lord, had he only known her for twenty-four hours? Was it possible she had turned his world upside down in less than a day?

"Do you expect me to believe you left my home today on a rope with every intention of returning?" he said in patent disbelief.

Her eyes met his in the mirror, brimming with innocence. "It's the truth."

He cast a cynical glance around the room. There was a white poodle curled up asleep on the bed, nestled cozily amidst a heap of bonnets, stockings, and a pair of well-worn satin ballet slippers.

"You're a dancer?" he asked, realizing with a vague sense of relief that she must have been talking to the dog and not a lover when he burst in.

"A private passion, not a profession. Papa would have disapproved. Robert would have been mortified."

He raised his eyebrow at the nuance of affection in her tone. "Robert?"

"My brother, the prude. Oh dear, Daphne, you aren't sitting on my good hat, are you?"

Connor frowned to cover his sudden fascination. A ballerina. He studied her covertly from beneath his brows. Well, that explained her alluring air of gracefulness. One piece of the puzzle in place. Against his will he pictured her practicing in his fifteenth-century Highland house, her perfect little body perspiring. Relevé. Plié. Tendu. It would be torture to watch her and not touch. There was something too erotic about a woman's body exercising with such focused strength. A glimmer of resentment entangled with expectation flashed through him. They would be alone most of the time except for the four servants who maintained the small estate. Trouble loomed ahead in spades.

So did possibilities.

She glanced at him over her shoulder. She was even lovelier with her hair caught back, elegant with the exquisite features of a doe, her eyes wide and expressive. Connor felt some of the resentment melt away as he studied her. "It's all right if I bring him, isn't it?" she asked in concern.

"Your prude—I mean, your brother?"

"My butler."

Not exactly alone then. But alone enough—why was he having so much trouble following this conversation? "Not the old man I met on the stairs?" he said incredulously. "He didn't look strong enough to make such a strenuous journey. I'm not going to be anyone's nursemaid."

"I should hope not," Maggie said. "Claude would be mortified if you mollycoddled him. He is, however, old and unemployable, my lord. He will not survive on his own. We have to take him. We have to."

She was so steadfast in her protective loyalty that Connor didn't know how to refuse her without sounding like a monster. He shook his head, exhausted and at his wits' end. He had to get away from her, and fast. She was addling his brains. "We're obviously headed for disaster, Miss Saunders, and I can see no alternative but to make other arrangements. One of the junior lawyers who works for me should be handling this. Donaldson is my best. He has a married sister in Aberdeen where you could stay indefinitely."

He didn't add that Donaldson wouldn't even notice if she danced naked on his dinner table. The young man's work obsessed him; women did not exist in his dedicated world. "You'll be safe with Donaldson," he concluded—safe in ways that Connor, dangerously attracted to her, could not promise.

Maggie walked over to her overstuffed trunk. "No."

Connor sensed a rebellion brewing. "What do you mean 'no'?"

"I am not going off with a total stranger."

He smiled insultingly. "*I* am a total stranger, Miss Saunders, in case that startling fact has slipped your attention. One housebreaking does not a friendship make."

She plopped down on her trunk in protest. "You're less a stranger than a man I've never met," she argued reasonably. "Besides, I have the utmost confidence in your ability to protect me. Apart from a few obvious flaws in your temperament such as beastly arrogance and a weakness for women, I believe you have an honorable heart."

Honorable was the last word Connor would use to describe the feelings she had stirred in his black heart so far. Smoldering lust seemed more accurate. She looked like Little Miss Muffet with her skirts spread out on her tuffet, and he, like the nasty big spider, would probably end up frightening her out of her naive faith in him. She needed a lesson in reality, this woman who'd broken into his house to help a homeless old peddler.

She gave him a look of unshakable trust. "I wouldn't feel safe going into hiding with anyone else but you."

"In spite of my beastly arrogance and weakness for women?"

"Well, nobody is perfect."

Connor snorted at that. Her self-composure amazed him. It made him want to master her. And he hated to admit it, but he still couldn't shake off that silly tingle of magic he felt when he looked at her, as if a wicked fairy had bopped him over the head with her wand.

He scowled to hide that embarrassing realization. "It will not be easy, traveling together under such strained circumstances, lass. I intend to use every opportunity to look for my sister." He paused, hoping for evidence that he'd intimidated her. If he had, she hid it well. "You and I know very little about each other."

"I know more about you than you realize," she said calmly.

His mouth tightened. "A kitchen maid's gossip. I knew I shouldn't have brought Emily into my house. I trust there won't be any more misjudgments between us based on what is said behind my back."

"I trust not, my lord." She smoothed down her skirts. "If that's understood, then we might as well be on our way."

Connor didn't feel like anything was understood at all. He was confused. He wanted to walk out of this room and pretend they'd never met. But then he remembered the stranger in the market asking about her. The men who'd injured her last night, the tragedy in her past that Sebastien and the old butler had alluded to. Perhaps at the moment there was little Connor could do to help Sheena. But he had the power, if not the inclination, to help this woman. She needed protection. If any harm came to her, the responsibility would lay in his hands.

For one small woman, she had stirred his life into a storm. He turned in defeat to the door. "Hurry up," he said brusquely.

She looked worried. "You never did tell me it was all right to bring Claude and Daphne along."

"Who the hell is Daphne?" He all but bellowed the question, then took a startled step back as the poodle bounced off the bed and hurled itself at him in a frenzy of tail-thumping friendliness.

Maggie clasped her hands, grinning in relief. "She likes you. That's a very good sign. Daphne is an excellent judge of character. So were her parents. I feel even better about my decision to go off with you."

Connor stared down in dismay at the dog, if you could call it that; it looked more like a hyperkinetic ball of hair, and it kept licking his hands.

He stumbled backward to open the door. Claude stared at him from the hall, pale with exertion. "Mademoiselle," he said weakly, "there is a man in the parlor who wishes to see you, a policeman, I suspect. I'm afraid I neglected to ask his name."

"It's all right, Claude." She had returned to the dressing table, adjusting a monstrous object on her head. "Will this hat do, Lord Buchanan?" she asked anxiously.

Connor glanced around, but he couldn't see her face. It was hidden beneath a huge veil that dropped from her forehead like a curtain. "Will it do what?"

"I'm wearing it to conceal my identity. I don't want anyone to notice me."

He thought that she couldn't have attracted more notice if a pelican had gotten caught in a fishing net and landed on her head. He couldn't bring himself to comment on it though because he was in shock, just beginning to realize what he'd gotten himself into. A dog that looked like a white powdered wig with legs, a hostile old man, a woman petite enough to tuck into his pocket. Helpless, dependent on him, expecting him to play the hero. He *was* a traveling circus.

"Do you think I should bring a bathing dress?" Maggie asked thoughtfully.

Connor rolled his eyes. A bathing dress, she'd said. "We're not going on a Mediterranean holiday, lass. We'll be in seclusion."

"I only wanted to be prepared in case you asked me to go for a little swim."

"Miss Saunders, I am protecting you from criminals, not overseeing a playful splash in the local stream. Furthermore, a Highland autumn can be not only damn cold but downright dangerous."

"Just like the Highlanders who survive them," she said sadly. "I don't know why you're being so nasty about this. If we're stuck together, we may as well be friends. Especially after last night."

"Friends?" he exclaimed. *"Friends?* You tried to rob me. We didn't exactly spend a lovely evening at the opera getting to know each other."

Maggie brightened. "Do you like the opera too? I never would have guessed. Well, at least that's one thing we have in common."

Connor could only shake his head at what aggravation lay ahead.

"Well, I'm going to bring a parasol," she said after a moment. "And don't tell me the sun doesn't shine in the Highlands. I refuse to be affected by your pessimism."

He expelled a sigh of exasperation. "Bring a parasol. What does it matter?"

"The gray-striped silk or the ivory lace? Oh, never mind. I'll bring them both. Will you carry down the trunk, or shall we have it sent to your house?" she asked politely as she began heaping hatboxes into his arms.

He grunted, struggling to see her over the rising mountain of millinery. "I'll have it picked up in the morning before we leave. Is all this stuff really necessary?"

"I will not embarrass you with inappropriate clothing."

He frowned. "There must be a fortune in hats here. How can a woman of your circumstances afford all this? Or am I carting around stolen goods?"

"Arthur has spoiled me horribly. He insists that all his boarders be well dressed."

"Stolen goods." Connor sighed. "I knew it. Now I'm a criminal."

Maggie hid a grin. "What about the dog?"

Daphne's tail started to wag.

"The dog," he said.

Maggie stuffed her ballet shoes into a black velvet reticule. "Claude, too?"

Connor clenched his jaw as she tucked a parasol under his arm. He felt like a damned hatrack. Lord help him. "Claude too."

There was a small crowd waiting for them at the foot of the stairs. The Chief; Janet; Auntie Mabel; Charlie Cameron, the famous jewel thief who had been released from prison last year; young Hugh, the housebreaker; and his uncle, Reckless Ronald MacTavish, the retired highwayman who'd lost an eye in the French and Indian Wars.

Maggie felt a lump rise in her throat at the sight of them, the only family she had. She remembered the times Charlie had brewed chamomile tea when she caught a cold, how Ronald would come out searching for her whenever she was a few minutes late from work, how Janet had warmed her slippers at the fire. And the Chief, the secrets they had shared late at night when no one else was listening, the tears they'd shed over losing their beloved homes.

She felt Connor behind her on the stairs, big and powerful, regarding her friends in blatant disapproval. Out of the frying pan into the fire. Why should she trust him? He needed her now, and she needed him. But what would happen to her after his sister was found? What was she giving up to go off with this man?

The Chief's voice broke the silence. "Ye'll need an escort back to his house."

"We will not," Connor said in horror. "The Lord Advocate can hardly be seen accompanied by the worst criminals in the city."

"They're the best criminals in the city," Maggie said with a catch in her voice.

"Aye." The Chief walked slowly forward to confront Connor until they stood chest to chest, Maggie like a wild daisy lost in the shadow of two towering oak trees. "A warning, lad," he said in a soft growl. "If any harm comes to that lass, I'll be sewing buttons on yer shroud and not yer coat the next time."

"No one is going to hurt her."

"And another thing." The Chief's voice dropped an octave. "If word gets out that I was mendin' clothes in my spectacles, I'll ken who come after."

Connor could barely restrain a grin. "I have a feeling that information will come in handy in the future when I need a favor or two."

"Dinna push yer luck, Connor."

Luck? Connor turned to regard the cause of all this consternation, admitting to himself that there could be worse things in the world than guarding a beautiful young woman in his Highland hideaway.

"Are you ready, lass?" he asked.

She nodded, then sniffed, flicking her veil back to dab at her nose with a handkerchief. "This is all so sudden and upsetting, my lord. I need a moment to say good-bye in private."

Connor looked around the hallway in disbelief. Hardened

criminals were clearing their throats, blinking back tears, stepping forward to embrace Maggie in rough hugs. He felt like a wolf stealing a baby lamb from its flock.

"For God's sake," he said. "It's not as if she's never going to return. I have to be back myself before the end of the month."

For some reason this made Maggie sniff all the louder. The Chief looked at Connor with sad condemnation in his eyes.

"For five years I have loved Maggie like my own daughter, but I cannot break the rules, not even for kin. Once you leave the clan of Heaven's Court, there's no coming back. When ye take Maggie away tonight, she becomes an outsider to us. Now give us a minute alone so we can make our farewells in private. Get the hell out of here, Connor."

Connor waited on the unlit doorstep, feeling like the cat that had been put out for the night. He wondered idly if there was some sort of ritual to be performed when you broke from the clan. Oaths made in blood, secrets sworn on a human skull never to be revealed.

Annoyed, he set down Maggie's silly parasol and walked around the side of the house, half hoping to peek into the parlor. He was anxious to return home to find out if there'd been any news of Sheena.

The sound of leaves rustling and a soft curse caught his ear. He sidestepped a weed-infested vegetable plot and walked quietly to the back of the house.

A man clad in dark clothing was in the process of climbing up an ivy trellis toward a second-story window.

An unpleasant tug of realization tightened the nerves of Connor's scalp. The man was scaling the ivy toward Maggie's bedroom window like a lover sneaking an hour with the woman forbidden him. Or was he not a friend at all, but a stranger with something more sinister in mind?

Was this one of the men who'd kidnapped Sheena?

Connor eased out of his coat and crept up to the trellis, experimentally testing its weight with his foot. As he suspected, it wouldn't hold him. Damn, the warped wood felt too fragile to bear even the intruder. He gave it a powerful shake.

Another curse broke the silence. A shower of dry leaves hit Connor on the head. Then suddenly the man on the trellis was treading air, arms flailing, and falling backward like a rotten apple shaken from a branch.

He landed at Connor's feet, swearing violently, entangled in the remnants of the shattered trellis. Connor stared down at him in thoughtful silence. The man was young and good-looking, clutching a bouquet of beheaded flowers to his chest. He didn't look like much of a threat, either.

"Hell." He sat up, looking dazed and disgusted. "Bloody hell. Damn stinking trellis."

"You should have used a ladder," Connor said.

The man jumped to his feet, startled to see another figure in the shadows. "Who the devil are you?" he demanded in indignation.

Connor stepped forward, towering over him by half a foot. "That's a question I should be asking you."

The man looked Connor up and down before apparently deciding cooperation was in his best interests. "Liam Mac-Dougall," he said reluctantly, cradling his bruised elbow. "Who the bloody blazes are you? You're not one of the clan."

Connor debated whether he should use restraint to talk the matter through, or simply obey a very tempting impulse to knock the little idiot senseless. "Why were you trying to break into Miss Saunders's window?"

"Why should I tell you?"

Connor gave him a malevolent smile. "Because I'm going to hurt you very badly if you don't."

"I wasn't trying to break in," Liam said in a dejected voice. "I was going to break Maggie out. The Chief refuses to let me court her, and there's a rumor that she's being taken off by another man, that she's gotten herself into some kind of trouble and has to leave the country."

Connor glanced up at the darkened window. "What kind of trouble?"

"I'm not at liberty to say." He brushed himself off, releasing a sigh of self-importance. "All I can reveal is that it has something to do with a ring of French spies."

"And you took it upon yourself to save her from this international intrigue?"

"Aye." Liam nodded uncertainly. "That's right."

Connor narrowed his eyes. "Let me see if I understand. You were risking your neck to save Miss Saunders from enemy agents using"—he gestured to Liam's left hand—"a bunch of headless flowers as a weapon?"

"Not exactly," Liam said with an offended look. "The flowers were for the wedding. I hoped we could elope. I've just taken a commission in the Horse Guard, and thought Maggie could live with my family in Glasgow. Mother is going to fuss at first of course, but that will change after the baby comes."

"The baby?" Connor said in a startled voice.

Liam looked embarrassed. "That's what usually comes after a honeymoon, isn't it?"

"Sometimes before."

"Yes, well, I thought if I left Maggie with a baby to look after, it would take her mind off more unpleasant things."

"Such as a ring of French spies?"

"That, and how much she was missing me."

Connor shook his head. "Romeo couldn't have done any better. Damn bad luck about the trellis giving way—"

Liam cursed.

"And the unfortunate fact that you're too late to save her."

"You mean she's gone?" Liam said in panic.

"Going even as we speak."

"Oh, my God." Liam leaned back against the shredded trellis, bereft and pale. "Now what am I going to do?"

"I suppose you'll have to find another damsel in distress."

"That isn't what I meant." Liam sounded terrified. "I won't be able to get out of here unless Maggie shows me the way. I'm a dead man. These flowers will adorn my grave."

Connor lifted his brow. "How did you manage to get in, lad?"

"Janet. The little witch. She charged me twenty pounds, too."

Connor tried to look sympathetic. "We can't put a price on love, can we? Anyway, take my advice, Liam, and try to sneak out of here however you can. If the Chief catches you, it won't be a pretty picture."

"You're telling me. Damn it, I'd like to get my hands on

the bastard who's taking her away. Here." He shoved what was left of the bouquet at Connor. "Perhaps you can use these. They're no bloody good to me where I'm going."

He stomped off toward the back gate, swearing and pausing once to glance up wistfully at Maggie's window. Connor watched him with amusement and something else that felt annoyingly like jealousy. Which of course it wasn't. Hell, the last thing he needed was to play intermediary between two star-crossed lovers with all the trouble he already had on his hands.

"I shouldn't have interfered," he said aloud, staring down at the broken trellis.

"Is that you, my lord?" a soft voice whispered behind him.

Connor turned to stare at Maggie as she walked cautiously through the garden. "Who are you talking to?" she asked, lifting her veil.

He caught her arm before she could trip over the trellis. He had every intention of telling her the truth. God forbid that his position as her protector took on any further significance. "It was—"

"Oh—oh!" She brought her hands to her face, noticing the remnants of the splintered wood at her feet. "You caught an intruder, didn't you?"

"Well, he—"

"He was climbing the trellis to my window, and you interrupted him." She grabbed his arm and gave it a grateful squeeze. "If it hadn't been for you, he would have broken into my bedchamber and done God only knows what."

Her blue eyes shone with admiration in the moonlight. Her breasts pressed against his hand, reminding him how close he'd come last night to taking her, how much he still wanted to. She was like a maddening melody he couldn't get out of his mind. "You weren't in your bedchamber," he said slowly. "He would have broken in to find an empty room."

"But he didn't know that when you pounced on him. Look at that trellis, my lord. He must have put up a fierce fight. You weren't hurt, were you?"

Connor hid the flowers behind his back, seriously tempted to leave her misconceptions alone. "Quite frankly, there wasn't much of a fight. I shook him off the trellis, he fell, and then he ran off."

"*You* frightened him away, and you didn't even have to hit him."

Connor swallowed hard, wondering why her unwarranted praise should please him. He was accustomed to flattery and flirtation. A compliment for a good deed he hadn't even committed was a novelty. She was twenty-three, he remembered suddenly, and a man had wanted to elope with her. Had she cared about Liam MacDougall?

"Miss Saunders, I must be honest with you."

"Of course you must," Maggie said graciously. "A man of your integrity could be nothing else."

"The intruder was—"

There were loud footsteps behind them, then the Chief bellowed, "Yer escort is ready, Connor. Are ye takin' her away or not?"

Connor turned involuntarily toward the house. "Yes, I'm taking her."

Maggie's gaze dropped to the straggly flowers in his hand. "Another bouquet for me?" she said softly, raising her eyes to his. "You must have picked them yourself in the dark. I don't know why you pretend to be so mean. That is the sweetest gesture."

"No, it isn't."

"You're far too modest," Maggie said. "I should have known you would keep your word about protecting me, although I have to admit that until this moment I had my doubts about this whole situation."

"I have my doubts too, Miss Saunders."

"I never doubted your ability to protect me," Maggie added, as if afraid she'd insulted him. "Only your willingness."

The Chief shouted at them again.

"Should we tell him about the intruder?" Maggie whispered.

Connor snagged her arm, herding her back toward the house. The last thing he needed was to get embroiled in an illegal manhunt for a misguided suitor. "I don't think he'll trouble you again. Let's just get out of here. I still have to pack before we leave for the Highlands."

"Did you get a look at him?" she asked anxiously. "Do you think it was one of the kidnappers?"

"It wasn't one of the kidnappers. It was Liam MacDougall." He waited after he'd dropped that bombshell to gauge her reaction, and he had to admit he was gratified by the utter blankness on her face.

"Who? Oh—*Liam*. What was that idiot doing on the trellis?"

Connor smirked. "Not exactly an encouraging response for a man who risked his neck to elope with you."

"Elope with me?" Maggie looked shocked. "But I hardly know him. In fact, I only met him twice while I was tutoring his niece."

"Then you won't mind missing the idyllic life of maternity and living with his mama that he had planned for you."

Maggie frowned in suspicion. "You didn't hurt him, did you?"

"I didn't lay a blessed finger on him. Can we go now?"

Maggie didn't argue with him. She glanced back thoughtfully over her shoulder at the trellis that lay in pieces on the ground. His lordship was obviously in control of the situation and took his promise to protect her to heart, which made her feel a little better about being alone with him.

It still didn't answer her concerns about the attraction smoldering between them, the sparks that ignited whenever she looked into his face. And it didn't alter the inherent danger in entrusting her life to a man who took what he wanted, who possessed the predatory instincts of a lion, and who from the start hadn't exactly made a secret of his sexual interest in her. His professional success hadn't been achieved on mere intellectual skill but on a combination of physical presence and calculated aggression. He had proved himself to be the most powerful male animal in the pride.

While he was guarding her, Maggie would have to be on guard against him.

He stopped abruptly. "From this moment forward you will do everything I tell you."

Maggie stared up at his hard face, realizing again how much she admired the way he took command of the situation. "Everything?"

"Yes," he said. "You see, I'm used to people obeying me, lass. It's one of the privileges of power."

"Which you intend to wield."

"Aye." Amusement glinted in his eyes. "I'll do the wielding, you do the yielding. That's the way I like it."

The Chief slipped on his spectacles at the parlor window to watch them leave the court. Both Connor and Maggie wore blindfolds which would be removed only when they reached the outskirts of the sanctuary.

His little French lassie was an outsider now. She had broken from the clan.

He turned back into the room, his huge shoulders slumped in dejection. "The Devil's Advocate has taken our angel away, and she's gone willingly too," he murmured, sliding a finger under his glasses to wipe the corner of his eye. "I never thought to see the day."

The young girl sitting on the hearthstone leaped up to fling herself into his arms. "Don't be sad, Papa. You still have me."

"Aye, lass," he said ruefully. "Isn't that a consolation?"

Chapter

16

❧

Maggie had made another serious mistake.

The journey into the Highlands with Connor Buchanan had taken on hazards she'd never anticipated. As they veered northward off the Stirling Road into uncivilized terrain, he'd shed the trappings of refinement like a pair of socks, the little things that mattered so much to a person of her upbringing. Little things like carrying on a polite conversation and giving her bouquets of battered flowers.

He shaved only when the mood struck him, which judging by the stubble on his square jaw, wasn't very often. He let his long hair loose over his shoulders. Between endless stretches of silence, he communicated to her with incoherent grunts and unfathomable looks which she caught when he thought she wasn't watching. Those looks made her shiver. They made her feel rather like a primitive woman who had been singled out by a hunter for mating purposes.

When they stopped, it wasn't to rest or admire the rugged scenery, the mauve-swathed hills or castle ruins, or to dine on fresh venison. It was for Connor to harass the local authorities or interrogate an innkeeper about his sister. He wielded his authority like a whip.

Maggie wondered how long a person of her refinement could tolerate the discomfort of traveling with him. The coach just couldn't seem to hold his restless energy. Not to mention his sheer physical being. His muscular legs were everywhere, and she had banged up against his right shoulder more times than she could count. Slamming into a body like his hurt. She suspected it left bruises.

The weather added another element of misery to their journey, cold and misty with rain on the horizon. The coachman, eager to reach their destination in record time, had decided to make a "detour" onto an abandoned coffin route.

The detour included hitting every rut, rock, and log that had lain on the Highland track since God was a boy.

But the worst part was that Maggie knew they were being followed, and Connor acted as if he hadn't noticed, even though she reminded him of that fact at least three times an hour.

"Call it a sixth sense, my lord, but there was something a little too familiar about that swineherd coming over the hill."

Claude, on the opposite seat, was sound asleep and snoring lightly. Daphne had cuddled up to Connor's side, a situation he barely tolerated. Connor himself didn't bestir himself to respond. He was rudely pretending to read the *Scottish Gazette*. She knew he was only pretending because he hadn't turned the page all day.

It was an affront to good manners. She reminded herself that no self-respecting de Saint-Evremond should have to suffer such treatment. "Excuse me." She tapped her gloved knuckles lightly on the back of the newspaper. "Aren't you at all concerned about the swineherd? There was something very suspicious about his eyes."

Connor buried his nose in the paper only to look up involuntarily as the coach ploughed into a rut. Maggie bounced forward, to the opposite seat, then shot straight back into Connor's lap.

He groaned as if she had mortally injured him with the impact. Then, as the coach gave another jolt, he put his arm around her waist to prevent her from flying forward again.

Maggie was astonished at how good it felt to settle back against his chest. It was also reassuring to learn that, despite his appalling rudeness, he was willing to protect her from harm when necessary. After all, it didn't matter what the man said or didn't say. Only what he did.

"Thank you," she said in a low, embarrassed voice. "I won't forget this."

Connor never knew exactly what the woman was talking about, but he did know that she talked too much and if she landed in his lap one more time, he wouldn't be responsible for his actions. She was far too soft and feminine. She smelled too delicious to resist. She was relentless in her quest to drive him to distraction.

The coach rocked to a teeth-jarring stop. Connor's grip on her tightened, and she clung to him like a wild rose that grew against a castle wall, fragrant and tempting if a man didn't mind a few thorns. He tried to pretend her derriere wasn't pressing into his privates, that a man of his experience ought to have some control over when he became aroused.

The coachman came to the door before Connor had shifted her back onto the seat. Daphne wiggled under his arm, determined to be included in his attention. Claude snored on.

"Sorry about the rut, sir," the coachman shouted. "It's this damned mist. Thick as porridge. A man canna see his own hands in front of his face." To demonstrate, he waved his fingers at the window.

Connor tugged his newspaper out from between himself and the girl on his lap, shredding it in half in the process. "Well, be quick about it this time. I don't want to be sitting here after dark."

"No, sir. Of course not, sir. I was wonderin' though if ye could all empty the coach. Just until I get us out of this rut."

Connor eased Maggie off his leg. He could smell the whisky on the blasted man's breath through the window. "He's a damned drunkard," he said to himself, wondering what else could go wrong. "I should never have listened to Ardath when she insisted I hire him. Everyone get out."

Maggie lifted her hand to tidy her hair, drawing Connor's attention to the fullness of her breasts and narrow waist. God knew there was nothing enticing about her crumpled gray velvet dress, but that didn't stop him from imagining the supple dancer's body hidden beneath it. A body that he was supposed to protect and not lust after like an animal, he reminded himself with a grunt of annoyance.

"Take your belongings," he said in resignation. "There's no telling how long it's going to take him to work us loose."

Maggie clucked her tongue in sympathy as she gathered up her skirts. "A good servant is worth his weight in gold but almost impossible to find nowadays. I suppose it's a sign of the times. That's why I treasure Claude so highly."

Connor watched in grudging admiration as she leaned over to gently shake the old man awake. She was so convincing in her pose as the exiled duke's daughter that Connor realized he could end up wrapped around her little finger just like everyone else if he weren't constantly on guard against her.

"Put your cloak on," he said in a gruff voice to disguise the fact that he'd been staring at her again. "You'll freeze to death out on the moor."

Startled, Maggie scooped up her dog and swung her head around to reprimand him for his abrupt tone. The words died in her throat at the look he gave her, and tiny flames ran down her backbone. Her eyes met his, and she wanted to tell him that it didn't matter if it began to snow. There was enough heat in Connor Buchanan's gaze to start a bonfire.

Connor climbed a hill and sat down on a large boulder to watch Maggie, Claude, and the driver argue about how to lift the wheel out of the rut. Actually, it wasn't a rut. It was more like a ditch, but he supposed if you were drunk enough, you wouldn't know the difference.

He wondered if getting drunk would make traveling with her more tolerable, or if it would only make it worse by lowering his inhibitions. His mind kept mulling over the images of tussling with her in his bed. That creamy skin, those lush breasts and muscular legs he could too easily envision wrapped around his back. His attraction to her was a frightening thing.

Traveling with the woman was making him mad. Every time she touched him, he jumped as if he'd been burned with a hot poker. The sweet huskiness of her voice sent chills down his back. The dog and the old man didn't help, either.

In fact, he had been forced to put his foot down on the road from Falkirk.

Not that it had done a damn bit of good.

"Daphne needs to go, my lord," Maggie must have said at least fifteen times an hour.

To which he would reply, "Good. Let her go. The farther, the better."

"I mean she needs to, well, she needs to use the privy, as it were."

"The privy? Dear Lord. We are not stopping again to let that animal spend an hour sniffing around every burn, brush, and boulder in creation."

And Claude would add, "I know it is not my place to say so, sir, but surely it wouldn't hurt to stop and admire the local scenery?"

"Yes, it would hurt." Connor realized that the time had come for a show of authority. "I am protecting a witness, not giving a grand tour of the Highlands to a dog. We are not stopping. Now, if that's settled, I do not wish to be disturbed again. I wish to sleep, hopefully until this wretched journey is over."

The poodle took her revenge while Connor took a nap.

"Oh, Daphne," Maggie whispered, "you didn't. Not all over his lordship's law briefs. Funny word, isn't it, briefs? Claude, open the window while his lordship is still asleep and hang his important papers out to dry. He'll be as cross as crabs if he finds out."

"He has already found out, Miss Saunders."

"Oh, dear." A sheepish smile crept across her face. "I hope those papers weren't terribly important."

"Of course not, lass!" Connor retorted. "They only represented months of blood, sweat, and tears on the Balfour case. But never mind. The Crown will understand if crucial evidence for the trial of the century is ruined because a poodle used it for a chamber pot."

He heaved a sigh of impatience and lifted his gaze to the sky. Darkness was dropping like a curtain. They'd never get to Kilcurrie at this rate, he thought in frustration. Frustration over not finding Sheena, over his increasing desire for a girl who at least outwardly represented everything he fought against. Deceit, criminal ties, emotional complications. What she might consist of deep beneath that surface appeal was another matter.

Certainly not like anyone, man or woman, he'd ever met before.

He glanced down, his gaze going straight to the petite figure with mist spangling her midnight hair. How could she think she was being followed? There probably wasn't a human being for miles around, let alone one associated with the kidnappers, who, if they had any sense, wouldn't be parading around disguised as the local swineherds.

But try to tell Maggie Saunders that. Try to inject a dose of reality into her make-believe world of deposed dukes and French castles and tenderhearted criminals. Connor still hadn't gotten over how everyone around her catered to her fantasy. Well, he wouldn't be counted in her story-book entourage, thank God. It was one thing for the country to view him as a hero. But it was quite another for that image to seep into his personal life.

Except that his association with her wasn't supposed to be personal.

He narrowed his eyes, then laughed out loud, the sound echoing in the hills. What the hell did they think they were doing now?

The driver had unhitched the horses. He had wedged a board under the stuck wheel and was pushing against the carriage with all his might. So were Maggie and Claude, their faces empurpled with effort, worker ants trying to roll a boulder up a hill.

In fact, from where Connor sat it looked like all three of them were pushing in different directions. If anything, the wheel only sunk deeper into the rut, spewing mud in the air.

He shook his head in chagrin. He buried his face in his hands, hiding a grin. He couldn't bear to watch. He was half afraid the old butler would take a heart attack. Maggie looked in grave danger of sinking up to her grateful neck in muck.

He rose, dropping his coat on the boulder, his voice brusque. "All right. Everybody get out of the way." He rolled up his shirtsleeves and slid down the hill. "Miss Saunders, keep that embarrassing excuse for a dog away from the carriage."

Maggie plucked her dainty feet out of the mud in relief. "What are you going to do?"

"Be careful, my lord," the driver said worriedly. "I near broke my spine tryin' to budge that wheel."

Connor turned to the carriage like David confronting Goliath. "Everyone stand back."

"Dear heaven." Maggie put her hand to her mouth as Connor positioned his forearms under the chassis and lowered his shoulders. "Don't you strain your sacrum, my lord."

He ignored her. He clenched his jaw in concentration, his golden hair falling in his face. The muscles of his back and shoulders strained against his white linen shirt. A groan escaped from between his gritted teeth and Maggie closed her eyes, praying aloud that he would not injure himself. He would have laughed if he'd a breath to spare.

Then all of a sudden, as she opened her eyes to peek, the carriage was free, bobbing slightly as he lowered it to the ground. Maggie, Claude, and the driver applauded politely.

"There is something to be said for brute strength," she said in grudging approval.

"That was quite impressive, my lord," the driver said. "You must have a physique like cast iron."

Connor rolled down his sleeves, shrugging off their praise. "You can all get back into the carriage now. With any luck there won't be another delay."

The driver pulled off his cap and gave Connor an abashed smile. "We do have another slight problem."

Connor looked up. "A problem?"

"It's the horses, my lord. I unhitched them to lighten the carriage. Then that dog chased them across the heath. Don't worry, though. They'll not have gone far. Old Claude here and I will have them back in an hour or two."

Maggie scrambled over a clump of brown heather to catch up with Connor's ground-eating strides. "Are you limping, my lord?"

"Yes, I'm limping."

She tugged her cloak free from a scraggly bush. "Why are you limping?"

"Because my foot is killing me, that's why. It feels like there's a damn nail digging into my instep." He stopped at the boulder where he'd left his coat and sat down to tug off his boot. "There *is* a damn nail in my foot," he said, looking up at her darkly. "How do you suppose that happened?"

Maggie clutched her cloak at her throat and stared out over the hills, guilt etched in every delicate feature of her face.

He stood, his hazel eyes hooded, and hobbled over to her. "Why did you put a nail in my boot?"

"I did nothing of the kind."

"You are lying," he said. "I can always tell when someone is lying."

She looked affronted. "I did not put that nail in your boot."

He stepped another inch closer, staring down unflinchingly into her face. "I'll probably die of tetanus. You'll be arrested for second-degree murder."

The reality of his physical proximity was more menacing to Maggie than any threat of future punishment. She gazed up at the underside of his jaw, caught in the current of charged air between them. "It was Emily, if you must know," she confessed in a small voice.

"Emily? Emily—the housemaid?"

She took a reflexive step back, noticing how the mist had wrapped them in a cocoon, how isolated they were, how his warrior's appearance fit so well into their surroundings. Claude and the driver had vanished from sight. She cleared her voice, aware that her nerve endings had begun to tingle in either warning or expectation. She had a terrible feeling that this was where the wielding and yielding were about to come into play.

"She . . . she wanted to make sure you weren't a devil," she whispered, realizing as she stared into his penetrating eyes how easily that rumor could have started.

Connor's gaze held her captive as the silence between them deepened. She noticed that he didn't deny the ridiculous charge. She also noticed that they were standing so close together that their breaths mingled in the mist.

"We are alone in a very isolated spot," he murmured. "If I *were* the devil . . ." He shook his head mockingly, allowing her own fertile imagination to fill in the disturbing details.

Maggie's toes curled inside her worn traveling boots.

"What would you do?" she inquired softly.

"Wicked things, Miss Saunders."

She moistened the edges of her mouth with her tongue. "How wicked?"

He caught her by the elbow just as she would have stumbled back against the boulder. A shock of alarm ran up her arm. She should have known better than to tease the Lion to test his temper, but she'd always believed it was better to get things out in the open.

His gaze flickered over her like a flame. "For my first demonical deed, I would probably take off all your clothes."

Something between a gasp and a giggle caught in her throat. "You wouldn't."

He drew her a little nearer, his fingers exerting faint pressure on her forearm. "Yes, lass, every stitch, well past the wee silk rosebuds to the mole on your left breast."

A white-hot shiver shot down Maggie's neck. "And then?"

He glanced around. "Let's see— Ah. I'd seduce you over there—under that outcrop of granite. The mist would curl around our naked bodies as passion consumed us. We'd probably bear scratches for days afterward from the gorse. One of us might catch our death, but it would have been well worth it."

Maggie disengaged her elbow and calmly walked over to the outcrop. She made a show of examining it, all the time trying to decide how to handle this situation. His eyes gleaming, he strolled up behind her.

"Well? Will it do, or shall I drag you by the hair into a nice cozy cave?"

She turned and forced herself to smile. "Have you ever seduced a woman here before?"

He laughed quietly, the deep tones of his voice raising goosebumps on her skin. "One hill looks like another when you've lived in the Highlands long enough."

His kiss was a flame in the mist, not totally unexpected but exciting, enclosing her in dangerous heat. Maggie couldn't lie to herself. She'd been hoping he would kiss her again since that first night. Of course, she'd also been hoping that if he did, she would have the sense to rebuff him. She didn't, though. She had clearly inherited the de Saint-Evremond weakness for powerful men from her wicked ancestors.

Instead of stiffening up, her entire body came alive like a string quartet, humming, throbbing, vibrating with secret little notes and harmonies that she'd never heard before. His kiss was hard and demanding, taking possession of her mouth. Sensation burgeoned in the pit of her belly, burnishing and bold. She moaned in enjoyment.

He groaned against her mouth. Then he gripped her harder, crushing the breath that was building in her lungs. Maggie sighed as he drew her bottom lip between his teeth. She barely recovered from the pleasant shock of that when his big hands slid under her cloak to cup her buttocks.

She thought he said something. She couldn't make out the words; she was busy wondering what his hands were doing to her derriere, how *her* hands had slipped inside his coat. She pressed her fingertips to his chest. Strong. Muscular and as hard as a mountain. It was a chest to snuggle against on a cold day, to hide behind when the world grew unpleasant. Her head swam with sensation.

"Maggie." He was shaking her, she realized as she resurfaced from her daze. "Miss Saunders."

She opened her eyes and stared up at him in bewilderment, the mist cooling her hot face.

"If you don't release me right now," he said with laughter in his eyes, "we're both going to regret it."

She wrenched her hands away from his coat as if she'd been holding live coals. "What did you say?"

"I said that in addition to not believing in rumors from unreliable sources, you had better learn a little self-control. I might not be a devil, but I am human, and a mortal man can only take so much temptation."

With that warning delivered, Connor picked up his boot, jammed his foot into it, and made his way back down the hill, whistling softly. He heard Maggie stumbling behind him, and he chuckled, resisting the urge to turn around. He could still see the look of wounded indignation on her face. Well, her innocent response might have taken them both by surprise, but he had won the first round.

He sobered as they reached the carriage, realizing he wouldn't have the last laugh after all. Because although he might not in actual fact be a devil, he was burning with desire for an angel, and by stirring up the smoldering embers between them on that hill, he'd just made sure that the rest of his journey would be sheer hell on earth.

Chapter
17

He woke up abruptly, wondering if the driver had hit another rut. It was pitch dark in the carriage, and it took him a few moments to realize that the soft whimpers of distress were what had disturbed him.

He leaned across to the other seat, frowning as he saw Maggie huddled into a little ball, her stocking feet exposed, vulnerable.

"Miss Saunders?" he said quietly, his own body cramped and aching from the confinement. He touched her shoulder. "Maggie, wake up. What's the matter?"

A man's voice, warm and unfamiliar. Maggie fought to follow it but couldn't find it in the dream. It didn't belong there.

Panic. Fear. She shied away from the intense heat, a blinding light at the center of the sun. Yet she knew that if she could only bear to look into the brightness, she would finally face the nameless horror that had haunted her for eleven years.

"Miss Saunders?" Connor was fully awake now, sensing her panic, helpless to end it. He wasn't sure whether it was better to let her sleep the dream out or interrupt it. Sheena, he remembered with a stab of dismay, could never be woken from her frequent nightmares.

"It's all right, sir," Claude said, bending stiffly to draw a plaid over Maggie. "She's only dreaming."

"Of what?" Connor asked in bewilderment.

"Of things best forgotten." The elderly man leaned down and whispered in Maggie's ear, soothing phrases in French that Connor couldn't hear. Intrigued, he realized that this was an established ritual between them. Within moments Maggie calmed, her body relaxing into an undisturbed sleep.

Connor couldn't rest after that, his mind struggling for answers. Maggie Saunders's secret terror didn't have anything to do with her witnessing the kidnapping at all, he realized. And, strangely, although it made him all the more determined to probe the mystery of her past, it wasn't because he distrusted her. It was because he cared.

Maggie stirred as they approached the inn. Pretending to just awaken himself, Connor watched her in concern. She gave no sign that less than an hour ago she'd been battling the private demons of a nightmare. But then the human mind was strange. Perhaps she wasn't even aware of her buried torment herself.

"Where are we?" she asked, yawning delicately and stretching her arms.

He forced his gaze to the window, determined not to become aroused by the sensual grace of her movements. "The Golden Sovereign. A friend of mine owns it. It's a little out of the way, but we're not likely to find anywhere else in the dark."

She climbed over him to peer out the window at the endless vista of uninhabited hills and heath. "Good heavens. It can't be quite seven o'clock, but it might as well be midnight. There isn't a shop in sight. It's not just out of the way. It's the end of the world."

"Which is precisely why I came here. This is exactly the place a carriage would pass if the driver was hoping to escape detection on the main thoroughfares."

Maggie drew her cloak around her as he opened the door to the misty courtyard, murmuring, "What a wild, desolate place." She felt a shiver go through her at the thought of a woman abducted, alone with a man in such an untamed setting. But, stealing a glance at Connor, she wondered if she was really that much safer herself.

"Would you mind bringing my hatboxes, my lord?"

"We are in the Highlands, lass. Where would you be wearing one of those silly hats?"

"Are you going to be this surly to me the entire journey?"

"Miss Saunders, I am tired. You and your dog refused to let me sleep. You will forgive me if my social skills are not quite up to snuff."

"I hadn't noticed that having a nap makes much difference to your manners," she retorted. "However, whether one is in an uncivilized setting or not, one can still take pains to look presentable. Kindly hand me that hatbox."

The innkeeper's pretty brunette daughter, Isabel, was delighted to be dragged from her supper chores to see Connor. "What perfect timing," she exclaimed, clumping down the stairs in a pair of leather brogues. "Papa is in Caithness. Evan, you'll see that we aren't disturbed for the rest of the night, won't you? The doctor for Mrs. Gloag should be here in a few minutes."

The rough-faced man polishing glasses at the bar stared at Maggie, who stood looking indignant and ignored in the middle of the taproom with Claude and Daphne. Connor glanced back at her helplessly as Isabel tugged him toward a private hallway.

"I got your message about your sister," Isabel was saying in a troubled voice. "We've put the posters up, but there hasn't been a single carriage by here in months."

The barkeep gave Maggie a curious look. "Sit by the fire, lassie, and have a hot whisky toddy on the house. There's no tellin' how long the pair of them will be in that parlor."

Maggie frowned. "I'd like to know what they do in the parlor that can't be done in the public room."

A grin lit the man's bearded face. " 'Tis a secret best left unsolved." He glanced curiously at Claude and Daphne. "Are they yours?"

"Yes." Maggie sighed, trudging toward the inviting peat fire. "They're mine."

Claude came up behind her and touched her arm. He was

hobbling badly from his arthritis, and his earlier trek across the heath after the horses. "Come sit by the fire and warm your feet, my lady."

"Warm your own feet, Claude," she said with uncharacteristic irritation as she stared down the darkened hallway. "You're in worse shape than I am."

"I can't balance you on my knee and drink a glass of whisky at the same time, Isabel," Connor complained. "Something is going to spill."

She grinned and bounced back down onto the sofa, curling around him like a kitten. "Who was that girl with the horrible hat?"

He took a sip of whisky. "Someone I'm supposed to be looking after."

"I thought she might be one of your sisters."

"She isn't." He glanced around the stuffy room, then closed his eyes, disturbed as the image of Maggie, as he'd abandoned her, popped into his mind. "What do you want to talk to me about?" he said wearily.

"I wrote a poem in honor of my tragically short-lived romance with Mr. Donaldson."

"I'm sure he'd be flattered," Connor lied. "Isabel, could you move a moment? I've pulled a muscle in my groin."

She laid her head on his shoulder. "You promised you were going to take me hunting with you and Donaldson this year. Did you forget, Connor?"

"The only thing Thomas and I will be hunting this year is a killer and a kidnapper," he said grimly.

She shuddered, drawing her knees to her sides. "Do you know who they are?"

"We know who the killer is, but we haven't identified the kidnapper—yet."

"And that girl you brought along with you is involved?" Isabel whispered. "You're supposed to keep her safe from the kidnapper?"

"Yes." He released a deep sigh. "I'm to keep her safe. I don't suppose you've heard anything from my sister Rebecca lately, have you?"

"Rebecca? I only see her once a year at the cattle drovers' fair. Did I mention I might be getting married in January?"

"Really?" Connor tried to look like he cared, but he felt grumpy and guilty for leaving Maggie in the taproom. Not that anything was liable to happen to her in an empty inn so early at night. And did he owe her every hour of the day? Did he have to hover over her like a nursemaid to make sure she didn't so much as break a fingernail?

No, he told himself. He didn't. Then again, he didn't have to think about her all the time either, but he did. "I'm happy for you, Isabel," he said, forcing his attention back to her announcement. "You can tell me the details in the morning, but for now I—"

"You can't go yet." She rose onto her knees to stop him. "I have to recite my poem first. I wrote it to immortalize the night Mr. Donaldson almost seduced me in the carriage house."

The way Thomas had related that night, it had been the other way around. Connor looked up. "Someone's knocking at the door."

"I don't care." She raised her voice. "Come back in a few minutes. We cannot be disturbed right now."

Connor frowned. "I think you should open the door."

"Not until after I recite my poem."

He wondered if it had been Maggie knocking, and what she wanted, and why she thought she had the right to interrupt his conversation. "Hurry up, Isabel. It's past my suppertime."

"All right." She drew a long breath, closing her eyes in concentration. "It's called *The Plucking of a Pretty Rosebud in the Carriage House.*"

"That's a hell of a title." Connor took another deep drink of whisky and dropped his head back against the sofa. He was in the Highlands now, the one place he felt free to be himself, but he couldn't relax. Not with so much on his mind. He glanced toward the window. "Do I hear people running about in the courtyard?"

"Not unless it's the doctor, or it's starting to rain. Do be quiet, Connor. 'Oh, pretty rosebud,'" she began, "'innocent rosebud, pink rosebud—' Why is that girl waving a ribbon in the window?"

He put down his glass. "Either this whisky is stronger

than I realized, or you've skipped a line. That doesn't make any sense."

She slid to the edge of the sofa, gesturing behind them. "Oh, my goodness, that *girl*—it's not a ribbon, it's a garter. She's waving a garter at us."

"Donaldson never took your garters off in the carriage house, Isabel, and don't you dare tell anyone he did." He stifled a yawn. "I'm not one for poetry, but it seems to me you could work a little more on—"

He didn't finish. He had just glanced past Isabel to the familiar silhouette waving at him in the window. Alarmed, he jumped up and crossed the room. "What in God's name is going on?"

He wrenched open the window and leaned across the sill. "Why are you waving a garter at me, Miss Saunders?"

"I was trying to get your attention," she whispered.

Connor wasn't about to tell her that the interruption had been a relief. "It couldn't have waited?"

She looked past him to Isabel. "There are some things more important than drinking whisky with a woman."

"Not that I can think of," Connor retorted.

Maggie frowned. "While you were enjoying a reprieve from your responsibilities, Claude, Evan, and I managed to catch the man who's been following me."

"What man?" Isabel asked, coming up behind Connor.

Maggie hesitated for effect. "The man in a dark cloak who demanded that I disrobe."

Connor didn't think he could have heard her correctly. "He *what?*"

"In my establishment?" Isabel said weakly.

Maggie nodded, clearly gratified by their reaction. "You heard me. I told you, my lord, and I must admit it was a terrifying experience, me sitting there helpless and—"

Connor turned, his face black with a fury that silenced the two women watching him. "Get back inside," he ordered Maggie, storming across the room. "Isabel, send a servant for the local magistrate right away. You two are to remain inside until I return for you."

Isabel nodded numbly.

Maggie, impressed by his response, found her voice. "Claude and Evan have got him locked in the stable," she called after him. "Be careful—the man is obviously deranged."

Energized by pure emotion, Connor didn't take the time to think. If he had, he might have reconsidered his hot-headed reaction.

He might have avoided disaster.

Chapter

18

❧

He thumped up against the headboard and watched her tiptoeing across the room. The rain pattering on the inn's heather-thatched roof drowned out the faint sound of her footsteps. She moved with the bewitching ease of a prima ballerina. How was it possible to be so attracted to a woman who had thoroughly humiliated you only an hour ago?

"What do you want now, Miss Saunders?"

She jumped, putting her hand to her heart. "Goodness, you gave me a turn. I didn't know you were awake."

His voice deepened in indignation. "Do you think I could possibly sleep after making a complete ass out of myself in front of the entire inn?"

"There's no need to use that tone," Maggie said. "It was a logical mistake, a misunderstanding. After all, the man did insist I go upstairs with him and disrobe."

"Because he was a damned doctor, and he thought you were the woman who had summoned him here for acute stomach pain." He raked her with a resentful glance, noting how her soft black hair curled over her shoulders, how tantalizing she looked in a pale nightrail with a frilly hem. "What do you want with me in the middle of the night, anyway?"

"It's only eleven o'clock," she said.

"Most people were asleep an hour ago," he retorted.

She crept to the edge of the bed. He imagined he could see the shape of her breasts through the thin ivory batiste. His body tightened at the enticing illusion. It didn't take much to excite him these days.

"I want to stay here until morning," she explained. "A man just knocked on my door."

She sat down uninvited on the edge of the bed. Her thigh brushed his. He leaned forward with a growl that sounded inhuman in the darkness. "You're imagining things again. It was probably a guest who'd returned to the wrong room."

She closed her eyes as the covers fell to his waist, revealing his broad shoulders and bare chest. "I am not imagining anything. The man at my door said that someone important wanted to talk to me, that I was in danger, and that if I knew what was good for me, I'd come with him right away."

Connor couldn't deny that the fear in her voice was genuine. He rose, a sheet draped around his waist, and dressed swiftly in the shadows. "Almighty God. I never heard of a kidnapper who bothered to knock. I don't suppose you got a look at him?"

"Of course not." She opened her eyes warily, hesitant to look his way. "I did, however, get a look at your torso, and while I realize that most virile men enjoy sleeping in the buff, it is not a practice I can recommend. What if the inn were to catch fire and you were forced to make an emergency exit?" She frowned down at her lap. "Are you dressed yet?"

"Yes, I'm dressed." He bumped back into a footstool, swearing to himself. "Did you think I was going to conduct an official investigation in the nude?"

"Considering your recent lapse in the social graces, I wasn't entirely sure. You haven't been at all yourself lately."

It was an absurd remark since she didn't know him well enough to comment on his past behavior. "I don't suppose anyone else heard this mysterious man at the door, did they?"

"I wouldn't know. I waited until I knew he was gone, then I ran to your room as fast as I could. I think you ought to keep your door locked in future. To be on the safe side."

Connor frowned at this useless piece of advice and combed his fingers through his hair. "I'll have to alert Isabel. She isn't going to like this."

"May Daphne and I stay in your room until you return?" Maggie asked nervously.

It was the first time Connor noticed the dog at the door, wiggling its behind in greeting at his bewildered glance. Was this a bad dream? Was he really going to disturb the entire inn looking for an anonymous man while a girl and her annoying poodle slept in his bed?

"Bolt the door behind me," he said testily. "Don't open it to anyone except me."

Maggie had already settled under the covers and made space for Daphne. "How will I know it's you?"

"By my voice, Miss Saunders."

"Perhaps we ought to have a secret password. The Chief always—"

Connor uttered a colorful obscenity.

"Well, I certainly won't forget *that* phrase," Maggie said to herself as he strode from the room, closing the door with a bang.

"Wake up, Miss Saunders. Rise and bloody shine."

Maggie roused herself and rolled onto her back, wondering if she'd imagined the rude slap to her rear end. Beside her Daphne wagged her tail in welcome, recognizing the unsmiling figure who leaned over the bed. The dog apparently didn't care that Lord Buchanan had been transformed into an untamed beast over the past few days. Or perhaps the pair of them had begun to communicate on some primitive level. Connor did exhibit quite a few animal tendencies.

"Did you find the man?" she whispered.

Connor stared at her for several seconds, his mouth curling into an insulting smile. Exhausted, embarrassed, it didn't do his temper a damn bit of good to see her snuggled in his bed, as dewy as a wild daisy in a meadow. "Well," he said slowly, "after your butler nearly decapitated me outside the door, because he, being half blind, mistook me for a stranger, I began the humiliating task of waking up every man, woman, and child in the inn. It wasn't enough to accost an innocent physician only an hour or so earlier. I had to make sure that I offended everyone in the bargain."

Maggie sat up with the covers wrapped around her. "You're upset because he got away again, aren't you? You've committed yourself to protecting me, and the very fact that he got close enough to knock at my door makes it seem like a dereliction of duty. You are clearly a man who cannot admit failure, which is not truly a flaw. It is a mark of greatness."

He leaned down lower, his voice like flint against stone. "Get your perfect little posterior out of my bed, Miss Saunders."

Maggie swallowed, struggling to keep Daphne from leaping up and licking his lordship's sternly clenched jaw. "I know you tried your best. You shouldn't blame yourself if he got away. The criminal mind is devious—"

A muscle ticked in that sternly clenched jaw. Daphne popped out of Maggie's arm and began running back and forth to the door, launching into a chorus of playful barks.

Maggie summoned a weak smile. "She thinks we're going out."

"We are." Connor gave her a chilling smile and reached down to pry the covers out of her hands.

"But it's almost midnight—"

"Yes. I'd noticed that."

"And it's raining."

He dragged the covers to the floor, his gaze traveling over her shivering form. "That was exactly what I told Isabel's father when he returned unexpectedly from Caithness and demanded to know what the hell I was doing interrogating his guests before he insisted I vacate the premises."

"What a stupid man," Maggie said sympathetically. "I hope you put him in his place. Doesn't he know you're the Lord Advocate of Scotland?"

"He's a Highlander, Miss Saunders. He wouldn't care if I were the Lord God Himself."

"Well, he can't throw us out at this time of night."

Connor stared down at her in exasperation. Virginal temptation, pale skin, a vision of innocence that conjured up thoughts of sin. She might be ruining his life, but she looked damn tempting in his bed. "He has already thrown us out.

The driver is bringing the carriage around even as you argue with me. We have been evicted, given the boot, shown the proverbial door."

Maggie pushed off the bedcovers and came to her feet. Rain beat against the roof in cascades. Connor felt a dangerous urge to force her back onto his bed and give free reign to the fever that burned in his blood for her.

"Do you want me to speak to Isabel's father?" she asked quietly. "I have a feeling you're not handling this as well as you could. I'm certain I could convince the man to let us stay here until morning. I have a way with people, or so I've been told."

The arrogance of the woman, the naiveté. She, with the tussled hair and physical might of a hummingbird, *she* thought she could manipulate a situation when he'd made a career of such matters.

"You're ridiculous," he said. Ridiculous. Desirable. The rain pounded the roof in rhythm with his pulse. The heat of her small body radiated to his. Before he knew it, he had pulled her against him and brought his mouth down on hers in a desperate, hungry kiss.

To his surprise she wrapped her arms around his waist instead of pushing him away. Her response plunged his thoughts into turmoil. He ran his hands down her back, learning the contours of her supple body, absorbing the little shivers she gave into his own.

"You're driving me out of my mind," he whispered roughly.

"I know," she whispered back. "It isn't on purpose."

He lifted his hand to her breast, groaning deep in his throat as she arched her back, innocently offering herself to him. He wanted to touch her all over, to rub against her, to force her down on the floor. His kiss grew fiercer. Sexual excitement sizzled down his spine. He drew her into his body; she was so light and agile it was like molding a swan's feather to his frame. Satin against steel. He walked her back to the bed, devouring her mouth, the soft cries she gave.

Maggie decided it was a good thing he was holding her so tightly. His kiss had melted her to the core, turning her insides into wax. She was in jeopardy of following in her forebearers' sinful footsteps.

"I think it's a good thing after all that we won't be staying here tonight," he said in a low, tortured voice as he tore his mouth from hers.

Maggie opened her eyes to look at him, breathless and unbalanced. "Why?" she whispered. "Are you ill?"

"Am I ill?" he said in a strangled voice.

Maggie studied him in concern. "I hope you haven't caught something. Perhaps you ought to lie down."

He removed her hands from his neck. "I definitely should not lie down. And you—"

A hard knock at the door interrupted them. "This is Isabel's father, Lord Buchanan," a gruff voice announced. "A guest has just told me he saw a woman sneak into your room, but I told him it couldna be true. I told him there was not a woman in your room."

"I'll handle this." Maggie stepped toward the door before Connor could stop her. "The man needs to be put in his place."

Connor, shaking off the sensual lassitude that had immobilized him, stared at her in disbelief. "What are you doing?"

She turned to him briefly before raising the bolt. "You might be a famous lawyer, my lord, but you clearly lack experience in dealing with people in day-to-day affairs. The line between our inferiors must be delineated, gently, but delineated all the same. This man must be reminded of his position on the social ladder."

He looked horrified. "You're in your nightclothes. You— You're only a girl. Do not open that—"

She did. She opened it with the practiced annoyance of a princess disturbed by a peasant.

"You don't know what you're doing," Connor sputtered, hopping backward over Daphne. "This is the Highlands, not the French court. We'll be tossed out on our ears."

Maggie shook her head, dismissing his concerns, and smiled with beguiling sweetness at the irate man who faced her.

"What is the meaning of this intrusion?" she said in the same voice she used when Daphne had made a puddle in a bad place. "Do you have any idea who you are disturbing?"

Connor swallowed a groan and sank to the bed in surrender, covering his eyes. Isabel's father was too astonished to reply. Not that Connor really wanted to hear his response. He'd suffered enough embarrassment for a lifetime.

Chapter

19

❧

Thomas Donaldson, junior counselor, felt like kicking up his heels in excitement. He made do with a low chuckle of self-satisfaction that went unnoticed in the tavern's din of drinking and conversation. Finally. He'd finally unearthed some crucial evidence on his own. He couldn't wait until the Lord Advocate heard about this. Thomas only wished he could tell Connor he'd found his sister too.

But Sheena Buchanan had vanished without a trace. Donaldson would have given his right arm to find her. He lived to please Lord Buchanan.

He finished his ale and threw several coins down on the tavern table. The two informants he'd just met had already melted into the crowd. He wasn't surprised. It didn't help to be seen consorting with the public prosecutor's assistant in this part of town.

He sauntered outside, too pleased with himself to notice the damp chill in the air. Or the shadows that fell into step behind him.

He wouldn't call a cab. He wanted to walk. His mother was visiting and would be waiting up for him to celebrate his birthday. He needed an hour alone to savor his success.

DARING

Motive.

He'd discovered the Balfour murderer's motive. Connor had been convinced of the man's identity all along, and now Donaldson had learned that Connor's prime suspect, a middle-aged nobleman, was being blackmailed for a sordid crime he'd committed against a child in the past. Lord Montgomery, pillar of the nobility, devoted husband, friend to the royal family. Secret gambler, child molester, and killer, had needed money. Desperate enough to murder his own banker and clerk and frame a disoriented vagrant who just happened to be in the wrong place at the right time.

Proving this would be Connor's job. Montgomery, despite wealth and connections, didn't stand a chance once Connor got him in the witness box.

Donaldson began to whistle. It was later than he realized, but he had never felt so awake, so hopeful for the future.

He became aware of the footsteps only a few seconds before the club struck the side of his head. He staggered into a parked carriage. The club fell again.

"That was for not minding your own business."

Pain exploded through his temple. He tried to speak. Blackness sucked him into a void. Another blow. He barely felt it this time. An impassive voice hissed in his ear.

"And that one was for Buchanan."

He sank gratefully into the numbing darkness. He never heard the carriage wheels scrape over the cobbles. He never saw the gentle giant of a man who found him in the gutter a few minutes later and hefted him into his huge arms.

A young girl in trousers stepped off the pavement. "Who is it, Papa?" she whispered.

"I think it's Donaldson, the silly bugger who works for Connor. Someone has beaten the lad half to death."

"Connor's friend?" Her eyes grew wide with alarm. "Do you think that he's in danger too?"

"I dinna ken, Janet, but he's man enough to take care of himself. It's Maggie we should be worrying about."

Chapter

20

It was as black as the bowels of Hades in the carriage, but Maggie didn't need a light to see the look on his lordship's face. Features cast in stone. Hazel eyes smoldering with anger. She'd thought he was going to suffer an apoplectic fit when Isabel's father had invited her to spend the night.

And told Connor to find lodgings elsewhere.

She leaned forward. She would probably be wise, under the circumstances, to keep her thoughts to herself. But she had to break the tension building between them.

"Try and look at the bright side, my lord."

"The bright side." His voice could have cut through granite. "By the 'bright side' I assume you mean that traveling through a thunderstorm in a leaky coach being driven by a half-drunken man, in the wee small hours over an unmarked road, that cramped between a poodle, a butler, and a hysterical woman prone to hallucinations, is preferable to the privacy and comfort of the room we just left?"

Maggie shook her head in admiration. "You do have a way with words. What I meant, though, is that we'll be at your sister's cottage that much sooner. Think of the time we're saving."

He grunted, turning his face to the window, clearly not in a mood to be reasoned with. Maggie settled back against the squabs, sighing as Claude covered her legs with a tartan blanket.

"More cheese and biscuits, my lady?" he asked solicitously.

"Yes, please, Claude. I'm famished. What a night."

"Another meat pie and glass of wine? Isabel's father insisted you should eat before setting out. He was most concerned about your health."

Maggie darted Connor a glance. "If his lordship doesn't want it."

Connor refused to acknowledge her. He had closed his eyes, folded his arms over his chest, and settled into a forbidding silence.

"Don't bother him again, Claude," Maggie said in a loud whisper. "His lordship is having his little pout. Can you imagine? A man his age."

Connor opened his eyes. "I am not pouting. I am exasperated." He nudged Daphne away with his shoulder. "Stop licking my damn face."

Maggie gasped. "Now you're swearing at my dog. You *are* heartless. Why, you've hurt her feelings. Look at her. She has big fat tears in her eyes. Just look at her."

"For the love of God." Connor turned his head to examine the poodle, feeling like a proper idiot. "She does not."

Claude leaned down. "I know it is not my place to say so, sir, but I have looked at that dog's face every day for a decade, and those are genuine tears."

"Apologize to her, my lord," Maggie said.

"Apologize to a poodle? I will not."

"Please, sir," Claude said, sotto voce. "If not for the heartbroken little animal, but for the sake of peace in the carriage."

"Heartbroken?" Connor said. "Her damn tail is wagging like a windmill."

"He swore again!" Maggie scooped the creature protectively into her arms. "Did his lordship scare you with his nasty-wasty voice?" She nuzzled Daphne's wet black nose. "Shall we have Claude give the bad, bad man a big, big spanking with a spoon?"

Connor covered his eyes. "Dear God."

"Don't let pride stop you from doing the right thing," Maggie urged him. "Apologize, and we'll forget the entire ugly incident ever happened. Daphne is willing to make friends."

Connor shrank down into the seat, a conquered man. What was the use? "Please accept my apologies, Daphne," he said gravely.

"Give her a kiss," Maggie said.

There was utter silence. Maggie smiled uneasily, holding the dog up like an offering. Claude watched with bated breath.

Connor's grin was menacing. "I will kiss the hind end of a hippopotamus before putting my lips to that poodle."

Maggie lowered the dog back into her lap. "I don't think he's going to do it, Claude," she whispered.

The old man nodded unhappily. "Even worse, he's made her cry again."

She wondered where they were, if Lord Buchanan would continue to ignore her the entire way. She flipped aside the leather curtains to look, leaning over him. She didn't expect to recognize anything in the dark, rain-washed landscape.

She certainly didn't expect to see a large black carriage lumbering down the road behind them.

Or was it only a circle of standing stones shimmering in the rain at the wayside? Goosebumps rising on her skin, she reached blindly back across Connor's lap for the field glasses on the seat.

"Wake up, my lord," she said urgently. "Wake up and look out the window."

Connor didn't need to wake up. There wasn't a nerve, muscle, or bone in his body that wasn't standing at attention after she'd slid across his legs, then groped his lap for the blasted glasses. He was a smoldering volcano of suppressed lust waiting to erupt.

"It is two o'clock in the morning, Miss Saunders."

"I realize that," Maggie replied, her bottom hitting his chest as she pressed her face to the window, "but we're being followed. See for yourself."

She thrust the field glasses back at his chin. Releasing a slow hiss of exasperation, he pushed her derriere out of his line of vision and lifted the field glasses to the window. Then he started to swear.

Maggie was more relieved than frightened by Connor's outburst. Now, at last, he would believe her. Now he would take protecting her more seriously.

"You see it, don't you?" She tried to subdue the triumphant note in her voice. After all, he'd brushed off her warnings like so many flies that annoyed him. "You realize that I've been right all along."

His mouth tightened into a thin white line. "What I realize," he ground out, flinging the glasses down beside her, "is that the idiot driver has wandered off the road. We're heading straight into McGonigle's bog. Almighty God, he's going to kill us."

"Sir," Claude said, "I know it is not my place to say so, but I couldn't help noticing that you haven't eaten a thing all evening. Would you care for that meat pie now?"

Connor started to bang with all his might on the roof. The carriage shook with the force of his blows. It slowed, descending down a shallow incline. Then it began to sink, a foot at a time, into the murky depths of McGonigle's bog.

The farmer's wife wrung her chapped hands in agitation at the bottom of the steep wooden staircase. "I wish I'd known to expect ye, my lord. I'd have cleaned up properly, but the bairns have been sick with coughs, and my husband's away buyin' sheep."

Connor gave her a reassuring smile. "We're the ones who should be apologizing, Mrs. Pringle, begging shelter like gypsies in the dead of the night. By the way, this is—" He glanced questionably at Maggie, uncertain how he should introduce her.

"There's no point in keeping it a secret," Maggie said quietly. "This kind woman deserves to know who she is sheltering in her home."

"Are you a princess?" Mrs. Pringle wondered, staring at the mud-stained Maggie in awe.

"Not quite," Connor said wryly. "She is, however, the daughter of a French duke."

The woman studied Maggie in dismay. "Look at the wee lassie, a duke's daughter no less, covered in stinkin' bog mud up to her knees. What could a lovely innocent like you have done to deserve such an unkind fate?"

Connor opened his mouth to explain, then closed it as a small boy in a nightshirt appeared at the top of the staircase. "Peggy's hackin' like a horse again, Ma. I canna sleep."

"Get back to yer bed," the woman said in embarrassment. "I'll be up as soon as I see to her ladyship's comfort." She turned back to Maggie, clearly awestruck that a member of the French nobility had descended on her humble home. "Just let me run up to make sure the room is suitable for ye. 'Tis as cold as a tomb to be certain. Dear me. I'll have to fetch some coals from the cellar. And towels—people like ye want them clean, I warrant."

"I'll take care of the coals, Mrs. Pringle," Connor said. "Please don't put yourself out."

The woman started up the stairs, shaking her head. "It doesn't seem right, my lord, making the likes of ye sleep out here in the barn wi' the beasts. I'll have the bairns move down to the parlor."

"You can't do that," Maggie said in alarm. "Not with those bad chest coughs. Why, they'll catch pneumonia."

Connor nodded in agreement. "I'm so tired I could sleep in a tree."

The woman bustled off. Maggie started up the stairs, then turned to regard Connor, swaying on her feet with fatigue. "I don't know, my lord. Perhaps she's right. The barn will be awfully damp and unpleasant in this weather. I'm really worried. Perhaps I should sleep there instead."

Lightning flickered behind the windows, illuminating her drawn features in a flash of brilliance. Connor found himself unwillingly touched by her offer, even though privately he blamed her for getting them in this absurd predicament. But he couldn't let her sleep in a bed of moldy straw, haunted by her mysterious nightmares. Without realizing it, he felt compelled to protect her again, and she cared about his comfort. He liked that.

"I've slept in worse places." It was true. Once as a child, he had hidden his orphaned family in a Highland cave for an entire summer. The girls had thought it an adventure, much like Miss Saunders did. Women, he thought, rarely had a grasp on reality, which was one of the things he liked about them. And she didn't want him to be cold. It was too sweet, especially in view of the fact that he had practically bitten her head off a few minutes ago. Absurd, the stab of affection he felt at that nurturing quality. Toss a few crumbs of concern his way, and he was ready to grovel at her feet. "The barn will do us for the few hours left until morning," he ended gallantly.

Maggie hesitated. "Actually, I was thinking more of Claude and his arthritis. I know you'll be all right, a man as strong as you. By the way, it was amazing how you lifted those horses from the bog. I don't know when I've ever been so impressed."

She stripped, teeth chattering, and washed with a bucket of water behind the crude wooden screen in the tiny dormer bedroom. As she was toweling off, the door opened and footsteps tromped across the room.

"Is that you stomping about, my lord?"

"Yes." He sounded understandably irritable. "I've brought the coals so her ladyship can toast her aristocratic toes for the few minutes left until morning. It is, after all, only five o'clock."

"How kind of you . . . but do try to make a little less noise. You sound like the giant at the top of the beanstalk." She shivered, rubbing briskly at her chilled skin. "Would you mind tossing me my nightdress? It's lying on the bed."

"I am on my hands and knees, groveling in the dark to get these wretched coals lit. Fetch your own nightdress."

Maggie looked up. "Fine. I only asked. I wouldn't want nasty soot marks on it anyway. You should be careful lighting that coal. Men who aren't used to menial chores often hurt themselves doing them. My uncle burned his beard off lighting coals. He was a count, a brilliant man like you. I think he scorched his eyebrows too. Perhaps there's a correlation between intelligence and clumsiness. Don't look."

She streaked past him to the bed, the skimpy towel clutched to her breasts. Connor, who had been deliberately ignoring her, glanced up just in time to see her bare white buttocks disappear under the covers, a heart-shaped moon vanishing behind the clouds during a total eclipse.

The sight jolted through his exhaustion like a spear thrust.

He grinned shamelessly; hoping for an encore, he rested his hand back down on the grate, and the tiny pile of coals that had just begun to glow. Small flames arrowed up his jacket sleeve. The intense shock of pain wiped the grin from his face. It made him leap up with a string of curses that could be heard throughout the house.

She pulled down the covers, struggling on with the night-dress as she threw her bare leg over the bed. "You looked, didn't you?"

"Hell's bells!" he shouted. "Maggie, fetch me the basin of wash water. I'm on fire!"

She shrank back as he jumped up and plunged his arm into the basin, splashing at the flames. "Well, thanks very much for the help," he said in a disgruntled voice. "I suppose you couldn't rouse yourself from the bed for laughing so hard. It's all right, though. I don't mind becoming a human bonfire as long as it entertains her ladyship."

He turned in annoyance, shaking his dripping sleeve. Maggie had left the bed and stood pressed with her shoulder blades against the wall. She wasn't laughing though, as he expected. Instead she looked panicked, the same pallor on her face as the morning she had fainted in his town house.

"Maggie." He came forward, fear in his voice. He forgot the pain in his hand. It was only superficial anyway. The truth was, he was more embarrassed by his reaction to the sight of her body than the burn. "Maggie, what is the matter with you?"

He took another step toward her. But he stopped instinctively as she shrank back, shaking her head in denial of an invisible horror. Daphne, as if sensing something amiss, clung to Connor's legs and whined.

"I'm not going to hurt you, Maggie," he said in a soft puzzled voice. "What's wrong? Why are you afraid?"

His voice seemed to penetrate whatever strangeness entrapped her. "Hurt me?" She blinked, giving him an odd look. "Of course you're not going to hurt me. I never thought you were. Let me take a look at your hand. I can't believe the fuss you were making. Surely it can't be that bad."

Connor wondered if exhaustion was making his imagination go wild. "My hand is fine, lass, but if I don't get some sleep, I'll be a raving lunatic."

"You're going to wake up the entire household," Maggie whispered as he walked away, completely herself again. "It wasn't my fault you hurt yourself. I did warn you not to look."

Chapter

21

❧

Maggie awakened less than an hour later after a brief restless sleep. She'd had another one of her nightmares—it frustrated her, never understanding what triggered them, what they meant. They seemed to be increasing in frequency lately. She wondered if they were caused by the strain of knowing someone was following her.

She willed her heart to slow down. Fire and ice. The aftermath of the nightmare ebbed through her, leaving a sense of loss and aching sadness. She concentrated instead on the sound of the rain washing against her window. Her room was cozy and warm, thanks to the coals Connor had lit. She smiled, feeling guilty. Claude and his lordship must be perishing cold in the barn while she lay there, snug as a bug on the heather tick. She hoped the two men could sleep until after breakfast.

She rose from the bed with a wistful sigh and pulled on the cloak she'd left to dry by the fire. She dragged the two extra goosedown comforters that Mrs. Pringle had brought in to lay across the bed in case Maggie took a chill.

Then she tiptoed downstairs, let herself out through the

kitchen, and made a mad dash across the yard in the rain to the barn. Dawn was just breaking.

The pungent aroma of straw, linseed oil, and animals assailed her through the gloomy shadows, reminding her of childhood summers. Tears sprang to her eyes, hot and unexpected. Memories broke across her mind of playing with Robert and Jeanette in the ancient barn, hiding from their nursemaid, then ambushing the poor woman and pretending to behead her.

They would never be the Three Musketeers again.

She wiped away the traces of rain and tears mingled on her face, forcing her thoughts to the present. She found Claude sleeping peacefully in an empty stall. She covered him with one of the comforters and gently lifted the sword he held across his chest, placing it at his side. He looked like an ancient alabaster knight resting on a burial chamber.

I still have you, old friend, she thought, but not for too many years. And then, with a lack of social decorum that would have horrified him to his dignified core, she leaned down and kissed his parchment-thin cheek. He was the embodiment of love and loyalty. He was the father she had lost.

His lordship was asleep in the loft. She struggled to pull the heavy comforter up the ladder—it was filthy by the time she finished—but it was so damp in the barn she decided the sacrifice was worth it. Connor would fuss like hell if he woke up, but she suspected that secretly he would appreciate the gesture.

She knelt in the straw and studied his face in leisurely detail. Even in rest the symmetry of bone and masculine planes made a striking impression. She wondered what he'd looked like as a boy, if his face had ever shown any softness. She wondered how such a hard man would respond to gentleness.

He didn't stir when she pulled the comforter over his threadbare quilt. He slept like the dead. She felt a wave of appreciation wash over her. No wonder he was tired, pulling those horses from the bog, always fighting to keep his emotions under control.

What did he really think of her? Feel for her? Aside from physical attraction, of course. Were there any other women in his life besides Ardath? Maggie didn't think so, but then with a man like him, it was hard to tell.

As she began to rise, she noticed his greatcoat folded inexpertly under his head like a pillow. She tried to re-arrange it and felt his pistol protruding from the pocket. This discovery horrified her. What if he shot himself in the temple while he slept? Perhaps, overfatigued, he'd simply forgotten where he had placed the gun. Why did a man who made a career of taking care of an entire country not take care of himself?

Connor woke to the sight of a pistol pointing at his nose. He exhaled slowly, staring Maggie in the eye. "Miss Saunders." His voice was deliberately steady, giving no indication he could scarcely breathe for fear she might squeeze the trigger at any second. "I've been meaning to talk with you . . . to apologize," he improvised. "It is true that I haven't been on my best behavior lately."

"No, you haven't," Maggie was forced to agree.

His hand crept up under the comforter. "I have been rude at times. I have lost my temper."

"You have been difficult," she said. "However, at least you have the grace to admit it."

Connor tensed his hand to strike, waiting for the perfect moment. It came when she went to brush a bit of straw from her cloak, gasping as she realized she was still holding the pistol.

He chose that instant to disarm her. He shot his hand up like a snake and grasped her wrist before she could react. "Give me the gun, Maggie," he said urgently. "Violence never solved anything. We can settle our differences in other ways."

Maggie had no idea what he was talking about. "You are hurting my hand," she said through her teeth.

"Let go of the gun, lass."

"Let go of my wrist."

He sat up carefully. She tried to pull away, and then, as his grip tightened, she felt her fingers flex involuntarily, and the gun went off, blowing a hole through the barn roof.

They looked up simultaneously, too shocked to speak. A waterfall of rain cascaded through the small opening the bullet had gauged. Particles of soggy heather and slate floated over them.

"Dear God," Maggie whispered, her other hand flying to her mouth. "Look what you've done. What was the point?"

Connor stared at her in disbelief. "Look what I've done? Is that what you said? Was I supposed to let you shoot me?"

The sound of straw rustling came from below. Then Claude's voice, feeble but alert, called up the ladder, "Is everything all right with you, sir?"

"Everything is wonderful," Connor said, glaring at Maggie. "Why wouldn't it be?"

"I thought I heard a noise, sir. Some kind of small explosion."

"Don't tell him I'm up here," Maggie whispered. "He'll challenge you to a duel in my honor."

"It was thunder," Connor said, not taking his eyes off Maggie. "Go back to sleep, Claude."

"Yes, sir. And thank you for the extra bedding, sir. It was most considerate of you. Most unexpected."

There was a pause, as if Claude suddenly found the conversation embarrassing, before he shuffled back to his make-shift bed. Connor laid the gun down behind him, his face taking on a pitiless look.

"Even if you were only trying to frighten me—I don't believe you're capable of shooting a man—it was a dangerous thing to do. You obviously don't know how to handle a firearm. That gun could have gone off and killed me. Wouldn't you have felt terrible then?"

Maggie stuck her nose in his face, biting off each word with emphasis. "That is why I removed the gun from your coat—so you wouldn't blow your pompous head off."

He stared down into her incredible blue eyes, aware of the subtle changes in his body, temperature, pulse, and heartbeat, aware that the tension that gripped him was generated by another primal emotion. The rain had brought out the sweetness of roses on her skin. A hot rush of blood flooded his veins. He ached to pull her down on top of him, to bury his face between her breasts.

"You came out in the pouring rain—you took the gun from my coat—because you didn't want me to hurt myself?" he said incredulously.

She raised her chin, enjoying his shamefaced expression. "I brought you the quilt because I thought you might be cold."

He glanced down at the heavy comforter, hesitant to hand her this victory. Finally he said, "Well, what would you have thought, if you'd woken up and found me pointing a gun in your face?"

"If," she said, her voice clipped, "*if* I had been either so careless or exhausted as to fall asleep with a loaded gun under my head, I would have been immensely grateful to you for saving me. I would have expressed my gratitude in any number of ways that did not include attacking you and blowing a hole in the roof."

"Gratitude?" Connor snorted derisively. "You really do have your own peculiar perception of things, don't you? Well, I'll show you gratitude."

Maggie never saw his kiss coming. There was no time to defend herself against it. She felt the power of it, though, in every pore of her unprepared body. She craved it, invited it, her lips opening beneath his.

His initial gentleness deceived her into believing she could enjoy the sparks that flew between them before they burned her. How wrong she was. His hand slid up her scalp to anchor her head as his mouth ate at hers. Pleasure pierced all the way to the pit of her belly like the point of a heated sword. She fell straight backward into the straw, the air forced from her lungs by the weight of Connor's body as he crawled over her.

"Merciful heaven," she breathed.

He kissed the underside of her jaw, nibbling at her throat. He moved his large hands over her as if he owned her, as if he knew instinctively where to find every secret pleasure spot on her body. Each brush of his lips made her shiver. When he loosened her nightrail and drew her nipple into his mouth, she arched upward from her shoulders only to sag back helplessly in submission.

"That," he said in a dangerously quiet voice as he drew back into the darkness, "is gratitude, and if you know what's good for you, you'll go back to your room before I am overcome with it."

Maggie pulled herself upright, dazed and flustered. "Hon-

estly, I don't know why I bother," she said, tugging her
cloak out from under him. "I should have let you freeze."

He closed his eyes, breathing hard, and heard her scurry
down the ladder, banging the barn door behind her. A second later a stream of chilly water hit him full in the chest
and dribbled down into his trousers. The final insult, he
thought with an ironic smile.

The next time she gave him the opportunity, he wouldn't
be so quick to let her go.

Maggie's agitation lasted only as long as it took her to
notice the man in black standing by the stone wall that encircled the farmhouse. At first, pondering the upsetting scene
in the hayloft, she almost walked right past him. It was past
daybreak but still dark, the drizzling rain muting her surroundings. His tall figure blended into the hazy background
of trees that bordered the farmhouse fields.

She froze in midstep at the edge of the muddied yard,
fear slamming into her chest. Rain splashed down around
her, icy, soaking into her hair. Her instincts screamed that
the man didn't belong here any more than she did.

She stumbled back a step. She was afraid to run, afraid
to cry for help. She doubted anyone would hear her anyway
in the rain.

"Marguerite. That is your name, isn't it?"

His voice was faint, indistinguishable from a hundred others. "I've been waiting for the right moment to talk to you,
to warn you. Connor Buchanan is a dangerous man."

She had to outrun him. The farmhouse was too far. Another step backward, toward the barn.

The man moved away from the wall. "Don't stay with
him, Marguerite. He's going to hurt you."

Chills crept over her body. Marguerite. He spoke her real
name with such familiarity. *Was* there something familiar
about him? Black hat, black cloak, black breeches, a face in
shadows. He could have been anyone. The murderer Connor
was chasing. Sheena's kidnapper. If she'd seen him before,
he wasn't someone she knew well.

"Let me take you somewhere where we can talk in private," he said almost tenderly. "Out of the rain. You need
a friend, Marguerite. You've been through so much."

He took another step. Then she was running, sloughing through the mud, clumsy, slow. Her cloak fell off. Somehow she reached the barn. She even managed to climb the rickety ladder back to the loft where Connor lay with one arm behind his head. Panic robbed her of speech. She scrambled through the straw, the strange voice ringing in her ear.

He's going to hurt you.

Connor's eyes were closed, but he hadn't been able to fall asleep. Kissing Maggie again had overstimulated him, and yesterday hadn't exactly been dull to begin with. He kept thinking about the innocent pleasure on her face. About touching her soft white skin. That delicious body and her sensuality, her legs parting under his. Imagining making love to her gave him the biggest erection of his life.

A moment later his secret fantasy came true. Well, half of it did. She hit him like a tiny cannonball in the chest. For a split second their bodies touched, melded, and he could feel every sensuous curve of her body like a brand. Unfortunately, it wasn't a sexual experience. The attack scared the life out of him, and he hollered in reaction.

"What the hell has happened now?"

"Protect me, my lord," she said frantically.

She had ripped the comforter from his warm, relaxed body and was clinging to him, soaking, shaking with cold and fright. Her feet felt like blocks of muddy ice. He pulled her upright, his hopes for an impromptu moment of passion dying as he saw the look on her face.

"What happened?" he said in a grim voice.

"M-man." She gritted her chattering teeth. "All in black. He knew my real name—said you wanted to h-hurt me."

Connor knew she needed calming down, but his anger overpowered the urge to comfort. He grabbed his coat from the straw and pulled it on over his bare shoulders. He stuck his pistol in his waistband. Mrs. Pringle's husband was out of town. The driver and Claude were snoring fitfully below. Unless Maggie had been imagining things again, no one on the farm should have approached her.

And no one should have tried to convince her Connor meant her harm.

* * *

She hurried after him, afraid to let him out of her sight. She was bound and determined that this time he would believe her. If he meant to protect her, he'd better start taking the situation more seriously.

The rain roared down on them hard enough to float Noah's ark. Maggie stumbled to match Connor's enormous strides with mud splashing up to her ankles. Threads of watery light were beginning to lace the sky.

The man wasn't standing anywhere by the stone wall. She could have screamed in frustration at the exasperated look Connor shot her.

"He was there," she said, tramping up to him. "I swear to you. He was standing right there. Look for footprints if you don't believe me."

"Footprints. In a sea of mud."

"Well, he wouldn't stand around waiting for you to come after him, would he?" she shouted.

He stared past the wall, past the shivering trees, to the lonely field beyond. Suddenly his eyes narrowed. A chill raced down Maggie's back as she followed the direction of his focused gaze. Thank God—he'd spotted him.

There was barely enough light to make out a man's figure in the middle of the field. Dark hat, dark cloak. The man's body seemed to be buffeted by the wind as if he were struggling to run against it. Maggie wondered if he'd gotten stuck in the bog.

Connor glanced back at her in frustration. "I told you to stay inside the barn."

"I wanted to make sure you believed me." She edged another inch closer to his back. "Do you?"

He didn't answer, his mouth a taut line of tension. He pulled away from her and took out his pistol. He looked rather fierce and frightening, standing there in the rain with a coat over his bare chest. Her stomach turned over as she realized he might kill that man, or worse, be killed himself.

"Do you have—" She stopped as a giant shudder racked her from head to toe.

Connor spared her a disgusted glare. "How can I go after him when I have to worry about you getting hurt? Hide behind that wall." His gaze returned to the dark figure in the field. "And don't get up until I tell you it's safe. I think he's waiting for me."

"It looks like he's motioning to you," she whispered. "Please be careful."

He set out in the rain, leaving her to take cover behind the wall. She wondered if she had just sent him to his death. Why hadn't she thought to run back to the barn and raise the driver to help him? She swallowed dryly, wishing she had never left her room.

It was hard to see in the diffused light, but she could pick out Connor charging across the field like a warlord. Obviously he couldn't see well either because he ran straight into a wagon. It didn't stop him for long. He circled with a primitive growl and continued forward.

Then suddenly the wind picked up. The man in the middle of the field began waving his arms, clearly trying to provoke a confrontation. Maggie straightened, her hand pressed to her mouth against the urge to scream a warning to Connor. The man seemed to be pointing a long brown object at Connor. It looked like a musket.

She climbed over the wall, rain stinging her face, but she scarcely noticed the cold anymore. She had to stop Connor. He glanced back at her once. The wind howled in her ears. Yet she kept running as hard as she could—until she stubbed her toe on a small boulder hidden in a clump of dying gorse.

The pain was unexpected and excruciating. It brought tears to her eyes. She doubled over, cursing fluently in French. She barely noticed Connor swing around to stare at her.

"What is it, lass?" He was panting, his face panicked. "Have you been hurt?"

"Yes," she wailed.

"Did he shoot you?" he said, or something like that; Maggie was feeling too sorry for herself to pay attention to anything else. "I'll kill him," he roared. "I'll kill the bastard with my bare hands."

Maggie sniffed; she thought she'd broken her baby toe. As the pain began to recede, she heard the bloodcurdling Buchanan war-shout, made famous at the Battle of Agincourt, rise from the middle of the field. Then there was a pistol shot, followed by the muted rhythm of rain and wind.

She straightened, half afraid to look around. Connor was staggering toward her like a bedraggled warrior, his long hair plastered on his neck like wet yarn, his pistol hanging limply from his hand.

Rain ran in rivulets down his rigid face. Her startled gaze flew to the figure of a man in the field. The figure who was suddenly missing a head. "Oh, my goodness," she whispered, her eyes widening with realization. "You've just killed—"

"A scarecrow."

He stumbled past her to the wall, coat hanging open, chest heaving with exertion and disgust.

"Thank you," he said, folding down numbly to stare through the trees. "I have just sunk to the lowest depths of humiliation. I have been outwitted by a bag of straw."

"But there *was* a man standing by the wall," she insisted. "He knew my name. He said you were going to hurt me."

"He could be right about that," he muttered.

Maggie bit her lip, glancing across the field and then back at Connor. "You look as if you're going to faint," she said in concern.

His head snapped up. "Well, would you blame me? I thought I had cornered a kidnapper. I thought he had shot you in the leg. I wanted to kill him. I emptied my pistol into him."

He rose to his feet, walking her backward into the wall. His eyes burned like a demon's. "And do you know what happened after I emptied my pistol?"

Maggie shook her head from side to side, her hand at her throat.

"His head exploded off his body and landed at my feet! His arms went flying in the air." His voice climbed, challenging the howl of the wind. "I caught his nose before it hit the ground. It was a carrot. A CARROT."

Maggie winced, closing her eyes in empathy.

He advanced another step, his jaw practically jutting into her forehead. "I saw what I believed was a human being blown into pieces before my eyes—"

"Oh, my—"

"I stumbled over its turnip head in shock before I realized what I had done. I murdered a bunch of vegetables on your behalf, Miss Saunders. So, yes, if I look like I might faint, forgive me."

"Perhaps you'd feel better if you put your head between your legs," she whispered hesitantly.

The suggestion earned her a furious scowl. She couldn't blame him, although Maggie, in her own defense, knew what she had seen and heard. She knew the man at the wall had been real.

She also knew that she'd been right about Connor Buchanan from the start.

He wasn't the beast of popular legend.

He wasn't simply a hero. He was a man to slay scarecrows. He was a man she could love for the rest of her life.

Chapter

22

"Ye've overpaid me for the hole in the roof, Lord Buchanan." Mrs. Pringle looked up respectfully at the somber figure on horseback. "And ye didn't have to pay me for the scarecrow at all. 'Twas just a silly old thing we'd sewn together with Daniel's old clothes. Half the time the crows just sat on his head and pecked on his carrot."

"It was the least I could do." Connor barely glanced at Maggie, mounted on a sturdy dun mare beside him. "You are ready, Miss Saunders?" he said in a glacial voice.

"Yes, I am." She smiled warmly at Mrs. Pringle. "Lead on, my lord. I'm looking forward to a stimulating ride after being cooped up in that stuffy carriage."

"Dinna forget the lunch I packed in yer saddlebags," Mrs. Pringle called after them. "And thank ye for helping with the children, Lady Marguerite. That herbal tea of yers worked wonders for the coughs."

"It was a wonder she didn't poison them," Connor said under his breath. "Or burn down the farm. Or shoot out all the windows. Or cause me to murder an innocent man."

Maggie spurred her horse after him. "That remark was uncalled for."

Connor would not even acknowledge her. He was never going to forgive her for mistaking that scarecrow for a man. "You have nothing to be ashamed of, my lord. It only proved you're perfectly capable, and willing, of protecting me when the need arises. The Chief always says that a man shows his colors in a crisis. I believe this incident will only end up deepening our friendship."

He stopped briefly at the stone wall, raking her with a faint sneer. Maggie rode up beside him. "He was standing right here in the rain, just as plain as the nose on your face." Mischief lit her eyes. "Or should I say carrot?"

He didn't appreciate the joke. He just set his heel to his horse and trotted off without looking back. Maggie hurried after him as realization dawned.

"Your male pride has been hurt," she said understandingly. "Well, you needn't worry about looking foolish in front of me. With my family history, I'm in no position to pass judgment. My great-grandfather liked to dress up like a shepherdess. My uncle wrote poetry in the privy. We all have our little secrets."

He was galloping away from her again, on one of the horses Mrs. Pringle had loaned them. Maggie caught up with him at the edge of the bog. The mud-encrusted carriage sat in the weeds where Connor and the driver had dragged it to dry. Maggie decided to make another attempt at drawing him out of his shell.

"It looks rather forlorn sitting here all by itself, doesn't it?" she said breathlessly.

Connor didn't say a word. In fact, he refused to speak to her for the next seven miles, even though Maggie did enough talking for both of them. She studied her surroundings with interest, the blue haze of the hills broken by an occasional castle ruin or burial cairn. The heath spread before her like a tapestry, the browning bell-heather interwoven with spaghnum moss.

Connor had deigned to mention earlier that if the mist didn't obscure the way, they should reach Kilcurrie before nightfall. Claude and the driver were bringing along the rest of her belongings in Mrs. Pringle's pony cart.

"I hope they don't get lost," she thought aloud. "Claude and I have that tendency in common."

By this time she didn't expect Connor to answer. She understood that his injured pride needed to heal, and that in time he would forgive her. Still, halfway down the hill into a wooded strath, she realized she could have a more serious problem on her hands.

After last night's embarrassment, he wouldn't be so quick to spring into action. The next time the man in black approached her, she might have to be ready to protect herself.

The coachman scratched his belly through his tunic and yawned into the mug of steaming tea Mrs. Pringle placed on the table before him. "Lord," he said, "what a night."

"And how would ye know what sort of night it was?" Her voice was tart. "It took me and this good man here an hour to rouse you from yer drunken stupor."

This good man was Claude, who was removing a half dozen oatcakes from the griddle. The coachman frowned.

"Aye, well. I may have had a dram too much, but 'twasn't whisky that interrupted me sleep. There was a gunshot, that's what it was."

"I did not hear any gunshot," Claude remarked from the stove. "It was thunder. His lordship said it was thunder."

Mrs. Pringle nodded. "If his lordship said it was thunder, then that's what it was. I'm not one to argue with the Lord Advocate of Scotland." Especially not when she had a thick wad of his lordship's bank notes tucked in her apron pocket to cover the cost of repairing the roof from the "thunder."

The coachman picked up his mug, his face dour. Drunk or not, he knew what he'd heard. And seen. That sweet little noblewoman in her nightdress and a man all in black beckoning to her by the wall. He'd thought it a bit odd, but since he'd been answering nature's call at the time, he hadn't exactly been in a position to interfere. Not that anyone would have believed him. No one had much respect for a professional coachman who had driven his coach into a bog.

Chapter

23

"At least my house is still standing," Connor said as he surveyed his estate from the crest of the Highland foothill where he and Maggie had slowed to rest their horses. "I don't know what I expected with so much turmoil in my life. Nothing would have surprised me at this point."

Maggie suppressed a tolerant smile. He was feeling sorry for himself again. Still, it was the first civilized thing he'd said to her all day, and she decided if he was going to extend the olive branch of reconciliation, she should graciously accept it. "It's a lovely place," she said. "Of course it's small compared to the château, but small houses have their charm, don't they?"

Connor turned his head to examine her in frosty silence, giving Maggie the distinct impression he'd hoped he had lost her along the way. "What château?" he said suspiciously.

"The one I grew up in, my lord. It was a Renaissance-style castle overlooking a river in Normandy."

He shook his head, dismissing her with a grunt, and urged his horse down the hill into the woods. Maggie followed him, bristling with annoyance.

"You don't believe me, do you?" she said.

"I don't know what to believe anymore."

"Just tell me one thing," she said. "Why would I make up a story about my past if it weren't true?"

"Why does anyone make up anything, Miss Saunders?"

"You are such a cynical man."

"Working with the criminal element does not predispose one to believing the best of people." He smirked at her over his shoulder. "By the way, I'd watch where I was riding if I were you. These woods are rather dense."

"Apparently, it is a common affliction."

He smiled at that and rode on slowly through the tangle of birch trees and thick undergrowth of fern. Then suddenly he stopped and swiveled around in the saddle, his gaze searching the shadows.

"Did you hear something?"

"Only Daphne running off after a rabbit."

"I heard footsteps," he said, frowning.

"I didn't." At this point in their relationship Maggie was determined to prove she was levelheaded and not prone to either hysteria or hallucinations. She promised herself she wouldn't utter a single scream even if a wildcat dropped onto her head.

Connor stared at her in critical silence. "Perhaps you should take off that hat. Someone could mistake those feathers for a bird in the underbrush."

"These are genuine ostrich feathers," Maggie said, stung. "When was the last time you saw an ostrich running about the Highlands?"

There was an unmistakable crunch of footsteps in the surrounding thicket. Connor narrowed his eyes, motioning her not to move.

"Those were human footsteps," he said quietly. "Get off your horse and take cover."

"I didn't hear any footsteps," Maggie argued, sounding more levelheaded than she felt.

"Poachers," a gruff voice grumbled behind the trees. "Damned poachers are coming out now before it's even dark. I'll teach them a lesson. Give me that gun."

Connor dismounted and, ignoring her squeak of protest, dragged Maggie off her horse. "I suppose you didn't hear that, either?" he whispered roughly.

"Didn't hear what?"

A loud crack interrupted them. Seconds later a pistol ball tore into the interlaced canopy of branches overhead, showering the clearing with broken twigs and dry leaves. Despite this alarming sign, Maggie managed to maintain her composure. She refused to obey the instinct to run for cover. She wasn't about to give Connor another excuse to accuse her of being a hysterical female.

Another shot broke a small limb from an adjacent tree and sent it crashing down between them.

"Get on the ground—down that slope." Connor pushed her behind him, shielding her with his body. "Someone is shooting at us."

"Are you sure?" Maggie whispered.

"Yes, I'm—"

He broke off as a woman with unruly silver-gray hair stomped out from behind the birches. She wore black leather boots up to her thighs and a pair of tartan hunting trousers under a belted tunic. A pack of assorted dogs swarmed at her heels, sniffing and panting to be free. She carried a smoking pistol in each hand. She was almost as tall as Connor.

"Oh, my God," he said, parting the branches that hid him for a better look. "We're being shot at by the Duchess of Kincarden, my lunatic neighbor."

"Is that you, Buchanan?" the older woman said in amazement, stepping around her dogs for a better look. "Good heavens, it is, and with a chit in the bushes. You haven't changed a bit."

"You shot at us," Connor said angrily. "Did it ever occur to you that it might be dangerous to charge through the woods like you're leading a lion safari? Did it ever occur to you that you could kill someone?"

"I intended to kill someone," the duchess admitted. "This is my property you're trespassing on, and I thought I'd caught a pair of poachers. Someone has to protect the innocent animals."

Connor pulled a twig out of his hair. "Be that as it may, you can't take the law into your own hands. That's what we have sheriffs and magistrates for."

A branch rustled behind the duchess as a young woman

with blond hair in a coronet limped into the clearing. Hefting her musket onto her shoulder, she stared past the duchess in astonishment.

"Connor!" she exclaimed.

He looked her up and down disapprovingly. "Rebecca. My God."

"I almost shot you," she said, hiding a lopsided grin that radiated irresistible Buchanan charm. "You might have warned us to expect you."

He wrested the musket from her arm and propped it up carefully against a tree. "Didn't you get my letters? I told you I was coming."

Her clear blue eyes danced with curiosity as she glanced at Maggie. "Well, I did receive them, Connor, I can't lie. But I didn't read them yet."

"Why the hell not?"

"Because they always say the same thing. You're like an old woman, forever fussing me to move into the city so that I can find a husband. Your letters are boring and bossy."

He crossed his arms over his chest. "If you didn't read my letters, then you don't know that your sister Sheena has been kidnapped, and that the kidnappers are threatening to make you their next victim."

Rebecca stared at him in disbelieving silence. "Sheena? Why would anyone want to kidnap Sheena?"

"I've no idea. Presumably it has something to do with my appointment to the Lord Advocacy." Connor turned to Maggie, his gaze meeting hers. "I have reason to believe the kidnappers might be in the area to pursue you, Rebecca. This young woman had the misfortune to be the only witness to Sheena's disappearance and is under my official protection."

The amusement faded from Rebecca's eyes. "If you're teasing me, Connor, you have the cruelest sense of humor. And if you're trying to frighten me into leaving here, it won't work. I won't be bullied."

Maggie brushed herself off and stepped forward, regarding Rebecca with sympathy. "I'm afraid he's telling the truth, although he did leave out a few pertinent details. Not only did I witness your sister's abduction, I also tried to rescue her by crowning the getaway coachman with a champagne bottle. I was assaulted myself in the process."

"A champagne bottle. That shows initiative," the duchess said in approval. "I'm honored to make your acquaintance. My name is Morna Mainwaring, Duchess of Kincarden."

Maggie dipped into an elegant curtsy. "I am Marguerite de Saint-Evremond, daughter of the late Duc and Duchesse de Saint-Evremond. The honor is mine, your grace. I apologize for trespassing on your property. His lordship led me to believe we had entered his estate. Poachers must be severely dealt with."

The duchess studied her in open appraisal for several seconds. Then she noticed the little white dog growling protectively at Maggie's feet. The woman's wrinkled face softened. Jamming her pistols into her waistband, she squatted with her gloved hand outstretched.

"What a splendid dog," she said.

"It's a poodle," Rebecca said quietly, her troubled gaze lifting back to Connor's face as if she were still hoping he was teasing her about Sheena.

"Nice doggie," the duchess said. "Good doggie. You won't let me hurt your mistress, will you? Well, that's as it should be. Good breeding shows."

She rose spryly to confront Connor again. "That dog is doing its job, Buchanan, protecting this brave girl. How dare you drag her into the woods where she could have been caught by dangerous poachers."

"Not to mention dangerous neighbors," he said in a dry voice.

The duchess put her hand on Maggie's arm. "You're looking peaked, my dear, and after your ordeal, I'm not surprised. Come back to the house with me and Rebecca for some bracing brandy—de Saint-Evremond, you said? You don't mean Simon de Saint-Evremond, by any chance?"

Maggie took a breath. "Yes. My father."

"Oh, my heavens." The duchess studied Maggie's face with a look of wonder. "It was Simon who introduced me to my own late husband at a charity ball in London so many decades ago. William and I lost touch with him over the years when we moved to Scotland to breed hounds. There were rumors your dear Papa was involved in helping Britain squash that little dictator Napoleon."

Maggie nodded proudly. "Papa was a Royalist until the day his enemies took his body away, madam."

A deep sigh escaped the duchess before she shook her head, words suddenly inadequate to express her sympathy. Connor couldn't believe it. He'd have sworn the old battle-ax didn't have a compassionate bone in her body, except when it came to her menagerie of animals.

And Maggie. Well, if he'd doubted her before, he didn't now. She was obviously everything she claimed to be. She was everything he'd hoped for that first night, and more. Yet she remained a mystery to him, a treasure entrusted to his care, and he didn't know when his sense of duty had gotten entangled with personal desire, probably from the beginning, but it was too late to do anything about it now.

Rebecca's troubled voice intruded on his thoughts. "Well, Connor, she's certainly not like the others you've brought home, is she? I daresay this means something serious. Come walk with me. Tell me everything about Sheena."

Connor nodded slowly. Maggie and the duchess strolled off arm-in-arm through the woods, lost in their own world. A world of lofty sentiments where noblemen laid down their lives for peace, and stouthearted women hunted poachers who hurt helpless animals.

A world where apparently a small blue-eyed girl was a beloved princess and he became the beast who watched her with fierce longing from the edge of a primeval forest, lured to her innocence and afraid of it at the same time.

Chapter 24

Evening had fallen when they reached the restored Tudor-style mansion, driven at breakneck speed by the duchess's robust female driver, Frances. Maggie, Rebecca, and the duchess embraced like long-lost relatives as they parted with promises to meet the following afternoon for tea. Connor staggered out of the coach covered in dog hair.

The friendship between the three women had been strengthened by the fact that, on the way back through the woods to the coach, Maggie's poodle had rescued one of the duchess's pups from drowning in the rain-swollen burn. The duchess had sent her driver back to her house to reward Daphne with a basket of venison bones. It occurred to Connor that the three women had only their association with him and a love of animals in common. He did not care to speculate what this meant.

"You mind that you protect that girl, Buchanan," the duchess warned him from the carriage window as she prepared to leave. Then she pulled out a pistol and fired a shot into the air. "If any kidnappers show up, send them over to me. I know how to take care of that sort."

Connor closed his eyes, shuddering at the thought.

DARING

The carriage barreled off into the dark with Rebecca, the duchess, and a half dozen hounds. Connor hadn't taken his first fateful step up the drive than a parade of servants came pouring out of the gray stone house.

"My lord, is that you?" someone shouted. "Thank God. At last."

"Well, at least your staff hasn't tried to shoot you," Maggie murmured, smothering a yawn. "That's reassuring."

Connor narrowed his eyes. "No, it isn't. I don't have that many servants. Only a steward, a housekeeper, and a butler. What the devil is going on?"

The steward, a short white-haired Highlander with a straggly beard that reached his chest, approached Connor first. He was out of breath and struggling to shove his arms into his wrinkled tweed jacket. "We were expecting you days ago, my lord. I was afeared you weren't coming after all."

"Is something wrong?" Connor said.

"Only everything that could be wrong, my lord," the steward replied.

"What the blazes is that supposed to mean?"

A trim brown-haired woman in brown muslin came forward to break into the conversation. "Ladies first, Dougie. His lordship will hear my side of the situation before you fill his head with a pack of lies."

Connor blew out a sigh of impatience. "Who are all these people in the driveway, Mrs. Urquhart?"

"Unfortunately, I am no longer Mrs. Urquhart," the housekeeper said. She pointed her finger at the steward's bulbous nose. "Two ill-fated months ago I married that awful man there."

"And my life has been hell on earth ever since," Dougie said morosely. "The nasty woman has taken over the house, my lord. I'm an outcast in my own domain."

Connor glanced up the driveway at the line of servants bowing and curtsying at him like mechanical dolls. "Who are all these people?" he asked in a clipped voice.

"That is your new staff, my lord, as befitting the most powerful man in Scotland," Mrs. Urquhart replied with pride.

Connor's lips thinned. "The most powerful does not mean I am the richest, Mrs. Urquhart."

"Well, one has to keep up appearances," Maggie said, empathizing with the housekeeper's efforts. "Especially a man in your position."

"I doubt there has ever been a man in my position, Miss Saunders."

Dougie scowled. "My wife, and I use the term loosely, hasna been the same since she visited her snooty cousin in London last summer. She says we Highlanders are barbaric and out of fashion, sir. She thinks I ought to shave."

Maggie, who had never been able to resist taking sides, regarded the man's unkempt beard with a critical eye. "She does have a point. I've seen rats' nests that were tidier."

Connor rubbed the stubble that shadowed his own jaw. "I advise you not to intervene," he said tiredly. "These trivial domestic matters are best left to be solved by themselves."

"On the contrary." Maggie suddenly saw a chance to repay Connor for protecting her, using her past expertise as the member of a tightly run noble household to put things right in his home. "These matters must be nipped in the bud before a rebellion ensues."

"Nipped in the bud?" Connor stared down at her, in her silly hat with the crushed ostrich feathers, and squelched the urge to kiss her senseless in front of everyone. The trouble was, he wouldn't be satisfied with just kissing her. He'd want to carry her up to his room, throw her on his big bed, and strip her naked, revealing one delectable inch of creamy skin at a time. Then, with only a bottle of whisky and a blazing fire in the background, he would make love to her. Hard and hot. Slow and tantalizing. His body tightened at the thought of her graceful dancer's legs spreading to welcome him, the soft cries she'd utter as he drove—

He thwarted the fantasy by scrubbing his hand over his chin, feeling Maggie's curious blue eyes examining his face. "Nip away, Miss Saunders. I'm going to drown my sorrows in some raw Highland whisky and then ride over to talk to the sheriff about Sheena. Settling a dispute between servants is the farthest thing from my mind."

"Well." Maggie turned to Mrs. Urquhart as Connor strode off toward the house, his male servants in tow and loudly registering their complaints. "It seems we have the makings of a crisis here."

Mrs. Urquhart took out her hanky and dabbed at her perfectly dry eyes. "I only want to improve the household for his lordship's sake. Is that such a crime?"

"Not in the least," Maggie said. "Men would never improve themselves without our prompting, Mrs. Urquhart. They would behave like perfect beasts if left to their own devices. But take heart. You shall have my full support in this situation. I do not think I am bragging when I say that his lordship and I, due to circumstances beyond anyone's control, have been forced to develop a close friendship in an unnaturally short time."

"Ah." Mrs. Urquhart nodded. "I see."

Maggie smiled sagely. "I am not without my influence on him. If you take my meaning."

"Bless you, miss. I think I do."

"The battle is half won already," Maggie said, squaring her small shoulders in a militant stance. "A de Saint-Evremond can be a most powerful ally."

Chapter

25

Maggie cradled her teacup in her hands and walked around the darkened pine-paneled room. She felt safe in the heart of this mellow Highland house. She felt safer than she'd felt since leaving France, knowing Connor slept just down the hall from her. A strange tingle went down her spine as she remembered the sensation of lying beneath him in the straw. She had never felt so defenseless and desirable as at that moment.

She sipped her chamomile tea and crossed the room to the window. The wooded hills that rose into the mist and moonlight isolated the house from the rest of the world, a comforting sight.

But did the hills hide danger and not discourage it? Were Connor's enemies waiting there, closing in around them?

She couldn't remember anything more about the men who had kidnapped Sheena. Even if she'd had time to scrutinize them, what would she have been able to tell from a masked face and nondescript clothing? They could have been anyone.

And yet there had been something oddly familiar about the figure at the stone wall, the man's voice at her door at the inn. *Had* he been one of the men in Connor's courtyard? Had something else happened that night, something so disturbing that she'd suppressed the memory like many other details in her past?

On impulse she put down her cup, turned from the window, and walked swiftly down the hall to Connor's room. His door was shut. She opened it. She didn't intend to wake him. She just wanted to look at him once before she fell asleep.

She knew now that this man would risk his life to keep her safe.

But could she do the same for him?

He lay sprawled half drunk across his bed, trying to think up a thousand excuses to enter her room. He could warn her about the warped windows. He could explain how to find the privy in the middle of the night. He could pretend he'd heard a noise and needed to check her wardrobe for a hidden intruder.

He wanted her. He wanted to fall asleep with her beside him, their bodies fitted together. He wanted to wake up in the middle of the night and make love to her, to breathe her bewitching scent, to soothe his black mood with her bright spirit. He was obsessed with her.

The meeting with the sheriff had depressed him. Yes, the man and his deputy had gotten Connor's letters. They were searching for Sheena, posting reward notices all the way to the Isle of Skye. Yes, they had been keeping an eye on Rebecca, but the stubborn woman refused to move from her isolated cottage. The sheriff intended to investigate a report of strangers in the area the very next morning. An unknown man had leased the old Jacobite castle on the hill, presumably for hunting purposes. Connor hated the thought of his Highland hideaway being taken over by outsiders, but there was no time to worry about that now.

And, no, the sheriff and his deputy didn't expect to find Sheena alive, if at all. Connor was experienced enough to read that grim suspicion, though they wouldn't dare voice such an opinion to his face. They didn't like him much, but they respected him. And Connor refused to accept the worst about his sister. She *was* safe. He believed it with all his heart.

Maggie was still awake.

He could hear her pacing, light troubled footfalls around her room. He pictured her undressing for bed, that perfect body burnished in firelight. Midnight-black hair tangled over her breasts. Delicate, a body made for loving. Made for him. Loneliness and longing combined forces against him in a challenge fiercer than he had waged in any courtroom. He had no defense prepared. He was guilty of loving her.

He didn't care anymore if she had lied about her past; she could be the daughter of a dustman for all he cared. They could both be a little mad. He was no longer a rational man. Since that humiliating night when he had assassinated a scarecrow in the rain, he knew how he'd react if he caught anyone trying to hurt her. A tide of hot fury swept through him at the thought.

His rivals had been right. Beneath his image of self-possession beat the black heart of a barbarian, a beast, with all its raging passion. The man who held the power to condemn or condone was capable of committing murder himself. He would kill anyone who touched her.

In fact, he would kill for the chance just to be touching her himself.

Maggie crept across the room, then stopped midstride as she caught a glimpse of Connor through the parted bed curtains. She picked up the quilt to cover him. She was afraid he never protected his health. At first she thought it was a touching sight, that fierce body sprawled out like a little boy's. Except that, on closer inspection, she was forced to admit there wasn't anything little about him. And he wasn't asleep at all, his hazel eyes glinting up at her with predatory anticipation. He was totally nude, shameless and doing nothing to conceal the unsettling fact.

"Touch me at your own peril," he said in a low conversational tone, leaning up on one elbow to watch her.

She lowered the quilt to the bed. "You're not going to assault me with your pistol again?"

He sat up without warning. "What are you doing in my

room?" he demanded quietly. "Is there a homicidal scarecrow in the house?"

"There is no need for sarcasm. I merely wanted to make sure you'd returned from meeting the sheriff and were well."

His teeth flashed in a grin. He reminded her of a dangerous tousled lion, an animal too unpredictable to trust. His room seemed to fit his personality, bare but for a few pieces of rough-hewn furniture and a leather armorial shield on the wall. "I am quite well," he said. "And you?"

"I'm feeling rather foolish if you must know," she admitted, turning away. "I don't know why I was worried about you at all."

"What did you imagine would happen to me?" he asked in an amused voice.

She glanced back in irritation. "I was raised by unconventional parents with liberal standards. Even so, I hardly think it's appropriate to be having a personal conversation with a naked man in his bedchamber. You ought to have a little more decency."

Connor snorted at this logic. "Who entered the naked man's bedchamber, may I ask?"

"That is beside the point."

He rolled onto his stomach, his mouth stretched into a smile of male superiority. "I think something other than concern over my welfare brought you into this room."

Maggie told herself to back away from the bed, but a perverse curiosity kept her rooted to the spot. "Such as?"

His smile deepened. "It's that sexual attraction I warned you about before."

She frowned, trying not to admire the breadth of his shoulders, his naked torso. What a magnificent man. "Not that nonsense between the virgin and the beast?"

"Precisely." He stretched forward, the sheet casually draped around his waist. "A powerful force, sexual attraction. It makes people do the most unreasonable things."

Maggie cleared her throat as he rose from the bed to face her, flexing his well-muscled arms above his head. Strong chest and shoulders. Narrow waist. One deep breath, he'd lose that sheet, and she could describe the rest of him in vivid detail, too. "Good night, my lord," she said decisively.

"I'm sorry I disturbed you. I am leaving before either of us succumb to the unreasonable."

She barely reached the door than she felt him stealing up behind her. The heat of his body ignited invisible sparks in the air between them. If she turned to face him, it would be like staring into the center of the sun. She would melt at his feet, in his arms. His whisky-scented breath brushed her hair. Desire rushed through her veins, temptation tingling in its wake.

"I don't believe I heard you putting on your clothes," she said with a catch in her voice.

"I don't believe I did, lass."

"Then, aside from the sheet, you are—"

"As naked as a newborn bairn."

"But bigger."

"Aye." She heard a hint of laughter in his voice. *"Much* bigger. In fact—"

"I don't need to know the exact proportions."

He brushed a strand of hair from her shoulder, the gesture seductive and sweet. "It's cold standing here by the door. Come back to bed with me," he coaxed. "We'll keep each other warm."

Maggie didn't feel cold at all. Especially not when he lowered his mouth to the nape of her neck. His kisses, scattered across her shoulder, scorched like wildfire. She took a steadying breath. She would be lost if she didn't leave soon.

"Do you still want to tuck me in for the night, lass?" he asked with a wicked chuckle. Then, "Maggie, darling, the next time you have the urge to sneak into my bed, you don't need to use such a pathetic excuse. You don't need an invitation. My door is always open. I know you want me, lass. I want you, too."

She swallowed a retort, realizing her good intentions had just been reduced to the most insulting motive imaginable. His male arrogance astonished her. She would have kicked him if she'd had the nerve to turn around.

"I think there's been a misunderstanding, my lord."

"Of course there has." He took delight in teasing her. She could sense him grinning like a satyr, so smug and confident of his sexual prowess. "But tuck me in anyway." He brought his hands upward, spanning her rib cage, to cup her breasts in his big palms. "I won't be able to sleep now unless you do."

Her smile was brittle. The need he stirred in the depths of her body was undeniable. "So you want to be tucked in for the night, do you?"

She caught her breath as he pulled her back against his chest, his thumbs rubbing in tantalizing circles across her breasts. "Yes, please," he said, nuzzling her neck.

Maggie felt the power and response of his body to her nearness, his hard shaft pressed against her hip. "Do you mind waiting for a few moments before you're 'tucked in'?" she asked thoughtfully.

Connor traced her earlobe with the tip of his tongue, his voice husky with arousal. "Don't be long then. I'm not at all a patient man."

Maggie leaned against the doorjamb, biting her lip against laughter at the loud shocked voice that resonated down the hall. He would never forgive her for sneaking downstairs to engage his housekeeper's help, but she hadn't been able to resist her own mischievous revenge. Didn't his ego deserve a little deflation? *I know you want me, lass.* Indeed.

"Really, sir! Not a stitch of clothing. I canna believe my eyes."

"Close your damn eyes, Mrs. Urquhart, or at least have the decency to turn around. You had no business barging into my room uninvited in the middle of the night."

Mrs. Urquhart raised her tone to a warbling soprano. "I was under the impression that you wanted to be tucked in for the night."

"Do I look like a child, Mrs. Urquhart?"

"Common decency forbids that I come close enough to give you an answer, sir."

"Miss Saunders is going to pay for this." His voice crackled like a thunderbolt through the house. "I hope she can hear me."

Maggie grinned, whispering in the darkness, "She certainly can."

"The considerate young woman was only following your orders, sir," the housekeeper retorted. "Your very peculiar orders."

"The hell she was. She wanted to embarrass me."

"Excuse me, sir, but you are embarrassing yourself, summoning female servants into your room in that disgraceful state of undress."

Connor sounded as if he were choking on his words. "Nobody was invited anywhere, you thickheaded woman."

"Now you're stooping to insults. I knew that would come next. But did you or did you not request that you be tucked in for the night, sir?"

Connor could be heard stomping across the room like an ogre and wrenching open his wardrobe door. "Stop using that ridiculous term. And who the devil moved all my clothes? What are these damn dresses doing here?"

"Kindly answer the question, sir."

Maggie winced as she heard the wardrobe doors slam, followed by Mrs. Urquhart's gasp of unadulterated horror. Surely he wasn't parading around nude in front of the poor woman?

"We are not in a court of law, Mrs. Urquhart," Connor said. "This is my house, in case you have forgotten. You are a servant in my employ, and I am not a criminal on trial. I do not have to answer your stupid questions. Hell's bells, where are my trousers?"

"Lady Marguerite took them to the laundry, sir."

"She did *what?*"

Mrs. Urquhart began retreating into the hall. Realizing the danger of being caught eavesdropping, Maggie turned to tiptoe back to her room. Too late. Connor stood cloaked in the darkness of his doorway, glowering at her with one hand on his hip, the other covering his naked torso with a huge leather shield that was emblazoned, appropriately enough, with the Buchanan lion rampant.

"Did you enjoy that, Miss Saunders?"

Maggie tried not to stare at the family crest that barely reached his massive chest. "Did I enjoy what?"

He slammed the door in her face. The reverberation echoed through the stillness of the house. It drew a cluster of curious servants in their nightclothes to the bottom of the stairs.

"Why is Lord Buchanan wearing a shield?" a chambermaid asked curiously.

"The lad has a fierce temper," Dougie said proudly. "That door almost came unhinged when he slammed it."

Mrs. Urquhart clattered down the stairs, flustered and muttering under her breath. "The lad has more than a temper wrong with him."

"Did you tuck him in for the night?" Dougie demanded.

"No, I did not!"

Dougie looked puzzled. "Well, why not?"

"Because he was stark naked, you old busybody, that's why. The man was lying in his bed like a . . . a—"

"A Greek statue." Maggie walked to the top of the stairs, gazing down at the small gathering. It was clear someone in authority needed to take a stand to set things right in this household, or chaos would ensue. Connor had obviously let matters deteriorate during his absence. Fortunately, Maggie could summon the benefit of her experience as a duke's daughter to help him.

"Everyone back to their beds," she said, lightly clapping her hands to get their attention. "His lordship's style of dress is nobody's business, and if he chooses to unhinge the doors in his own house, we shall not question him. Obviously he has changed his mind about being tucked in. That is also his right. Your jobs are the only matter that should concern you. Is that understood?"

The male servants grumbled a bit at this explanation, resenting taking orders from the little sprite of a thing who had upset their master. The women, however, seemed almost relieved that order would be restored to the house.

Maggie nodded in satisfaction, then turned from the stairs only to cringe at the sound of Connor banging about behind closed doors like a wild creature in a cave. Clearly no one had taught him the value of setting a good example. Well, at least she had taken a stand on the side of authority.

Tomorrow she would tackle taming the beast himself.

Chapter

26

The note from Sheena arrived the following morning. Connor sat down on the steep wooden staircase to read it in grim silence. His uncle had forwarded it from Edinburgh by private messenger. The scribbled missive was short, but by no means sweet. He sighed with relief as he immediately recognized the handwriting.

> Connor,
>   By now you are probably aware that I have been kidnapped. I am alive. My kidnapper is treating me well. As a matter of fact, he's nicer to me than you ever were.
>   Your long-suffering sister,
>
> Sheena
>   P.S. I hope you feel guilty for ruining my life.

"Perhaps it's from another impostor," Maggie said over his shoulder, taking the liberty of reading it when she saw how dejected he looked.

"It's Sheena." His voice was flat. He leaned his left arm

210

against the railing, staring into space. He didn't bother to hide the note from Maggie, or to pretend he'd enjoyed a perfect relationship with his little sister. His personal life was a mess, and Maggie had become part of it. But Sheena wasn't dead, thank God at least for that.

"Well, at least she's alive," she said awkwardly.

"Yes."

She laid her hand on his back. "Don't worry. Everything will turn out well in the end."

"I hope to God you're right. She didn't sound very frightened, did she?"

Maggie looked at him in concern. "I know you're hurt by her note, and probably wishing she weren't your responsibility, but in my opinion you're very fortunate."

"Fortunate? With a family like mine?"

She paused. "I wish I had a family to upset me."

He studied her for a long unguarded moment. "Isn't it enough that you're the most desirable woman I've ever met? Do you have to be so damn understanding too?"

"You look tired," Maggie said gently. "You must not have slept well."

He narrowed his eyes. He'd been awake again all night, reviewing the names of every criminal with a grudge against him, waiting for some instinct to point him to the kidnapper.

Waiting for Maggie to slip back into his room and give him another chance to talk her into staying. Waiting for her to make him laugh when he wanted to cry, for her to make him feel strong when he was helpless. He could be so persuasive when he put his mind to it. Why did his power of speech fail him in her presence?

"Did you expect me to sleep after being humiliated in front of the entire household?" he said grumpily.

"Ah." She bent to untie her ballet shoes. "The tucking-in incident still bothers you."

Connor frowned, staring in frustration at the curve of her rump. He'd been working in his office when the messenger arrived. Maggie had been practicing ballet in the gallery directly outside his door, using the banister as a barre. He hadn't been able to get a thing done.

Her black hair was still carelessly gathered back in a pink ribbon, a few curls falling around her face. Her flowing muslin costume emphasized every sculptured curve of her body, from her rounded breasts to her delightfully proportioned derriere. It was scandalous and erotic. Just looking at her made his mouth dry.

"I'm going for a walk in the woods," he said. "I can't work now. Tell Mrs. Urquhart I won't be back until dark."

She straightened, her eyes distressed. "A walk alone in the woods? What if someone follows you?"

"I will be perfectly fine by myself."

Maggie stepped down beside him. "You shouldn't be alone at a time like this."

"A time like what?"

"I'm going to walk with you in the woods," Maggie said firmly.

Alone with her in the woods. He felt temptation tug at his soul. "You can't come with me. The woods are too dangerous."

"Dangerous?"

"Wild animals." He gazed longingly at the slope of her shoulder. He could almost taste her. "Beasts," he added. "Poachers and lunatic women with guns. But it's the beasts I'd worry about. They hide behind trees and boulders just waiting to devour innocent young women."

Maggie raised her face to his, calmly accepting the challenge. "I'm not afraid of wild animals. However, I am worried about Claude. He should have reached the house long before now. What if he and that drunken driver are wandering about lost? Besides, you and I can protect each other, can't we? Wait here while I change."

Connor released his breath, watching her provocative costume-clad figure dart up the stairs. Lord, she had a gorgeous body. No wonder her father had forbidden her to dance. "I'm warning you now," he shouted. "I'm going to be bad company. I will be rude. I will be silent—I will totally ignore you."

It was impossible to ignore Marguerite Marie-Antoinette de Saint-Evremond when she did not want to be ignored. She chattered endlessly. She gave unsolicited advice on topics he didn't give a damn about like handling servants and poachers and which mushrooms would kill you if you ate them. She hopped after him like a little bird in her blue cotton dress and limp-feathered hat. He kept walking in circles, plunging into thickets, hoping to tire her out, or at least quiet her down.

"I love walking in the woods," she said, breathless to keep pace with his restless strides.

"So do I," Connor said. "Alone."

"We played every day, rain or shine, in the woods around the château. Jeanette was always a princess, and Robert was the knight who had to save her."

"What were you?" Connor asked dourly.

"The witch or dragon who'd taken her prisoner."

He glanced back in curiosity. "A dragon?"

"I used to borrow Uncle Paul's pipe and make smoke come out of my nose—oh, dear, watch out."

In his eagerness to teach her a lesson, he'd led them into an overgrown trail of old broom and bracken. Her warning saved him just before he would have tripped over a mass of mossy roots and landed at her feet. He caught his balance in time and stretched back to help her make the crossing into the woods.

Maggie gave him a grateful smile. "You're quite a nice man when you want to be."

"You are naive, Miss Saunders."

"I am not."

"Yes, you are. You believe there is good in even Edinburgh's worst criminals. You risked your life and reputation to rescue a demented old man who can't remember your name. Well, in reality nobody is nice to anyone unless they expect something in return. It's a cardinal rule of life."

"You're not the first person to tell me this," Maggie said. "However, I've been quite happy as a jinglebrains for over twenty years, and I'm not about to change now. What is it *you* expect from me, by the way, or are you the exception to the rule?"

"I expect you to help me find my sister."

Maggie stopped in her tracks. "Any decent human being would do that."

"I expect more than that, actually," he said in a low voice.

Maggie tilted her head back to study his face, the chiseled planes, and powerful jaw. He took her breath away. He was tugging her against him by the hand. Her heart fluttered in her chest, a butterfly emerging from a chrysalis. There was no mistaking the dark passion in his hazel eyes. There was no resisting it either.

She lowered her gaze. "Are you asking permission to court me?"

"I *am* courting you, lass," he said in amusement.

He brushed his mouth over hers, gripping her hard against him. Maggie sighed and snuggled in the wall of his chest, bliss tingling in her blood. He groaned and crushed her closer until her eyelids fluttered shut. She could have died happily in his arms.

"I think you ought to know that the Chief won't let any man touch me in an improper manner," she murmured.

"Neither will I." He closed his eyes and ran his hands down her hips, shuddering at the feel of her. Then he deepened his kiss, eliciting a response from Maggie that tested the limits of human restraint. Instead of drawing away from him, she arched against him in invitation. In fact, Connor was afraid he would slip on the damn roots again and bring them both crashing to the ground in a frenzy of unthinking lust.

"I'd feel terrible if the Chief hurt you for courting me," she whispered.

"So would I. God, you taste sweet."

He went to his knees, dragging her down onto the ground. Soft moss cushioned their bodies, redolent of earthy mould and moisture. He leaned over her, his heart pounding in his chest.

"I can't sleep at night for wanting you," he said quietly. "I can't work. I can't even think straight."

Happiness glinted in her eyes. "I'm sorry to hear that."

"Aye, you look it too, lass."

"Well, I can't say I'm displeased. After all, when we first . . ."

Her voice trailed off on a sigh as he traced his long fingertips down her throat, then her breasts, deftly unbuttoning her jacket bodice. His face had changed, shadows obscuring his smile, angles pulled tighter across the strong bones. The playfulness had deepened into a darker emotion that Maggie intuitively recognized as passion.

Then she felt his hand under her skirts and heard his harsh intake of breath. "You aren't wearing any stockings," he said in astonishment.

"I never do when I walk in the woods," she said, sitting up to face him. "I like to feel the earth under my toes. My dancing master used to claim it strengthens your muscles."

She reclined against the peeling birch trunk, closing her eyes with a beguiling smile. Connor wondered if she was deliberately trying to look seductive, or if it came naturally. Her mouth was as moist and tempting as a wild cherry. Her hair fell in untamed curls over her shoulders, drawing his gaze to the deep cleft of her breasts. He ached to bury himself inside her. He had to make her his.

"You should try it yourself," she murmured, digging her toes into the ground with childlike abandon.

He rubbed his thumb against the underside of her knee-cap. "Maggie, if my muscles were any stronger right now, I'd have to arrest myself for indecent exposure."

She opened her eyes to stare at his downbent head. His touch raised shivers over her skin. "What did you just say?" she whispered, spellbound by the sensations he evoked.

"Nothing." The yielding softness of her skin made him groan. Even the little sigh that she gave excited him. Her eyes had drifted shut again. Appalled, he wondered how she could fall asleep when he was this aroused. Was she going to start snoring halfway into his seduction? "There's a bothy about a half mile from here," he said. "We can be alone for as long as we like. Maggie, I can't wait. You're tormenting me."

The urgency in his voice broke her relaxed trance. She opened her eyes reluctantly. Although she considered herself unschooled in sexual matters, she knew exactly what he was asking. Yet before she could even consider giving him an answer, something stopped her. A prickle of apprehension crawled down her spine that had nothing to do with the ramifications of losing her virtue.

The woods. The unguarded way she and Connor were sitting together. It reminded her of the tapestry, the lion and the princess so engrossed in each other that they didn't sense the presence of an enemy.

He drew a breath. "I'll understand if you say no. It won't

stop me from having you, because there is always tonight, and—"

"We are not alone," she said quietly.

He shifted, instantly in control. "Where?"

Maggie stared over his shoulder, too afraid to say another word. It wasn't her imagination. Someone was watching them. Why hadn't she realized it before?

A shadow fell across the copse. The shadow of a man.

Maggie spotted him only seconds before Connor turned his head and saw the figure standing behind the trees, a sword glinting at his side.

Chapter

27

✍

It was only Claude.

Later Connor would insist that he knew it all along, but Maggie noticed that he turned chalk-white and leaped up to shield her. At any rate, Claude's untimely appearance had certainly spoiled Connor's plans for a sylvan seduction. To her shame, she felt more disappointed than relieved. Her body still throbbed with those forbidden urges.

"Who the hell would expect a butler to be wandering about the woods?" Connor said under his breath.

Maggie pulled her bodice together and scrambled to her feet. "He's probably lost," she whispered. "Don't say anything to hurt his feelings. He can't help it."

"I am not lost, my lady," Claude announced, pretending not to have noticed the provocative scenario he had interrupted. "I came looking for you to warn you."

"Warn her of what?" Connor demanded, breathing deeply.

Maggie gasped as she took her first good look at the elderly man emerging from the trees. Always immaculate in appearance, Claude's hair stood up in spikes from his head like a hedgehog, and his black broadcloth jacket was shredded from shoulder to hip.

"What on earth happened to you?" Maggie cried.

Connor was more concerned about the lethal weapon in the man's hand. "Put that sword away, Claude. There are no dangers in these woods."

"Yes, there are," Maggie said. "You told me yourself. Remember the beasts hiding behind the trees?"

"I am living proof of those dangers." Claude resheathed his sword with dramatic flair. "I fought myself with one of the kidnappers less than an hour ago. I left his body down by the stream and went immediately to the house where I was told you had taken my mistress into the woods."

Connor tried to make sense of this. The power of his desire for Maggie had left him disoriented. "Left his body? Left *whose* body?"

"He just told you," Maggie said, shivering lightly. "He's killed one of the kidnappers. Oh, what a relief. Now all we have to do is find your sister."

Connor sagged back against the tree. Between Maggie and his family, he'd be lucky if he lived to see fifty. "Oh, God. How do you know it was a kidnapper? It couldn't have been. Oh, my God. You know what he's done, don't you? He's gone and killed one of my neighbors."

"Are you all right, sir?" Claude asked, shuffling through the leaves to examine Connor. "You're looking a bit green in the gills."

"I think he's going to faint," Maggie said in concern. "For a man who works with murderers, he seems to have a sensitive nature. You've given him a shock."

Connor looked insulted. "I have never fainted in my life."

"Don't fight it, sir." Claude gave him a consoling pat on the shoulder. "It's nothing to be ashamed of. Perhaps you should sit down on this stump."

"Yes, sit down, my lord." Maggie was shoving with all her might to force him down into a sitting position. Then Claude started to help her, prodding Connor in the chest.

This irritated Connor so much that he swatted at them in self-defense. "Leave me alone. I'm not sitting down."

"Sometimes you do not know what's good for you," Maggie said in a slow, deliberate voice as if he were incapable of understanding normal speech. "You've had a shock. Sit down, stop behaving like a baby, and put your head between your legs."

Naturally, there was no body.

Well, what had Connor expected? Maggie believed Claude's story because she was high-strung and traumatized from witnessing Sheena's abduction. Claude believed his own story because he was senile, unable to see properly, and lived in a bygone time of swordplay and chivalry. For all Connor knew, the old fool had probably attacked a tree. After all, he'd mistaken a scarecrow for a man himself. Imagination played nasty tricks on the mind.

"But I left his body right here after I ran him through the shoulder, sir," Claude said in confusion.

"Perhaps it happened at another stream," Maggie said gently.

"It happened here." Claude was adamant, poking the tip of his sword into the turf where Connor, on his hands and knees, sifted through soggy loam and leaves for the missing corpse.

"Put that blade away, Claude, before you hurt someone," he said sharply.

"He's already killed someone," Maggie reminded him, peering through her fingers over Connor's shoulder as if she were afraid of a grim discovery.

"I suppose it's possible that I only wounded him," Claude conceded reluctantly after a long hesitation.

Connor stood and dusted himself off. "It's possible that you imagined the whole incident."

"He called me by name, sir," Claude said thoughtfully. "He asked me where Lady Marguerite was, and that was when I decided that enough was enough and I ran him through."

Connor felt compelled to humor the old fellow if only for Maggie's benefit. "Did he put up a fight?"

Claude brightened. "Oh, yes, sir. He was an excellent swordsman—of the Angelo school. We parried for quite some time, and then I think I tired him out. He executed his engagements with admirable style."

Connor pursed his lips, trying to picture this.

"He tore Claude's clothes," Maggie said. "You cannot deny the physical evidence of that."

Claude gave a faint smile. "Actually, I tore my jacket when the coachman drove the apple cart into a hedgerow. The kidnapper did not hurt me. I was too swift for him." He snatched a branch from the ground and lunged, his elbow slightly flexed. *"En garde!"*

Connor shook his head. He could see that nothing he said would dissuade Maggie and Claude from believing the worst. Perhaps he should just pretend to go along with them. After all, he knew now that Sheena was alive, if still missing, and if he wanted to win Maggie's favor, which he did badly, it was clear he'd have to be nice to Claude. It couldn't hurt.

"Good work, Claude." He gave a manly nod of approval, then turned away. "It's reassuring to know that you can protect your mistress when I am not around."

"Thank you, sir," Claude said gravely to Connor's back. "I only wish I could say the same of you."

Connor continued as if he hadn't felt this barb. "And since you have handled the matter so efficiently, without spilling a drop of blood, we can all sleep soundly in our beds tonight."

Maggie and Claude exchanged troubled glances.

"But obviously I did not kill him, sir," Claude said slowly. "Unless of course I *did* kill him, and his cohorts sneaked back to carry his body away. I did not consider that possibility."

"His cohorts?" Connor glanced back, a cynical smile twitching at the corners of his lips.

Maggie did not share his amusement. "You're going to have to find him. A wounded madman is the most dangerous sort."

Connor thought she was carrying her loyalty too far. "I don't even know what he looks like."

"Neither do I," Claude confessed. "He was darkly cloaked, and masked. Of course, he is mortally injured now. That should make him easier to identify."

Maggie regarded Connor with unwavering confidence. "Find him, my lord. Find him before it's too late."

Connor released a loud sigh. If he hadn't been interrupted, he might be in heaven this very moment, alone, and naked with her in the shepherd's hut by the loch. Well, so much for sexual fantasy. She and Claude kept glancing around as if they expected a band of armed brigands to assault them at any second. It probably had something to do with Maggie's past. Her entire world had been destroyed in a single evening. She had good reason to look over her shoulder. She'd lost her home, her family, her security.

He understood this. It was a secret pain they shared, but in his case losing his parents had forced him to develop a tough outer shell. Maggie's strength lay within herself, an emotional fortitude he envied. It had enabled her to survive. But she was still fragile. And she still needed a protector.

They needed each other. This woman was what had been missing from his life.

He threw up his hands, relenting. "Oh, fine. I'll look for the wounded man." Not that he thought there was such a thing, although God forbid, the possibility still existed that Claude had attacked a poacher or one of Connor's neighbors. "But first I want to take Maggie back to the house."

He didn't really. A single-minded male, he still had his evil heart set on the bothy, although Maggie didn't look like she would succumb to his seductive powers right now. It was a damn shame. Being with her was the only thing that would put him in a good mood.

He stalked off, resigned to his sacrifice. He was obviously beyond help, chasing after a nonexistent villain to please a fanciful old man and his enchanting mistress. He felt like a beast on a long rope.

Maggie waited a few moments, then turned to Claude in concern. "This whole thing has upset him more than he'll allow to show. He's the type who has too much pride to admit he's afraid."

"He didn't look at all himself," Claude agreed.

"Perhaps you should follow him, just to make sure he doesn't walk into an ambush."

"Or stumble upon the wounded man."

"Go with him, Claude. He's strong as an ox, but he did

look pale when you told him about the swordfight. Sometimes I think he doesn't have a true grasp on reality. He spends so much energy taking care of others, he doesn't take care of himself. He seems to think he's invulnerable."

"I will protect him, my lady."

"I know you will."

Chapter

28

Connor was worn out when he finally returned to the house. He had hiked over hills and sloughed through streams scouring every inch of his estate, the surrounding woods, and unmarked roads that led into the Highland wilds for the wounded man. He probably wouldn't have had the strength to confront him if he'd found him. Still, the instant he saw Maggie hurrying down the hall, he felt a jolt of energy go through him like an electrical charge.

She was the reason he'd spent five hours humoring a doddering old butler and pretending to look for a dead body that had never been alive in the first place. He had already forgiven her, though. He grinned inwardly at the thought of how she could repay him.

"Thank heavens you've come home unharmed, my lord." She hugged him as if he'd just returned from the Crusades. "Did you find anything?"

They stood in a candlelit recess of the narrow hallway. He turned deliberately, aware he was trapping her against the wall. She felt small and defenseless. He felt aroused and uninhibited, remembering the delicious warmth of her body, how easily she had responded to his touch.

"Do you think the wounded man is lying in wait somewhere?" she whispered anxiously. "Do you think he'd dare break into the house?"

"We can't be sure, lass, but you'd better not leave my side just in case. It might even be a good idea if you slept in my room tonight."

Maggie pressed her shoulders to the wall, trying not to smile. "That sounds like a good idea."

"Doesn't it though?"

He liked the way her eyes caught the candlelight, reminding him of the sun reflected in the sea. He liked her hair loose and tangled in wild curls over her shoulders because she looked as he imagined she would look after a night of hard loving in his bed. He slid his arm around her waist, breathing in her fragrance, dragging her against him to kiss—

"I hear people in the drawing room," he said, lifting his head abruptly. "Why do I hear people?"

Maggie made an effort to break away from him. "I had to alert the neighbors of the danger of a wounded man in the area."

"Why did you do that, Maggie?"

"Because— Are we on a first-name basis now, my lord?"

"Yes, I think we are. We crossed a line today in the woods, and there's no going back. I haven't been able to stop thinking about you."

"I'm touched to hear you say that, Connor, especially when I know you had more important things on your mind like finding the—"

He silenced her with a slow, sensual kiss. Maggie melted against him as his tongue penetrated her mouth, as he pressed her against the wall, molding their bodies together. He made her so light-headed, she would have collapsed if he hadn't held her upright. His presence overpowered her.

"Tell my neighbors to go away," he said in a hoarse whisper. "Tell them the woods are safe again. I'll meet you upstairs in my room in a few minutes. We can sit in front of the fire with a bottle of—well, I don't have any champagne, but there's wine."

Maggie closed her eyes as he buried his face in her neck, sighing with pleasure. "I'd like that too, my lord—*Connor,* but it's rather impolite in view of the fact they were about to launch a search party to find you."

"My neighbors hate me." He moved his mouth down her throat, leaving a trail of little love bites. "Why would they want to help me?"

"I've spent almost five hours convincing them you aren't as bad as you seem." Swallowing a groan, she gave him a nudge toward the drawing room. "It's up to you to prove I'm not a liar."

Connor avoided his neighbors whenever possible. He knew they hated him. They resented him because he lived in Edinburgh most of the year, and when he did return, he either went hunting or secluded himself with a woman. They didn't really understand what he did for a living, or the importance of his position, but they had always been afraid that some of the criminals he'd prosecuted would descend on their Highland haven to cause trouble.

The threat of a stranger in the woods had confirmed their worst fears. Connor drew danger to him wherever he went.

He strode into the room, determined to send them all packing; he had other more enjoyable plans for the evening. The duchess and her hounds had taken over the sofa. Captain Balgonie, a retired soldier, was warming his behind at the fire, and Sir Angus McGee, a rotund and well-to-do sheep farmer was dozing in a wing chair, tiny snores escaping him. Connor shook his head. It was amazing that Maggie had kept them from one another's throats for almost five hours. They didn't just hate him. They hated each other too.

He took off his coat and poured himself a glass of whisky from the sideboard. His long golden hair fell around his shoulders. The firelight accentuated the deep hollows of his face. He looked more like a pagan warlord than a civilized Highland laird. Indeed, he didn't feel the least bit hospitable. "I'm sorry you were dragged from the comfort of your homes. It was apparently a false alarm." He downed the whisky in one swallow, trying to decide which of his wines Maggie would prefer. "You can all go home now," he said bluntly.

The duchess pushed a dog off her lap. Another immediately took its place. "Don't tell me you failed to find the wounded man, Buchanan."

"The wounded man is a figment of Claude's imagination," Connor said very quietly, just in case Maggie was outside listening.

"We should have gone after him ourselves," Captain Balgonie said. "Probably too late now."

Sir Angus opened his eyes in annoyance. "We decided against looking ourselves. You'd remember if you didn't drink as much. We voted to stay here to protect Lady Maggie."

Connor was pouring another whisky when Maggie slipped into the room. Heat flooded his body as she brushed past him. He clenched his jaw to control the urge to grab her. He wanted these people out of his house. More precisely, he wanted this woman in his bed. A knot of desire tightened his throat, deepening his voice as he spoke.

"I am perfectly capable of protecting Miss Saunders should the need arise."

Maggie sent him a pleased glance.

Sir Angus scowled at Connor, apparently unconvinced of this. He grew heavier every year, a short oval-shaped man with skinny legs and buckled shoes who reminded Connor of Humpty-Dumpty as he sat perched on the edge of the chair. "How could you protect her if you're prone to fainting at the mere mention of bloodshed? I must say I was surprised when Lady Maggie told us how sensitive you were."

Connor almost choked. The look he threw Maggie as she hurried over to slap him on the back was black enough to wither an evergreen.

"Some of my best men passed out on the battlefield. A man fainting isn't anything to be ashamed of," Captain Balgonie said.

The duchess snorted. "Yes, it is. It's a damn disgrace. Men were men in my day. Maggie's father was the heart of valor, wasn't he, my dear?"

"Yes, your grace," Maggie said dutifully.

Connor put down his glass. "I'm sorry you were all inconvenienced, but you must be eager to return to your own homes. I'll ring for Dougie to show you out. Sleep well."

Maggie made a face at him. "That isn't polite," she whispered behind her hand.

"I don't care. Stop telling people I'm a fainter. The whole

time I was in the woods, Claude kept asking me if he should return to the house for smelling salts." He walked toward her, his eyes glittering with unholy determination. "Would you like me to embarrass *you* in front of everyone?"

Maggie swallowed nervously, slipping behind the unoccupied wing chair as if a piece of furniture could save her from the rugged Highlander who was slowly stalking her with seduction in his eyes. The devil would disgrace them both.

"Stop it, Connor," she whispered. "There are people in the room."

He grinned, advancing on the chair. "If you don't get rid of them," he mouthed, "I am going to be a very bad boy."

"I-I'm afraid there's been a misunderstanding," Maggie stammered, terrified he would indeed carry out his threat. "His lordship doesn't faint at the mention of bloodshed. In fact, he has only come close to fainting once in my presence, and that was when he shot a scarecrow into pieces."

"That's even worse," the duchess exclaimed. "How would he react if he had to shoot a real man?"

"He thought it was a real man at first," Maggie said, smiling despite herself at the memory. "And he tore off his coat, shouted like a Viking, and went berserk in my defense. I've never seen anything quite like it."

No one said a word. Maggie thought they were probably too impressed to comment. Connor looked like he wanted to disappear into the woodwork. "We've held you here long enough," she added tactfully. "Please don't let me keep you from your beds another minute."

Connor seized the advantage and took her by the wrist, propelling her to the door. "The servants will be glad to accompany anyone who is afraid to ride alone. You will excuse us now. Miss Saunders has offered to serve as my secretary for the evening to help me catch up on my work. All those depositions, you know."

Maggie stared up at him. "I have?"

"Yes, you have." He stroked the inside of her wrist with his thumb. "Our after-supper appointment? The court is counting on your cooperation."

"I'm afraid there isn't going to be any supper," she said after an awkward hesitation. "The servants won't be seeing anyone home either. You see, your male and female staff are in a state of civil war. Neither sex will lift a finger to help the other. The men won't bring the coals to the cellar so the women won't cook. The women won't cook so the men claim they don't have the energy to bring up the coals."

"Good God," Connor said.

"I am working on the problem," Maggie continued, "but I must say you need to take a firmer stand. You're the one they're afraid of."

Connor's brows drew into a frown. "I'll tell you what stand I'm going to take. I'm going to sack the whole aggravating lot of them."

"That is a rather drastic measure," Maggie said. "It shows little understanding of human nature."

A muscle tightened in Connor's jaw. "My capacity for understanding human nature has reached its limit. So has my attraction to you. Are you going to meet me later tonight or do I have to get forceful about the situation?"

Maggie pretended to ponder the matter, wondering exactly how forceful he intended to be. "I suppose I'll have to discuss the matter with Claude first."

"With—you're going to discuss your private life with a butler?"

Maggie turned away before giving him an explanation. A commotion had broken out among the guests. The duchess and Captain Balgonie were bent over Sir Angus's chair, making distressed clucking noises like two oversized chickens. Sir Angus was grimacing as if he'd been mortally wounded.

"Now what is it?" Connor said in an aggrieved undertone.

Maggie moved away from him. "I think Angus has aggravated his lumbago. His doctor warned him this would happen if he got up too quickly. You shouldn't have insisted he leave, my lord."

She hurried over to see if she could help, Connor following with reluctance. "What happened, Angus?" she asked in concern.

"I hurt my back when I tried to get up." Angus grimaced for effect. "These overstuffed chairs weren't made for a man's physique."

"It's not the chairs, Angus," the duchess said unsympathetically. "It's your body. You're built like a damn egg."

"Let me help you up," Connor said, elbowing his way forward.

"No. No. Nooo." Angus let out a howl of agony and shrank deeper into the chair, holding out his hand in warning. "Don't anyone touch me. I can't bear it. The pain makes me wild."

Connor frowned. "You can't sit in this chair all night, Angus."

"I know how to handle this," Maggie said confidently. "He needs a hug."

Angus raised his head, regarding her with interest.

"I'll need your help, my lord." She motioned to Connor, positioning herself behind the armchair. "Put your arms around him. As if you were going to give him a great big hug."

Connor's frown deepened into a full-fledged scowl. "I don't want to put my arms around him."

"I don't want you to either," Angus retorted. "I thought Lady Marguerite was going to put her arms around me. Having your big hairy arms around me is another matter."

"I'll help." The duchess stationed herself at the other side of the chair. "One good heave should get the egg on his feet."

"Perhaps we shouldn't move him at all," Captain Balgonie said, standing in the background. "You might end up doing him a permanent injury."

"Nonsense," Maggie said briskly. "Come, my lord. Let's get him out of this chair."

They did, Maggie supervising as Angus dangled like a rag doll between the duchess and Connor. "Now you must embrace him," she instructed Connor, demonstrating on a startled Captain Balgonie. "Then you lift like this, and give him an enormous squeeze, as if you were two friendly bears who meet in the forest."

Balgonie grinned from ear to ear, hugging her back without prompting. Connor scoffed in naked contempt. "I am not hugging another man. Let the captain do it."

"The captain doesn't possess your brute strength," Maggie said quietly. "And if you don't, it may be weeks before Angus can be safely moved."

Angus's round face brightened. "I don't mind staying here

if it comes to it. My daughter can move in to take care of me. You remember her, Buchanan. Louise with the mean streak. She used to chase you through the woods with a whip. Knocked out her front teeth when she ran into a tree."

Connor hugged him. Angus's spine gave a loud crack like lightning, and for a moment he swayed as if he might swoon. Then a look of utter bliss spread across his face. He straightened. He stretched and tested his back, turning this way and that.

"Why, it's better. I'm cured. You are amazing, my dear," he said to Maggie, totally underplaying Connor's part in the procedure. "That's the first time anybody has ever been able to give me such immediate relief. Where did you learn this invaluable skill?"

Captain Balgonie nodded approvingly. "Of all the chits you've paraded in and out of this house, Buchanan, she's the only one worth a walk to the altar."

Maggie looked up slowly. "The chits, eh?"

"It's high time you got married," the duchess said in agreement. "It's a damn disgrace that a man your age is still playing peekaboo in the bushes with young girls."

"I do not play peekaboo in the bushes," Connor said hotly.

"Of course," the duchess continued, "what a man does with his wife after they're married is nobody's business."

Maggie arched her aristocratic brow. Her voice was composed. "Be that as it may, your grace, I'm afraid that a marriage between his lordship and myself is out of the question. My family would never have approved."

"That's him coming now, Mrs. Urquhart," Maggie whispered. "What did I tell you? Men are the most predictable creatures. His pride has been hurt. It needs building up. Hide before he spots you. You'll see how it's done."

"His lordship never seemed to me to need building up, my lady." The housekeeper glanced uneasily as the heavy footsteps stopped outside the bedroom door. "He'll be furious if he catches me eavesdropping."

"Then we won't let him catch you." Maggie sprang up from her desk and pushed the woman behind a silk-paneled dressing screen. "Don't move a muscle."

"Oh, dear." Mrs. Urquhart touched her cheeks. "I'm going all hot. This is dangerous."

"Nonsense. If you want to regain control of your marriage, not to mention this household, you must be able to bring the men involved to their senses." Maggie returned to the desk, carefully drawing her dressing robe together at the throat. "If there was one thing I learned in Heaven's Court besides swearing, it was how to bring a man to his senses. Nobody could calm the Chief like me when he was on one of his rampages."

She sat at the walnut writing desk, illuminated like a medieval figure etched in stained-glass by a soft circle of candlelight. Her unbound hair cascaded to her hips. Her feet were bare, toes tapping the polished wooden floor. She paused, pen in hand, as she heard Connor enter the room. A smile flitted across her face. The beast had taken the bait.

She didn't need to glance around to ascertain it was him. She knew the feel of his presence, the dark, exciting energy by heart. Her body, pulses, and temperature knew it too, and reacted accordingly.

"You left before you explained yourself," he said curtly.

She pressed the pen to her lips. "Oh, I'm sorry. You were wondering about the technique for the back. I learned it from a Swedish physician Papa employed to strengthen Robert's spine. Actually, I learned the procedure from Robert. He used to experiment on me, the wretch, and some days—"

Connor cut her short. "I meant you did not explain why a marriage between us is out of the question, and you know it."

He moved deliberately between her and the candle sconce on the wall, blocking her light with his broad frame. Maggie stared down at the letter on her desk. The words were blurred, overshadowed by the massively built figure who hovered over her.

"I took your answer to the duchess as an insult," he said, managing to sound hurt and intimidating at the same time.

She began to write again. "Well, I didn't mean to hurt your feelings. However, to state the obvious, I am the daughter of a duke, and you are only the public prosecutor."

She could feel the indignation rising off Connor like steam. She bit the edge of her lip to stifle a chuckle. "I am not an 'only' anything," he said. "I have just been appointed Lord Advocate of Scotland, damn it."

"Congratulations, my lord."

"Quite a few women consider me a prize catch."

"Those would be the chits?" Maggie murmured, her expression impassive.

"I'm not responsible for the asinine remarks of my neighbors."

"But you are responsible for the parade of aforesaid chits and playing peekaboo in the bushes, aren't you?" Maggie asked matter-of-factly, not interrupting her writing.

Connor smirked and sat down on the edge of the desk, making it impossible for her to see. She nudged his heavy thigh with her elbow. He did not give an inch. A slab of marble sat beside her, commanding her attention. This man would not be moved.

"The chits are neither here not there," he said, leaning over her with an infuriating smile. "There's no reason for you to be jealous of them."

"Jealous? Me? What an imagination. What conceit." She made a show of trying to hold her letter up to the light to re-read it, but after a while it became impossible to even pretend. "Is it necessary for you to perch on my desk like a hawk?" she said in annoyance. "I find it difficult to concentrate in your presence."

"Good. I have the same problem around you."

She started to lean to the side to study her letter, then gasped as he plucked it out of her hand and flicked it negligently into the air. "Do control yourself, my lord."

"I am tired of controlling myself," he said. "I've been controlling myself ever since I met you."

"You certainly didn't in the woods today."

"You have no idea how I controlled myself." His face looked fierce and chiseled in shadow. His silhouette appeared enormous and menacing against the wall. He lowered his head to hers. "We didn't finish what we started."

"The courtship business again," Maggie said, frowning. "This is all very sudden."

"What do you mean it's sudden?" he said in amazement. "I haven't been able to keep my hands off you since we met."

"So I've noticed," Maggie murmured.

Connor brushed a strand of hair off her shoulder. "You didn't seem to mind."

"I can't argue that," she said, holding back a smile.

He leaned forward on his elbow, closing the space between them. Maggie suppressed a shudder, breathing in his evocative scent—musk, male, and wood smoke. "You do care for me," he said. "I know it. And you're a woman—"

"I can't argue that either."

"—and I want you to be mine."

She rose slowly from the desk, feeling a tingle of anticipation as her breasts brushed his shoulder. His eyes glittered with irony as he watched her. Maggie reminded herself that she was supposed to be setting an example for Mrs. Urquhart on the fine art of male-female negotiations.

"What exactly are your intentions toward me?" she asked somberly.

His white teeth flashed in a wolfish grin. "I usually follow my instincts in these matters, lass. But since you've demanded a plan of attack, I suppose I'd start by kissing your adorable mouth. Then, while you were swooning from my kiss, I'd untie your robe—"

She glanced in alarm at the dressing screen, praying that the prudish housekeeper wouldn't drop into a dead faint. "I was referring to the future," she said with starch in her voice.

"I—hell, I don't know."

She sighed. "I see."

"You've got me so turned around, I don't know night from day anymore." He forced her chin up with his big knuckles. "Let's follow our instincts, lass. This is not a usual situation with rules to follow."

Maggie curled her fingers into fists. She sensed he was going to kiss her. "It most certainly is not," she said.

"I am going to make love to you all night long," he announced unexpectedly.

There was an almost inaudible squeal from behind the dressing screen. Connor seemed not to notice it, but Maggie dropped her pen and backed away from him, hitting the desk with her hip. Connor grasped her by the forearms before she could collapse into the chair.

He pulled her up into his arms and kissed her deeply. Then he brought his hands down her shoulders, sculpting her body through the thin silk of her dressing robe. He knew exactly what he was doing. She felt his palms grazing her breasts, circling the tender peaks until she responded. Arousal bubbled in her veins. Her legs were folding under her like the sticks of a fan.

His calculated aggression brought out something daring inside her, a longing that matched the dark hunger in his eyes. She suppressed a groan and leaned into him. Her reaction wasn't part of her strategy for awakening his more reasonable side. In fact, it seemed that instead of bringing him to his senses she had surrendered control of her own.

Connor swallowed with difficulty, pressing his forehead to hers. "You're warmhearted and wonderful. You make me look forward to the next day instead of dreading it. This house was a tomb before I brought you here. I was dying inside until you came along."

He sat down heavily in the chair, drawing her down into his lap. "Now I've embarrassed myself completely, but it's the truth. I've never met anyone like you, Maggie."

She rested her face against his shoulder, whispering mischievously, "Not even among the chits?"

He chuckled, cupping the curve of her bottom in his big hands. "Not one of the chits could hold a candle to you," he said with a sigh. "I think I'm in very serious trouble."

Maggie raised her face to his, whispering, "I think we both are."

His conscience tried to rear its head, but his desire for her overpowered it. He understood he had sworn to protect her, and God knew seducing her could hardly be considered a government duty, but somewhere between Edinburgh and the Highlands, she had stolen more than a confession from him. She had stolen his unsuspecting heart.

He was flooded, all at once, with a disconcerting wave of affection and raw arousal for the woman who had brought such turmoil into his life. His little tapestry virgin. He ran his hand up her hip to her inner thigh, feeling her muscles tremble at his touch. He loved how she responded to him. He had a feeling that he wouldn't have to teach her how to reciprocate in bed. She was as natural a temptress as Eve, eager and passionate.

"Let's lie down together," he whispered, tugging the robe off her shoulder.

She yanked it back up, horrified at the thought of the housekeeper witnessing this. "But I'm not tired."

"Neither am I." He blew lightly in her ear and pulled her against him until her robe rode up to her hips. "I'll rub your back. My hands are very strong."

"Why don't we play a nice game of . . . of chess instead?" she suggested brightly.

"Chess? In bed? Naked?" He sat forward and began to unbutton his shirt, grinning at the thought. "Well, that will be a first for me, but I like it. Very original. Intellectually stimulating and sexual at the same time. What a naughty imagination you have, lass."

Maggie blushed and wriggled backward onto her feet. "I do not have a chessboard, and I've never played chess naked, either."

"What about whist?"

"Oh, honestly, my lord. I wish you wouldn't say such things in front of people."

"In front of people. Maggie, you come out with the silliest things." His eyes sparkled with gentle mockery. He threw his shirt over his shoulder. "I can't very well play chess naked with myself, can I?"

"It is not an endeavor I care to discuss," she said stiffly. "However, there's something else I've been meaning to talk to you about."

"Does it involve taking our clothes off?"

She stared at his muscular torso, momentarily distracted by the sight. "It most certainly does not."

"Go ahead, lass," he said good-naturedly. "I'm listening."

She backed away from him, stealing a glance at the dressing screen.

Did she want to undress in private? Connor wondered, excited by her modesty. It occurred to him that she was acting a little strangely, but then she was a virgin, for all of her exposure to the criminal element. He warned himself not to spoil her first experience with his impatience.

"Well," he said, shrugging his wide shoulders. "I'm all ears."

She forced her gaze to his face. "We had a statue in the château pleasure garden that looked exactly like you. It was of some Greek god carrying a young woman away in a chariot."

Connor glanced over at the dressing screen. "How interesting," he said politely.

"In fact, we had several statues," Maggie continued, her face softening as it did whenever she discussed her family. "The gardeners always complained about having to trim around them. One day Robert took it into his head to cover all their privy parts in gilt paint. He—"

"Excuse me. Whose parts are we painting?"

"The statues." Maggie paused, frowning at the interruption. "Robert thought they were indecent. He thought that since Papa was away so often on private business—actually, it was espionage—he should protect the family."

Connor sprawled back in the chair. "Robert—your brother?"

"Yes, he was such an awful prude. The funny thing was that the gilt paint drew your eye right to the very spot he meant to hide. The statues were nude, you see."

"Yes, I gathered that."

"Well."

Silence then as Maggie struggled with the emotions she had evoked.

Connor studied her, aching with lust, yet surprisingly touched by the images she had conjured. He could see her childhood, could sense her sorrow. He could see the young girl she had been, playing on the grounds of a story-book château. Innocent. Secure. Sheltered until her world had been shattered. He wondered about her nightmares. What had she witnessed? What horror had her young mind repressed?

"What happened to Robert?" he asked after a moment.

"I don't know." Her anguish was palpable. "That was what I wanted to talk to you about."

Connor swung around in the chair. The dressing screen had moved. He was sure of it. "The dressing screen moved," he said quietly.

DARING

"Oh." Maggie bit her lip. "The dog is probably hiding. You know how playful Daphne is. Will you help me?"

He thought he saw a tear tremble in her lashes. The sadness of that single teardrop tore him apart. Seducing her in her current mood was not looking like a good prospect. Besides, this was more important, an intimacy he had not anticipated or planned.

"What do you want me to do?" he said softly.

"Use your legal talents to help me find Robert. You must have connections all over Europe."

He couldn't refuse her. He couldn't stand the pain in her eyes. "I'll do everything I can. How long ago did you leave?"

"Ten years."

Ten years. By his calculation she would have been only thirteen at the time. The same age as when he'd lost his parents. A woman-child alone in a frightening world. At least he'd been left his sisters, although it was small consolation in light of the fact they had survived to make his life miserable.

"I have several friends in France."

"He isn't in France," she said quietly. "I've learned that much."

He braced his elbows on his knees, thinking. "We'll find him," he promised her. "I'll do everything—"

She rushed forward before he could finish, flinging her arms around his neck. "You're not at all the beast everyone believes you to be," she whispered fiercely.

"Don't be so sure of that, lass." He kissed her, hard and deep, plundering the sweetness of her mouth, running his hands over her little body until her breath came in uneven gasps.

"Do you really think you can find him, Connor?"

No, he didn't, but if this was a sampling of her gratitude for small favors, he was damn well going to try.

"I can't do anything about finding your brother tonight." He traced his forefinger down the slope of her breast, pleased when her nipple puckered in response. His own body shuddered in anticipation. "Let's start on it in the morning, all right?"

He wanted for her to give him permission to resume his

love-play. If she'd been anyone else, they would have been cavorting in bed an hour ago. But Maggie only blinked as if he had sprinkled ice water in her face. She rolled off the chair and retreated to the desk to rifle through a small rosewood box.

Connor clenched the sides of his chair to keep from physically assaulting her. "What are you doing, Maggie?" His skin burned where the imprint of her body lingered like a brand, heating his blood.

The candlelight cast her into an alluring silhouette, thighs, hips, breasts. He rubbed his face with both hands. She didn't hear him, preoccupied with the clutter on her desk. She shoved back the curly black hair that fell into her face.

"I don't want to make love our first time in this room," he said, staring around as if seeing it for the first time. "My bed is more comfortable. It's bigger too. I can't fit my legs into this one."

"Of course you can't," she murmured, obviously not listening. "Aunt Flora kept all our family papers for me. Secret documents, she called them. Spies and secrets—that was my father's life. Perhaps you can make sense of them. You're an intelligent man, even if you don't always act it. Here."

She waved a wad of yellowed correspondence in his direction. Feeling undignified in his half-nakedness and unrequited lust, he stood and strode forward to take them. "Thank you," he said dryly.

Her face was anxious. "I hope they help. Let me know if you have trouble with the translations."

His mouth flattened at the thought of the lonely night ahead. "This is not what I had in mind."

She picked up his shirt from the floor and hung it over his arm. "I'm sure you're eager to start. Would you like Mrs. Urquhart to bring you up a pot of tea and oatcakes? Mental work is such a strain, isn't it? Don't stay up too late."

"I don't need tea," he said. "I want you. Naked and helpless beneath me. I doubt I'll be able to get much sleep after practically disrobing and panting at your feet like a—"

The dressing-screen shook. Connor stared at it in suspicion. Maggie, noticing the direction of his gaze, took his arm to steer him to the door.

"I don't know how I'll ever repay you for this," she said, nudging him to walk.

"Well, I do. I want to bed you."

"You have such an earthy sense of humor, my lord."

He stared over her head at the screen. "You're keeping something else a secret, aren't you? Do you have a man hiding back there?"

"A man? Where would I find a man? She forced all six-feet-three inches of him out into the hall, breathless with the effort. "And if I had one, why would I hide him behind the screen? I am offended."

"And I'm frustrated. I—"

She closed the door with gentle finality, her strained smile the last image in Connor's mind before he turned to see Dougie and three other male servants staring agog at him from the hall. He grunted; he was in no mood to explain why he was standing bare-chested in the dark and having a discussion with himself about his sexual frustration.

"Why are the lot of you skulking about at this hour?" he demanded.

Dougie whipped out his handkerchief and began polishing the life out of the banister. The two other men hastened to straighten the family portraits on the wall. "I'm dusting, sir," Dougie said in a martyred voice. "No one else in this house will do it. The women won't lift a finger."

Men dusting at midnight.

Connor walked sedately to his room, pretending he was not naked to the waist. No one said a word. The Emperor in his new clothes. The most powerful man in Scotland. Lord save him, what a joke. The most helpless was a more apt title. Helpless and hopelessly besotted.

Maggie plopped down in the chair with a weak sigh of relief. "You can come out now, Mrs. Urquhart. He's gone."

The housekeeper crept toward the chair like a mouse after the cat had disappeared. "That was brilliantly done, my lady. You had me all a-quiver with the suspense. I wasn't sure which of you would win in the end."

"Neither was I." Maggie closed her eyes. "I'm ashamed to admit that I almost lost control of the situation several times."

"That would have been during the silences."

"It must have embarrassed you horribly."

"Not really," Mrs. Urquhart said. "You become accustomed to that sort of thing when his lordship visits."

Maggie lifted her head. "You must be talking about the chits again. Well, I trust there will be no more of that nonsense in this house."

"Oh, I shouldn't think so," Mrs. Urquhart agreed. "His lordship never treated the chits the way he treats you. He never treated Mrs. Macmillan like any one of the chits either."

Maggie heaved another sigh. "I can't see Ardath allowing a situation to get out of control, which brings us back to the problem of you and your husband, and the example I meant to set tonight. A woman must use subtle tactics to prove a point. She must be alluring and aloof at the same time. She mustn't give away everything at once."

The housekeeper looked doubtful. "But I've been married to Dougie for months. There isna much left to give, in the biblical sense, I mean."

"Then you'll have to create a little mystery, a little conflict."

Mrs. Urquhart lowered her voice. "Is that what you've done?"

"There's been enough mystery and conflict in my life for ten women," Maggie admitted sadly.

"If I may be so bold, my lady, may I ask you another personal question?"

"Under the circumstances, it would not be inappropriate."

Mrs. Urquhart whispered, "Are you in love with his lordship?"

Maggie's lips slanted into a wistful smile. "Undoubtedly. But things between us are in a bit of a muddle, what with him trying to find his sister, then protect and seduce me at the same time. Not to mention the difference in our backgrounds. My family would consider that I was marrying down."

"But he is the Lord Advocate."

"It is a point in his favor."

"He's a very determined man," Mrs. Urquhart said, looking worried. "I feel an obligation to warn you. I've never known a woman to refuse him."

"It does seem that I am resisting the inevitable, doesn't it?"

Mrs. Urquhart shook her head. "I must say that once he removed his shirt, I never thought he'd leave this room without insisting he have his way with you."

Maggie shivered, trying not to imagine what "having his way" entailed—and what she had missed. "I experienced a few moments of intense anxiety myself." She had experienced intense longing too, but the housekeeper didn't need to know that.

"I can't imagine how anyone so young has garnered this much experience in relations with the opposite sex. You have obviously learned a lot living with the criminals."

"None of the criminals I dealt with were anything like his lordship," Maggie said, staring worriedly at the door. "I hope to heaven I haven't overestimated my abilities."

Chapter 29

Rebecca swung from the hearth and stared through the open door of her cottage, the fine hairs on her nape lifting. She put down the horn spoon she had been stirring her gruel with, a nightly treat for her nocturnal friends, the hedgehogs. A shadow had fallen across the sunken stone doorstep.

The shadow was too large to be one of the animals who came to her for food and shelter. At one o'clock in the morning, it was late for a friend to visit.

Her young deerhound, Ares, growled deep in his throat, rising from her left side. The hare Rebecca had released from a trap with the injured hind leg pressed back deeper in its pine hutch under the sink. The raven with the broken wing stirred in its cage.

"Who is it?" she asked in a voice that betrayed no fear. "If you are hurt, please come inside."

It wouldn't have been the first time that a stranger had taken refuge in her cottage, a servant unexpectedly discharged from her position, a homeless Highlander, or simply a lonely traveler who'd heard of Rebecca's unconditional hospitality and healing skill.

She hurried to the door. She was more afraid she'd scare

off the poor soul than that he was some kidnapper skulking about in her beloved woods. She couldn't imagine anyone abducting Sheena. The girl was spirited enough to take on a shipload of pirates single-handedly and emerge from the encounter unscathed.

"I don't think you're taking this at all seriously," Connor had scolded Rebecca as they'd walked through the woods together. "You're far too easy a target, a defenseless woman living by herself."

Connor. Her big brother, protector, friend, and all-around pain in the neck. Rebecca was secretly proud of him. She still suffered a shock of delight every time she saw him, that handsome, strapping Viking of a man who had guided her clumsily through puberty and her first painful romance. Connor, an adolescent himself at the time, had dispensed advice with an ignorance that made her burst into giggles to this day. She didn't know how either of them had survived.

"If a boy sticks his tongue in your mouth, give him a good kick in the privates."

"Stay away from the parson's son, Rebecca. He had his hand down his trews during the sermon."

He had fought for his sisters. He had bullied them, bored them to tears with his lectures. He had changed Sheena's nappies, and now that ungrateful girl had repaid him by getting herself abducted. In Rebecca's mind there was no doubt that Sheena had brought this evil thing upon herself, either because of her own recklessness or by associating with the wrong people.

Rebecca could have throttled her. Not only had Sheena embarrassed Connor by getting herself abducted, she was now threatening Rebecca's happiness. In typical fashion, Connor was using the kidnapping as an excuse to force Rebecca back into the city where he could keep her under his thumb.

And, where, like a transplanted wildflower, she would promptly die.

"You won't die in the city," Connor had said in exasperation. "What a preposterous notion. You need a husband."

"I'm never getting married, Connor. Never. You control the country. You may not control my life."

He couldn't understand this. Her unconventional passion

for solitude, her lack of desire for the security of marriage, flew in the face of the orderly existence, the traditional position of male dominance that he had fought to represent. He enjoyed being the epitome of power and authority.

Her dog, Ares, rushed past her to the door, teeth bared, hackles rising. She gently nudged him aside with her foot. "Stop that. You'll frighten off our visitor. Sit, you great silly beast. No one is going to harm us."

But she felt a flash of fear slide down her spine before she could suppress it.

There was no one at the door.

She released a deep breath, grasping the hound by the scruff of the neck. "Well, how stupid. It must be all the talk of Claude's wounded man. We won't mention this to Connor, Ares, or he'll stage a manhunt in the woods and frighten off all our animal friends."

Chapter

30

Connor shoved the hillock of papers to the side of his desk and glanced in surprise at the window, wondering when morning had broken. Even here in the Highlands the weight of his responsibility gave him no rest. His preparations for the Balfour case, his petition to Parliament for jury improvements, the letters that had begun to arrive from legal associates who'd heard about Sheena. Finding Sheena. The queries to France for Maggie.

Seducing her. Making her fall in love with him. Plotting excuses to keep her in his life when the situation with his sister got straightened out.

He studied the note from Sheena that sat on his desk, mocking his worry for her. Somehow its rudeness reassured him. The tone was so much like his impertinent sister, rubbing his nose in their strained relationship. Could Rebecca be right? Had Sheena staged her own abduction to punish him for breaking up her romance with that convict? It was an agonizing thought.

Well, whether he found her or not, he would have to return to Edinburgh within a fortnight. He intended to take Maggie with him, not as a witness but as a wife. She was the only silver lining in this cloud, and he didn't intend to lose her.

He glanced up at the forceful knock at the door. "Come in."

He wanted it to be her. Maggie, in her ballet costume, come to brighten his mood, to tease and tantalize, and take his mind off his worries. A smile of anticipation formed on his face only to fade as he recognized Claude, looking as stiff as a gravestone.

"Can I help you?" he asked, sensing trouble.

The butler exhaled through pinched nostrils. "I know it is not my place to say this, sir, but—"

"No, it isn't. But we both know you're going to say it anyway so get it over with."

"It is about the matter of your seducing my mistress."

"Good grief. I think I must be hearing things."

"I have taken the aforementioned matter into consideration, sir. A decision regarding my permission will be issued in due time."

"Your permission?" Connor grinned and gave the globe on his desk a dizzying spin. "You're having me on."

"No, sir. It would be inappropriate for a man in my position to display a sense of humor."

"Come on, Claude. You can tell the truth, man to man." He winked broadly. "Maggie put you up to this, didn't she?"

"If by 'Maggie' you are referring to Lady Marguerite, then I believe the situation is understood between us." Claude hesitated. "Is there something wrong with your eye, sir?"

Connor clapped his hand down somewhere in Asia, bringing the world to an abrupt halt. "Great God. You're serious."

"Your reputation does not work in your favor, my lord, if I do say so. However, the biggest obstacle, in my opinion, is your background."

"This is absurd," Connor said. "You are a butler. I am the Lord Advocate of Scotland. I could have you—do you know the extent of my power?"

"Threats will not work on me, sir. I cannot be bullied or bought. My loyalty runs deeper than that." Claude began to back toward the door, his dignity intact. "But all is not lost. I have taken note of several character points on your side."

"What a relief. I was beginning to worry."

Claude frowned. "A light breakfast will be served in fifteen minutes. I have volunteered my help until this dispute with your staff is settled. Lady Marguerite is expecting you in the winter parlor. May I suggest, sir, that you change into fresh attire?"

"What's wrong with my attire?" Connor said darkly.

"Hunting boots at the table, sir." Claude gave an imperceptible shake of his head. "It just isn't done."

Connor scowled. "Yes, it is."

"Not if you want my approval," Claude said in a sly undertone.

With a formal bow, he left the room, abandoning Connor to his amused belief. "Hell," he said aloud, "I think I'm being blackmailed by the butler."

Connor threw down his napkin and pulled out his pocket watch. "We've been waiting for breakfast for over an hour. It's almost time for supper. How long does it take to make a simple meal?"

"Quite a while if Claude is overseeing the preparations," Maggie answered patiently. "He insists on perfection."

Connor studied her across the table, thinking the word perfection applied to her. She looked as fresh and radiant as a rosebud after a rainstorm. Clearly she hadn't lost any sleep over thwarted lust last night. He released a sigh. "Why is your butler overseeing not only my breakfast table but my life? How have I allowed this to happen?"

She smoothed a wrinkle from the yellowed wrinkled tablecloth. Her hair was arranged in a loose chignon, secured with several pearl-headed bodkins. Connor's gaze followed the graceful arch of her neck down into the deep indentation of her breasts.

She smiled at him. "It was my idea that Claude should serve as a neutral party in the house until the domestic crisis is resolved."

He leaned into her, draping his arm possessively over the back of her chair. "Did you know that there is another crisis brewing in this house, Maggie? In approximately twenty seconds I am going to attack you."

"Not during breakfast."

"I don't see any breakfast." He sneaked his hand under the table to touch hers. Electricity tingled between their fingertips. Connor drew a sharp breath as heat suffused his body. He was enamored of her and didn't give a damn who knew it. "Let's go for another walk in the woods."

"Do you think that's wise? The wounded man might still be lurking about."

He ran his hand along the inside of her forearm, drawing her toward him. Her lips parted in expectation. Unfortunately, before he could kiss her, Claude appeared in the doorway, announcing, "Breakfast is served."

Maggie straightened up like a schoolgirl. Connor settled back in his chair with a disgruntled sigh. He could have sworn Claude had interrupted them on purpose, probably waiting just outside the door for the perfect moment to prove he took his role as surrogate guardian to heart.

Connor still hadn't figured out how to deal with him. The man was too old to physically subdue and too stubborn to reason with, and there were Maggie's feelings to consider. It was a prickly situation.

Claude shuffled up to the table bearing a large silver teapot with all the solemnity of a courtier presenting the Crown jewels. He was so slow and stiff, the teapot trembling in his hand, that Connor just couldn't envision him engaged in serious swordplay.

"I see you have changed out of those nasty boots, sir," he intoned in such a voice of parental authority that it made Connor wonder whether he'd be checked next to see if he'd washed behind his ears for breakfast. "You are having tea?"

He nodded meekly, amazed to realize that he was being intimidated by a man employed to polish the silver. Well hell, old habits died hard. He still struggled against the Highlander in him that felt faintly bewildered in a formal setting. Ardath was always kicking him under the table for using the wrong spoon.

"No." He raised his voice, taking a stand. "I've changed my mind. I do not want tea."

Claude eyed him disapprovingly, not saying a word.

"I think you should take the tea," Maggie whispered behind the napkin.

"I do not want tea," Connor said, practically shouting.

Claude's upper lip curled at the corner. "His lordship does not want tea. Can you imagine?" he said to no one in particular. He held the trembling teapot over the table. "Are you sure, sir, that you do not want tea?"

"It seems important to him," Maggie said thoughtfully.

"It isn't his business." Connor stared at the dripping teapot. "Oh, hell. I'll have tea if it makes everyone happy."

"Very good, sir." Claude's hand hovered over Connor's cup. "But are you sure you wouldn't rather have coffee?"

"I want tea," Connor shouted.

Claude took on a martyred expression. "I know it is not my place to say so, sir, but you would have made it easier all around if you had stated your preference to begin with."

Connor didn't look at his watch, but he swore it took a good five minutes for Claude to pour that cup, half of it splashing into the saucer. Of course, by the time Connor tasted it, the beverage tasted like lukewarm well water.

"Where is the rest of the breakfast, Claude?"

"It is coming, sir."

"It is coming. I see. Do you have any idea when it is coming? A week? A month? By Christmas?"

"As soon as I return to fetch it, sir."

"Then Christmas is a distinct possibility," Connor said. "May I ask what the other servants are doing?"

"They are on strike, sir," Claude replied.

Maggie took a tiny sip of tea. "The domestic conflict in the household will never be resolved until Mrs. Urquhart and Dougie make up, my lord. I thought you understood this. I have done my share to advise the female contingent. It's time you took a hand to represent the manly point of view."

Connor didn't particularly care about the domestic conflict, but it was clear that he and Maggie would probably starve to death within a week with Claude serving their meals.

"This cannot be tolerated," he said. "Claude, you are to bring Dougie to me as soon as I have eaten, assuming that my food arrives sometime in this century. I will not have my authority undermined in my own house."

Which, of course, was a joke.

Connor could no more control his staff than he could his

desire for the delicate young woman who sat beside him, the woman he ached to dominate and had sworn to protect, the woman whose inadvertent touch made him tremble like a boy on the verge of his first sexual experience.

Connor stared in trepidation at the toast and sausages on his plate. By the time Claude brought them to the table, they could have been put on display as prehistoric fossils.

"How am I supposed to eat this?" he wondered aloud. "Do I look like I live in a cave and hunt wild boars with a club?"

Maggie meticulously spread a spoonful of marmalade over her toast. "Well, since you asked, I have to admit that at times there is a little of the primitive about you. As to eating your breakfast"—her voice took on a conspiratorial tone—"I don't think it would be a good idea to criticize Claude's culinary skills. Not if you want him to decide in your favor about courting me."

Connor grimaced. "Are you telling me I have to eat your butler's cooking—his petrified breakfast—in order to even qualify as your suitor?"

She laid down her knife. "It would be a good start."

"Maggie, he is only a servant."

"Oh, no. He's much more than that. Yes, I know he's ancient, but like a Ming vase he is priceless, irreplaceable." She glanced fondly at Claude, who was weaving back toward them with another teapot, leaving great stains on Connor's costly Persian carpet. "His family has served my family for generations. Anyway, he swore to Aunt Flora on her death-bed that he would defend me with his life."

Connor snorted at this sentimental confession and tried to spear his sausage with a fork. It was like stabbing a stone. Then he tried to chew it, and as he did he realized that if anyone had told him a month ago he would be eating rocks to win a woman, he would have laughed his head off.

Suddenly Claude was at his side with the teapot again. "Shall I refresh your cup again, sir?"

Connor nodded in resignation. Another mouthful of cold tea brewed as black and foul as Satan's breath was just what he needed to wash down the rock caught in his throat. Lord, what a man wouldn't do for lust. Or was it more than that?

DARING

He glanced at Maggie in an ivory lace-trimmed day dress that mocked his carnal intentions. He remembered how soft her skin was in those secret places. A shiver of raw desire danced down his spine. Never in his life had he exercised this much restraint. Frustration was taking its toll. Still, he wanted more than a string of sexual encounters. He wanted full possession of this woman. He even wanted her butler to like him.

He swallowed the rock. It was definitely more than a simple case of lust. He was heart-deep in love with her.

Claude bent over him, placing the teapot precariously at the edge of the table. Then, unexpectedly, like a magician performing a sleight of hand, he snapped out a napkin and settled it over Connor's lap. "We must remember our etiquette, sir, mustn't we? Will there be anything else?"

Connor could only shake his head, afraid to wonder what would happen next. Would Claude insist on spoon-feeding him? If Connor didn't finish his food, would he be sent up to his room? He looked across the table then and raised his brow at the sight of Dougie hovering in the doorway; the silly fool was dressed like an overgrown gnome in a moth-eaten suit of livery he must have found in the attic complete with puffy velvet pantaloons and braided jacket.

"What are you doing in that ridiculous costume, Dougie?" he asked with a frown.

"I'm doing my job, sir." Dougie's beard bobbed over his high starched collar. "I'm dressed like a butler."

"A butler?" Connor didn't like the sound of this. He caught Maggie smiling knowingly as she stirred sugar into her tea. "You are my steward, Dougie. Kenneth is the butler."

Dougie put his tray on the floor. Then he bent to inelegantly pull up his baggy stockings before he clomped across the room and banged a bowl of scorched porridge on the table. "Not anymore. Kenneth is gone to work for the duchess, and I canna say I blame him. This is yer breakfast. Dinna complain about it. I did my best, but I'm a steward, not a damn butler."

Connor stared down at the bowl in distaste. "What, pray tell, happened to the cook?"

"The last I heard she was playing cards with the scullery

maids," Dougie answered. "All the women are on strike for better working conditions."

"I'll take care of this right now." Connor started to rise from the table only to hesitate as Maggie stayed him with her hand.

"It isn't a good idea, my lord."

"It isn't?"

She wagged her finger at him. "I told you to take action earlier. The strike is too well established now to thwart. I do suggest, however, that you intervene to stop the crisis smoldering under your very nose before it too blows up."

"Crisis?"

"In this very room."

Connor turned his head to see Claude and Dougie sizing each other up across the table like a pair of Roman gladiators. There was definitely a rivalry brewing between them. A battle of the butlers.

"Eat up, my lord." Dougie was standing over him like a mother hen. "A man your size needs his oats to start the day."

Claude stepped forward, straightening the lapels of Connor's jacket with a possessive tug. "His lordship is having *des saucisses* this morning. A man his size needs his meat."

Dougie sniggered. "Day—sew what?"

"Des saucisses," Claude replied solemnly. "That is sausages to the ignorant."

"Sausages. These are sausages?" Dougie made a face. He picked up a link from Connor's plate and dropped it on the table with a loud *plink*. "And here I thought they was skinny brown stones from the burn."

A militant gleam lit up Claude's faded gray eyes at this insult. "Undercooked pork can kill a man." He handed Connor a fork. "Enjoy your meat, sir."

Dougie pushed the bowl of porridge in front of the plate. "Have some healthy Highland ambrosia, sir. 'Twill put the roses back in yer cheeks, as my granny used to say."

Maggie nudged Connor's foot under the table. He turned to her, catching his breath at the unexpected jolt of sexual desire that struck him as their eyes met. "It's time to assert yourself," she whispered. "Let it be known who's the master."

He gave her a roguish grin. "Follow me up to my room and I'll show you who is the master."

"Master of the house," she added softly, staring into her lap.

His dark gaze devoured her. His need for her was so powerful he didn't care if he ever ate again. "What do you suggest I do?" he asked reluctantly.

"Well." Maggie pursed her lips as she contemplated his dilemma. "If you offend Dougie, you'll turn the domestic crisis into a full-scale civil war, and that could be very unpleasant all the way around. On the other hand, if you offend Claude, then he probably won't give you permission to court me."

Connor frowned. "This is not sounding very hopeful."

"It is a bit of a pickle," Maggie admitted. "I suppose if I were you, I'd consider doing something along the lines of what Solomon did. Do you understand what I mean?"

"No. I don't." He leaned a little closer. "I do know that I'd like to pull you onto my lap and nibble on your neck," he said in an undertone. "Your skin reminds me of fresh cream. And your mouth—"

"Restrain your baser side, my lord. Claude is staring at you. I suspect he learned how to read lips in Heaven's Court."

Connor slumped back in his chair. "What in God's name does Solomon have to do with this, anyway? Am I supposed to divide myself in half to please two butlers?"

"No," Maggie said. "You're supposed to eat both their breakfasts."

Connor didn't have a chance to comment on her unsatisfactory suggestion because Claude had elbowed Dougie aside to reclaim his authority. "A fresh serviette, sir?" he inquired, whipping away the spotless napkin on Connor's lap to replace it with another.

Dougie took exception to this. He barreled his way back between Claude and Connor's chair, muttering, "This French fellow is getting on my nerves." Then he snatched away the square of linen from Connor's lap and proceeded to tuck it into Connor's cravat like a bib. "No need to be layin' the blasted thing over yer legs like we was diaperin' ye. A man wants his nappie where it'll catch the dribbles and spills."

Connor's face reddened. "Enough is enough," he said, tearing the napkin from his throat. "Claude—"

"Your cravat is crooked," Maggie murmured.

Connor shot her a look. "Claude."

The butler straightened, regarding Connor with a challenging air. "You wish something of me, sir?" he inquired with a meaningful look in Maggie's direction.

Connor gripped the edge of the table, unable to articulate what exactly it was he wished at that moment. A new identity? To wake up and find it was all a bad dream? Was his love life really dependent on the whims of an eighty-four-year-old butler? Yes, it was. And he was helpless to do anything as long as he coveted the demure young thing trying to conceal her enjoyment of his predicament beside him.

"I wish to compliment you for breakfast." The breakfast that was sitting in his stomach like a sack of coal. He rose, looking resolute but feeling a trifle queasy. "Dougie, I would like a word with you in my study. And pull up those stockings before you fall flat on your face."

Dougie shook his head in dejection. "I canna control the women in this household, my lord. I canna control my own wife. That's why I've decided to seek a divorce. I've chosen ye to represent me."

Connor paced in front of his desk. "I can't represent you in a divorce. I only handle criminal cases."

"Well, my marriage is a crime, my lord."

Connor glanced out the window, catching sight of Maggie walking toward the woods. Where was she going? he wondered in amazement. He watched her vanish between the trees, hips swaying, the breeze teasing the glossy black curls that spilled down her back. She was as alluring as a wood sprite. Even the way she walked drove him wild.

He pushed the curtain aside. He didn't like the thought of her wandering in the woods all alone. She could get lost. She could trip over a tree root and hit her head, or she could fall into the gorge. She could stumble over the wounded man—

He sighed in frustration. The truth was, *he* was the biggest beast who'd ever lurked in those woods. Maggie had as much to fear from him as anyone. He was determined to learn all of her secrets if it killed him.

Dougie's voice broke the silence that had fallen. "Do ye think I have grounds for divorce, my lord?"

Connor edged closer to the window, half listening. "Has your wife been unfaithful to you?"

"Not that I know of. Who would want her? She's so mean."

"Has she refused you relations?"

Dougie looked uncertain. "She wasna happy about my mother visitin' last month, if that's what ye mean."

"That is not what I mean," Connor said in annoyance. "Has she refused to have congress with you?"

"Well." Dougie scratched his head. "She might have. Then again she might not. 'Tis hard to say."

Connor turned reluctantly from the window, losing sight of Maggie in the landscape. "That doesn't make sense. Hell, man, can't you remember whether you've had congress with your own wife?"

"I suppose it depends." Dougie toed the edge of the carpet, his voice a sheepish mumble. "What exactly is congress, sir?"

"Congress is . . . well, it's coitus." Connor closed his eyes, wondering if he could take the shortcut through the woods to meet her. "Intercourse. Connubial bliss."

Coitus. Intercourse. Bliss. Maggie open and vulnerable beneath him, willing and warm, the essence of woman. A treasure no man had ever touched before. Desire crashed over him in waves. A predatory growl rose in his throat at the thought of taking her innocence the way his Highland warrior ancestors had taken their women.

He opened his eyes in irritation and looked around. "It's sex, damn it. I'm talking about your sexual affairs."

Dougie gasped, shocked to the tips of his pointed ears. "I dinna think that's any of yer concern."

"Neither do I," Connor said tightly. "In fact, I don't ever want to discuss the distasteful subject again. Just do the job you were hired to do and make the most of your marriage while you remain in this house. Is that understood?"

"Aye, my lord," Dougie said unhappily.

Connor nodded in relief. "Now get on with your work. I'll deal with the women later. I've some pressing business of my own to attend to."

He hadn't taken two impatient steps toward the door when Mrs. Urquhart herself appeared, bristling with self-importance. She dismissed her husband with a contemptuous look, then cleared her throat. "There is a visitor to see ye, sir."

Connor suppressed a string of curses. Not his neighbors again. What did he need to do to have Maggie to himself? "Tell whoever it is that I am unavailable for the rest of the day."

The housekeeper paused a moment. "He's come all the way from Edinburgh to see ye. He said he has a verra important message. Something about a dangerous development in the murder case."

Connor experienced a jolt of excitement mingled with resentment that reality was intruding on his life. Of course he wanted a break in the case, but the timing was terrible. Instead of chasing after Maggie in the woods, he'd had to send Claude out to watch over her.

It was the only sensible thing to do. Sensible but a damned strain and sacrifice. He was astonished at the emotions a single woman brought out in him. Sacrifice was not a concept he applied to his dealings with the opposite sex. As a rule he took what he wanted, and it usually was offered to him before he had to ask.

He wouldn't be able to think straight until he knew how she really felt about him. Or at least until he'd gotten her into his bed. Her feelings could wait until later. Connor had confidence that once they'd gotten that far, their future together was assured. He was a damn good lover if he did say so himself.

He paused before he entered the drawing room, clearing his thoughts. As he was halfway through the door, the visitor seated before the fire turned to acknowledge him.

"Sebastien," he said in surprise. "You're the last person in the world I expected to see here. I thought you were leaving the country."

"So did I." Elegant in a knee-length cashmere coat and

straight-legged trousers, Sebastien gave a little shrug. "The affair I was working on became more complicated than anticipated."

Connor took the opposite chair. Logic as well as intuition warned him something was wrong. Sebastien looked rather gray and unwell, glancing repeatedly at the door. "What happened?" Connor said bluntly. "Have you brought information about my sister?"

"No." Sebastien slid to the edge of the chair, grimacing slightly as if the effort pained him. "But I do have some disturbing news, news that will officially reach you in a few hours—Connor, are we completely alone? I prefer not to be seen."

Connor did not immediately question the man's strange request. He understood that in Sebastien's profession, anonymity was desirable if one wished to assume different identities. Such a precaution, however, did seem rather out of place in this isolated setting. "I have a small staff of local servants." Connor paused. "All of them put together couldn't scrape up the brains to be involved in any espionage, though."

"What about the girl?" Urgency laced Sebastien's voice. "Is she still here?"

"What girl?" It took Connor an instant to remember that Sebastien knew about Maggie, that in fact he knew more about her mysterious background than he did himself. For the first time the thought struck him as strange, and he felt both jealous and concerned, resenting that there was still so much about her he had to learn. "Yes, she's still here," he said guardedly.

"Well, aren't you supposed to be protecting her?"

"I have been protecting her," Connor said with a touch of irritation.

"Then where is she?" Sebastien demanded. "Who is watching her while you're sitting here alone with me? Is she with people you can trust?"

The ormolu clock on the stone mantelpiece ticked in the silence. Connor's brows drew together as he struggled to understand. "She went for a walk. I sent her butler out after her as a precaution. But what is this odd preoccupation you have with my witness? She's perfectly safe on this estate."

"I hope so," Sebastien said.

Connor felt a prickle of unease, confused by the man's demeanor. "My housekeeper said something about the murder case. Why are you here, anyway? What is all this secrecy, Sebastien?"

"Donaldson was brutally attacked in an alleyway several days after you left," Sebastien explained slowly. "I gather he had been on the docks gleaning some crucial information on the Balfour murder case. Something that implicated your suspect. Donaldson is expected to recover, but I'm afraid he'll need a long recuperation. It was Arthur Ogilvie—the Chief, they call him—who found your colleague in the gutter and probably saved his life."

Connor didn't speak for a moment. The room seemed suddenly darker, the temperature chilling by several degrees. "Then Sheena isn't safe," he said. "I got a letter from her—it sounded so natural I'd half convinced myself that whoever kidnapped her wasn't going to hurt her."

"We still don't know if there's a connection. Frankly, I suspect not." Sebastien was studying him with unnerving intensity. "It would seem, however, that in light of this alarming development, you are perhaps not the best person to protect Miss Saunders."

"Why the hell not?"

"Because you are apparently a magnet for danger, Connor. Your sister has been abducted, your young protégé viciously beaten."

Connor stood abruptly, resenting the criticism. When it came down to it he still believed in his own invulnerability and power, and he couldn't bear the thought of entrusting Maggie to anyone else. "Donaldson knew the danger of visiting the docks alone. I warned him not to take chances on this case. Poor bastard—he'd better recover."

Sebastien gripped the arms of the chair to rise. This time Connor could not miss the man's subdued groan of pain, but he was too distracted to comment on it.

"I had no idea you had formed such an attachment to her," Sebastien said, standing to face him.

"It wasn't exactly something I planned," Connor said in self-defense. "One thing led to another, and I fell in love."

"I see."

DARING

Connor swung around to the fire, swearing under his breath. "I *am* going to take care of her."

"But you have to return to the city in a fortnight to assume office." Sebastien sounded calmer now. "The Lord Advocate of Scotland can hardly seclude himself for an extended romantic interlude while a murderer runs loose in the capital city."

"Romantic interlude. I should be so fortunate. I can tell you quite honestly that the prospect is looking bleaker and bleaker."

Sebastien raised an eyebrow. "Indeed?"

Connor paced in front of the fire, his leonine head downbent in thought. "You're sure Donaldson will recover?"

"That is what I was told," Sebastien said. "Unfortunately he can't remember much about the events leading up to his attack."

"It was good of you to ride all this way by yourself."

Sebastien pulled a pair of gloves from his pocket. "As it turns out, I had unexpected business in the area."

"In this area?"

Sebastien offered nothing more.

"Aren't you at least staying the night?" Connor said after a moment. "Your shoulder is obviously bothering you, Sebastien. Don't tell me all this cloak and dagger business has given you bursitis."

Sebastien forced a smile. "Just a run-in with an old friend. Besides, that other affair I mentioned is more urgent than I realized."

"So it does have ties to espionage?"

"Something like that." Sebastien walked to the door, then paused. "Your relationship with Miss Saunders . . . it hasn't crossed any serious boundaries, has it?"

The smile froze on Connor's face. "I can't believe you asked me that."

For an instant something dark and threatening flashed in Sebastien's eyes, and Connor realized how little he really knew of the man. "Be careful, Connor," he said, his expression once again masked. "I wouldn't want to see anything happen to either of you."

Connor was disturbed by the interview. He was fond of Donaldson and furious at the same time that the young fool had risked his life to gather information. It was the reckless sort of thing Connor had done when he worked for the court as a legal clerk. It was the mark of a man who would go far.

He was also more worried than ever about Maggie and his sisters.

He threw on his black greatcoat and left the house to cut across the estate to the woods. It was a cold November day, the wind carrying the tang of peat and decaying leaves. Maggie couldn't have gone far with Claude accompanying her. They shouldn't be hard to find. He knew the area well, the hidden bridle paths, the maze of hazel coppice, the hilly lanes.

An hour passed.

He started to retrace his steps. Back to the gorge in case one of them had slipped on the path above the waterfall. Back to the old wooden bridge to make sure it hadn't collapsed beneath their weight.

After another hour he returned to the house, charging into room after room in the hope he'd find her. He refused to believe she had vanished. By the time he burst into the kitchen like a cannonball, his long hair disheveled, leaves stuck to his coat, he had worked himself into an uncharacteristic panic.

"Did she come back?" he bellowed.

A scullery maid dropped a saucepan in fright at his dramatic entrance. Mrs. Urquhart and Dougie, apparently having reached some sort of truce, looked at him as if he'd taken complete leave of his senses from the long oak table where they sat sipping tea.

"Did who come back, sir?" Dougie asked in bewilderment.

"Lady Maggie," Connor shouted.

Silence answered him. He suddenly felt like a moron, his emotions exposed, his legendary control shattering, but he couldn't help himself. What if something had happened to her? "She went for a walk in the woods several hours ago! It's almost dark, and she isn't anywhere in the house! Neither is Claude."

Another silence. Then Mrs. Urquhart glanced around to the petite figure on the floor behind the chopping block. Connor, breathing hard, followed the direction of her amused gaze but did not immediately register a connection.

DARING

The petite figure had its head stuck in the oven. It also had a familiar shape, a pleasantly rounded posterior that wriggled back toward him. A delicate face appeared between the chairs, flushed with heat and annoyance. Maggie rose like Venus with flour on her nose instead of foam.

"Who, may I ask, is doing all the shouting and dropping of saucepans on the floor? It took me three hours to get that soufflé right and now the whole thing's collapsed like a damn pancake."

"It was me." Connor's voice, hoarse with relief, shook the herbs and onions tied to the soot-blackened rafters. "I've been looking for you for hours."

"You were worried about me?" Maggie looked altogether too delighted at the thought of him spending an entire afternoon of self-torture on her account. "That was sweet of you, my lord. Sweet but rather silly. Claude and I went for a drive with the duchess. You know she wouldn't have let anything happen to me."

"You might have informed me," he said, walking her back against the table. "At the very least you could have left a note . . . a trail of bread crumbs or—or lace. I've wasted an entire day's work because of you."

Maggie stared at him in wonder. He'd obviously been more frightened than he could show, and his concern was manifesting itself in a very bad mood. This was such a good sign. He cared deeply. She felt like celebrating with champagne.

"Would you like a cup of tea and some collapsed mushroom soufflé?" she asked him softly.

Connor braced his hands down on the table with a defeated sigh, overwhelmed by a sudden rush of emotion. The mischief and self-awareness in her dark blue eyes mesmerized him. He *never* again wanted to experience that sick rush of fear he'd felt when it seemed she had vanished. She meant more to him than he realized.

"Go out into the garden," he ordered her. "I need to talk to you in private."

They stood on either side of a lichen-speckled sundial in the blue-violet haze of a Highland gloaming. An owl called softly from the nearby woods. A badger rustled through the blackberry brambles. Maggie rubbed a spot of flour from her nose and searched Connor's face in the lengthening shadows, shivering a little as his eyes bored into her.

Intense. Magnetic. Possessive. She had been awed by him from the first day she'd spotted him in the street with a line of smitten admirers in tow. Well, she was one of those smitten by his charisma now. More than smitten if the truth be told. She loved the beast with every beat of her heart.

He lowered his head, frowning at her across the sundial. She sighed, sensing a lecture coming on. "As of today, there will be no more walks in the woods."

"I wish you would make up your mind, Connor. I thought you wanted me to walk in your woods."

"Not without me," he said fiercely. "It isn't safe anymore. Donaldson was brutally attacked and left for dead."

Maggie drew in a shocked breath. "Attacked—in your woods? I had no idea he was even in the area. I wonder— dear heavens, you don't suppose Donaldson is the wounded man we've been trying to find? The man Claude ran through with his sword? It could all be a tragic misunderstanding, like Romeo and Juliet. Oh, Connor."

He lost several moments trying to decide at which point in the conversation her train of thought had derailed. "I am not talking about these woods. Donaldson was attacked in Edinburgh, presumably by someone who hopes to thwart the murder investigation."

Maggie rolled her eyes. "I realize you are renowned for your courtroom eloquence, my lord, but frankly there are times when your logic eludes me. Did you or did you not just state that these woods weren't safe?"

"I meant that they might not be safe."

"Were they safe yesterday?"

"Yes." What the hell was she getting at? "I assumed so."

"And being safe yesterday, they are no longer safe today because a man was beaten in Edinburgh?"

Connor suddenly wished for a glass of whisky. Arguing with Maggie was as exhausting as appearing before the High Court of Justiciary.

"The woods aren't safe because whoever attacked Donaldson could have followed us here," he said in exasperation.

"There is no need to use that tone," she said. "This is

exactly what I've been trying to explain to you for the past fortnight."

She had him there.

"Yes," he conceded, "and I've done some serious thinking on the subject—"

"So have I," Maggie interrupted him, circling the sundial like a lawyer summarizing a case before a jury. "And I realize now that Claude and I have probably overreacted. I don't feel threatened here at all. If there was any danger to me, I would surely sense it. I have good instincts about such things."

Connor frowned. "What about the wounded man?"

"Ah, yes. Well, neither Claude's eyesight nor his mind is what it used to be. It is entirely possible he imagined the whole incident. I would never tell him this, of course."

"And the figure in black at the farmhouse? The man who knocked at your door at the Golden Sovereign?"

She wandered over to the garden wall. "I can't really explain it," she called over her shoulder. "All I know is that I'm not afraid anymore."

"But I am," he said quietly, looking past her into the woods. "I have come here every autumn for seven years straight, and I, too, have good instincts. There is someone watching us. I can sense it at this moment. There is someone in those woods who does not belong."

Chapter

31

Connor stared into the fire, savoring the late-night silence. In Edinburgh he rarely allowed himself time for contemplation. But he'd bought this house as a retreat, which he rarely used. There were no unpleasant intrusions here to bother him. There were no happy ones either.

No children, no wife, no meddling in-laws. No complications, or commitments.

He took a drink of whisky. "Oh, God," he whispered. "Let her love me back. Don't let me lose her. I've never cared like this before."

He lifted his head, hearing the servants joking in the garden where Claude was giving fencing lessons.

For the first time since Connor could remember the house seemed alive, lit by the foibles of human interaction and laughter. Maggie had brushed angel wings of warmth and brightness over his life. How had he come to need her this badly? Need her to the degree that instead of protecting her, he risked putting her in greater danger.

The door creaked open behind him. Light footsteps approached his chair. He drew an expectant breath, releasing it into the darkness. A knowing smile spread across his face.

He'd been waiting for her. He had willed her to come to him. Sensual tension thrummed through his veins.

"Sit down beside me, lass," he said with deceptive calm. "I'll pour you a glass of wine."

"That would be nice, my lord, as long as you aren't going to give me another one of your scoldings."

She sat down in the wing chair opposite him and took the glass of wine he gave her. To his surprise she was wrapped in only a dark burgundy velvet dressing robe. In fact, all he could see of her was her face and finely boned hands and feet. It was, unfortunately, more than enough to stimulate his erotic imagination.

Her delicate sensuality stirred a desire in him that bordered on savage. He didn't know how he managed to maintain a facade of detachment. Dangerous undercurrents roiled beneath his surface calm. He watched in a pretense of composure, calculating his next move, while she propped her feet on the tapestried footstool, wriggled her toes in abandon, and took a sip of wine.

"This is just like old times, isn't it, Connor?" she said with a blissful sigh.

He resisted the urge to run his hand along the instep of her foot to her thigh. She wouldn't be so relaxed if she knew what he had in mind. "Old times?"

"You trying to get me drunk in front of a fire. It reminds me of the night we met."

"Do you know a man named Sebastien?" he said unexpectedly.

Maggie lowered her wineglass to give him a long critical look. "I hope you pay more attention to what other people are saying in the courtroom than you do to me. It's very disconcerting to talk to you sometimes."

"Do you know anyone named Sebastien?" he repeated.

"I've known several Sebastiens," she replied. "The first one was my father's secretary. He disappeared the night Papa died. We suspect he may have been executed in Marseilles. Then there was old Sebastien, the gardener's uncle. He was caught in a compromising position behind the privet hedge with Maman's seamstress." Maggie sipped her wine, smiling. "Apparently, this lascivious conduct was a family

trait because young Sebastien, the gardener's son, was
caught in—"

"Do you know a man named Sebastien who lives in Edinburgh? He may have had dealings with the Chief."

She mulled this over for a moment. "No. Why?"

"Because he seems to know quite a bit about you," Connor said with a scowl.

"That's very flattering."

"It isn't flattering," he said. "It's disturbing. I don't like
other men being that interested in you. You're daft if you
think I'm going to allow it."

She put down her wineglass and reached for his hand.
"You're turning dark in the face, my lord. I wish you
wouldn't worry. I told you I wasn't afraid anymore."

"But I am," he said quietly, grasping her hand in his powerful grip. "I'm afraid of what I feel for you, that someone
will hurt you because of me. I'm afraid for my sisters."

He slid out of his chair and pulled her down against him,
gripping her against his massive chest. "I need you so
badly, lass."

The brilliant arguments, the veneer of sophistication
crumbled to dust in her presence. He was the lion captured
by the princess. The beast that would lay down its life for
the chance to win her love.

Maggie came without resistance, stroking his face with her
hand. A shudder of raw desire went through Connor's large
body at her touch. Everyone assumed he had no weaknesses,
but he did. He yearned for tenderness. He yearned to be
accepted for his flaws as well as his strengths.

"You're seeing me at my worst," he said, embarrassed
by his emotions. "When everything is over, you're going to
marry me."

She leaned back to look at him. "That's a nice thought,
Connor, but you'll have to ask—"

"I'm not asking anybody," he said forcefully. "The matter
is not open for debate. Especially not after tonight."

She looked intrigued. "What's going to happen tonight?"
she whispered, unconsciously holding her breath.

Devilish lights danced in his eyes. "You aren't leaving this
room until I make you mine."

Before she could react to this display of male assertion,

Connor worked her robe open to the waist, loosening the sash with a skillful tug. Maggie gasped in astonishment at his audacity and sat bolt upright in his lap.

Connor himself was in shock, immobilized by a powerful surge of desire that robbed him of speech. She was naked under her robe. Sinfully, deliciously, temptingly nude. He drank in the sight of her like a beggar drowning in a fountain of wine, her full rose-peaked breasts, her belly, the dark triangle of hair between her legs. He had trouble breathing.

She was lithe and tiny, perfectly fashioned. Soft, sensuous, unique. His throat closed over an animal growl. His heart thundered against the wall of his chest.

"Dear God," he exclaimed, shaking his head incredulously. "Where are all your clothes?"

"Upstairs," she said in irritation. "I'd just taken a bath when I realized I hadn't let Daphne out for her evening puddle. I popped in to wish you good night, never dreaming that I was to be rendered naked for ravishment." She yanked the robe back together at the neck.

He gave her a beastly grin and, with a flick of his wrist, rendered her naked again to his hungry stare.

"Ravishment, is it?" He untied the sash at her waist, using it to drag her into him. "Am I expected to live up to my reputation?"

"I am inexperienced, my lord," she said primly, drawing her knees into her body.

"Oh, I know." His voice was tender; the passion in his eyes was not. "My very own little virgin. Mine to ravish and enjoy."

She caught her lower lip between her teeth. Her hair tumbled down over her bare arms and breasts. It was such an erotic sight that Connor couldn't help himself. He cupped her chin in his hand and bent to kiss her. Then, grasping her wrists in his other hand, he gently forced her back down onto the rug. The firelight illuminated every inviting swell and hollow of her supple form. Aroused beyond belief, he brushed his lips back and forth across hers with deliberate sensuality. She arched upward in anticipation.

"How can anyone so small have such an unsettling effect on me?" he mused aloud. He smoothed the curls from her face, his deep voice amused. "Why are your eyes squeezed shut, Maggie? Am I really such a beast that you can't bear to look at me when we make love?"

She cracked open one eyelid at a time. "You are not a beast at all," she said. "You're the most beautiful man in the world, if not a little overpowering. It's just that you're so good at this sort of thing. I'm nonplussed, that's all."

"What sort of thing?" he teased, blowing in her ear.

"Seductions—well, at least I can't accuse you of stealing my virtue because you have a trial in the morning."

"What does a trial—ah, yes, the virgin on the eve of battle." A smile flickered across his face. "I'd forgotten about that particular rumor."

Maggie hoisted herself up on her elbow to frown at him. "I notice that you aren't denying it. Is it true?"

He took his sweet time before satisfying her curiosity. "Well, lass, like most rumors, I suppose it had its origin in a kernel of truth."

She nudged his hand off her hip. "How big a kernel?"

"I suppose that somewhere in the hazy past I might have seduced a woman who was passing herself off as a maiden on the eve before I opened a case."

"You don't remember?" she said crossly.

"I don't remember any of the women I met before you came along," he answered, settling his hand back on her hip. His thumb traced the fragile curve. "Was there anyone else?"

He moved his mouth down her throat to her breasts. Everything about her aroused him. The breathy sigh of enjoyment that escaped her only made him more excited. When she arched against him, he felt his body harden in answer. His hands trembled when he touched her. "You've changed my life, Maggie," he whispered. "I never used to do things like shoot up scarecrows, and lift carriages out of bogs."

She smiled. "I can't take all the credit. The Chief always says a man never knows his mettle until he's pushed to the limit."

Connor exhaled through his teeth. "I'm pushed to the limit right now."

"You mean . . ."

He began to unbutton his shirt. "Yes, lass. That's exactly

what I mean. No, don't shy away. I want to feel your body next to mine."

The warmth of her soft flesh against Connor's bare chest was a delightful shock to his system. He took his time exploring the contours of her body. He marveled at how flawless and fragile she was.

"Maggie, we have a problem." He breathed a sigh into her hair. "A serious problem. It's been on my mind since this morning."

"I know." She cuddled up contentedly against his chest. "Breakfast nearly killed me, too," she confided. "I didn't want to hurt Claude's feelings, but I had indigestion for hours."

He skimmed his forefinger across her buttocks, tracing the sweet cleft. "Breakfast, although an abomination to the human stomach, isn't the problem."

"You're right." She shivered as he splayed his hand over her belly, his thumb circling her navel. "The burnt salmon we had for supper was. I haven't felt well since."

"In two weeks I have to return to Edinburgh to take office," he continued. His hand drifted lower. He began to stroke the downy softness between her thighs. "I had been considering asking Donaldson to come here and take care of you. Of course that's out of the question now. Everything has changed."

"It certainly has." Maggie's breath rushed out. What *was* he doing to her? "I can't go back to Heaven's Court."

"Good God, no. The Lord Advocate's wife? I should hope not."

"Assuming that I agree to marry you. I might just prefer to remain a witness."

He smiled darkly, his eyes burning with an emotion that made her feel like he was holding her heart over a red-hot flame. "Then I'll have to put you under arrest," he said with mock regret. "The Court is bringing a charge against you for the malicious mischief you inflicted on the night of October twentieth.

"And"—he dragged his hand over the tangle of curls between her thighs—"for the mischief you've inflicted on me every night since. How do you plead?"

"Who is to be my judge?" she whispered.

"I am."

"And the jury?"

"Judge, jury, and jailer. This is a one-man courtroom, lass."

"In that case, I suppose I shall have to throw myself at the mercy of the court."

He laughed softly. "This court is not known for its mercy."

Maggie stiffened as he slipped his finger inside her, stroking, rubbing, stretching her tender flesh. His mouth went dry as he stared down into her face. He loved her reaction, her blend of inexperience and instinctive passion as she moaned, her muscles tightening around his finger. He loved the wet heat of her.

"Are you—" She caught her breath. "Are you sure this is legal?"

"Search and entry," he whispered with a wicked smile. "The Court is exercising its right to make sure you aren't holding anything back from us."

"As if I'd dare."

"Is that a smile I see on your face, Miss Saunders? I assure you the complaints against you are quite serious . . . and my cross-examinations have been known to go on for days."

"Days?" she whispered, shaking with pleasure.

"Sometimes weeks. Oh, Maggie." His husky voice wove a spell over her senses. "I don't think I can wait. You've destroyed me."

The fire shadows played up the size and virile strength of his body. She could sense the power he held in check, the passion.

He sat back to take off his trousers. Maggie's gaze lifted to the mantelpiece. "I hope Claude remembers to let Daphne in for the night. Do you think that I should remind him?"

"Right now?" Connor said in horror.

"It will only take a moment."

He sighed. His trousers hit the floor. "I'm trying to seduce you, Maggie."

"I know," she whispered. "You're doing a remarkable job of it too."

"If I were doing that good a job, you wouldn't be worrying about your poodle."

Her voice cracked. "I hate to admit it, Connor, but I do believe that infamous de Saint-Evremond sangfroid is deserting me."

"It's only natural," he said gently. "This is your first time. I'm a little on edge if the truth be told."

"Are you?" she said in surprise. "It certainly doesn't show."

He gave her a slow, easy smile. "Actually, it does if you know where to look, which being innocent, you don't."

Maggie glanced down without thinking, her eyes widening. "Yes, I see what you mean. Good gracious. How did we get ourselves in this position?"

"It was inevitable. I wanted you, and I got you. I never lose, lass. Never."

"So I've heard, you conceited devil."

He laughed low, moving over her, determined to enjoy his domination to the fullest. Trailing butterfly kisses over her breasts and belly, he brought his mouth to the fragrant hollow below. The female scent of her tantalized his senses. The taste of her intoxicated him. He was drunk on his desire for her. When she arched in surprise to escape him, he clamped his powerful forearms down on her legs and pinned her to the floor, immobilized her with the seduction of his mouth.

"Connor." The pleasure, piercing and raw, took her unaware. She was trembling from shoulder to toe, wild impulses overwhelming her.

"Inevitable," he murmured, savoring her fragrance. "Inescapable. I'd save my strength for later if I were you. You're not going anywhere unless I take you there."

"Monster," she said, struggling now not to escape but merely to breathe. "Beast."

"Beauty." He gripped her wriggling white bottom, loving her with his tongue. "And every delicious inch of you is mine to enjoy."

"I suppose there's no point in arguing with you—"

"None at all."

She suppressed a groan. "Or pretending to resist."

"Do be quiet, Maggie," he murmured, lifting his head to

grin at her. "I don't like to be interrupted when I'm having so much fun."

She burned with need, unable to stop him. She stared into his beautifully rugged face, the face of a male conqueror, the man who had chosen her for his own, who would kill to protect her. Wicked desire smoldered in his eyes as they locked with hers.

"Are you ready for me to prove my mastery, lass?"

He lowered his head at her soft whimper of submission, and he hadn't lied when he promised he would show her no mercy. The pleasure he gave her broke down every barrier, every inhibition that stood between them. Maggie suspected it probably broke a couple of laws too.

"Yield to me," he commanded, and she did. "Love me."

"Yes," she whispered, because she always had.

He raised himself up over her, his voice dark and compelling. "Touch me."

She obeyed, running her fingertips down his back, teasing the ridged indentation of muscle until he trembled. Then suddenly he felt her hands closing around his bulging sex. He stared down in fascination, then squeezed his eyes shut, shuddering with pleasure. His mind went blank. He was lost. Her soft touch was his undoing. She had tamed him with tenderness.

"No one has ever made me feel like this . . . I'll die if I'm not inside you . . ."

Then his body was covering hers, and he kissed her again, his mouth tasting of whisky and sin. "I can't wait anymore," he said roughly, tangling his hand in her hair. "Don't be afraid."

"I wasn't afraid until you said that. Why should I be afraid of you?"

Still, she was frightened for a moment, that final moment when she hovered between innocence and becoming his. "Connor," she said in a hesitant voice, "I might want to think this over just a little long—"

His look of raw determination silenced her. His long hair swung forward as he straddled her, spreading her thighs. When she felt his thick shaft penetrate her, branding her his own, she shivered and pressed her shoulders to the floor to anchor her. He thrust, and she arched with an age-old instinct, caught in an internal storm of thunder and lightning, electricity racing down every nerve ending. She couldn't control the wild beating of her heart.

He took possession of her body until he touched her woman's soul, until he found solace, forged the bond, made the alliance his lonely heart had ached for. He drove into her until there was no part of her that did not answer to him.

"And now we belong to each other," he said with a long-drawn groan of pleasure as he surrendered to pure sensation. "I'll never let you go."

Chapter

32

❧

He was trying to sneak her up to his bed when the midnight summons came. His shirt was slung around his shoulders, entangled with the sash on Maggie's robe. They were a wee bit tipsy on blackberry wine and each other.

He'd even made it halfway up the stairs, Maggie snuggled in his arms. They probably would have reached his room sooner if he hadn't stopped every ten seconds to kiss her. The house was utterly black, the lights extinguished hours ago. Uncensored fantasies filled his head as he contemplated the hours left until morning. He wanted to devour her. He wanted to debauch her on the landing. He felt powerful and insatiable.

Then Dougie, clomping up the stairs behind them with all the subtlety of a warhorse, ruined everything.

"There's a letter just come for her ladyship," he announced loudly enough to awaken the entire household. "Thought it might be important."

"Not now," Connor said through his teeth. He made a meaningful signal with the hand hooked around Maggie's bottom. "We're on our way *upstairs*. I'm carrying Lady Maggie to my room."

Dougie raised his candle to her face. "Dinna tell me the lassie's no feelin' well," he said worriedly. "Best to put her in her own bed, my lord. My granny always said ye'll catch a nasty chest cold switchin' beds—"

Connor snatched the expensive vellum envelope from Dougie's hand. "When did this come?"

"A few minutes after midnight," Dougie answered dourly. "Looks like an invitation. Hell of an hour to be sending letters if ye ask me."

Connor let Maggie slide down to her feet. "What is it?" she asked, covering her mouth to hide a hiccough.

Connor's face darkened as he tore open the envelope. " 'Dear Miss Saunders,' " he read slowly. " 'The honor of your company is requested tomorrow morning at nine o'clock in Glamhurst Castle on a matter of the utmost secrecy. It is advised that you come alone. Most sincerely yours, Lord Anonymous.' "

Maggie wobbled backward, balancing herself against Connor's arm. "Lord who?"

"Anonymous." Connor stared down at the note, cold fury glittering in his eyes.

"Glamhurst Castle has been empty for nigh on twenty years," Dougie said quietly.

Maggie met Connor's gaze. "The duchess mentioned that someone had moved in a few days ago," she said. "A man no one has seen or heard. She thought he might be a rich American. He brought quite an extensive retinue with him, footmen and maidservants. She was afraid he means to use the woods for hunting."

"Funny name, Anonymous," Dougie said. "I dinna trust him."

Connor's voice rose into the darkness from the depths of the brocade-curtained bed. "You're not going to that castle, Maggie."

"Of course I'm not going. Do you think I'm quite mad?" She scooted back against the carved pine headboard, then bent over him in alarm. "You aren't going, are you? Not by yourself."

"No." He avoided her eyes, drawing her back down against his chest, his big hand wrapped possessively in her hair. She sighed in obvious contentment. He, on the other hand, was a burning tangle of anger and anxiety.

"Do you think it's from the man who has Sheena?" she whispered.

He stroked her shoulder, absently staring across the shadowed room at the door. "I don't know, lass."

"Why would he be so open if he meant me harm?" Maggie thought aloud. "Would he dare to hurt me knowing I was under your protection?"

"You'd be surprised at what some people are capable of." He looked down at her thoughtfully, his chest tightening with emotion. "Or perhaps you wouldn't. You've seen your share of sorrow, haven't you?"

He set out for the castle at dawn. When he left the room, Maggie was dead to the world, curled around a goose-feathered pillow with her dainty feet hanging over the bed. She didn't so much as twitch an eyelid when he bent to kiss her. She was safe, and he meant for her to stay that way.

"No more bad dreams for you," he said with grim resolve. "I'm putting an end to it today. Nothing is going to hurt you again if I can help it."

He dressed in his heavy woolen hunting clothes and took his pistol from the bureau drawer. As he tucked it into his coat pocket, the meeting in the parlor with Sebastien broke into his thoughts.

Your shoulder is obviously bothering you, Sebastien. Don't tell me all this cloak and dagger business has given you bursitis.

Just a run-in with an old friend.

I ran him through the shoulder, sir. . . .

What did he really know of Sebastien? Letters of character could be forged, even from the Prime Minister and members of Parliament. Seals could be stolen. Connor had never bothered to check Sebastien's credentials. Why would he have? The man moved in elite circles. He'd always gone out of his way to help Connor, and until recently, Connor had no reason to suspect him of any malice.

After all, even a spymaster had to retire sooner or later, and Sebastien certainly wasn't the first Frenchman to settle in Scotland. The two countries had been political allies for ages.

But suddenly he realized that Sebastien knew far too much about Connor's life than he needed to, and he was undeniably interested in Maggie. Obsessed with her, perhaps. Nothing else could have brought him all this way across Scotland. There hadn't been a spy in these remote hills for almost a hundred years.

The truth hit him like a thunderbolt.

Sebastien was the elusive wounded man, and whether or not he was linked to the Balfour murder, he had to be insane to think Connor would let him get to Maggie.

Maggie surfaced from the dream, fighting for breath. Tears of frustration burned her throat. She'd been so close this time. She had actually reached the bedchamber door at the château and opened it. She had seen her sister's silhouette against a backdrop of brilliant light, and the answer to all her questions had been just within her—

Connor was gone.

She sat up in the bed and stared, bewildered, around the room. The bureau drawer was half open, and with a flash of panic, she remembered awakening to watch him load his pistol during the night.

"I'm going hunting in the morning," he'd said when she sleepily inquired what on earth he was doing.

A shiver of fear shot through her.

Hunting an enemy. He would shun the laws he represented in order to handle the matter like a Highlander. She should have known he'd been too composed last night when he'd read that note. A man like Connor would always confront danger.

By the time she'd dressed and rushed downstairs, she discovered that Claude and Daphne, as well as Connor, had been missing for hours.

The three of them had been spotted by the kitchen maid shortly after sunrise on the hilly road to Glamhurst Castle. The man she loved, her butler, and her pet. All she cared about in the world on a mission to protect her, to confront a madman. Panic washed over her like a tidal wave. What if she was too late to do anything? Why had she not sensed the fury beneath Connor's deceptive calm?

It was market day, and Dougie and Mrs. Urquhart would not be back until late afternoon. Most of the servants had accompanied them to bring home supplies. It took two hours to reach the nearest village on horseback. She didn't know where to turn. She only knew she had to help Connor, or go mad with helplessness and fear.

She was on her way to the stable to saddle a horse, intending to ride to Rebecca's cottage when the duchess's coach rolled up into the driveway. Before the woman could plant one booted foot down on the steps, Maggie rushed over to meet her, her face white with worry.

"Good morning, Maggie," the duchess said in her brusque voice. "Claude's promised to give me fencing lessons in the garden. Thought I'd improve my riposte. I've brought Rebecca along with horse liniment in case my shooting shoulder gives out."

"Claude isn't here." Maggie blinked hard, pulling the sinister note from her cloak pocket. "Neither is Connor. They've gone off to confront Lord Anonymous in the castle."

Rebecca leaned across the seat to look through the opened door. "Lord who, dear?"

The duchess scanned the note, shaking her grizzled head in grim pronouncement. "Considering everything that has happened so far, I don't like the sound of this."

"I don't either," Maggie burst out. Hadn't she once been afraid that somehow she would indirectly lead Connor into danger? Hadn't he himself sensed a threat in the woods?

"Odd seal. Quite impressive." The duchess ran her callused thumb over the blurry blob of wax on the envelope. "It looks expensive."

"It isn't a black rose, is it?" Rebecca asked in alarm.

"I don't think so," Maggie said. "At first I thought it looked a little familiar, but it's too smeared to distinguish."

"Presumptuous bastard, this Lord Anonymous," the duchess murmured.

Maggie drew a steadying breath. "We're not helping Connor by standing here in idle chitchat. His life might be in danger at this very moment."

"I rather doubt it," Rebecca said reassuringly. "Connor could make micefeet out of any man stupid enough to confront him. Besides, Maggie, the note was written for you. This person doesn't seem to be interested in my brother."

"Which could be a trick," the duchess said. "For all we know, the madman might have Connor hidden in the castle dungeon right now."

Maggie's composure began to collapse. "Along with Claude and Daphne. They've been gone for hours. Anything could have happened to them."

Rebecca and the duchess shared concerned looks. "The wee doggie is missing too?" Rebecca said. "Morna, why are we wasting time blethering? We can devise a plan to rescue them on the way."

The duchess gave Maggie a gentle prod toward the coach. "Frances can drive us halfway there, but after that the road narrows to a footpath. Damn good thing I brought my guns. It looks like we're going to do battle, girls."

Maggie climbed into the coach, her face pinched with anxiety. "Shouldn't we alert the authorities—perhaps ask Captain Balgonie or Sir Angus to join us?"

"I don't see why," the duchess said, climbing in after her. "Angus would complain about having to walk. Balgonie would complain that he was getting his trousers dirty, and the delay could cost us at least an hour. What do you say, Becky? Do we need the men to help us or not?"

Rebecca gracefully drew in her skirts to allow room for Maggie on the seat. "I shouldn't think so. After all, you have your guns and I have Ares. That ought to be more than adequate protection. It's not as if we haven't tackled trouble before."

"True," the duchess said. "It won't be much different than the time we rescued those foxes from Lady Rosyth's wretched hunt in Nairn two years ago."

"Or set all those hedgehogs loose last summer when the gypsies were hunting them for stew," Rebecca agreed, flipping her braid over her shoulder.

"Then it's settled." The duchess rapped against the roof with her rifle butt. "The men would only be in the way."

Chapter

33

"I don't believe it," the duchess said, pulling her head in from the window as the coach shuddered to a stop. "There's another carriage blocking our way. Don't the idiots know this is private property? Frances," she shouted, "take care of this immediately."

An athletic-looking grandmother in her fifties, Frances jumped down obediently from the box to confront the driver of the obstructing vehicle. A friendly argument ensued in the middle of the road, and then a woman's plea for peace rose above the furor.

"I know that voice." Maggie leaned over Rebecca and Ares to draw back the leather curtains. "It's Mrs. Macmillan."

"Mrs. Who?" the duchess said, pulling out a flask of whisky from her cloak.

"Connor's mistress," Maggie said as she slid off the seat to the door.

The duchess almost choked on her wee nip. "His what?"

"You remember Ardath," Rebecca said with a smile. "Connor brought her here last spring. She got in a fight with that horrid old man at the fair who was trying to sell his daughter's favors. She had him thrown in the clink and found the girl a good home."

"Ah." Morna nodded in remembrance. "A lovely woman. But I thought she planned to give Buchanan the mitten when they got home."

"She did." Maggie stepped very carefully over Morna's guns to reach the door. The woman was a walking arsenal. "However, despite the end of their romantic association, they've decided to remain friends. I wonder what on earth she's doing here."

"I've brought news about Sheena," Ardath explained a few minutes later when Maggie asked her that very question.

They were huddled together on the hillside road a few yards before it ended abruptly in a densely wooded footpath. The previous Jacobite rebels who had owned the castle had done everything possible to block access to their stronghold, intending to repel British soldiers. Enormous boulders had been rolled down the hill like bowling balls to prevent easy passage.

Maggie felt a gust of wind rustle through the skeletal beech coppice behind them. "Sheena isn't dead, is she?" she asked in dread.

Ardath, who looked travel-worn and frazzled, absently stuffed an unruly red curl under her hat. "She is not, but I daresay she will be when Connor finds out what she's done. I'm terrified of how he'll take this."

"What has the little fiend been up to now?" Rebecca asked, limping up behind them.

Ardath turned. "She planned her own abduction and eloped to Gretna Green with the man Connor had forbidden her to see. The criminal I defended to Connor's face turned out to be a cad. Or half a cad. At least Henry had the decency to marry her."

Maggie was indignant. "Oh! To think that they dragged me into their nasty plot, and I was so concerned about her."

Ardath sighed. "The silly girl is quite sorry she involved you. It seems she mistook you for Philomena Elliot. She thought you'd be the perfect witness to the abduction because Philomena had never seen Henry before, and, quite frankly, Philomena isn't known for her brains. The whole wretched affair was an act. You were used to convince Connor she'd been kidnapped."

"I can't believe I risked my neck trying to rescue such a deceitful creature," Maggie exclaimed.

Ardath nodded in agreement. "The carriage driver also sends his apologies for his part. The man was truly concerned that you were hurt when you fell in the courtyard."

"This is a criminal act in itself," Rebecca said angrily. "Connor will certainly have the marriage annulled. And if he has any sense at all, he'll thrash Sheena soundly for what she's put us all through."

"He will do neither," Ardath said, "although she is doubtless deserving of both. The brat is pregnant, married, and worried sick about his reaction. So is her husband. They have employed me as an intermediary, a position I resent but have accepted to protect Connor's name. He does not need another embarrassment at this stage of his life. The public is already clamoring for safety in the streets."

The duchess frowned at Maggie. "We'd best not repeat the story about the scarecrow then. It doesn't make him sound very competent."

"What scarecrow? No, don't tell me. I don't think I could stand another shock." Ardath sank down wearily on a rotten pine stump, taking a swallow of whisky from Morna's flask. Then she noticed the rifle tucked under Rebecca's arm and the deer hound slavering at her heels. "Something else has happened, hasn't it? What's wrong?"

Maggie lifted her eyes to the bulk of the castle, encircled in gray-violet bands of mist. It looked like a medieval stronghold, faraway and forbidding. "Connor went up there to confront the person he believed was Sheena's kidnapper," she said slowly. "He went to handle the matter man to man."

Rebecca looked up in sudden horror. "But there is no kidnapper. He never existed in the first place and couldn't have sent that note."

"Which means that someone else wanted to lure either me or him there." Maggie shook herself out of her trance.

"Someone who has gone to a great deal of trouble and expense to spring a trap. But who?"

"The Balfour murderer." Ardath came to her feet, her face as pale as chalk. "Connor always said his suspect was a wealthy nobleman without a conscience. Only a man with money could afford to lease a castle. Somehow he must have guessed that the way to get to Connor was through you."

Chapter

34

They had the castle surrounded.

Rebecca and Ares took the rear. Maggie, the duchess, and Ardath positioned themselves at the east wing of the keep where, apparently to counteract the November gloom, the inhabitants had lit candles which glinted through the cracked mullioned windows. The three women had stacked several empty wine kegs to use as a ladder beneath what appeared to be the parlor window.

At any rate, it was one of the few rooms in the castle that looked occupied. Thistle and bracken fern grew waist-high in the once-grand courtyard. Merlins and jackdaws nested on the parapets where Scottish rebels had waited for their Stuart prince. A thin wind rattled the shutters of the abandoned dovecote. The west turret bore black gauges in its side from a long-forgotten battle. The east tower looked no better. Even the ghosts of Glamhurst's former glory had faded away into obscurity.

The duchess tore off her leather gloves with her teeth. "Maggie will have to climb up to have a look-see. I'll serve as a crow while Ardath holds these barrels steady. Whatever you do, don't let them fall."

"Perhaps we should knock at the front door," Ardath suggested. "I could pretend to be a gypsy selling apples."

The duchess gave her a leveling look. "Do you have any apples?"

Ardath pursed her lips. "Well, no, now that you ask, I don't."

"Then that takes care of that. Help me give Maggie a leg up. There's something queer going on in that house. It's too quiet. I hope they haven't killed Buchanan yet. He's a hard-hearted bastard, and there were times when I've been tempted to shoot him myself, but he has his good qualities."

She and Ardath hooked their hands together to hoist Maggie into the air, then steadied the tower of barrels while she scrambled to grasp the window ledge for leverage.

"Well," Ardath said anxiously, "what do you see?"

Maggie blew a wisp of hair from her eyes. "There are . . . three men, no, there are four of them. Good God, these are the filthiest windows I've ever looked through in my life."

The duchess glanced up. "Do you see Buchanan? Is he alive?"

There was silence. When Maggie spoke again, her voice reflected both profound relief and bewilderment. "He's sitting on the sofa. His feet are propped on a footstool."

"He's dead?" Ardath whispered, closing her eyes.

A scowl tightened Maggie's face. "Not unless that's his ghost who just stuffed a wedge of cheese into his mouth and washed it down with a glass of wine."

"Cheese and wine?" The duchess lowered her rifle in confusion. "That's a peculiar way to do away with someone. What manner of man is this murderer anyway?"

Maggie rubbed the heel of her hand across the grimy windowpane, clenching her teeth as if to stem the tears that slipped silently down her face. It was an eternity before she could trust herself to speak, and then the words came in halting snatches of breath. "He is . . . a prude and a . . . tyrant. A snob of the first water. The man holding Connor captive is my brother. Robert Phillipe . . . the sixth Duc de Saint-Evremond."

"Your brother?" Ardath said in amazement. "The one you've been trying to find for years? What on earth is he doing with Connor in a castle?"

Maggie slowly slid to the ground. "That's exactly what I intend to find out. Stay here. I'm going inside."

Chapter

35

~~~

"Robert. Robert Phillipe." She kept repeating his name in disbelief, hardly aware that Connor had jumped up to support her until the three other men in the room rudely bumped him out of the way.

Claude, Robert, and a third man she did not know at first. Tall, elegantly dressed with his arm in a sling, he guided her to a chair. *"Assieds-toi,* Marguerite," he said with a sympathetic clucking of his tongue. "Sit, chérie. I warned your brother this would be difficult, but he simply couldn't wait another day to see you. There was truly no easy way to do this, and of course, he needed to be sure."

His voice faded into the buzzing of a hundred bees in her ears. She stared at him as he knelt, his concerned face coming into focus. "Sebastien," she said numbly. "Sebastien the spy. Papa's secretary. *That* Sebastien. *Mon Dieu.* I thought you were dead. Oh—the wounded man. It was you. You're the one who followed me here from Edinburgh."

"Yes, it was me," Sebastien admitted. "Claude ran me through in the woods before I could unmask myself. I have been in Scotland for months, waiting for the right moment

287

to approach you. I must say you've developed quite a nose for trouble."

"For months?"

Connor hunkered down in front of her, grasping her cold hands in his. "You've had a shock, lass. So did I. I knew Sebastien as a retired spy, a friend to the British. I had no idea he was so closely connected to your life."

"Oh, Connor."

"Take a sip of wine," he urged her. "Everything will be all right."

She drank the entire glass that Claude solicitously brought her; in the back of her mind she kept thinking that Connor was due for a little shock himself when he heard about Sheena's selfish prank. But even her concern about that vanished as she gazed across the room at the silent man who dared not approach her, his face hidden in shadow.

Her brother. He was alive. *Thank you, God. Thank you, God.*

"I know it's you, Robert. Why are you hiding in this old castle? Is this intrigue still necessary after all these years? It was you that followed us across the moor, wasn't it? Robert, answer me. Oh, you've made me so angry. You and Sebastien in your frightening masks."

"The last thing I wanted was to frighten you," he said softly.

She handed her empty glass to Sebastien, rising to her feet. "I never gave up hope. Why did it take you so long?" She gripped his hands, trying unsuccessfully to turn him toward her. "Why?" she whispered. "Why won't you look me in the face?"

"The soldiers torched the house that night, Marguerite," he explained solemnly, refusing to move away from the window. "You were correct in remembering that you ran up the staircase to warn Jeanette. Unfortunately, the soldiers had gotten there first. You burst in before I had a chance to help."

She was grateful for the wine that had warmed her as Robert began his story, filling in the gaps in memory that had haunted her since her last night in the château. She did not acknowledge how much she appreciated Connor's powerful arms around her shoulders, but she doubted that she would have been able to endure the truth which Robert painfully revealed.

"The room was on fire," Robert continued in a voice so low she had to strain to hear it. "Jeanette had been burning Papa's papers when the police arrived. They incriminated several of our friends."

Maggie closed her eyes. "They killed her."

"They raped her," Sebastien corrected gently. "They interrogated her, then left her to burn to death while they searched the rest of the château."

Maggie shook her head in frustration, tears burning her throat. "I still don't remember. Why can't I remember?"

"It's a blessing, perhaps," Robert said, turning finally to regard her. "I shall never, ever forget the look on your face when I found you. You were kneeling over Jeanette's body, a little tigress trying to defend her with an ancient sword. Claude and I had to drag you outside to get you to safety."

Maggie rubbed her cheeks with the back of her hand. "Why did you keep this from me, Claude?"

The elderly servant bowed his head in heartfelt remorse. "Your mother made me swear I would protect you from pain at all costs. I did not know what happened to Robert and Jeanette after that night. I prayed you would not remember what you had seen. I . . . I hoped you would forget. Keeping you safe was all that mattered."

She shook her head dazedly. "Deep inside, a part of me remembered. Those scars never healed."

"Nor mine." Robert raised his face to hers, allowing the candlelight to reveal the brand he bore from that night. When she did not flinch in revulsion, but only lovingly raised her hand to his disfigured cheek, he smiled in sadness and relief.

"The doctors did not think I would survive," he said. "My back and legs were burned as well. Sebastien sent me to the West Indies, where Papa had modest land holdings. For years I dared not try to track you down. I was sick in body and mind. I hoped that with Aunt Flora you would assume a new identity and forge a life free from fear."

"You might have sent me word, if only to let me know that you were alive."

"It took time to trace you," he replied. "And who was I to draw you back into a world of danger and subterfuge?"

"Your father left behind documents that implicated many highly placed people in treason," Sebastien added gently. "It was my job to make sure that none of the family's enemies had survived."

"Including members of the British nobility," Connor guessed.

"Yes." Robert released a deep sigh. "I had to be certain that by revealing my identity, I was not endangering her life. And, of course, that she was not an impostor posing as a de Saint-Evremond."

She gave a faint sniff of resentment. "Why would anyone bother?"

He raised his brow in astonishment. "To lay claim to the family fortune, naturally. The estates have been restored, Marguerite. It is time to resume our old life. I am here to take you home."

Connor could practically feel the excitement shoot through Maggie's small body like an arrow, and it was all he could do not to grab her and run from the castle when she worked her hand free from his.

Home.

I am here to take you home.

He gazed at her in dread, waiting to hear her protest, to refuse, to insist she had already found her home. Instead, she stared at her brother's scarred face and contemplated his offer as if he had just handed her the world on a platter. Love and loyalty blazed in her eyes. He felt desperate to draw her back to him, to remind her of what they had shared. He knew how much she loved and needed her family. He could protect her from danger, but could he prevent her from leaving him of her own free will?

"What happened to Jeanette?" she said in a pained whisper.

Robert averted his face. Claude gave a mournful shake of his head and began to polish the sideboard with the cuff of his sleeve. Sebastien contemplated a spot on the floor. The agony in Maggie's voice made Connor want to shake Robert until his teeth rattled. Hell, if there was bad news, why drag it out any longer?

"She . . . she's dead?" Maggie said, folding down into the chair.

"She is not dead," Robert said stiffly, "although for the disgrace she has brought the family name, she may as well be. I am seriously considering disowning her."

Maggie shot to her feet. "This is unconscionable, punishing our poor sister because she was the victim of a brutal crime. She couldn't help being assaulted by those soldiers."

Connor's upper lip curled in contempt. "As one man to another, I find your attitude repugnant. In fact, I'm seriously considering taking you by the lapels of your fancy jacket and throwing you out the window."

"I'm not talking about *that*," Robert said in horror. "I would never blame Jeanette for her bravery that night. It's what she has made of herself since then that I abhor."

Maggie cast a bewildered look at Sebastien. "Don't tell me my sister has become a prostitute."

"Not quite," Robert replied. "However, I venture to say it is the next step. Jeanette is engaged to a butcher, but the worst part is what she is doing to support herself." He took a quivering breath like a dragon about to blow fire from its nostrils. "It's with the deepest shame that I inform you Jeanette has become a professional dancer. Your sister is a ballerina."

"I'm shocked to my toenails," Connor said with a straight face.

Maggie dropped her head back against the chair. "Somebody bring me a glass of water before I expire of the embarrassment."

Robert smiled grimly, the unmarred side of his face with its aquiline features actually handsome in the half-light. "Very amusing, infants. Marguerite, you are no better yourself—breaking into houses, giving deportment lessons for a living. I can see I have my work cut out for me before the wedding."

"Wedding?" Maggie lifted her head and glanced questioningly at Connor, who froze in mid-motion with another wedge of white cheese halfway to his mouth.

"Are you offering to pay, your grace?" he asked hopefully.

Robert ignored him. "I think it might be better for us all if your acquaintance took his leave now, Marguerite. I understand that he is involved in a criminal case and probably will appreciate a reprieve from guarding you."

Connor pushed aside the tray Claude held out, his thick eyebrows gathering in a scowl of displeasure. "This is my wedding. While you might be a person of rank in your country, I am also a man of some importance who must consider public opinion. I want to be in on planning the ceremony."

Robert looked away.

Connor looked upset. "I am the Lord Advocate of Scotland. Does that mean anything to you?"

"I can't say that it does." Robert turned to Maggie. "Have I met him before today? He does seem vaguely familiar."

"He looks like the statue in the garden that you covered in gold paint." She braced both hands on the arms of the chair. "What are you planning, Robert? I have had more than enough trouble in my life."

Robert withdrew his handkerchief from his vest pocket and pressed it to his nose. "Trouble," he said with a sniff. "Could anyone possibly have gotten into more trouble than you?" He gestured to the thick dossier of papers on the sideboard. "The Chief, Marguerite? Heaven's Court? And that name . . ." He tsked.

"Name?" she said darkly.

Disapproval deepened his voice. "Maggie Saunders? Was there ever anything so common? I shall have to whisk you off to Marseilles for a good six months to scrub the taint of the sewers off you. With any luck Bernard won't hear about your scandalous past until you're a blushing bride and in the family way. He believes you have been safely locked away in a convent all these years."

"Bernard." Maggie paled. "Bernard is still alive?" she asked weakly.

Connor's head snapped up. He couldn't decide whether it was hope or horror that had caused that quivery catch in her voice, but he did know he didn't like it. "Who is Bernard?" he demanded.

"Bernard is very much alive," Robert said in answer to

Maggie's question. "He is also the heir to his father's titles and Norman estate. He has been loyal to your memory, Marguerite. He never married. He always believed in his faithful heart that you two would be reunited."

"So he finally became the seventh Comte de la Tourette." A secretive smile crossed her face. "I can't believe it. Do you remember the time he built that pirate ship and sailed downstream to besiege the château?"

Claude coughed into his hand to suppress a chuckle. "You counterattacked him with a barrage of arrows, mademoiselle. It was a grand battle."

Sebastien smiled. "You were a very good shot, Marguerite. He didn't sit for a week, as I recall."

Robert was grinning from ear to ear. "And when he locked our German tutor in the dungeon? He was the bravest boy we knew."

Connor glanced around the room in disbelief. "Excuse me. Before we break into a rousing chorus of 'Auld Lang Syne,' would someone tell me who the bloody hell Bernard is?"

Claude rolled his eyes in disapproval.

Sebastien grimaced in embarrassment.

Robert muttered something about "Scots barbarian" and proceeded to continue his conversation with Maggie. "The nuptials will be held in Paris, of course. Bernard's eldest brother is a priest now."

"Nuptials?" Connor smiled nastily. "I have the distinct impression that I'm being ignored. Do you have any idea what Maggie and I mean to each other?"

Maggie sprang out of her chair to grasp his arm, talking in an undertone. "I'll handle this in my own way, Connor. Just allow us an evening together to straighten everything out."

He shrugged off her hand. "We'll straighten it out now. I want your brother to understand how you and I feel about each other."

"I'll tell him tomorrow," Maggie whispered.

Connor glared at her. "Tell him now."

"Yes, tell me now," Robert said quietly.

Maggie raised her face. "We're in love, Robert. I should think it was obvious."

He swallowed hard as if this were more than he could accept. "People in strained circumstances sometimes fall prey to feelings they would not normally entertain. You have both feared for your lives. You have been forced into an unnatural relationship."

Maggie shook her head. "It's the most natural relationship I've ever known. I love him, Robert, and I would have loved him if we'd been two strangers who bumped into each other at a ball."

Robert stared at her. "But he was only your body-guard—"

"I'm not giving her up," Connor said. "I can't."

"Are you trying to tell me that you have ruined my sister?" Robert said softly.

Sebastien smiled uneasily. "What a question. Can't we just enjoy our reunion for now?"

Connor squared his shoulders, aware of the anger simmering beneath Robert's silence. He couldn't admit that he and Maggie had been intimate. Not to her own brother. He would never humiliate her that way.

"Tell him the truth," Maggie said. "Connor, let my brother know what we did last night."

"We drank wine and played cards," Connor said stiffly. "Your sister is as pure as the day I met her."

"No," Maggie whispered.

Sebastien shot Connor a grateful look. "What did I tell you, Robert? His reputation is undeserved. He's an honorable man."

Robert grinned at Connor. "Forgive me for even asking. You see, I love Marguerite so very much, and if you had ruined her, I'm afraid I'd have had no choice but to call you out. She would have lost one of us to a duel."

Connor blinked. "Are you serious?"

"Oh, quite," Robert replied, gazing at Maggie with tears in his eyes. "I saw one sister dishonored and was helpless to save her. I would cheerfully die before allowing that to happen again."

Connor felt Maggie touch his arm again. "Please don't fight him, Connor. Oh, please, please don't," she whispered. "I'll handle this in my own way. Just allow us an evening together to explain how I feel."

Numb, he shook his head. "No."

"Yes." She dug her fingers into his arm. "He means it. You don't know him."

He turned his head to stare down at her. "I'm not letting you go."

"I won't go. I promise."

Connor's throat tightened. She loved him, but she also loved her brother. What if Robert persuaded her to return to France for just a little while? What if, once she saw her home, she began to forget her bodyguard?

"Don't leave me, Maggie," he said.

"Let me be alone with my sister," Robert said. "We have many things still to discuss."

"Your coat, sir?" Claude said in blatant distaste, holding out Connor's favorite hunting jacket with his face averted.

"I've enjoyed knowing you, Connor," Sebastien called from the sideboard. "I hope you will keep in touch."

A maid flittered into the room with a platter of petits fours.

Four burly footmen appeared to usher Connor out. He pushed them away, backing into the hall with his eyes never leaving Maggie's face. "Who's Bernard?" he shouted.

"He was my betrothed," Maggie said hesitantly as, once again, a door to her was closed in his face. "You know how these old families are, Connor. Tradition, engagements made over the cradle. Don't worry, though. I'll straighten everything out."

As Connor stood, stunned, in the dark unlit corridor, he could hear Robert's voice ringing behind those closed doors.

"What a beast that man is, Marguerite, involving you in a kidnapping and murder case. I half expected him to start swinging a battle-ax at our heads. But then Scotland has never been a civilized country, has it? Ah, well. It is a good thing, perhaps, that we are in such a remote spot. It will make our departure in the morning that less conspicuous. We will have to contrive a respectable past for you, of course. The convent is safe, and Bernard will be none the wiser."

Connor's blood boiled as he waited outside that door for the refusal from Maggie that never came. And he was still standing there, burning with betrayal twenty minutes later, listening to the cheerful sounds of family celebration within when the duchess found him.

He gave her a grim smile. "Robert is right about one thing. We Scots are still primitive in our rituals. By law Maggie and I would only have to pledge our troth to each other to be legally wed."

"Then pledge it and get on with the bedding, if you haven't taken care of that part already, which I suspect you have." The duchess nodded briskly at Connor's silence. "I thought so."

"Hell, hell, hell." He broke away from the door to kick the dark stone wall, stubbing his toe for his trouble.

The duchess yanked off her cap and ran her hand through her untidy mop of silver-gray curls. "Stop creating such a fuss. You're the Lord Advocate. Make up a law about Frenchmen inhabiting Scottish castles."

"What damn good would that do?" Connor paced the narrow perimeters of the twisting passageway. "He'll either take her away in the morning to marry this Count of the Toilette, or I'll be forced to shoot him. And if she objected, I didn't hear it. She's going to leave me, Morna."

"She loves you, Connor."

"I know that, but if her brother persuades her to postpone marrying me, I won't be able to stand it. I need her now. Once he convinces her to visit France, I'll have to fight to get her back."

"Family ties are powerful. There's a chance you're right."

He gave her a black scowl. "It's not a chance I care to take."

"Then just be a man about it and abduct her," the duchess said practically. "That's what my husband did when my fa ther was holding out for the crown prince of Hartzburg. Climbed a ladder to my bedroom and had me breeding be fore my father ever realized I was gone."

"Don't think it hasn't crossed my mind."

The duchess gave him an encouraging thump on the back. "Do it, lad. You can use my coach as a getaway. Becky and I will cover you. Ardath can make the arrangements for a ceremony back at the house."

Connor frowned. "Ardath? Ardath is here?"

"I'll explain it to you later," she said quickly. "You take care of rescuing your bride first. Come on. We've got to plan this thing properly. I'll find a way to alert Maggie to expect you."

The duchess was right. Connor had no choice but to marry Maggie immediately and take the matter of her future out of her brother's hands. Once Connor was a member of the family, Robert would have to accept him.

He realized it would be wise to plan an escape route if he had to abduct Maggie in the dark. Obviously she would have to sleep somewhere in the east wing since the rest of the castle was crumbling and uninhabitable. He'd have to strike tonight unless he wanted to end up chasing her across the Channel and all over France. He wasn't going to wait for her to be pushed back into Bernard's welcoming arms.

He knew the castle's history and that the previous tenants had converted the roundtower chamber into a bedroom before their final defeat. Secluded, it was the perfect place to hide a princess. Connor almost wished he'd thought to keep Maggie there himself, away from the world. While he was glad that her heart's wish at finding her brother had been realized, he went insane at the thought of her belonging to a man she'd pledged her heart to in childhood. Perhaps Connor couldn't insert himself in her past, but he was damn well going to dominate her future.

His hunch proved correct. The chamber had been dusted and aired, the stone floor swept of the leaves that blew in the unshuttered window. The heavy bedstead boasted fresh lace-trimmed Belgian linen. A bowl of nuts and imported fruit sat on the nightstand. A virginal white-ivory nightrail lay over a chair.

Daphne dozed by the hearth where a cheerful fire blazed blue and gold flames. She thumped her tail as Connor entered but didn't bother to rouse herself from her cozy spot. The room had been prepared for royalty, for the newly recovered de Saint-Evremond heiress. Connor was an intruder.

His face defiant and determined, he pushed open the narrow door to the stairwell onto the battlements and ran up the winding steps. Wind stung his eyes as he walked to the edge of the crenellated wall.

He leaned over, contemplating the sobering drop to the wooded ravine below. It would be quite a feat to sneak her down that turret wall without risking life and limb. Not impossible, but perhaps with a decent rope and ladder—

"*Sacre-bleu!*" a horrified voice shouted behind him. "Thank the good Lord I am not too late!"

Connor nearly jumped out of his skin as he swung around to see Claude charging toward him like a bull. Before he could react, the older man grabbed him by the scruff of the neck, spun him around, and dragged him away from the unshuttered crenellation.

"What are you doing, you cabbage head?" Connor shouted.

"This is not the answer, sir. You must be strong!"

They did a sort of shuffling dance across the walkway, Claude trying to shove Connor behind one of the merlons, Connor struggling to free himself without hurting the older man. The wind battered them unmercifully, heightening the sense of melodrama.

In the end they stumbled across a rusty Jacobite cannon, landing flat on their backs like a pair of breathless tortoises with their arms still locked around each other.

"Do you mind explaining what that was all about?" Connor said as he stared up, stunned, at the sky.

"No woman is worth such a horrible end, sir." Claude gasped weakly, placing his hand over his heart. "Not even my mistress."

Daphne bounded across the battlement, leaping over Connor's chest to cover his face in slobbery kisses. Connor scooped the dog to his chest and sat up in irritation. "How many glasses of champagne did you have, Claude? What in God's name are you ranting about?"

Claude struggled into an upright position, wringing his hands. "Suicide, sir. Think of those you'd leave behind. Think of my poor mistress."

"Leave behind?" Maggie called from the depths of the turret doorway. "Did you get lost on your way outside, Connor? Why are you and Claude sitting on a cannon?"

Claude shook his head in sorrow. "His lordship was contemplating suicide over you, my lady. I never realized he cared so much. Oh, sir. I have misjudged you. It appears you have a passionate heart, after all. I feel terrible."

Maggie hurried toward Connor, her small body buffeted by the wind, her face white with alarm. "Dear God, *I* never realized he was that sensitive a man, either. Suicide. You beast, Connor. Don't you care how I would have felt when I had to identify your body?"

"Claude? Marguerite?" Robert had apparently followed his sister up to her room. "Why is everybody gathered out here in this bitter wind? Why is that Scotsman sitting on a cannon?"

Claude rose stiffly to his feet. "Don't be too hard on him, your grace. He is under extreme emotional duress." His voice dropped in sympathy. "He was about to"—he made a somersaulting motion with his hands toward the wall—"you know."

Robert compressed his lips. "No, Claude, I do not know."

Maggie gestured covertly at the crenellation. "The tower, Robert." At his blank look, she gave a little hop on the balls of her feet. "Over the edge. . . ."

"He was doing acrobatics on the battlements?" Robert said in bewilderment. "Jumping rope?"

Connor leaned back against the cannon with Daphne in his lap to watch this impromptu game of charades played out. He saw no reason to interrupt. He couldn't very well admit he was plotting an abduction, anyway. Hell, let them think he was Lady Macbeth.

"He was trying to take his own life?" Robert finally guessed. He regarded Connor with a newfound respect mingled with contempt. "Well, I would not have guessed he had it in him. But, alas, Marguerite, this only proves me right. I could never have handed you over to a man who is that emotionally unstable."

Chapter

36

Connor sat in the moonlit castle garden and listened to Ardath in horrified silence. He felt betrayed, humiliated, enraged. That Sheena would put him through hell for almost a month. That she would defy and deceive him when he had only wanted her happiness. She couldn't have devised a better way to hurt or publicly embarrass him.

"She's afraid of you, Connor," Ardath explained gravely. "She got pregnant and was terrified to tell you. He married her. They're a family. You really have to accept it."

Rebecca, standing behind the bench, touched his slumped shoulder. "Poor big brother. You always think you know what's best for everyone."

"I do know what's best." He lifted his head, his hazel eyes bright with anger. "I've seen more of life than all of you stubborn women put together. Who do you think she'll come crawling to when her criminal husband can't pay the rent? And you, Rebecca, who will take care of you in your old age? Your helpless animals?"

"I will take care of myself," she said. "Oh, Connor. Stop worrying about us. Can I not simply be the family's eccentric old auntie who watches your children while you and Maggie are on holiday?"

Maggie.

He lifted his head to the roundtower window where she stood, framed in candlelight, imprisoned by the shackles of family obligation. She gave him a forlorn little wave. He didn't have the heart to wave back. He wanted her back in his arms, and he was going to get her if he had to tear that castle apart stone by stone.

He glanced around as the duchess returned from heaven-knew-where hefting a ladder over her shoulder. "The coast is clear, Connor. What are you waiting for?"

He eyed the rickety ladder she propped up against the garden wall. "What good is this thing supposed to do?" he said indignantly. "That won't reach halfway to the turret window."

"That's why I sneaked up to Maggie's room and gave her a nice long rope to knot around the bedpost," Morna replied. "She agrees that an abduction is probably the only way to avoid a duel. Good Lord, Connor, where is your initiative?"

"Morna, I love Maggie more than life itself but I am not climbing up on that ladder, rope or not."

The duchess squared her shoulders. "That's what I was afraid of. Therefore, prepared for every eventuality, I have drawn a map of an alternate abduction route."

Connor frowned down at the wrinkled parchment she pulled out of her trouser belt and spread beside him on the bench. "What are those little X's suppose to mean?" he said suspiciously.

"That's the way from Maggie's chamber through the unoccupied west wing. It's a bit of a walk but you'll manage."

"And all this scribbling over here? 'Thread. Salt. Horse liniment.' Is this some kind of secret code?"

The duchess peered down at the map. "No. It's the list Frances took to market. Just ignore it."

Connor's frown deepened. "There's something about this I don't like. The west wing is falling apart. And the east—"

"For heaven's sake, Buchanan," the duchess said. "Don't be such a twiddlepoop. One can't have a fairy tale castle at a time like this."

He sighed, rising to his feet. Thunder growled overhead, which didn't surprise him. Nothing would surprise him ever again. At least the foul weather was fitting.

A stormy Scottish night was perfect for an abduction.

Maggie was all packed and waiting to be abducted. There had been more to bring along than she'd anticipated, what with the wedding trousseau and family keepsakes Robert had thoughtfully left in her room.

He had planned everything to the last detail, much as Connor had tried to plan his sisters' lives. The trouble was, both men meant the best but usually ending up making a mess by interfering.

Even if Sheena stayed happily married to her embezzler husband for life, Connor would never admit he'd been wrong. And Robert would probably hold a grudge for the rest of his days because Maggie had defied tradition for the man she loved.

Connor. She did love him, too, so much she ached with it. She loved him for going to such lengths to prevent a duel with her brother. There was no doubt in her mind that a confrontation between the two men would end up with one of them seriously wounded if not dead. Robert was forcing her to defy him.

She leaned out of the turret window to search for Connor in the darkness. She hoped to goodness he knew what he was doing. He wasn't the sort of person prone to wildly romantic gestures.

She sighed as she watched him steal through the shadows of the ravine. He looked strong and powerful, a Highlander determined to carry off his bride. This was one Scottish tradition Maggie approved of, although she would have preferred to have her brother's blessing. Still, it was sweet of Connor to go to all the trouble of rescuing her. She only wished he'd hurry up before Robert realized what was happening. With all the racket Connor was making, someone in the castle was bound to hear him.

Her heart was so full of love and gratitude.

Robert and Jeanette were alive, and Connor didn't know it yet, but as soon as the murder trial ended, he was taking Maggie to Paris for their honeymoon.

Maggie suspected he would need a rest after winning the case of the century. Perhaps by that time Robert would have softened enough to at least let them stay in the château. She was dying for Connor to meet her sister, to admire her ancestral home.

A stone sailed through the window, the prearranged signal that the abduction was about to get under way.

Maggie ran back to the bed to test the rope that the duchess had brought her under the pretense of saying farewell. Then she hurled it out the window, hearing Connor curse as it hit him on the side of his head.

She started to crawl over the ledge, then stopped. "Where is the ladder?" she called down in confusion.

"There's been a change in plans," he shouted back. "We'll have to escape through the west wing garderobe."

"Into the drains?" Maggie said to herself, pulling her leg back over the ledge. "Whatever you say, Connor. But it doesn't seem nearly so romantic."

He appeared at her door nearly three minutes later. Maggie's breath caught as she turned toward him, her ruggedly handsome Highlander.

It seemed ironic that not long ago she had climbed a rope to rob him, and now he was stealing her, heart, body, and soul.

The Devil's Advocate abducting a woman.

She knew it would only add to the allure of his reputation.

She could hardly wait to see what other scandals they could brew up together as man and wife.

Chapter

37

"The trunk is going to break if you keep banging down the stairs like that, Connor."

"Maggie, the only thing that will break is our necks, and if you don't hold still, it is a distinct possibility. Please don't put your hands over my eyes when I'm carrying you. I can't see a damn thing in the dark as it is." He kicked the trunk down another step. "What on earth do you have in here anyway? A year's supply of cannonballs?"

"My wedding trousseau. Robert had it made for me. It's ever so lovely, all seed pearls and Valenciennes lace."

"Well, if that doesn't tickle me pink. I'm killing myself carting the trunk of clothes you were meant to wear to marry the Toilet Count. How long is this staircase anyway?"

"These types of stairs were built originally to repel invaders," Maggie said conversationally. "They're made narrow so that an enemy would have a hard time climbing up with a sword."

"Yes, well, they don't do much for a man going down with a woman, dog, and trunk either. Did we really have to bring Daphne along?"

"But she adores you." Maggie grazed his cheek with a

kiss, whispering sweetly, "So do I. Do you have any idea how much?"

He grunted, tentatively hooking his right foot over the trunk to feel for the next step. "Show me later, lass."

"I love you more than the de Saint-Evremond family code, more than chocolate éclairs and champagne, more than—"

"Is that a light I see flickering at the bottom of the stairs?" Connor asked worriedly. "Or is it a pool of water?"

"—pearls and diamonds, more than silk sheets and—"

"Quit licking my ear, lass. It's getting me aroused. This is no time for loveplay."

"That wasn't me. It was Daphne. Aren't you going to tell me you love me even once while you abduct me?"

Connor leaned his shoulder against the wall to rest his muscles. They had reached the halfway mark, but it was still a dangerous plunge in the dark if he fell. And something kept nagging at his mind. Something about the castle's history. "Maggie, I'm risking my neck to marry you. Hell, yes, I love you." He raised his voice to a shout. "I love you."

The shouting startled Daphne. She squeezed upward, paws flailing wildly to escape back into Maggie's arms. Unfortunately, Maggie had her arms laced around Connor's neck and couldn't grab hold of the dog in time.

She gave a horrified shriek. "Connor, I'm losing her!"

He jerked his left arm upward to grasp the poodle's wriggling posterior. In doing this he caught the dog, but lost his grip on Maggie. The trunk started to bump away from him as he locked his arm around her neck. Connor extended his leg to catch it only to realize there were no more stairs. He was treading air. The trunk was plummeting into a black void, and he was plunging forward to follow it.

Maggie released a shriek loud enough to be heard around the world. "Connor, the staircase is gone! We're all going to fall!"

He regained consciousness to see Maggie leaning over him on the stone cold floor of the garderobe, tears of concern wet on her cheeks. Her features slowly came into focus. "Connor, say something. Let me know you aren't dead."

"Non fit raptus propriae sponsae," he murmured.

Jillian Hunter

"Non—" She frowned, searching his face. "What are you trying to tell me?"

"Cannon law is quite clear on this point," he said calmly. "There is no illegal abduction if a woman consents to being carried off by her abductor. I could not be tried in a criminal court. The popular press is another matter."

"Can you move your feet?"

He lifted his head a few inches and wiggled his toes. "Apparently so. Just don't ask me to do a Highland reel. Daphne, stop licking my damn face."

"You sustained no permanent injuries?"

"My pride will never be the same. I do suspect, however, that I will live."

"Good." She paused a heartbeat before falling backward with Daphne into the clothes scattered about her. "Then you won't mind if I have a good laugh at your expense? Oh, Connor, that was the silliest thing I've ever seen. One moment you were standing there, and the next—"

Torchlight flared across the garderobe as she burst into a fit of giggles. Connor sat up with a scowl to watch Robert running through the doorway in his dressing robe and silk slippers. "What's going on?" he called out in panic. "Marguerite, is that you? Do we have burglars?"

Robert lurched to a halt and held the torch above Connor's head, gasping in shock as he surveyed the garments strewn about the floor. "I should have known. An abduction. This is an abduction."

Connor sighed. "Yes—no—oh, hell. What does it matter? I had to get caught. There isn't a lawyer in Europe who won't laugh his head off when he hears about this."

"Well, Marguerite," Robert said, "if you weren't ruined before, you certainly are now. What shame and scandal you have heaped upon the honorable house of de Saint-Evremond."

Maggie stood, clutching her wedding veil to her chest. "There doesn't have to be a scandal if we keep this a family secret, Robert. Please don't do anything rash. I really love this man."

"Do you?"

Connor rose unsteadily to his feet. "I would appreciate it

if you'd get that torch out of my face. I have a splitting headache."

Robert involuntarily retreated a step at the sight of the tall, blond Scotsman towering over him. "Well, I suppose we'll have to make the best of it," he said quietly. "I daresay Bernard would have called off the wedding once he learned of her criminal associations."

Maggie threw down her veil to give him an exuberant hug. "Oh, Robert, you darling. Are you giving us your blessing?"

"Not exactly," he said. "You're as incorrigible as your sister. Still, if you are going to marry a Scotsman at least he is a person of position." He looked up at Connor. "However, as far as abductions go—"

Connor grimaced. "I know. Very gauche. I remember now what was bothering me about the west wing as an abduction route. The former occupants turned their own cannons on the turret rather than surrender to the British. They planned to blow the stairs to bits."

Furtive footsteps crept through the doorway toward them. Three curious female faces peered into the torchlit shadows. "I forgot to tell you about the west turret staircase, Buchanan," the duchess said sheepishly. "Despite this oversight, everything obviously went well with the abduction."

Connor drew Maggie back against his chest, laughing in triumph. "Everything is fine, Morna. Please don't shoot anyone."

The wedding was performed at midnight by the village justice of the peace. The sleepy magistrate blinked in the candlelight and yawned through the ceremony. He wore a kilt over his nightshirt and apologized for forgetting his spectacles.

Robert acted as best man and even managed to strike up a friendship with the duchess, who accepted an invitation to visit the château sometime next spring.

Claude served Highland whisky and Maggie's collapsed mushroom soufflé.

Ardath served as maid of honor and was on her best behavior.

Connor wore a hunting coat and several fresh bruises from his fall down the staircase. He supposed he should be grateful he hadn't killed himself. His eyes were riveted to his bride during the impromptu reception that followed. For once his celebrated eloquence failed him. He'd always assumed that this sort of personal happiness was an illusion that people chased but never found.

But suddenly his life was complete. He couldn't imagine a future without Maggie. With her, he felt capable of conquering the entire world, which was a good thing since he would soon be returning to a murder trial and this tangled mess with Sheena. He would have loved to press charges against her husband, but as he'd told Maggie earlier, a woman can't be abducted if she goes willingly with her abductor. His feelings were still hurt. He wasn't sure he could forgive his sister.

Connor knew the fine points of the law. He had quite a few things left to learn about love, though, and after all these years, he still found himself unsettled by the women in his life.

"I have brought you a birthday present, Connor," Ardath announced as the tired but cheerful party began to disperse.

He slipped his arm around Maggie's waist, impatiently controlling the urge to drag her out of the room. Nobody was going to stop him from taking his bride to bed. "My birthday was in August."

"In that case, it's a wedding present." She motioned to Morna and Rebecca, who dragged a large rectangular object out from behind the sofa.

The present turned out to be a beautifully woven tapestry of the lion dancing with his princess at their wedding; it was the last in the sought-after series. Robert removed a monocle from his pocket to examine it and declared it genuine. His scarred face looked soft and faintly sad in the candlelight.

"I wish you a lifetime of peace together, and I envy you for finding each other." He kissed Maggie gently on the forehead. "You have my heartfelt blessing. Be happy, *ma petite*."

The tapestry was hung in a place of honor in the bedroom of Connor's Edinburgh town house, where an angel had taken on the devil and come away with quite a lot more than she'd bargained for. In fact, they both had.

The priceless tapestry looked down on the two figures lost in each other on the bed below. Tangled sheets. A masculine growl of aggression. A woman's sigh of delight. The Lord Advocate of Scotland making love to his abducted bride, so engrossed in pleasuring her that they would be late to host the party that was already in progress.

He didn't care.

He strained over her, his head thrown back in fierce absorption. He lost track of time when he was with her. She made him forget that a world beyond her mischievous smile had ever existed.

He collapsed on the bed with a loud groan of satisfaction. Maggie smiled, tingling all over, and prodded his foot with her big toe. "I hope no one heard that. Don't fall asleep again, your worship. We have to get dressed. Everyone in Edinburgh is here."

"Give me five minutes."

"Connor, you've been saying that all day."

"Have a heart." He grinned, his hand stealing up her rib cage to her breast. "The Balfour case is opening tomorrow. According to rumor, my 'activities' the night before determine my degree of success."

Maggie studied him for a moment. "If one were to go by your 'activities' you should win every case for the next seven years."

He winked at her. "Shall we try for a nice even eight?"

They were quiet for a moment. They both knew that this might be the last night for a long time when Connor would be free to enjoy himself.

"Two reliable witnesses have finally come forth to testify against Lord Montgomery," he said in a subdued voice.

Maggie released a sigh. "Who?"

"Montgomery's former secretary and a prominent apothecary who remembers seeing him walking past his shop shortly after the time of the murders."

"What about the men who attacked Donaldson?" Maggie asked worriedly.

Connor laughed. "The Chief found them—let's just say

that Arthur used his own, not entirely legal, methods to make them admit they worked for Montgomery."

"I think Thomas works too hard," Maggie said.

Connor only smiled. The minute Donaldson began to recover he had tracked down the letters that proved Montgomery was being blackmailed for his past sins. As a reward for all his dedicated work, Connor had appointed his protégé to the prestigious Faculty of Advocates.

Connor himself could hardly wait to confront Montgomery in court. The newspapers predicted that the newly appointed Lord Advocate would stalk justice like a lion in the jungle.

It was true. The scent of victory tantalized him. He would win this case as a tribute to his wife.

He had just trapped her beneath him again and was kissing her senseless when Ardath knocked quietly at the door.

"I know you're both in there," she said. "Nobody is going to believe that tired cravat story again, Connor. Tear yourself away from your lovely wife and hie it downstairs before I run out of excuses. There is a limit to even my charm." Her voice faltered. "Donaldson is here with his mother, he looks well, and Sheena just arrived, as big as a barn and weeping like a waterfall. Be kind to her, won't you?"

Connor fell back on his forearm. "The hell I will."

Maggie scooted to the edge of the bed before he could stop her. "You'll have to forgive her eventually. After all, you're going to be an uncle to her child. Who are you to deprive our baby of its little cousin as a playmate?"

His eyes met hers in the mirror, shocked, hopeful. "Our baby?"

"Yes. Sometime at the end of the summer."

He grinned arrogantly. "That must mean that you conceived—"

"The very first time we made love." She pursed her lips at his wicked expression, but she was delighted by his reaction. "There is no need to look so smug. It was bound to happen. Men sire offspring every day."

He dragged her back into the bed and possessively lifted her into his arms. "Not with my wife they don't. Are you going to get dressed, or shall I explain to our guests that Lady Buchanan is indisposed?"

DARING

"Who will rescue you from Philomena Elliot if I don't?" she asked with a grin. "The poor woman all but published your engagement to her in the papers."

"I should bring libel charges." He reached behind him for her petticoats and drawers, forcing himself not to touch her. "Stop torturing me with your body. In fact, if you don't get dressed right now, the party will have to be canceled, and I mean it."

Sighing, she dressed in an apple-green silk gown and followed him across the room, pausing halfway to glance around. Several loud taps sounded at the balcony door. "Connor," she said in a low voice.

"What is it?"

"There's someone rapping at the balcony door."

"I can hear that, Maggie. I was hoping we could ignore it."

"Well, I think you should see who it is. It might be important."

He frowned and moved around her to open the door. Frosty winter air crept into the room. Connor couldn't say the intruder's identity came as much of a surprise. "What do you want, Arthur?"

The Chief grinned and leaned around Connor to wave at Maggie. "I've brought ye a wedding present, lad. Sorry it's a bit late, but I had a job putting it all together."

"That's thoughtful of you," Maggie said, waving back.

Connor pulled Arthur into the room. "I hope to God no one saw you. Didn't it occur to you to knock at the front door like a normal person?"

"Oh, I couldn't do that, lad," Arthur said with a deep sigh. "You and I both have our images to uphold."

Maggie came up behind Connor. "I love presents. What did you bring us?"

"Just a wee gift to welcome ye home." Arthur opened his heavy black coat to reveal an entire silver service stuffed into the coat's satin lining. "It might come in handy, Maggie, now that ye're the Lord Advocate's wife and have to act as hostess at these fancy parties."

"Arthur, you are the kindest man."

"No, he isn't," Connor exclaimed, studying the platter Arthur had just unloaded onto the bed. "These are my initials.

This is the service I ordered from the silversmith last month that was stolen from his shop."

Maggie smiled. "It's amazing how things work out, isn't it?"

Arthur placed a gravy boat in Connor's hand. "I'll be off now, lad, before I'm caught fraternizing with the enemy. Remember what I said about taking care of Maggie. I'd hate to make yer life hell."

Then he was gone.

Connor quickly closed the balcony door and ushered Maggie across the room. "Giving me my own stolen silver as a wedding present. The gall of it."

"Connor."

"Now what is it, Maggie?"

"The strangest thing." She drew him back toward the bed, her face lifted in wonder to the wall. "It's the tapestry. Did you notice that the lion is laughing now? I'm sure he was scowling before."

He gave her an indulgent look. "Whatever you say, my pregnant little wife. Come on. We're late."

He guided her gently ahead of him, stopping in the hall when he noticed the figure staring up at them from the bottom of the stairs. He still hadn't decided how to deal with her.

Sheena.

She watched him with shame and hope and a little-girl-lost look in her eyes. Then Henry, her husband, came up behind her, placing his hand protectively on her shoulder. Connor felt a strange rush of anger and admiration that they thought their love powerful enough to fight him.

"Good evening, your worship," Henry said with an uncertain smile.

Maggie glanced up at Connor plaintively. "For me," she whispered.

He sighed. "Good evening, Sheena. Henry. I'm glad you both could come. I—" He glanced at Maggie. "I was wondering whether you would like to live at Kilcurrie until you're on your feet."

Donaldson and his mother appeared behind Sheena. Maggie hurried down to join the group, throwing her husband a look of gratitude that melted his heart. But he didn't follow her, glancing back at his bedchamber door. So much had happened since that first night.

Something drew him back into the room. Frowning, he walked past the bed and stepped closer to the wall. By damn, it hadn't been Maggie's imagination.

The lion *was* laughing.

But that wasn't what impressed Connor at all.

The amazing thing was that he understood exactly why the big beast looked so pleased with himself. He felt the same wicked exhilaration.

He and the tapestry lion shared a secret. They had been tamed by an innocent lady. They had won the love of a woman whom they surely did not deserve.

But, being beasts, they would claim that love anyway.

They would guard their women with their lives, and the many offspring that came of their mating. Possessive husbands, proud and protective papas to their cubs.

After all, the golden threads of the medieval tapestry promised a happy ending to their tale and a love that would endure forever. Their fate had been woven centuries ago, waiting for the perfect moment to unfold.